CW01514355

DIVIDED LOYALTIES

BY

CARON HARRISON

Published by

Caron Harrison
Ballabunt Croft
Cooil Road
BRADDAN
Isle of Man
IM4 2AQ

Copyright © 1998 Caron Harrison

All rights reserved. No part of this publication may be
reproduced, stored in a retrieval system, or transmitted in
any form or by any means, electronic, mechanical,
photocopying, recording or otherwise, without prior
permission in writing from Caron Harrison

Caron Harrison has asserted her moral right to be identified
as the author of this work.
All the characters in this book are fictitious, and any
resemblance to actual persons, living or dead, is purely
coincidental.

ISBN 0 9531155 1 8

Produced by
Axxent Ltd
The Old Council Offices, The Green,
DATCHET,
Berkshire, SL3 9EH

Also by Caron Harrison
Shades of Grey

In memory of my father,
Howard Wagner

Auf dem Grunde aller diesen vornehmen Rassen ist das Raubtier, die prachtvolle nach Beute und Sieg lustern schweifende blonde Bestie nicht zu verkennen.

At the base of all these aristocratic races the predator is not to be mistaken, the splendorous blond beast, avidly rampant for plunder and victory.

Friedrich Nietzsche.
Zur Genealogie der Moral, I, 11

CHAPTER ONE

Even if she could find a button, she had no needle and thread. Ilse Brünninghaus clutched the lapels of her threadbare jacket to keep out the numbing air. On her lap her son, Siegfried, looked balefully up at her, his grey eyes searching hers for some kind of nourishment. She had nothing to give him. No food, no shelter, no warm clothing at winter's approach. No hope. As though seeing her despair he let out a wail of his own. She hugged him to her breast, trying to keep him warm.

"At least I've spared you the Russians, Liebchen. At least I've done that much for you," she whispered into his tiny ear.

Siegfried knew nothing of the recent war or his mother's flight westwards from Dresden, through the American lines then north towards her home city of Hamburg in the British Zone. He did not know his mother now sat in a gutter in Kassel, exhausted, starved, terrified of contracting tuberculosis, the pauper's disease. All Siegfried knew were the pains of hunger, the cold of the night and his mother's hot tears.

She had rested long enough. Weak with hunger she rose from the gutter. Siegfried was almost too much to carry now, even though his ribs showed clearly under his skin. They had not eaten a decent meal for months, existing on scraps begged at doorways and gleaned from forests. Now the October nights were drawing in and she must find shelter soon. Around her on the shell-shattered streets, others were scurrying about, collecting firewood to drag down to their cellars, foraging for a cabbage or a lucky bag of potatoes. It was the same wherever she went. Germany was in ruins, her people kept starving by her well-fed conquerors.

"Nowhere to go?"

Ilse spun round, immediately feeling the giddiness of hunger.

"Steady on," the man said. He took the child from her while she clung onto his arm. As her eyesight cleared she noticed the arm was clothed in stained and faded field grey. Yet another defeated soldier.

"Thank you. I feel better now." Ilse reached for her son, and the gaunt young man returned him to her. His cheekbones were as prominent as her own, the pale skin stretched tightly across them. She could not guess his age, not that it mattered. They were all old now; sick and infirm. His brown, wavy hair needed cutting, but he looked clean and vermin-free. "I'm looking for somewhere to shelter for a few days. Do you know of anywhere?"

He grinned, and Ilse immediately felt warmer. "I don't normally drag young ladies in off the street, but if you don't mind sharing with half a dozen others, you'd be welcome for a few days. Where are you heading?"

"Hamburg."

He grimaced. "Do you have family there?"

"I used to," Ilse said softly.

There was no need for further comment. The young man knew the fate of Hamburg. He grasped her arm. "We'd best get going. Heinz Stadlbauer's my name. Let me show you to your quarters."

As she followed his lead down a narrow street, Ilse introduced herself and Siegfried. It was good to have someone to talk to at last. "I don't know why I'm heading for Hamburg," she prattled. "I suppose it's my home and I need some kind of return to familiarity, even if there's nothing recognisable there. When my parents were killed in the bombing of August '43, I went to live with my sister, Gudrun, in Mannheim. Siegfried was born there." She stepped over a pot-hole filled with muddy water. "Then Mannheim was bombed. Gudrun and I went to stay with an aunt near Dresden. Gudrun was in the city when it was bombed. I had stayed with Siegfried and my aunt. We watched the fires lighting up the whole sky. Gudrun never returned. Shortly afterwards my aunt died of bronchitis. I didn't want to stay to meet the Russians, so I headed back west, along with thousands of others."

"And here you are!" Heinz stopped in front of a derelict three-storey house, bounded by iron-railings and an overgrown garden. Some attempt had been made to clear a corner for vegetables, but nothing grew as yet. "The house itself isn't safe to live in, but the cellars are fine. A bit damp, that's all."

It was a palace after what Ilse was used to. She picked her way carefully in the dusk over fallen masonry and down the cellar steps. She could hear voices in the gloom, both male and female.

"We have a visitor," Heinz declared cheerfully to the assembled company. "This is Ilse. And little Siegfried."

Around a stove three men and two women looked up at her from assorted armchairs gleaned from the house. It looked quite cosy apart from the lack of welcome.

"For God's sake! Why did you bring a child here, Heinz?" one of the men asked gruffly. "He'll cry all night long and keep us all awake."

"Ilse's only staying a few days," Heinz explained. "She was on the street with nowhere to go. We must all help each other, or we won't have learned anything from this wretched war."

Ilse drew back towards the steps, but Heinz reached for her arm. "Stay, Ilse. Jens doesn't mean it. We were all in your situation once." He unbuttoned his tunic and, with a magician's flourish, produced a loaf of bread. "See. There's plenty to go with our soup. Now Ilse, you sit on that box near the stove and warm up a bit, while I find another bowl for you."

Timidly Ilse sat on the wooden crate. There seemed to be no more protest from her companions. One of the women, a still attractive red-head, passed her a blanket to wrap around Siegfried. Siegfried, however, could smell food and began to whimper.

Heinz quickly broke the loaf into eight, passing two pieces to Ilse, followed by a small bowl of cabbage soup. "You'll have to share that with Siegfried." He settled himself on another crate next to her, watching as she blew on the soup before feeding most of it to Siegfried.

It was dark outside now. Curfew for the German population. In the cellar was a single candle, its flame flickering in the draughts. Ilse watched it with half-closed eyes, Siegfried asleep on her lap now his stomach was warm, if not full. Beside her, Heinz was talking with the others. A sudden laugh jolted Ilse from her dozing.

Heinz noticed her waken and smiled at her. "Your payment for your supper, Ilse, is to tell us your story. We've all heard each other's a dozen times. Tell us about your life in Hamburg, where you met your husband, that sort of thing."

"I'm not married." Ilse lowered her eyes uncomfortably, not in her own shame but because of what she was about to tell of Siegfried's father. She saw Siegfried twitch in his sleep, his fine blond eyebrows wrinkling in a dream. She tucked back a strand of her own lank blond hair as she looked up again at her audience.

"Early in the war I was sent as a Kindergarten assistant to a small town not far from here. Medebach." She saw a few nods of recognition of the name. "There I met Karl. He was everything a girl could hope for: tall, handsome, well-respected – his father owned a local saw-mill. Karl was a corporal in a Mountain Division, home on leave. When he returned to Norway we wrote frequently. I was so proud of my soldier hero. He was soon promoted to sergeant, and in Russia became a lieutenant, awarded the Iron Cross, First Class. In February '43 he was wounded, and in the spring of that year came home on leave. It was heaven. We were so much in love and decided we would marry the next time he had leave. Siegfried was conceived then. I next heard from him in Yugoslavia, but after June came nothing. There were no more letters from him. I found out finally from his parents at Christmas that he was being held in a labour camp here in Germany. You can imagine my horror and anger at the danger he had put us in! There was I, just given birth to a son, and I find the father is a traitor. I was devastated. I refused to link my name with his again, and severed all contact with him and his family. For all I know he's dead now, and good riddance. It's men like him who brought Germany to the desperate position we're in now!"

Ilse's anger brought a flush to her cheeks. She could never think of Karl now without cursing his name. She looked around, realising there was silence in the cellar. No one was looking at her. Were they embarrassed by her shameful connection with a traitor?

At last Heinz met her eye. "What exactly did this Karl do?"

Ilse looked blank. "Do? I've no idea. His parents didn't know when they told me. All I know is he must somehow have betrayed the Fatherland."

"Perhaps you ought to go to his parents now, if they're so close, and find out. It might have been different from what you think, Ilse. People ended up in prison camps for the most spurious reasons," Heinz told her gently, despite his own anger at her callousness.

"Rubbish! There must have been a good reason. I'm not going crawling to the Drieslers' door, begging shelter for their grandson after what I've had to suffer because of Karl! I want nothing more to do with that family."

"I think you should reconsider, for the boy's sake. If there's the chance of a proper home for him, you ought to take it."

"Never!" Ilse's pride was the only thing she had. Her beauty was lost on the road from Dresden. "Siegfried must never be tarnished by his father's crimes."

"Aren't you making him suffer now?"

The debate was between Heinz and Ilse only. The others listened in stony silence. Ilse felt their censure.

"What's the matter with you all? Why are you against me? Don't you understand what it's like to love someone and then find he betrayed you?"

"I thought it was Germany he's supposed to have betrayed?"

"We are Germany. All of us. He betrayed me, he betrayed us all. Can't you see that?"

Heinz did not answer. Ilse could see he was regretting bringing her to the cellar. It was too late to leave now. Siegfried was fast asleep and she felt dog-tired herself. "Where can I sleep?" she asked.

Heinz pointed to a dark corner where there was a pile of old curtains. She laid Siegfried carefully down, then made herself ready for bed.

"Goodnight," she bade them from her corner.

There was a long silence, then a reluctant reply from Heinz. "Goodnight, Ilse."

In the morning she would leave.

*

Leaving Kassel was a wrench. She had no energy to face the long haul to Hamburg. Despite her tiredness she had lain awake, mulling over what Heinz had said. Perhaps she ought to seek shelter with Siegfried's grandparents. Now she stood at a road junction, looking first north then west. Hamburg lay to the north. In her arms Siegfried gave a weak cough. That decided her. Hamburg was too far. Medebach was so close. As she took the road west, through Istha, a convoy of British trucks passed by. She scowled and cursed the victors. At Korbach they wanted to know her destination. She gave them Dieter and Gisela Driesler's address. Another day and she would be there, despite her snail's pace. Her strength was giving out. She had nothing to barter for food, relying on kind-hearted farmers' wives to take pity on her and her sickly child.

The tall, grey tower and spire of Medebach's parish church of St Peter and Paul rose above the surrounding houses. Its familiarity brought a lump to her throat. So many memories here. Happy memories. She still knew many people in the town. They could tell her whether Karl was still alive, before she risked turning up at his door. She made her way up Korbacher Strasse, not recognising any faces, then crossed over to Ostwall where her friend, Margit Witter, lived with her parents. It was already late in the afternoon. Darkness would soon fall. Ilse hoped someone was at home in the old, half-timbered house. She knocked on the broad front door, over which was carved a Latin inscription, its meaning now forgotten to Ilse. Margit's mother opened the door. She had aged tremendously since Ilse last saw her over two years ago. Her thin body was wasted, her drawn face barely recognisable.

"Yes?"

"Frau Witter? It's Ilse Brünninghaus. You remember? I worked with Margit at the Kindergarten."

"Oh! Goodness me. Ilse! I scarcely recognised you. Come in. You look exhausted. Margit will be home soon, I hope. She's gone to try to find some bread."

Frau Witter led Ilse into a crowded room. Every chair was occupied. "My relatives from the east," Frau Witter explained. She spoke to a girl of about fourteen, busily knitting. "Rosa, would you mind letting Fräulein Brünninghaus sit for a while?"

Rosa stuck her needles in the knitting and slowly stood with a glance at the child Fräulein Brünninghaus carried. Ilse gratefully took her place on the upright chair. Frau Witter returned from the kitchen with a cup of ersatz coffee. "I have a little milk, if the child would like some?" she offered.

Ilse looked doubtful. There were so many other hungry children here. But Siegfried seemed in most need. "Thank you."

She did not have long to wait before Margit arrived back. Ilse heard her screech of excitement from the hall as her mother told her of their visitor. The door flung open.

"Ilse! You're back! Wherever have you been? We thought you were dead." Fluffy-headed Margit embraced her old friend, taking a quick peep at the pale and silent child by her. "So this is Siegfried. Poor little thing. However do you manage to find food for him?"

Ilse felt overwhelmed by Margit's welcome. Her exhaustion poured out in a long sob and she broke into tears on Margit's shoulder.

"Come into the kitchen, Ilse. We can talk there." Margit soothed her friend, leading her out of the crowded room. She noticed Siegfried totter and fall with scarcely a murmur, too weak to cry. Margit stooped to pick him up. He was as light as a feather. What a state they were in!

Ilse sat on a stool by the stove and dried her eyes, settling Siegfried on her lap. Margit drew up a stool next to her and pre-empted her questions.

"Are you on your way to Karl's family, Ilse? They'll be thrilled to see you and Siegfried."

"How are they?"

Margit smiled. "Overcrowded with refugees like the rest of us. Rudi's home too. Luckily he lasted till the surrender, so he was released quite soon."

Rudi was Karl's younger brother. If Karl survived the labour camp he would certainly be home, but Margit had not mentioned him. Ilse's thoughts soured at his name. She had a hefty suspicion Karl would be a martyr in his family's eyes. Her anger began to burn.

Margit saw her changed mood. "What's the matter, Ilse?"

Ilse gave a deep sigh and contained her anger. "It was stupid of me to come here. How can I face his family and politely talk about their son? I'll never forgive him, so how can I ask his family to take us in? It's impossible. They'd only end up throwing me out. It would be better not to see them."

Margit began to understand. "You still believe in Nazism, don't you, Ilse?"

"Don't you?" Ilse retorted. "Germany failed Adolf Hitler, not the other way round. I don't want Siegfried being brought up amongst defeatists. We'll keep going until we find somewhere we can be proud to call ourselves German."

Margit was horrified. "You'll die first. Please reconsider, Ilse. Think of Siegfried."

"I am. That's why I can't stay in Medebach. He'll be swamped by his father's family. Please don't mention we've been here, Margit. Promise me. Your mother too. She mustn't tell them. I don't want them trying to contact me."

Margit saw argument was useless. "There's none so blind, Ilse, as those who will not see. All right, I promise not to tell them, even though I think that's the wrong decision. If you ever change your mind, remember me. You must have some need for them to have come here in the first place."

"I can't deny that. In Kassel I thought Siegfried was ill. He began to cough, but he seems better now. I'll go on tomorrow."

"Where to? Oh, Ilse, I wish you could stay here with us, but as you can see ..." She gestured hopelessly towards the crowded living room.

"I know. I must leave Medebach."

"You'll have to stay tonight at least. You can share the floor here with Rosa and Hilde. It's warmer in the kitchen. We don't have any spare blankets."

The offer was tempting. Siegfried had fallen asleep, lulled by the warmth and the milk. "Thank you, Margit. But only tonight. I should never have come here in the first place."

*

After sharing a meagre breakfast with the fifteen others in the house, Ilse followed Margit to the Oberstrasse, hiding her face under a headscarf to avoid recognition. They waited for the bus, Margit having given her friend a few precious Reichsmarks. "Not that you can buy anything with them," she said. "Except a bus ride."

The bus went as far as Winterberg, where Ilse used the rest of the money to take the train north to Dortmund. She wanted to get as far away as possible from Medebach.

Arriving in Dortmund she wondered why she bothered to try her luck in a city. All that remained of the centre was the pattern of the old streets and city walls. It was Kassel all over again. She would have to find another cellar or derelict house tonight and then move on to a country town next day. At least in the country there was some food. She wandered down the streets. Piles of rubble were gradually being cleared by gangs of ex-soldiers, or anyone with enough strength to attempt such heavy work. She continued walking into the suburbs. More houses stood with fewer gaps between. As she rounded a corner where a queue of women stood outside an empty shop, her nostrils caught the warm, yeasty scent of baking bread. Perhaps what the women were waiting for. But she had no money now. A cup of coffee at the station took her last coins. Perched on her hip, Siegfried too could smell the bread. He began to moan and wriggle.

"All right, Schätzlein, I'll find you something. Even if I have to steal it," she whispered. She lifted her nose into the air and breathed hard. The scent came from across the street, not the shop. Tracking it down, Ilse found a narrow alley leading to a courtyard backed by yet another bombsite. One of the buildings in the courtyard was a small bakery. Ilse peered through a grime-smeared window. She could see an oven against one wall, and, stacked against another, crates of crusty, steaming loaves. Saliva rushed to her mouth, her stomach churned in anticipation. She stood on tiptoe and scanned the whole room. Incredibly there was no one in sight. Hugging Siegfried close to stifle any cries, she opened the rickety door, took a quick look round, strode up to the nearest crate and lifted the top loaf.

"What do you think you're doing?"

Ilse spun round, clinging on to the loaf, despite her fright. She was confronted by a sweating, coarse-featured and balding man who glowered at her.

"I'm sorry," she said quietly, quickly gathering her wits about her. "I'm so hungry. I couldn't stop myself coming in here." She blinked at him from underneath her lashes, wishing her once fine blond hair was not so lank and matted.

"Every loaf must be accounted for," he explained, a little less gruffly. "But if you want to share my lunch, you're welcome."

His gaze dropped to the front of her jacket, and Ilse knew the payment demanded for such kindness. It was common currency these days, but so far she had avoided spending it. Siegfried's hunger demanded she use it now. She nodded assent to his unspoken demand.

"You can wait in the flat upstairs until I've delivered this lot." He moved towards her and removed the loaf from her grasp. "This way."

Ilse followed him outside to the courtyard. Adjacent to the bakery door was another door, its pale blue paint peeling off in sheets. The baker unlocked it and led her up a bare wooden staircase to another door which he also unlocked. He stepped into the flat to allow Ilse access.

"I won't be long," he said, with another glance at her jacket.

Ilse shuddered, then sank onto the only chair not covered by dirty laundry. She kept Siegfried on her knee. The flat was filthy. Even Heinz's cellar was cleaner than this. The curtains hung in shreds at the opaque window, the bare floor was thick with fine flour dust, filtering up from below. There was a small kitchen area to her left which she dared not investigate, and another door, through which she saw grey covers on a tangled bed. The baker had no wife; that much was obvious.

Siegfried began to fidget and finally to grizzle. Ilse thought a drink of water might help stave off his hunger until the man returned. She set Siegfried on the floor and went over to the kitchen area. It was as bad as she feared. A single tap fed into a cracked, grease-coated sink. In a cupboard she found an old cup, which needed a good rinse first. She turned on the tap. It gave a shudder and a clank, before emitting a gush of rusty water. After a few moments the water ran clear and Ilse filled the cup. She tried it first. It tasted clean enough. After giving Siegfried the cup, she hunted around for some food. She did not intend waiting for the baker if she could help it. The cupboard contained only a few chipped plates and a handful of cutlery. Next to it was a taller cupboard, holding the unused cleaning equipment, a broom, dustpan and brush, bucket and mop. She wondered where the food could possibly be. Returning to the main part of the room she saw a large metal trunk in one corner. Lifting the lid she discovered the baker's treasure hoard. Tins of meat and vegetables, a bag of potatoes, even a large chunk of garlic sausage were kept here, safe from mice and cockroaches. Ilse had not seen so much food in a year.

"So you've discovered my little store."

Ilse slammed the lid. She had been so overwhelmed she had not heard his return. She saw he was carrying a loaf which he put on the table.

"Get a plate and knife," he said, removing the sausage from the trunk.

While Ilse did as she was told, Siegfried made a grab for the bread. The baker slapped the infant's hands hard. "Keep that child under control or you're out!" he snapped.

"I'm sorry. He's not yet two. He doesn't know any better." She put down the knife and plate and watched hungrily as the repulsive man sliced the bread and sausage into thick chunks. He only gave her one portion, but there was enough for herself and Siegfried.

The man gave her a few minutes to satisfy her hunger before demanding information. "What's your name and where are you from?"

"Ilse Brünninghaus. Originally from Hamburg, lately from Dresden and all towns west of it to here," she said succinctly.

He grunted. "I'm Röbel. Erich Röbel. Always of Dortmund." His eyes swivelled to where Siegfried sat on the floor, stuffing bread and sausage into his mouth. "Where's his father?"

"Dead, I think. At least I hope so."

"What do you mean?" Erich Röbel glared at her with his almost transparent blue eyes.

Ilse stared back with her own clear blue eyes and hoped her intuition proved correct. Now she had fed it did not matter if she were wrong.""He betrayed his country and his Führer."

Erich held her gaze a long time, then slowly smiled, revealing crooked, yellow teeth. "To keep my job I had to convince the British I was never a part of all that, despite what others maintained. I succeeded, so why are you not fooled?" He shifted his chair nearer hers and put his hand on her knee.

Ilse resisted the impulse to flinch. With a good scrub and a coat of paint this could be a home for her and Siegfried. She rested her hand on Erich's.

"I could sense a like-minded person," she said.

His hand squeezed her thigh more tightly. With the other he threw the remaining bread at Siegfried. "Keep him quiet for a bit," he sneered. He stood up, dragging her away from the table towards the bedroom.

Siegfried saw them go. "Mutti!" he called, holding up his arms.

"You finish eating, Schätzlein. I'll be back soon," she told him. She tried not to feel disgusted by Erich Röbel's body as she shut the door behind them. He was a good man, a loyal Nazi moreover. Appearances were not everything, she told herself. She felt her jacket being removed – easy since there were no buttons to undo. His hands groped for her shrunken breasts as his mouth closed over hers. She closed her eyes, trying to imagine it was someone else making love to her. She only had Karl's image to put in Erich's place.

No other man had slept with her. Thank God. It might have been different had she stayed in Dresden. The Russians!

She kept her mind busy until, with a last shudder, Erich slid off her. Ilse opened her eyes and breathed freely again. She watched as Erich tucked his shirt into his trousers and did up his belt.

"You can stay here longer if you like, Ilse."

*

Ilse was terrified when she discovered she was pregnant. Erich did not seem to like children. If Siegfried cried, Erich shouted. He showed no interest in him whatsoever. Would he throw her and Siegfried out? She could not bear the thought of hunger and cold again, after four months in the sanctuary of the warm, now clean, bakery flat. She delayed telling him for another three months until her condition became obvious.

She cooked a meal of his favourite goulash and waited until he had finished. Siegfried was quiet for once, tearing up paper in the corner.

"Erich, you may have already guessed. You're going to be a father." It was a deliberate attempt to make him feel involved and it seemed to work.

"Ilse! That's wonderful! A father after all these years! Well!" He patted her gently rounding belly. "It's about time we got married then."

Ilse's heart sank. She did not want to marry this man. She did not love him, and could not face living the rest of her life with his coarse, vulgar ways. But at least it was a home. And there was the new baby to think about.

"Yes. We must."

*

As Frau Röbel she acquired a new status in the community. Gradually the neighbouring women stopped and chatted more freely to her in the warm spring sunshine. Siegfried left her side to go and play with other children on the bombsites, revelling in his new strength and vitality after a winter cooped up in the flat. He suffered his share of cuts and bruises as he fell over rubble, or squabbled with his playmates, but he soon toughened and quickly learned not to go running to Mutti up in the flat. He would never run to Erich, even though he was nearer in the bakery. Erich only ever gave him a cuff round the ear, or a kick up the rear. Erich was horrible.

By September, when baby Margit was born, Siegfried was spending most of the day outside, out from under his mother's feet. Because Erich began work so early, he usually had a nap in the afternoon. Siegfried knew he would receive a wallop if he woke Erich, so it was safer to stay outside and throw stones at the local cats. Not yet three, he tagged along with the older children, learning stealth and how to steal. Money was almost worthless, there were few goods in the shops, but cigarettes were valuable currency on the thriving Black Market. A carelessly discarded man's jacket would be emptied of its contents in a flash. As youngest and least suspicious member of the gang, Siegfried was frequently used for pickpocketing. By the time he was four he was well-versed in all manner of petty crimes, and was well able to stand up for himself in a fight with his fellows. His mother was used to apologising to yet another neighbour whose child Siegfried had injured. Erich did not involve himself with his stepson's misdemeanours until they began to affect his own family.

Baby Heinrich appeared on the scene early in December 1948, just before Siegfried's fifth birthday. What little hope Siegfried had of some kind of celebration was dashed. Moreover when his mother was resting in bed, Margit was left in his care. Siegfried had no shop toys, so learned to make his own model aeroplanes and boats from paper or lumps of wood. When Margit grabbed his latest effort, breaking the wings, Siegfried's rage was noisy and violent. He lashed out at the little girl, cutting her lip. Siegfried's shouts and Margit's cries woke baby Heinrich. The noise was deafening. Ilse rushed in from the bedroom to pull Siegfried off Margit before he seriously hurt her.

"Outside, Siegfried! And don't come back in until I call you!" she yelled.

It was too much. Ilse did not know whether to comfort Margit or Heinrich first. When Erich came up to the flat after work, he immediately noticed Margit's cut and bruised lip. He turned on Ilse.

"What happened?"

"She and Siegfried had a fight over a –"

"Where is the little bastard?" Erich's fists balled. He scanned the living area, then poked his head round the bedroom door. There were no cupboards to hide in, no one under the bed. He slammed the door. "Outside?"

Ilse nodded, biting her lip anxiously as her husband strode towards the street door. A couple of minutes later she heard scuffles up the stairs. Siegfried was dragged into the room by his ear and deposited on the floor. Erich began removing his belt.

"No, Erich. Please," Ilse begged, grabbing his arm.

He shook her off. "Quiet, woman! He's got to learn a lesson. No bastard son of yours is going to hit my little girl." Wrapping the end of the belt round his hand, Erich let fly the other end across Siegfried's back. Siegfried yelped and made a dive for the sofa, but his stepfather grabbed him, holding him down to deliver a further dozen lashes. Afterwards Erich dragged the sobbing boy back downstairs.

"We'll have some peace now," Erich declared upon his return.

Ilse was appalled. "What have you done with him?"

"He's locked in the flour store. Perhaps he'll have learned his lesson by tomorrow."

"Tomorrow! You can't leave him there all night. He'll freeze. Erich, be reasonable. He's only just five."

"Old enough to learn from his mistakes." Erich sat on the sofa and picked up the newspaper. His attitude was obvious to Ilse. Let the boy freeze to death. It would be one less mouth to feed.

"I'm not letting you do this to my son!" She made for the door, but Erich grabbed her, swinging her round to meet his hand in a slap on her face.

"Leave him!" he bellowed.

Ilse was frightened by Erich's violence. Perhaps it would be best to let it all blow over. Hopefully Siegfried would learn his lesson.

In the store room Siegfried huddled amongst the sacks of flour, his back burning as deeply as his rage. "I hate him!" he shouted at a sack, punching it hard, despite the pain this caused. "I hate Erich!" He punched the sack again. There was another name he hated. One his mother used when she felt particularly resentful and blamed all their troubles on Siegfried's real father. He punched the sack again.

"Karl!" he screamed at it. He repeated the names and punches over and over in the cold, dark room.

Siegfried did learn a lesson from the experience of the store room. He learned the desire for vengeance.

CHAPTER TWO

With Edeltraud's arrival in February 1950, pressure for space in the cramped flat became extreme. Ilse and Erich slept in the bedroom, with Heinrich and Margit sharing a mattress on the floor, next to Edeltraud's cot. Siegfried was moved out to the sofa, but it meant he was in the adults' way in the evenings. The lack of privacy ground everyone's nerves to shreds. Ilse and Erich frequently argued and it came to a head, a month after Edeltraud's birth. Ilse could find nowhere to hang the mountain of washing her children produced. It was already draped over the stove, on two clothes horses, as well as over every chair back. The warm bakery would have been ideal but Erich refused to allow her to use it as a laundry.

"Why can't we look for a larger flat?"

"Because this is handy for my work, and there isn't anywhere else as cheap."

"How do you know? You haven't looked. I can't stand it any more here, Erich. We've got to find somewhere else!"

"And I can't stand your constant moaning. If you didn't have that bastard, it wouldn't be so bad."

Ilse threw the damp washing on the floor. "You took him on as well as me. He's part of the deal. And I don't like the way you always blame him when the children fight. It's not always his fault."

"It bloody well is! He's a thug and a villain. Don't forget who it was who set fire to old Cornelius' shed. And he steals. He's a bad influence on my children."

Their raised voices woke Siegfried. He watched the scene from under half-closed eyes. His mother stood face to face with Erich, trying to impose her point of view on him.

"You're a bad influence, you mean, the way you lash out at him all the time. No wonder he's learned to do the same."

"Don't you criticise me! He needs discipline, and you don't give it to him."

"He's *my* son. I'll treat him how I like."

This was too much for Erich. He grabbed Ilse's hair and yanked hard, pulling her down to her knees in front of him. "This is *my* flat and you'll do as you're bloody told."

Fury burst from the sofa behind him. Siegfried jumped on Erich's back, punching his neck and eyes. "Leave Mutti alone!" he screamed.

"You little shit! Get off!" Erich caught hold of Siegfried's arm and hurled him to the floor. There was no stopping Erich now. He kicked at the boy, then pulled him to his feet, only to send him smashing into the door-frame. Siegfried did not know where the next impact was coming from. He was sent hurtling about the room, only dimly aware of his mother's screams above the crashing of his body into walls and furniture.

At last it stopped. Siegfried opened his eyes to find he was lying back on the sofa. His mother was spongeing blood from his face and hair. "Mutti, I –"

"Shh. Don't talk, Schatz," she whispered with a glance towards the table where Erich sat drinking a beer. She finished cleaning him up, then gave his hand a soft squeeze. She knew what she had to do. For Siegfried's own safety he had to leave this flat. Next time Erich might kill him. She gazed into those familiar grey eyes, ruffled the fine blond hair. He was too like his father. Perhaps that was why she loved him so. He was a reminder of a love which was all-consuming in its time; a love shattered by treachery, yet still she felt the pain of its destruction. She bent and kissed Siegfried. He was asleep now. She could not bear to part with him, but she had no choice. She was a fool before to leave Medebach without seeing Karl's parents. Her stupid pride had clouded her judgement. What good was ideology to a child? Siegfried needed safety and a loving home. The Drieslers would give him that. They were kind people.

While Erich finished his beer, she found some paper and a pen.

"Who are you writing to?"

"Siegfried's grandparents."

"Oh." Erich smiled with satisfaction into his beer.

*

The reply came by return of post. Ilse had to wait for a quiet moment, when the older children were playing and the younger ones were asleep, before she could read it.

Dearest Ilse,   *28.3.50 Medebach.*

Your letter came as such a surprise to us. We knew that Margit Witter had managed to keep in touch with you and that you married a baker, but she mentioned nothing about Siegfried. We assumed he had not survived the war. Imagine our joy at discovering we still have our second grandson!

Before we say anything about having Siegfried, we must correct a false assumption of yours. You seem to believe that Karl is dead, but he is very much alive and well.

Ilse's heart skipped a beat as she read those words. Why had she and Margit shied away from talking about Karl? This could change everything! After all these years she could forgive his treachery. She could leave Erich! Karl was a decent man, intelligent too. And a tender lover. But however much she wanted him back now, could she really expect him to take on three other children? Erich could not tolerate another man's child. Maybe Karl would be the same. She turned back to the letter.

We did not know where to find you to tell you of Karl's release from the labour camp. It was his friend, Paul Zopf, who got him out. Paul was well-placed in the SS, but Karl's release was conditional upon him joining the SS. Once he had recovered his strength he was sent to the Ardennes in the last push there, but was eventually captured in February 1945 and taken to England as a prisoner of war. When we heard from Margit you were married we told him the news. He was desperate to hear what happened to Siegfried, but of course we knew nothing.

In England he worked on a farm, staying with the farmer and his daughter, Katherine. Karl and Katherine married in November 1947, deciding to stay in England as Katherine's parents were by then both dead, and the farm was hers. We have not yet been able to meet our daughter-in-law, but now that travel restrictions have been lifted, they are planning to visit us this May with their daughter, Sabina.

So you see, dearest Ilse, Siegfried can be looked after by his own father. Of course that means he will live in England, but there will be future visits here when you and Siegfried can see each other. In the meantime, if you want Siegfried to stay with us until Karl arrives, he will be more than welcome. However you may consider there is a risk he will settle with us, only to be uprooted again to England. We leave the decision up to you. Siegfried's safety is paramount in all this.

We have already contacted Karl to tell him the news. If you wish to write to him, his address is as follows: Lane Head Farm, Penchurch, Herefordshire, England.

Let us know what you want to do. We can come and fetch Siegfried if necessary.

With our love and best wishes to you and our grandson,
Gisela and Dieter Driesler.

Her hands trembling, Ilse read through the letter again, scarecely able to believe it. Karl was married to an Englishwoman and living in England. That was terrible! How could he live in the land of his enemy? More to the point, how could she let Siegfried go and live there? It had seemed such a good idea and suddenly it was all so complicated. She put her head in her hands in despair and sat down to think.

Erich came in and found her still sitting at the table. In one of his rare tender moments he sat down next to her and put his hand on her shoulder. "What's the matter? You've been crying."

She showed him the letter. He read it through with a final snort of disgust. "Well that just goes to show what a traitor he is. Taking up with an Englishwoman of all people!" He realised Ilse's tears demonstrated second thoughts on her part. "The boy's still going. He's not staying here."

Ilse sniffed. "I know. It just seems so far away. It would all be so strange for him."

"Are you going to send him to his grandparents first?"

Now the reality of sending him away was approaching, Ilse wanted to hang on to Siegfried for as long as possible. "No. I'll wait until May. It will be less unsettling." She hoped Erich would be more restrained with Siegfried, now he knew he was going.

The problem Ilse now faced was explaining to Siegfried he would be leaving her to live with his father, the man she had taught him from infancy to hate.

"Liebchen, I've got something very important to tell you," she began that evening, as she tucked him into his bedding on the sofa.

Erich had gone out for a drink with his friends, knowing there would be emotional scenes in the flat. Ilse sat on the sofa, stroking her son's brow, trying to show how much she loved him. "You know how difficult it is here, with us all living so crowded together. You have no toys, no proper bed. We all get in each other's way sometimes, don't we?"

Siegfried nodded, eyes wide, wondering what was coming to make his mother look so sad.

"Well, how would you like to go and live on a farm? There would be lots of space to run around in, fresh air and green grass to play on."

Siegfried smiled. This wasn't so bad after all! "When are we going?"

Ilse's heart bled to break the news. "I won't, Liebchen. Only you will."

"Why?" he wailed, all illusions shattered. He began to sob. "I don't want to go on my own. Are you sending me away? Have I been bad?" He remembered the thrashing he received when Herr Cornelius' shed burned down.

Ilse hugged him to her breast, smothering his tears. "There's just no room for you here." She waited a moment, letting his sobs die down. She had yet to tell him the worst. "You're going to live with your father. In England." There was silence. Total silence. She wished he would say something, so she knew what he was thinking. "Your father loves you, Siegfried. He'll look after you well. Much better than I can. We must forgive him what he did, mustn't we? It's all in the past now."

"You said you would never forgive him," Siegfried finally shouted. "You said he was a traitor and should have been shot. I won't live with him. I won't. I hate him!"

Ilse knew this would happen. She had conditioned the boy to hate his father. How could she expect him to change his opinion so suddenly? He was too young to reason with. She would have to be cruel now to be kind. "If you don't live with your father, you'll have to go to a children's home, where they'll beat you just like Erich does. You can't stay here, Liebchen. It's not safe. You'll be much better off with your father."

Siegfried dived under the bedclothes to hide from her. "I won't go. I hate him. And I hate you for sending me away," he shouted at her, hot tears streaming down his face.

Ilse gave up. She patted the lump under the bedding then rose to her feet. She had ironing to do, clothes to mend. Then Erich would come home the worse for drink, and force himself upon her.

"Oh, Karl. Why did I ever leave you?" she sobbed over the ironing.

CHAPTER THREE

Siegfried sat quietly in a corner of the carriage, sulking. Ilse allowed herself a few moments to remember her first journey to Medebach from Hamburg. 1941. So long ago. It was her father's doing. He arranged the position for her, away from the dangerous cities. He must have anticipated even then, in those days of glorious victory, the bombing that was to come. He had saved her life and lost his own.

Her first meeting with the tall, blond, charming corporal on leave from Norway was indelibly printed on her mind. He had held open the butcher's shop door for her. She had smiled. He was waiting for her when she came out. He only had a few days leave, but in that short time they became a couple. He was twenty-one, she nineteen. Now she was twenty-eight, haggard and worn from bringing up four children in poverty and misery. What would *he* be like?

Out of the carriage window, Ilse caught sight of Winterberg's four-storey station. Her heart began to race and she fussed about, gathering together Siegfried's two parcels of belongings.

"Come on, Siegfried. We're here." Ilse pulled him to his feet, making him take hold of one of the parcels. It had been a struggle all morning to get him ready. She could hardly blame him. Ilse sniffed back a tear, determined to be brave in front of Siegfried. The train rolled to a halt. She opened the door, helped Siegfried onto the platform, slammed the door, delaying the moment when she would have to meet her former lover. She took a deep breath and looked along the already emptying platform.

"There's your father." She felt Siegfried draw back. His reluctance mirrored her own. She would have jumped straight back on board the departing train, if it could have achieved anything. She did not move, but watched the approaching figure, English wife at his side. Ilse noted their smart outfits; Karl in a well-cut navy suit and hat, his wife in a light wool checked two-piece. Her chic chestnut brown hat perched jauntily on curls of similar hue. Karl had done all right for himself in England, but then he was the sort who would do well wherever he ended up. This had to be the best thing for Siegfried. She squeezed the boy's hand encouragingly. He only drew back even further behind her.

From behind his mother Siegfried heard his father's voice for the first time.

"Hello, Ilse."

It was deeper than he expected, softer too compared with Erich's usual bark. Siegfried would not be fooled by the gentle voice.

"Hello, Karl." His mother's reply was cold and distant. Her fingers tightened nervously on Siegfried's hand.

There was a moment's awkward silence, then his father squatted down in front of him. "So this is Siegfried."

Siegfried saw smiling eyes as grey as his own. His stomach heaved in disgust. He looked exactly like his father!

"Shall I carry your parcel for you, Siegfried?"

He hugged his parcel close, gripping tightly onto his mother's crumpled skirt.

"Answer your father, Siegfried," Ilse told him, trying to draw him out from behind her.

Karl placed a hand on her arm. "Don't worry, Ilse. I can see he's unsure of everything. How about us all having lunch together? It'll give him time to get more used to us before you go." It was the last thing Ilse wanted. A quick hand-over and be gone was what she had hoped for. "I really ought to catch the next train back to Dortmund. I've had to leave my other children with a neighbour –"

"Surely you can give us an hour, Ilse? We need to know a bit about him. His likes and dislikes."

It was the way he said her name. Before leaving that morning she had consciously hardened her heart. She could not allow herself to feel anything for Karl, be it love or hatred. But her heart was melting already.

"Very well," she agreed brusquely.

The English wife had said nothing so far, and Ilse avoided looking at her as they walked through the station to the adjacent hotel. The four of them sat at a table, and Ilse found herself opposite the Englishwoman. Karl introduced her.

"This is Katherine, my wife. She only speaks a little German, but has been trying hard to learn more since we got your letter."

Ilse studied the young woman opposite. The soft green eyes showed no animosity towards her, as she would have expected. Instead there was interest and concern, and a smile.

Ilse looked away. The waitress was coming to take their order. Ilse wanted something quick so ordered pea soup for herself and Siegfried. Karl took the hint and ordered likewise. Another awkward silence threatened until Karl started the conversation again.

"How many other children do you have?"

"Three. Two girls and a boy. I think another might be on the way. And you? You have a daughter, I gather."

"Sabina. She's not quite two. We left her today with her Oma and Tante Anna to spoil her. She's quite excited about seeing her new brother."

Siegfried sat quietly in his corner seat, observing and listening. The soup arrived and he pretended to be engrossed in eating, but all the while he kept his ears and eyes open. He could see his father's face more easily now his hat was removed. There was no doubt this man was his father. The likeness was striking. The Röbel children were all dark-haired like their father. Siegfried always felt superior to them because he took after his mother. Now he discovered his blond hair came from his father too. As his mother and father talked, Siegfried felt his stepmother watching him. He stared coldly back at her over his soup spoon, until she dropped her eyes. He turned his attention back to his father.

"You said in your letter your husband was mistreating Sigi. Does he treat you badly too?"

Ilse swallowed hard. The last thing she wanted was sympathy from Karl right now or the tears of self-pity would start to flow. She was determined to keep control of herself.

"My life has been hard. Erich saved me from the gutter. He is a worthy man."

Despite herself she began to relate the events of the past six years since Siegfried's birth. She concluded: "I have the three other children now and it is impossible for me to take care of Siegfried any longer. I can't guarantee his safety from Erich."

Karl did not press her to answer his question about Erich's treatment of her. Despite everything she was loyal to her husband –

had called him a worthy man – which made her abandonment of himself all the more surprising.

"Why didn't you go to my parents when Mannheim was bombed?" he asked her gently. "They would have been only too pleased to have you and Sigi stay with them. You would have saved yourself an awful lot of pain and suffering."

Ilse put on a brave show for Siegfried. "You don't seem to consider the pain and suffering we would have endured had we been arrested like you. The Gestapo would have thought I shared your traitorous ways. Then where would we have been? I had to cut myself off from you totally, to demonstrate my continued loyalty to the Führer. At least Erich was loyal to the end. I can be proud to call him my husband."

Her voice which had been low until now, filled the restaurant so that other guests turned to stare at the blond couple and their son, who were accompanied by a silent and distraught auburn-haired young woman.

Karl was not daunted. "How can you say that – now you know how evil the Nazis were?"

Katherine touched him on the arm. She spoke in English. "Karl, this isn't doing Siegfried any good."

Karl looked across at his son and saw he was hanging on to every word that was said. Ilse noticed too and began to gather her hat and coat together. "Thank you for the meal. I hope Siegfried is not too much trouble for you ... both," she managed to add, with a glance at Katherine as she stood up. "I hate to think of him so far away. Will you adopt him properly? Give him your surname?"

"Naturally. What else would we do?"

"I see." Ilse's emotions at finally losing her son were beginning to show. Karl hurriedly paid the bill, so they could escape the prying eyes of the restaurant, as Ilse struggled to hold back the tears.

Once outside Ilse bent down to kiss her son goodbye. "Remember what I told you, Schatz. I'll always love you. Try to be good for your father."

Before Siegfried could protest she had turned and was walking briskly towards the station. She did not look back.

"Mutti! Mutti!" Siegfried shrieked and began to run after her, but his hand was held too tightly. In a moment he found himself whisked up into his father's arms. Siegfried pounded him on the chest. "I hate you! I hate you!"

Leaving Katherine to gather up the parcels, Karl carried Siegfried towards the borrowed Volkswagen. "It's all right, Sigi. I won't hurt you. Just stop your struggling, then I won't have to hold you so tightly."

His words had no effect on the boy, who wriggled like an eel to escape. Karl had to stuff him into the back of the car, holding him down until Katherine could sit with him.

Once they were under way, Siegfried abandoned his protests and became determinedly uncooperative. He sat quietly enough on the back seat of the car, but remained sullen and uncommunicative. Katherine offered him some chocolate, which he refused, and Karl drove the short distance back to Medebach without once succeeding in getting Siegfried to talk to him.

There was at least some response from the boy when he saw Haus Fichtenblick. The half-timbered house seemed to front the road for ever. A long row of windows was tucked under the grey slate roof. At the far end, at right angles to the road, a barn stood with its large doors invitingly open. The house was surrounded by meadows and forest – all so different from the bombsites and poky flat Siegfried was used to in Dortmund. He stared wide-eyed, ignoring the members of his new family who had come out to welcome him, then ran across to the rail fence around the meadow where two cows stood.

Karl waved his parents back from approaching Siegfried too quickly. They understood the situation instinctively and allowed the boy time to set his own pace. Only six-year-old Uwe showed impatience and ran over to tell his cousin the cows' names.

"Uwe! Would you show Sigi your room and tell him where everything is, please?" Karl called over to his nephew as he helped Katherine carry the parcels to the house.

"All right, Onkel Karl. I'll show him the kittens first, though!" So saying, Uwe led his cousin off to the barn, and the two small boys disappeared inside.

"Well, it looks like those two have hit it off together, thank heavens," Katherine remarked. She laid out the meagre contents of the parcels on the extra bed installed in Uwe and Monika's room.

"Yes. It's a start at least," Karl replied. "Is that all there is?" The pile of clothing on the bed was pitifully small, with not a single toy included.

"Yes. Not much, is it? It looks like we'll have to buy him some clothes pretty soon."

Karl went to the window. Katherine stood by him, slipping her arm round his waist, as he watched his son exploring the garden at the back of the house, guided by Uwe.

"He's like you. He'll adapt well to his new circumstances. You'll see," she reassured him.

He looked down at her. "I hope so, for all our sakes. Otherwise we're in for a rough ride."

*

In bed that night, Karl lay listening to the sounds of the night and to Sabina's snuffling breath in the cot beside them. He was alert to the silence in the rest of the house. Sigi was bedded down and asleep with his cousins, but Karl hoped he would not wake in the night and forget where he was. Karl would have liked to have been nearer, but Anna and Stefan's room was in between, so they would be more likely to hear any disturbance.

"You're restless," Katherine whispered. "Are you worried about Sigi?"

"Yes. I wish he would speak to me. He seems to regard me as some kind of man-eater."

"Ogre," Katherine automatically corrected him. "I expect it's what Ilse's always made you out to be, and I don't suppose his stepfather was a very good example. What was it Ilse said today? I didn't quite catch all of it and I didn't like to ask in the car. Sigi seemed to get even more frightened when we spoke English."

"The language of the enemy – which only proves to him how much of a traitor I am," Karl said miserably. He quickly related what Ilse told him of her experiences during and after the war.

"The poor woman!" Katherine exclaimed. "What a life they've both had. Yet I got the impression she's still a bit of a Nazi."

She felt Karl tense before he spoke. "I think you're probably right. Even now she still can't see the truth."

Katherine shuddered. "Does that mean Sigi believes in all that."

Karl shrugged. "I don't know. I suppose I'll find out when he starts to talk to me."

"He will soon. I'm sure," Katherine soothed, then broached the awkward subject of Karl's first love. "She wasn't what I was expecting – Ilse, I mean."

"No. Nor me. She's aged a lot, but then so have I. I'll have to show you tomorrow the family photo album – what she and I used to look like."

Katherine was not so sure she wanted to see pictures of a uniformed Karl with the beautiful Ilse. But it was a part of his history she had learned to come to terms with and she agreed to his suggestion. "It might make an impression on Sigi, too."

"What, that his father wasn't always a traitor?" He laughed half-heartedly. "I suppose you're right. There are several pictures of myself with Ilse in there. It might help him accept the fact that once she loved me."

He sensed her discomfort at such talk of Ilse and pulled her closer towards him. "Don't worry, Schatz. I've got you and Sabina now. You're both more than I could ever have asked for." He caressed her hair. "But I think it's about time we had another child, apart from Sigi, don't you?"

Katherine smiled to herself in the darkness. She guessed Karl was sentimentally determined that their second child should be conceived in Germany. Either that, or the holiday here was doing him good. He had been working very hard on the farm over the winter, and then had come lambing. Some evenings he was asleep even before she was in bed.

He was making up for that now. She responded eagerly to his approach. It never ceased to amaze her what power he had over her, melting her body with his caresses.

"Let it be a boy!" she whispered afterwards in his ear.

"You really mean that, don't you?" he smiled.

"Of course!"

Karl laughed and kissed her nose. "I will ask my gods to grant your wish," he joked.

"And I will ask mine too," she replied.

*

Without Uwe, Siegfried's assimilation into the Driesler household could have been more traumatic. The two boys took such an instant liking to each other that Karl felt less apprehensive the following day, even though Siegfried still refused to speak to him. Anna managed to hold a conversation with him, and as they all sat at the table at midday, Siegfried followed Uwe's example and spontaneously called Gisela 'Oma', which delighted her no end. The men of the house were still regarded with deep suspicion, however. Karl wondered more than ever what kind of ill-treatment Siegfried had received from his stepfather.

After lunch Karl got Rudi to help him build a small go-cart for Siegfried. Uwe already had one, and Karl thought the two boys could race each other down the lane to the sawmill. Siegfried grudgingly accepted the finished item from his father, but Karl was pleased nevertheless by its success. When the boys finally lay exhausted on the grass, Karl remembered the photograph album. Katherine was busy tucking Sabina into bed, but when she returned he called her over to sit with him in the early evening sunshine and browse through it. His mother came and joined them in the garden, helping persuade Siegfried to sit with them. It was she who did the talking, telling Siegfried which of the two small boys was his father and which Onkel Rudi. As the uniforms – first Hitler Youth, then Wehrmacht – began to appear in the photos, Katherine felt a kind of unreality creep over her at seeing her husband's past opening up before her eyes.

"Who is that?" she asked, pointing to a dark-haired youth with his arms over both Karl's and Rudi's shoulders.

"Paul Zopf," Karl answered her quietly.

"The one who got you to join the SS?" she asked, looking again more closely at the man who possibly saved Karl's life, but in doing so once condemned him in her own eyes.

"The very same." Karl turned to his mother. "Do you know what became of Paul? Presumably you still have contact with his family, if they're still alive."

Gisela Driesler had wondered when her son would ask about Paul. As boys they were close friends, and it was she who asked Paul to try to do something for Karl when he was held in the labour camp in 1944. Now Paul was suffering the same fate.

"He was tried for war crimes and given seven years by the Americans," she told Karl.

33

He felt an immediate conflict of emotions. "I suppose I shouldn't feel sorry for him, but I do, after the way he stood up for me. What was he accused of?"

His mother shrugged. "His administrative duties covered many areas. I never liked to ask his parents what the specific charge was. Paul was always a good boy, and I'm sure it was only his association with his SS superiors that got him into trouble."

Karl had heard such excuses before, but he let the matter rest. Like his mother, he did not want to think ill of Paul.

Bored by these photos, Siegfried spotted a more interesting one over the page. There was a cry of recognition from him and a gasp of amazement from Katherine as Ilse's face stared up at them next to Karl's from the album; a fresh-faced and beautiful Ilse who patently adored the young Wehrmacht soldier beside her.

"1941," Karl said noncommittally, trying in vain to catch Siegfried's eye.

Nine years ago, he thought in amazement. He would have been a mere twenty-one years old, completely unsuspecting of the horrors to come. He had only just met Ilse then, but he knew from the start he wanted to marry her someday. By the spring of 1943 they were seriously thinking about it, but the war, and his own part in it, had changed everything. If he had any regrets, he managed to dismiss them.

CHAPTER FOUR

"We'll have to make a decision about Sigi soon," Katherine said, struggling to dress Sabina for church. "We can't leave it until the last minute."

Karl held Sabina still, while Katherine did up the buttons on her frock. "I can't see what decision there is to make," he replied. "He's coming back to England with us."

Satisfied the frock was buttoned at last, Katherine let the wriggling toddler escape and run downstairs to her grandmother. "That's your father in you talking. I know he feels the same way. But the others think differently."

Karl looked at her in surprise. "How do you know that?"

Katherine shrugged. "Call it a woman's intuition, if you like." She smiled, then confessed the truth. "No. Really I understand more German than your family thinks. They say things in front of me, they wouldn't say in front of you."

"Such as?"

Katherine sat down on the edge of the bed, and plucked up the courage to suggest to her husband that, like Ilse, he too should abandon their son.

"They think it would be best if he stayed here."

"What? Why should they think that? I know Sigi still won't talk to me, but once we're in England and I'm the only person who speaks his language, he'll soon learn to treat me as his father!"

"Don't forget Werner will be there," she reminded him. Werner was an ex-POW who worked for them. "I hate to say this, Liebling, but I think I agree with your family," Katherine said delicately. "You're looking at this from your own point of view, not Sigi's. You feel it's your duty to look after him, even if he's unhappy living with you. He'll have to go to school with English children, who'll no doubt tease and bully him."

Karl dismissed her argument. "There's no time now to talk about this. We'll be late for church. I can see everyone waiting outside." He picked up his hat and waited for her.

Reluctantly Katherine let the matter rest. She followed him down to the front of the house, where all the Lipinskis – Anna, Stefan, Uwe and Monika – had already set off in the horse-drawn cart, Siegfried amongst them. Dieter and Gisela Driesler had the Volkswagen warmed up, with Sabina sitting on the back seat. Karl and Katherine joined her for the three kilometres to the church of St Peter and Paul.

Karl gave a her a proud squeeze as they walked inside. Many of the residents of Medebach had already seen him and Katherine about the place, but some of the inhabitants of outlying hamlets gave Katherine a good long look as the Driesler entourage entered the church. Siegfried too attracted attention, but Katherine sensed he was accepted into the congregation more readily than she. His mother had been well-known hereabouts. Katherine had a good idea now of how Karl must have felt during his early days with her in Penchurch, subjected to the scrutiny of all and sundry.

She sat on the pew next to Karl, with Sabina on her lap, and studied the light and airy interior of the Roman Catholic church. The white walls and honey-marble floor contrasted with the sombre gloom of Penchurch's St Michael and All Angels, where she was a regular member of the congregation. It was seldom she managed to persuade Karl to attend. Here in his home town he seemed more willing to indulge in the Sunday ritual, despite his lack of faith.

After church, a shooting competition was held in a field near the town. Karl was in his element here, Katherine knew, and watched proudly as her husband demonstrated his superb marksmanship. Siegfried refused to be impressed, turning his back on the proceedings.

The beer flowed freely and a band played all afternoon. As a local event it was totally unlike anything Katherine had ever experienced in Penchurch, bar the rigid formality of the local Hunt. With Sabina happily entertained by a horde of other children, Katherine was able to relax and soak up the unfamiliar scene. She was struck by how changed Karl was in his home-environment. Although in England Karl was a keen member of the new village hall construction team, he was always very restrained. Here he was letting himself go, singing bawdy songs at a pig-roast, exuberantly playing bowls in the

Kegelbahn, and getting more than a little merry on several occasions. She had herself developed a surprising taste for the light German beer, and could well understand why Karl was downing it in such quantities. He would be denied the stuff until their next visit to Germany.

She watched Siegfried playing leap frog with a host of other children, rolling in the meadow grass like a horse loosed from the confinement of its winter stable. He was enjoying himself here. Was it right to drag him off to a foreign land, away from everything he knew? Even after five years in England, it was obvious Karl was happier in Germany. Why should it be any different for Siegfried?

She appreciated now exactly what Karl had given up to allow her to keep her little kingdom of Lane Head Farm, and she was grateful. Of course, they were their own bosses there, but she would miss the benefits of the extended family available here, with a babysitter almost always on hand. Werner, bless him, sat for them often enough, but he was developing his own social life now that he lived down in the village, and he was not as available as he used to be.

Anna sat down on the bench next to her and handed her a glass of white wine together with a plate of sausage and potato salad. Like her brothers, she was blonde and grey-eyed, but was not as angular in her features. There was a softness to her face which complemented her caring nature. During Karl's absence on the shooting range she was making sure her sister-in-law was well looked after.

"Our men are good shots, are they not?" She spoke slowly and clearly for Katherine's benefit.

"Yes. Very good." Katherine pointed to Siegfried. "He is very happy."

"Yes, at the moment, but I think not for much longer. He doesn't want to leave here to go to England with you."

"I know. But Karl says he must come."

Anna looked doubtful, but only shrugged, then called the children to come and eat.

*

The children were all asleep after their busy day. The adults sat quietly in the heavy carved chairs of the living room, drinking schnapps. Karl was brooding over what Katherine had said before church. He turned in his chair to face Stefan.

"Sigi seems to like it here. He's certainly taken to you and Uwe, although I rather think that's because you're not Drieslers."

Stefan, a fun-loving yet hard-working young man, his dark curly hair a sharp contrast to his wife's family, eyed his brother-in-law shrewdly.

"Yes, and Uwe is not a Lipinski but a Schwerte. He was suspicious of me as a new father at first, but when he realised his own father wasn't ever coming back, he soon decided I was the next best thing. Perhaps Sigi will accept you eventually – especially as you are his real father."

Karl detected a lack of conviction in Stefan's voice. "It sounds as though you think I'll have to wait a long time. Sigi seems to have decided he can do without a father; he's got enough grandparents, uncles and aunts to look after him here."

Grandmother Gisela was thrilled to have all her family around her at long last. The prospect of an additional grandchild to look after was not in the least daunting. With a hopeful smile she asked her son: "Would you like him to stay here with us?"

"No, of course not. I want him to be with me. But I get the impression you don't all think the same as I do."

Anna spoke her mind next. "You said yourself, Karl, that Sigi is happy here. Why risk all the upheaval of taking him to England, away from everything he knows? Stefan and I would be more than happy to take care of him, and perhaps we could influence him to love you. If you dragged him to England now, he might hate you for ever for it."

There was an expectant hush about the room as all eyes turned to Karl. Katherine had followed some of the conversation, her ear having become tuned over the past week to the dialect of the region. She too looked at Karl, trying to urge him to agree to Anna's suggestion.

"No." Karl had made up his mind. "How can he learn to love me from a distance? It may take a little time, but he deserves the effort it will take. I want my son to grow up with me."

*

Siegfried watched his father cross the meadow towards him. The two brown cows looked up from their grazing.

"Sigi! Can I have a word with you?"

Siegfried jumped to his feet, leaped the stream where he had been building a dam, and ran off up the track into the forest.

"Sigi!"

He heard his father call, but he was not going to come back to be lectured to. The track was broad but rutted. He soon found a side path leading off to a stand of silver-barked beech trees. Their coppery leaves crackled under his feet and he kicked up piles of them as he ran through their welcoming midst. He liked the forest. Uwe had brought him up here, shown him the deer trails, the squirrel-chewed fir cones, the buzzards soaring over the tree-tops. But Uwe was at school now. Siegfried sat on a mossy beech log, soothed by the rustling voices of the trees. "Fatherland", they seemed to be saying. "Fatherland".

Siegfried suddenly understood what his mother meant by the word. He truly felt part of the country he was born to. He had no father but this. Erich was just a dark memory, but Karl – it was impossible to call him 'father' – Karl cast a monstrous shadow over the future. He was bigger than Erich. Cleverer maybe. Harder to fool. "I'll never let him get me," he told the forest. "I'll kill him first!"

Hunger eventually made him wander back to the black and white house he was already thinking of as home. When Onkel Stefan beckoned to him after lunch, Siegfried hesitantly followed him to the barn. Onkel Rudi was there. And his father!

Stefan shut the barn door and picked up one of the ginger kittens from a pile of hay, depositing it in Siegfried's arms.

"Don't run away this time, Sigi," Stefan pleaded, kneeling in front of him, stroking the kitten's ears. "We want to talk to you, man to man."

Siegfried cast a sidelong glance at his father, then dropped the kitten, which mewed and scuttled away to find its siblings. Siegfried folded his arms in a defiant gesture across his chest, a scowl on his face. Stefan ruffled the boy's hair to try to reassure him. Karl refrained from touching his son. He cleared his throat instead.

"I know you don't want to, but you must listen to me, Sigi. It's important you know exactly what is going on."

"My name is Siegfried." It was the first time he had spoken to his father since his mother's departure.

Unabashed, Karl continued, aware that a small step at least had been taken. "All right. Siegfried then. I want to do what is best for you, but it may be very difficult for you just at first. You know that Katherine and I live in England?"

Siegfried stared across the barn, giving no hint that he heard the question.

"England will soon be your home too," Karl persevered. "We have a farm there, with sheep and hens, a horse you could ride, and a sheepdog called Joss, although he's getting a little old now." He remembered Siegfried's initial interest in the kittens. "We have a new dog too. I'll need your help to train Meg to work as well as Joss does. You could help me with that, couldn't you?"

"Would I have to learn English?" Against his will, Siegfried found his attention drawn to the prospect of having a puppy to look after.

"Yes, of course. You will go to an English school," Karl replied quickly, sensing a stumbling block.

"Then I don't want to live there. I want to stay here with Uwe and go to a German school, like he does."

Rudi tried to help out. "Perhaps I can bring Uwe over for a holiday to stay with you? I'm keen to see your farm, now we're allowed to travel again."

Karl smiled in gratitude to his brother. "That sounds a wonderful idea, don't you think, Siegfried?"

Still ignoring Karl, Siegfried looked wistfully at Rudi. "Won't I ever see Mutti again?" he asked.

"I'm sure you will," Karl replied. "We'll come here often to visit Oma and Opa and everyone. I'm sure you'll have the chance to see her then."

"I don't want to live with you – ever!" Siegfried shouted. Deciding that the discussion was over, he jumped up and ran to the door.

"Shall I stop him?" Rudi asked.

"No. Let him go," Karl said wearily.

Stefan and Rudi exchanged glances. The matter was out of their hands. They had made the offer to have Siegfried, but Karl had declined. Only he could sort out this problem now.

"I gather your talk with Sigi wasn't a great success," Katherine said when Karl joined her and Sabina by the stream. Sabina was paddling, trying to catch minnows.

Karl sat down on the grass beside Katherine and playfully splashed Sabina's chubby legs. "At least he spoke to me. He doesn't want to be called Sigi, it seems. I don't think Ilse can have ever called him that." He gazed up at the clear blue sky. "I just hope I'm doing the right thing. I'm sorry you're going to have all this extra worry, Schatz. I never dreamed we would end up with –"

"Think nothing of it, Liebling. He's your son, and as such is already precious to me. Another 'Schatz' for our family." Katherine's reassurance was genuine. "He's so like you in many ways. There's certainly no doubt you're his father. He's the image of you in those old photographs."

Karl fondled Sabina's short, auburn curls. He was rewarded with a wet hand on his leg as she proudly showed him a shining black pebble.

"Stone!" she told him, before her attention was caught by a new distraction. "Daddy! Fish! Fish!"

It still thrilled him to hear her call him 'Daddy', but he now recognised a new longing. To be called 'Vati'. Perhaps Siegfried would oblige once they were settled in England.

Departure day dawned. Katherine packed Siegfried's new case with clothes, books and toys, bought over the past few days. The go-kart would have to stay. Karl tried to pacify Siegfried over breakfast.

"I promise I'll make you a new one in England." He passed the plate of *Aufschnitt* to Siegfried, who took several pieces of smoked ham, before grabbing an equivalent number of slices of rye bread.

"I'm not going to England."

No one made any comment, but Siegfried laughed at them inside his head as he hid slices of bread and ham under his jumper when he was sure no one was looking. Everyone was too busy after breakfast to notice him slipping off up the forest track. He would hide up in the forest until the English left, then come back to the house to stay with Oma and Opa. They wouldn't send him to England all on his own.

Karl stuck his head round the bedroom door. "Have you seen Siegfried?"

"No." Katherine finished pinning Sabina's nappy. "Isn't he with Stefan and Rudi?"

"No. They said he was with you."

"Oh. He's probably saying goodbye to the kittens with Anna and Monika."

"I'll go and look."

Karl ran downstairs and out through the kitchen to the yard. The barn door was shut. His mother and Anna were pegging out washing, with Monika picking daisies nearby. "Have you seen Siegfried?"

The two women looked at each other. "No," Anna replied anxiously. "We thought he was with you."

Karl ground his teeth in anger. The little monster had said he wasn't going to England. He must have meant it!

"Not found him yet?" Rudi asked from the kitchen door.

"No. I have a horrible suspicion he's run away."

"Oh dear God," Gisela moaned, dropping her handful of clothing back into the laundry basket.

"Where would he go?" asked Anna.

Karl scanned the house and grounds. He wouldn't be here, so close. "The forest, I reckon. He ran off up there the other day when I wanted a word with him."

"He could be anywhere," Anna said, her eyes already searching the surrounding forested slopes.

"We'd better get the men from the sawmill and search the area," Karl told Rudi. "Where's Stefan?"

"With Vater inside. I'll fetch them."

It took a few minutes to comb the entire house thoroughly then organise the half dozen men from the sawmill into groups and allocate search areas. Rudi and Karl went together along the south side of the valley.

"Blast him!" Karl swore, as he and Rudi scoured the undergrowth by the small lake where they had learned to swim. "We'll never make it in time to catch the train now."

"Don't blame him, Karl," Rudi admonished him. "The poor lad's frightened to death of leaving here. I'd probably have done the same thing in his position."

"I know. I don't blame him," Karl replied more calmly. "It's his stepfather and Ilse I blame for maligning me to him. Siegfried hasn't given me the chance yet to show him how much I care for him."

He called out his son's name again, not expecting an answer from the runaway. A faint cry from the hillside beyond the lake startled them both.

"Siegfried?" Karl shouted again.

"Here!" came the reply from within a thick stand of fir trees.

The two brothers raced round the edge of the lake and tore into the dense, dark plantation, brushing the branches from their faces as they ran. Siegfried called every once in a while to give them his direction. At last they spotted him at the base of a small rocky outcrop, over which he had fallen.

"Thank God we've found you!" Karl exclaimed as they knelt down beside the tearful boy. "Are you hurt?"

Trying unsuccessfully to quell his unmanly tears, Siegfried rubbed his left ankle, but remained silent.

Gently Karl felt the ankle, which had started to swell. It did not seem to be broken, but clearly could not be stood upon.

"I'll carry you back to the house and Oma can put a nice cold bandage on that for you," Karl told his son.

"Aren't you cross with me?" Siegfried asked in a small voice, as Karl lifted him into his arms and began to push his way carefully back down through the fir trees, Rudi one step ahead to hold back the larger branches.

"A little bit," Karl answered honestly, "but more than that I'm glad you're safe. You could have been stuck there all night long."

"I know." Siegfried's tears were clear evidence of his fears at such a prospect. "I'm glad you found me, *Vater*."

As an overture of friendship it was small enough, the word 'Father' uttered with a certain reluctance, but Karl was touched by Siegfried's effort. "And I'm glad I found you, Siegfried." At last, Karl added under his breath.

When they got back to the house, Rudi immediately blew three blasts on a whistle to let the other searchers know Siegfried was found. Karl deposited Siegfried on a kitchen chair, to be ministered to by Katherine and Oma, before going out with Rudi to check that all the searchers were returning.

Now that he was safely back, Siegfried felt able to allow some of his former truculence to return. He scowled at Katherine when she tried to take off his shoe, but accepted the piece of chocolate she gave him, after his grandmother told him not to make such a nasty face.

"We were all so worried about you, Siegfried," she told him as she applied a cold compress to his ankle. "Katherine too. She cares about you very much, as does your father. They love you, and don't want you to come to any harm."

"Then why are they taking me to England?" he protested relentlessly.

"Because we love you, and want you to live with us," Katherine replied in German.

Siegfried looked at her in amazement, as if seeing her for the first time. "How can you love me? You don't know me! I can be horrible when I want to, so Erich says."

"And what did Erich do to you when you were horrible?" Gisela asked gently.

Siegfried hung his head and would not answer, but Katherine could see the fear on the boy's face. So like his father, she thought ruefully. Unwilling to trust or confide in anyone, bottling up his feelings until they exploded uncontrollably. Karl was still a bit of a minefield at times. She hoped Siegfried was not going to prove such a problem as Karl once was.

*

The journey back to England was tedious but uneventful. Disabled by his sprained ankle, Siegfried was unable to run away again. His farewells to his new-found relatives were wooden as he tried to hide his emotions from them, and grimly accepted the new path his life was taking. Sabina proved more trouble on the journey than did the broodingly quiet Siegfried.

As he began to hear English spoken more widely around him, first on the channel crossing and then on the train from Harwich to London, the scowl on the boy's face darkened and his refusal to speak became more marked.

To break the journey to Hereford they were stopping a night at the home of one of Katherine's cousins in south London. Evelyn Bagnold had received Katherine's telegram, announcing their day's delay, and was awaiting their arrival with intense interest and speculation. She had met her cousin's German husband only once, on their wedding day, and been very favourably impressed by him. But now it seemed he had a son to complicate matters.

She greeted Katherine with affection and Karl with some shyness, when the weary and travel-stained party arrived on her doorstep mid-afternoon, the day after setting out from Medebach. The little blond boy with them refused to let her near him, so Evelyn left him for Karl to cope with. The strain of the journey was only too apparent on all their faces.

"Come on in!" Evelyn told them, helping with the numerous bags which the taxi driver was unloading.

Sabina woke up and began to grizzle in her mother's arms.

"Do you mind if I go straightaway and change Sabina's nappy?" Katherine asked, clinging on to the wriggling child. "I'll say hello properly in a minute."

Evelyn grinned. She had two school-age children of her own and recognised well Katherine's predicament. "Go on up to the bathroom! Give a shout if you need any help."

She turned to Karl, who was helping the boy off with his coat, and began to make polite conversation about their journey until Katherine returned with a sweeter-smelling Sabina.

As Katherine and her cousin exchanged family news over cups of tea, Karl noticed Siegfried's growing boredom and restlessness. "I saw a park with swings down the road. I'll take Siegfried and Sabina there, if that's all right?"

Katherine was grateful for his suggestion. Sabina was also growing fidgety and was in danger of breaking Evelyn's numerous delicate china ornaments.

Through the front window, Evelyn watched the trio setting off up the road at Sabina's snail's pace with Siegfried hobbling along on his still-swollen ankle.

"That's quite an interesting family you've got now, Katherine," Evelyn commented, her eyes more on the tall figure in the middle of the group. "A handsome bunch too!"

She hoped Katherine would take the bait and supply her with all the details she was longing to hear.

Katherine grinned, sensing the unasked questions. "Siegfried's very like Karl was at that age. He's going to turn some heads when he's older, just like his father does."

Evelyn's ears visibly pricked. She had never been particularly close to her cousin from Herefordshire, but they were of a similar enough age to understand each other well. "Is that a problem for you, Katherine? Karl's good looks, I mean."

Katherine bit her lip, wondering whether to confide her uncertainties to Evelyn, who also had trouble keeping her eyes off Karl. At least Evelyn would understand the problem, she decided.

"Not really," she began. "Until now it just made me more proud to think I was the one who could walk beside him and know he was mine. But when I met Siegfried's mother, Ilse, and realised she had a prior claim to him, I suddenly felt very insecure."

"Does she want him back then?" Evelyn asked in horror.

Katherine remembered that day in Winterberg and Ilse's apparent disinterest in Karl. She had gone over that day in her mind many times, each time becoming more convinced of her suspicions about Ilse.

"When I first saw her, I would have said definitely not. She wanted nothing to do with him, except hand over their son. But after a while her attitude seemed to soften. Because I couldn't really understand all that was being said, I concentrated more on watching her face, her reactions, and more to the point, her emotions. By the time she left, I'm convinced she realised she still loved him, although she hid it well from Karl."

Although secure in her marriage to an insurance salesman who had never given her any cause for concern, Evelyn recognised her own compelling and involuntary attraction to Katherine's husband. She could understood Katherine's fears.

"Are you worried Karl might start to think about this Ilse again, now that he's seen her?"

"No," Katherine denied, rather too hotly in Evelyn's opinion. "But it may be that Ilse starts to pester him. I don't think her marriage is particularly happy, and she may see Karl as a way out for herself, with Siegfried her access to him."

Evelyn grimaced in sympathy. "It certainly looks as though you're in for trouble of some kind now. Siegfried doesn't seem very happy to be here, does he? He's going to be a handful for you." She glanced at the clock. Her own children were due back from school at any moment. "I'd better go and make some sandwiches for Trevor and Shirley. They're always famished when they get back from school."

Katherine followed her out to the kitchen. She was glad to have mentioned her fears to someone. Back home in Penchurch she would have been reluctant to even hint at such fears to people who knew Karl well. It would be disloyal in the extreme, even if the fault was not Karl's ... yet. She angrily dismissed the thought the instant it came to her. Since their marriage he had not looked at another woman. She felt wholly confident in his fidelity. Or had done so until she met Ilse. When she heard that name, she no longer pictured the exhausted woman at the station, but the carefree, smiling young woman close to Karl in the family photo album.

By the time Bill Bagnold arrived home from work, his three-bedroomed, semi-detached suburban house was almost bursting with noise. Trevor and Shirley were squabbling because Trevor had been moved into Shirley's room, and she would not let him build his Meccano set on the floor there; Evelyn was shouting at them to behave; her cousin's baby was squealing in rage from the bathroom. Hiding from the rumpus, Bill Bagnold entered the comparative peace of the front room, only to find it occupied by the two Germans.

Bill held out his hand awkwardly in greeting to the man who had married into his wife's family. He had not approved of the marriage, but did his best now to be polite.

"Good evening. I trust you had a good journey. Can I get you a drink? Scotch, gin, sherry perhaps?"

His host's abruptness was an indication to Karl of the man's nervousness. Karl would have infinitely preferred a beer, but he opted for the scotch.

The two men eyed each other over their drinks, aware of the tension between them. Siegfried sat sullenly on the sofa, watching a goldfish swimming round and round in its bowl on top of a bookcase. Conversation was almost non-existant until Evelyn entered the room and kissed her husband in welcome.

"A sherry for me, please, darling," she begged him, as she sank onto the sofa next to Siegfried, who shied away. "Those two are playing up as usual. You'll have to sort them out in a minute. I've had enough!"

"Yes, dear. In a minute," Bill replied, slowly getting up to fetch her drink, and putting off the moment when he would have to go and lay down the law. Ineffectually as usual. Why Evelyn expected him to have any more control over them than she did, he had no idea.

"I am sorry we are putting you to so much trouble," Karl apologised to Evelyn.

"Oh, it's no trouble, I assure you, Karl. Trevor and Shirley are always fighting over something or other. It's lovely to have you here as a distraction from them." She settled down with her sherry, smiling warmly. "Katherine's been telling me all about the outhouse you've been converting into a holiday home. We'll have to come up some time soon and make use of it. It will make a nice change from Bognor. Now the children are older they want more than just a bucket and spade holiday, don't you think?"

"Yes, I'm sure they do," he replied, wishing Katherine would hurry up bathing Sabina. He sensed Bill Bagnold's disapproval of his wife's suggestion.

"Does your son want a drink of anything, while we're waiting?" Evelyn asked. "He's sitting there so quietly, poor dear. I don't suppose he understands a word we're saying, does he?"

Karl's question to Siegfried met with silence. Karl shrugged, and made his apologies for his son's attitude. "I am sorry Siegfried is so quiet, but this is all very strange for him, and no doubt he misses his mother."

Evelyn's curiosity was instantly aroused by the mention of the intriguing Ilse, but before she could ask any questions, Karl's smile told her that Katherine had stepped into the room.

Really, Katherine had nothing to worry about, Evelyn thought enviously to herself. She glanced across at her own insipid husband. No other woman would look twice at *him*. Karl might be handsome but he also loved Katherine. That much was quite clear.

*

It was a relief to be on the final stage of the journey at last. When the bus pulled into Penchurch and they saw Werner Gimpel waiting with the Land Rover to take them home, both Katherine and Karl sighed audibly.

Werner too had received a telegram, warning of the day's delay. "Welcome home at last," he greeted them, with a pat on the head for Sabina. Feigning ignorance of the situation, he turned politely to Siegfried. "And who is this?" he asked in his heavily accented English. Werner was not as dedicated about perfecting his accent as his boss.

"This is my son, Siegfried," Karl explained, holding the boy lightly by the shoulders, aware of the gaze of several villagers who had also travelled on the bus. "Let's get these bags into the Land Rover, Werner. We're all keen to get home."

Not to be hurried, Werner held out his hand to Siegfried and declared: *"Es freut mich sehr dich kennenzulernen, Siegfried. Ich heiße Werner Gimpel."*

Unaware until now that there would be another German about, Siegfried grinned back at Werner, making an instant ally of him. As Karl drove them all back to the farm, Werner quizzed Siegfried on Germany and his impressions of England so far, while Karl listened to his son's confident and friendly answers. It was the same as with Uwe. Siegfried instantly accepted the fatherly Werner, sensing no threat in him.

It was Werner who helped the boy out of the Land Rover at Lane Head Farm, and it was to Werner that Siegfried ran for protection when he saw Joss and Meg, the Border Collies, come running towards them.

Katherine made a big fuss of the dogs, then persuaded Siegfried to stand his ground while they sniffed him out. Karl watched approvingly as Siegfried's tension diminished by the second with Werner, Joss and Meg's help. For himself, he felt impotent to help Siegfried. He concentrated instead on getting Sabina and the baggage into the house. He must be patient with Siegfried, he reminded himself. But the pain at seeing him respond so readily to Werner hurt him deeply.

CHAPTER FIVE

They had given him a fortnight but the inevitable could no longer be avoided. "School." Siegfried said the English word out loud to his reflection as he combed his hair. He had refused from the outset to let his stepmother do it for him. He didn't need nannying like Sabina. They didn't seem to realise just how much he could do for himself. He put down the comb – he already knew its English name – then ran out of his bedroom and down the stairs to the kitchen.

"Are you ready now? *Fertig*?" Katherine asked him.

"*Ja. Fertig.*"

His refusal to speak English would soon have to change, she supposed, once he got to school. She went to the back door and called to Karl by the toolshed. "He's ready now."

For his first few days Karl was driving Siegfried to and from school until the boy got his bearings and more confidence. Then it would be the school bus each day. They arrived at the little primary school in Penchurch at ten to nine to meet the headmistress, who then showed them to the infants' classroom.

Silence fell. Twenty inquisitive faces stared at him from the low desks. Siegfried's cheeks burned. He almost reached for his father's hand, but stopped himself. This was no time for cowardice.

The class teacher, Miss Humphries, stood up to welcome her new pupil.

"Good morning, Siegfried." She smiled warmly at both the boy and his father, patted her wiry grey hair to make sure it was safely gathered into its bun, then turned to the children. "Class, this is our new boy, Siegfried Driesler. I'm sure you're going to help him settle in and make his first day a pleasant one. Matthew Powell, you can be in charge of looking after Siegfried today."

The formidable Miss Humphries had twenty-six years' experience teaching infant school children, but never before had she dealt with a child who spoke no English. It would be a severe test of her ability.

His nationality was no less of a problem. She had no illusions about how difficult the new boy would find settling in. Children could be very cruel to anyone the least bit different. She pushed her glasses back up her hooked nose for a good look at him. Small for his age, she decided, casting a comparative glance at his tall father. Most likely malnourished in Germany, poor little mite.

Siegfried felt pinned under the gaze of a voracious eagle. The slightest movement and she would swoop in for the kill. His only hope was to outstare the beast. It seemed to work.

"Well, Mr Driesler, if you would like to leave Siegfried with us now, I'm sure we can make him happy here. We've got lots of things to do today – there's painting and games after lunch."

"Thank you, Miss Humphries. Siegfried's already learned a few English words, but I expect we'll hear a few more this afternoon."

"No doubt," she smiled, ushering him to the door. She noticed Siegfried did not give his father a second glance. That was a good sign. Perhaps he would settle in easily.

"Right, Siegfried. Let's find your peg. Then you can hang up your shoe-bag and coat."

Siegfried's hand was grasped and he was pulled towards the corridor. The teacher showed him a peg with the name 'Siegfried Driesler' written boldly on a label above it. It was wrong. He was Siegfried Brünninghaus, no matter what his father told him. Back in the classroom again, Miss Humphries sat him next to a chubby, freckle-faced boy.

"This is Matthew, Siegfried. Say hello to him."

Siegfried was surprised he understood what the eagle-beaked teacher said. Without thinking, he did as he was told. "Hello, Massew," he said politely. Laughter rippled round the class. Siegfried scowled.

Miss Humphries realised her mistake and was quick to divert attention. "Come along, children. Let's get back to work now. We were copying some words off the blackboard." She placed a slate and chalk in front of Siegfried, hoping he would join in.

Siegfried watched Matthew pick up his chalk and write the word 'cat' on his slate. There followed a list of words with similar endings, and Siegfried found himself enjoying the task. 'Cat' was a word he already knew from a picture book Katherine had shown him, but the other words were all meaningless.

At morning break he learned the words 'milk' and 'play', before being led out into the playground by Matthew. Once there, however, Matthew ran off with another lad. Siegfried began to follow but found himself at the centre of a circle of older boys and girls. Taunts began to fly.

"Look at the baby Jerry!"

"'e's so frigh'ened 'e'll wet 'isself."

"Who's a pretty boy, then?"

Siegfried regarded them disdainfully. He knew how to handle bullies. Showing no fear, he approached the toughest-looking boy, kicked him on the shin, then elbowed him out of the way. There were gasps of astonishment as he escaped the circle, but no one followed him.

He seemed to have made the right impression. They left him alone after that, apart from the occasional verbal taunt from a safe distance. If any other children tried being friendly with him, they were promptly picked upon by the older children for fraternising with the enemy. In class it was another matter. Under Miss Humphries' eagle eye Siegfried was tolerated. He joined in lessons enthusiastically having decided that one way of getting his own back was to come top of the class. He soon discovered he had no problem with sums, and he found more and more English words springing to mind in the weeks leading up to the summer holidays.

On the last day of term, Siegfried handed Katherine his end of term report. She could see Siegfried was agog to know what it said, so she opened it, rather than wait for Karl to come in for tea.

Siegfried has made an impressive start to his school life here, Miss Humphries had written. *Despite the language difficulties he is an intelligent and industrious pupil and tries hard in all subjects. His spoken English is developing well, while his written work is neat and well-presented. He is always polite to the staff, although he has yet to establish any relationships with other children.*

Katherine put down the report and smiled at him. "That's very good, Siegfried. Well done! Vati will be very proud of you."

She spoke in German, to show her pleasure. Normally when Siegfried came in from school, she spoke English for the sake of continuity. It was only when Karl and Werner joined them for tea that the conversation lapsed into German. Katherine decided it might be better to stick to English from now on, then Siegfried would pick it up even quicker. He could save German for his moments alone with Karl and Werner.

Karl was equally full of praise for his son, when he read the report a few minutes later. This time Siegfried did not smile. He ignored his father's praise.

"Please may I have another scone?" he asked Katherine.

She handed the plate to him. "Pass them round. Vati wants one too."

Siegfried took a scone then pushed the plate halfway across the table to his father, making Karl reach for it. Karl knew not to make an issue of it. It would only antagonise Siegfried more.

*

Over the summer Siegfried spent as much time with Werner as possible, adopting the little grey-haired man as an uncle.

"Why didn't you go back to Germany?" Siegfried asked him one day as they rested during haymaking.

"Ach, it's a sad story, little one. You wouldn't want to hear it."

"Yes I would. Please tell me, Onkel Werner."

Werner settled himself on the grass and braced himself to relate his tragic family history. "I used to have a lovely little house in Berlin. It was a little cramped with myself, my wife and our four dear children, but we were happy. The end of the war brought so much bombing and shelling of the city. All I know is that my family did not survive. Not one of them. Whether they were killed by the bombs or the Russians, by illness or hunger, I don't know. I was a prisoner here by then and no post was getting through. The Red Cross informed me later they had perished, and that was it. I had no desire to return to a Germany ruled by the Russians. When your father said he would need help on the farm here, once he was released, I asked for permission to stay in England, and was lucky to get it. I couldn't have ended up in a better place. They're lovely people, your father and stepmother."

Siegfried snorted derisively. Werner was only too well aware of the boy's animosity towards Karl. Perhaps because of it, he found himself treating Siegfried as one of his own children, telling him stories, giving him more time than he deserved. Siegfried learned to exploit Werner's soft-heart. But it was thanks to Sabina he found a means of causing conflict between his father and stepmother, something he found very entertaining.

It was a muggy August evening. The family gathered in the kitchen to admire the results of Siegfried's afternoon spent painting. He was particularly proud of a scene showing a Messerschmidt 109 shooting down a Spitfire. He stood holding it up in front of him, so the others could see it. The burst of flame from the British plane looked almost real. It reminded him of Herr Cornelius' shed. That was a sight worth remembering! Suddenly his picture was snatched from his hands by Sabina. He tried to grab it back and the picture tore right down the middle. Siegfried lashed out, just as he had done once at his other half-sister, Margit. The result was almost the same.

"Siegfried!" Karl yelled at him over Sabina's wails. "How dare you hit Sabina! Say sorry to her."

"She tore my picture," he muttered. "She should say sorry to me."

"Nevertheless you shouldn't have hit her. That's a spiteful thing to do. Now say you're sorry."

Sabina was beyond listening. Siegfried knew the apology was demanded as a form of punishment. He kept his mouth tightly shut.

Karl sensed stalemate and changed tactics. "If you're going to be like that, you can go up to your room."

Siegfried insolently stood his ground, deliberately testing his father's patience.

"Go on! Upstairs!"

Katherine was busy cuddling Sabina, but Siegfried noticed her keeping an eye on the developing confrontation.

Karl's temper broke. He grabbed Siegfried's shoulder and spun him round. A more than gentle push sent him flying out towards the hall.

"Karl! Don't!" he heard Katherine cry out. Siegfried clattered noisily upstairs then crept down again to listen at the kitchen door, catching the end of Katherine's speech.

"... as bad as Ilse's husband."

"Don't talk rubbish! I only pushed him. It wasn't as if I hit him."

"It was a jolly hard push. He could have collided with the door or something."

"I knew what I was doing. We mustn't be too soft on him, just because Röbel was too hard."

The angry voices continued for some minutes. In the end Siegfried decided Katherine must have won, as his father's voice sounded conciliatory. Siegfried grinned. He would not have minded a beating if it got his father into trouble too!

The next day Siegfried was bent on disrupting the mens' work. With his favourite German story-book under his arm he begged of Werner: "Read me a story, please!"

Soft-hearted Werner obliged, leaving Karl to continue copse-clearing on his own for the next quarter of an hour, wishing Siegfried would ask *him* for once.

The only time Karl had his son's full attention was during their training sessions with Meg. Karl had never trained a sheep-dog before and was relying on Katherine's help as well as tips from a neighbouring farmer. These he tried out with Siegfried's assistance. Karl gave a certain whistle, Siegfried pulled Meg on the lead to the left, another whistle and Meg came right. They had to develop a system different from the one Joss knew, so each dog had its own set of commands. Siegfried enjoyed working with the dogs, making them obey his instructions. It gave him a satisfying sense of power.

Another thing Siegfried loved were his mother's letters, which his father read out for him. Siegfried longed to be able to read them himself. Having heard a letter through once, Siegfried would try reading it himself.

My darling boy, he read.

I still miss you so much, but with every day that passes I know I did the right thing sending you to your father. At least you have lots of space to play in, and your own room too!

I am always so pleased to receive your letters. Please thank your Daddy for helping you write them. Soon you'll be able to write all by yourself, my clever boy!

I am busy making a new dress for Margit. Do you remember when she was first born, I had to borrow her clothes from a neighbour? Perhaps you don't. Germany is recovering quickly now. You wouldn't believe the number of new buildings around the flat. I keep hoping Erich will find us somewhere bigger to live, but I don't think he will.

Well, my darling, I must finish here, as Erich will be in soon. Please write again and tell me how Meg is doing. My love and best wishes to you and your family.
Mutti.

It was the last line which made him determined to read her letters for himself. He did not want his father receiving her love and best wishes. He devoted his evenings to his German books, curled up on the garden seat under the big pear tree. Every so often he would have to find Katherine or his father to help with a word, but Siegfried found German far easier to read than the curiously spelt English.

After a summer concentrating on reading German, his English spelling acquired German characteristics. His new teacher, Mrs Chambers, had problems reading Siegfried's attempts at written English. 'I wend vor a work,' was bad enough, but the word 'sru' stumped her, and she had to ask the boy what he meant.

"Oh! You mean 'through'!" she laughed. "Well, I'm not surprised you had trouble with that one." She wrote out the correct spelling and made him copy it out ten times.

Siegfried looked at the word in disbelief. "Stupid language!" he said to himself, but it only made him more determined to conquer it.

He tended to avoid the playground at break, preferring to loiter inconspicuously behind the coke heap, or as today, in the cloakroom. He was not always successful.

"Hey, you! Jerry!"

Siegfried took a deep breath and braced himself. He recognised the voice of one of the older boys, who regularly took great delight in increasing Siegfried's vocabulary of words of abuse.

John Winters saw the bait being taken. For all his measly six years, the German knew how to fight. Winters had made sure he had supporters on hand this time before beginning his Jerry-baiting.

"What you doin' all by yourself, Kraut? Hidin' from us? I've got a little test for you. Bet you can't say 'the Leith police dismisseth us'. Go on! Let's hear you try an' say that, Kraut. I bet you anything you like you can't."

John Winters proceeded to give a rendering of the sentence in a diabolical German accent, which sent his pals into fits of laughter.

Despite the provocation, Siegfried held his tongue. He could not yet argue to his own satisfaction in their language. The only language they all understood was that of his fists. Suddenly, at a signal from Winters, three boys made a grab for Siegfried, hoisted him into the air and hooked his belt over a coat peg, leaving him suspended, arms and legs flailing in space. The boys then all stood back and jeered at their captive.

A part of Siegfried's rage was directed at his tormentors, but a deeper, hidden part was also directed at his father for bringing him to England and making him have to suffer such indignities.

A shout from the end of the corridor warned the boys of an approaching teacher. They fled into the playground before Miss Smith, the headmistress, could identify the perpetrators of the racket emanating from the cloakroom.

"Oh dear!" she sighed quietly, as she spotted the pathetic, dangling figure. She hurried to his aid and lifted him awkwardly down to the floor, sensing his burning anger.

"Who did this to you, Siegfried?" she asked him gently.

Siegfried looked straight through her, his lips set in a determined line. He was not going to be accused of telling tales, as she surely knew who it had been. It was always the Winters boy and his gang. The other children in the school only made fun of him and rarely pushed him around.

Miss Smith gave up the inquisition. "Run along outside now, Siegfried. I'll have a word with Miss Warner on playground duty and tell her to keep an eye open for trouble."

Siegfried fled Miss Smith's presence. Finding a secluded spot in the sunshine by the coke heap, he sat on the ground planning his revenge on John Winters. His eye was caught by a nice pebble, smooth and round at one end, but with a wickedly sharp point at the other. He picked it up and ran his finger over the jagged edge. Pocketing the stone, he sauntered across the playground to where Miss Warner stood holding the hands of two five year-old girls, new to school that term. Making sure she had seen him near her, he dodged behind her back, took quick aim at his target, before stepping back into the teacher's field of vision.

A scream of alarm from across the playground alerted Miss Warner. Dropping hold of the little girls' hands and side-stepping round the loitering Siegfried Driesler, she hurried over to the prone figure of John Winters.

Siegfried smothered a self-satisfied grin behind his hand and joined the crowd of children quickly gathering round the casualty.

"Stand back, children!" Mrs Warner ordered. "Julia, you go and fetch Miss Biggins," she told one of the older children. Miss Biggins, the school secretary also functioned as the nurse.

Siegfried allowed himself to be shepherded back, as the children watched John Winters groggily open his eyes and try to sit up. He noted with even more satisfaction the blood trickling from deep within Winters' hair. Revenge was sweet, and he savoured its flavour for the remainder of the day.

*

"You're in a good mood today," Katherine remarked as Siegfried came home. "Did you have a good day at school?"

"Yes." Such was Siegfried's pleasure, he actually smiled at her as he helped himself to the milk and biscuits left out for him.

For once Katherine refrained from reminding him not to dump his satchel on the kitchen floor. Now into her fifth month of pregnancy she was careful to rest for a while each afternoon. Karl looked after Sabina for an hour, giving her a breathing space before having to cope with Siegfried.

Sabina came running in through the door, followed by her daddy and 'Uncle' Werner, and made a grab for the biscuits.

"One at a time, Sabina!" Karl told her, extracting two crumbling digestives from her grubby fingers.

"Siegfried says he had a good day at school today," Katherine told him, pouring out tea. "Didn't you, Siegfried?"

Siegfried nodded through a mouthful of biscuit. There was no way he was going to tell the adults why he was so pleased. He gulped down his milk, then ran out to the yard and on up to the woods. In his hideout in a thicket of old-man's-beard, Siegfried's jubilation waned. Seeing his father again reminded him of his earlier rage when suspended from the peg.

"It's all his fault!" He stamped on a scurrying beetle. "I've got to get back at *him* too."

It was not easy thinking of ways he could hurt his father. He searched his memory for experiences which might be of help.

*

Over their cups of tea, the adults congratulated themselves on Siegfried's apparent adaptation to life in England.

"Perhaps he's made some friends at long last," Katherine suggested. She looked pointedly at her husband. "Which is more than can be said for you, Karl. I hadn't realised until our trip to Germany just what a sociable person you really are. I've always thought of you as a loner, but you're not, are you?"

Karl lifted Sabina onto his knee. "You know what the problem is. Only you and the Murdochs really accept me. To everyone else I'm still 'that German who had the mental breakdown and nearly killed Mr Kellett'. I always feel they're watching me for signs I'm going crazy again."

Werner nodded in agreement. "It's the same for me. I try to be friendly, but always I know I am different from the others. After a few beers it is better."

Katherine giggled. "What a pair you are! Even an Englishman would feel the same way moving to the village from outside. Surely it's the same in small towns and villages in Germany?"

Karl frowned. "Come on! Our nationality is the problem!"

"So why is it different for Werner when he's had a few beers?" Katherine persisted. "Surely it's then that he's letting himself go. We need to find a way for you to do the same, Liebchen. You need to become more involved with some village activity, instead of concentrating all your time and energy on the farm."

"I've spent a lot of time helping build the village hall!"

"Yes, but even there you tend to work by youself. You need to become a regular participant of something."

He laughed. "Don't you dare suggest the church choir!"

"I wouldn't dream of suggesting such a thing to a pagan. Even one as nice as you." Inspiration suddenly struck her. "How about helping backstage for the next Penchurch Players production, making scenery and suchlike? That would be just up your street."

"As if I haven't enough work here," he moaned jokingly. "All right. When is their next play?"

"At the end of this month. I'll tell Vic Threadgold, shall I, that you're keen to help backstage?"

Karl grinned. "Yes, all right, Schatz. They can let me know when they need me." He turned to Werner, who was already on his feet ready to get back to work. "How about you? Are you an actor, Werner? Perhaps they can use you too!"

Werner dismissed the idea outright. "My English is not good enough. You know that! But my evenings are with Vera. She is enough for me!"

Karl slapped him heartily on the back. "I know just how you feel."

From his hideout Siegfried watched the two men walk back to the newly constructed feed-store, replacing the converted holiday home. The two-storey building was virtually complete, blending in with the reddish-pink stonework of the other outhouses. Siegfried watched his father climb a ladder to the roof. Werner hoisted up a basket of tiles using a rope and pulley before joining Karl on the roof. Siegfried grinned. He knew how they worked. His father would come down first to fetch more tiles.

"Just you wait, father," Siegfried quietly promised, his excitement growing. "I'm going to get even with you. You're going to learn a lesson just like John Winters did today."

The ladder had given him an idea. After some struggling, Siegfried managed to detach a sturdy length of creeper from his hide-out. Certain that Katherine was busy with his pest of a half-sister, he furtively made his way down to the new feedstore, unobserved by the men on the roof.

He could hear the men talking as he crept up the ladder to examine the rope securing it to a roof joist. Perfect! A quick release knot made the task simple for him. He left the rope loosely wound about the joist, descended the ladder then knocked away the chocks. Next he carefully wound the creeper round one foot of the ladder. He tugged gently on the creeper. The ladder moved slightly towards him before steadying itself. With the weight of a man on it Siegfried knew it would be much harder to pull, so he placed a large, rounded stone under the foot of the ladder. He grinned in anticipation and thanks to his young teachers of such tricks in Dortmund, then hid himself around the corner of the feed-store, the two ends of the creeper clutched tightly in his hand.

"My turn to go down for some more tiles, I think," Karl said to Werner. "If we're lucky we should finish by this evening. The weather's not going to be so good tomorrow." He cast his eye westwards to where the flat-topped mass of Hay Bluff was shadowed by approaching cloud.

Easing himself carefully over the edge of the roof onto the ladder, Karl felt an unaccustomed wobble. He grabbed for the roof but his movement only seemed to upset the ladder more. His fingertips brushed the roof's edge as the ladder fell away, taking him with it. He hit the ground with his right foot trapped between the rungs.

The sickening noise made Werner fear the worst. He peered down over the edge of the roof. Karl lay twisted over the ladder, his right foot lying at an odd angle.

Stuck on the roof, Werner filled his lungs with air and yelled. "Katherine!"

He called again, watching Karl struggling to sit up, but there was no sign from the house that Katherine had heard. A groan from Karl made him abandon his attempts to alert Katherine. Karl would have to help himself.

"Karl!" Werner saw a slight nod. "Katherine doesn't seem to have heard me. I'll have to get down from here somehow. I daren't jump in case I break something too. If I throw the rope from the tile-basket down, can you tie the end to the ladder, then I can haul it up."

Still winded, Karl got himself onto one elbow and tried to make sense of his injuries. Werner's voice gave him something to work on and he looked down at his legs, the source of most of his pain.

"*Scheiße*!" he swore on seeing his foot. He steeled himself to sit up properly, unable to stifle a gasp as he did so. Now he could see his foot caught between the rungs. He had to get it out somehow. Once his entire leg lay on top of the ladder, he would then have to shift the ladder out from beneath him.

Werner watched helplessly as Karl slowly manoeuvred his broken leg. At last his foot slipped over the edge of the ladder onto the ground. He sank back, exhausted by his efforts.

Werner sighed in relief. A trained paratrooper might have considered jumping from the roof, but at forty-eight he felt he was well past gymnastics and was glad Karl had managed to extricate himself successfully. He called to Karl to warn him the rope was coming down, then hauled it up once Karl had tied the ladder to it.

"I'll go and find Katherine," Werner said, once he was safely down. He set off at a run towards the half-timbered farmhouse.

Karl lay on the ground, waiting helplessly. Despite the pain, he sensed a presence near him. He looked up to see Siegfried standing over him.

"Where've you been?" Karl demanded sharply. "Didn't you hear Werner calling for help?"

Siegfried made no reply but bent down to inspect his father's twisted right leg, pleased his plan worked so smoothly. The creeper had released itself from under the ladder as it fell, enabling him to withdraw it out of sight to where he was hidden around the corner. He heard with delight the crack of breaking bones and his father's groans and curses. Upon Werner's departure he left his hiding place to gloat over his success.

"Does it hurt?" he asked innocently. "Is it broken?"

"Yes." Karl closed his eyes in the hope it would stop Siegfried from asking any more stupid questions. He did not see the smile which finally escaped his son's control.

Siegfried noticed Katherine trotting towards them, dragging Sabina behind her. He wiped away his smile and hung back out of the way to observe the rest of the drama as Werner too rejoined the scene.

Katherine dropped down at Karl's side. The first thing she noticed was his chalky face and his lips drawn tight in pain. She held his hand. It felt clammy. "Werner said you fell off the ladder," she said, trying to sound calm. "There's an ambulance on its way, and Donald's coming too. He should be ... Sabina! Get back! Don't touch Daddy's leg. It's hurt."

Sabina sat down in fright at the sudden reprimand and began to cry. Daddy's leg looked odd. Werner picked her up and cuddled her.

"We'll go to wait for the doctor, little one," he said lightly, walking off with her back to the house. "We must tell Uncle Donald where to come, eh?"

Karl watched their retreat. He felt so foolish lying there. He turned his head back to look up at Katherine. "I can't imagine how it happened, Schatz. The ladder was steady when we went up it. But when I came down it moved. The ladder fell, not me."

"Don't worry about it now. You won't be going back up it for quite a while yet."

"No." The pain was mounting. Karl closed his eyes to concentrate on overcoming it. Pain had been a large part of his life during the latter part of the war, but that didn't seem to count for anything now. "I must be getting soft," he muttered through clenched teeth.

"Rubbish. You're doing very well. Donald will be here soon. Perhaps he'll give you something for the pain."

Katherine had thought Karl's face white before, but it paled further at her remark. She knew why. "Dr Goldberg said you would be able to face injections, didn't he? The hypnosis cured you of your fear, didn't it?" she said firmly, hoping her confidence would carry over to Karl.

"I don't know. We never had time to test it."

She felt a rising panic. Was pain relief worth the risk of another mental breakdown? Hoping she sounded confident she tried to reassure him. "You'll be fine, Schatz." She cocked her head. She could hear Donald's car driving up the lane. A minute later she saw Werner leading Donald Murdoch towards them.

The Scottish doctor was approaching retirement age. Heavily built, he was breathing hard after his brisk walk from the road. "That's a nasty break," he declared after a swift examination. "But you've not damaged an artery, thank heavens." He checked Karl's pulse and grunted. "Hmm. We'd better give you something for the pain before the ambulance gets here."

Karl caught Katherine's eye. He gave a slight shake of his head. Donald Murdoch noticed it too. "Ah. Yes. I'd forgotten. Injections are a problem, aren't they? Though you've never told me why."

Boldly Katherine intervened. "Karl should be cured of his fear, Donald. We've just never had the chance to test the cure. Now seems as good a time as any." She squeezed Karl's hand confidently. "I'm with you, Schatz. You'll be fine."

From his vantage point close by, Siegfried listened in amazement. His father *was* a coward! Frightened of injections indeed! He watched closely his father's face as the doctor prepared a syringe. Yes! There was definitely fear there. But despite his ardent hopes to the contrary, his father received the injection without a murmur. Siegfried felt deprived of a spectacle and momentarily disappointed.

As the ambulance arrived he reminded himself of what he had achieved that day. This was even better than John Winters! It was a glorious victory, especially since his father clearly had no idea his fall was not an accident. Now he would know what it was like to be helpless and in pain. He must pay for all Erich's cruelty. This was only the beginning!

CHAPTER SIX

Werner had put Sabina to bed and was listening to Siegfried reading when Katherine arrived back from the hospital.

"How is he today?" he asked as she took off her coat and hung it up by the back door.

"Fed up with lying in bed. He asked me to take some paperwork in for him to do. He's going to write home and ask if his brother, Rudi, would like to come and help us out while he's laid up."

Siegfried's ears pricked up. "Onkel Rudi comes here?"

Katherine smiled at him. "Maybe. We'll see." She sat down in the rocking chair and laid her hands over the growing mound of her belly. She was rewarded by a hefty kick from inside. "He's going to be a footballer, this one," she laughed.

Werner left to cycle down to his lodgings in the village and Siegfried disappeared up to bed. Katherine switched on the wireless and put her feet up to do some knitting for the new baby, due in early February. She should be back on feet in time for lambing in March. That would be an exhausting time. She would be up all hours with the baby, and Karl would be up all night with the ewes. The winter was not a good time to be at the end of a pregnancy. Remembering the winter of 1947, when Lane Head Farm was cut-off for weeks, Karl had recently insisted on buying one of the new Land Rovers to replace the old Austin. It seemed an awful lot of money at the time, but it was proving its worth many times over.

She thought over all the changes since Karl took over the running of Lane Head. Given his forestry background, it was only natural he was making more of the woodland than her father had done. And not only at Lane Head. Other farmers in the area were asking him to fell awkward trees near to buildings, to thin out woodland or do a spot of coppicing. She would have to cancel some of Karl and Werner's engagements, until Rudi could come over to help. In the meantime, Karl could perhaps get on with his animal woodcarvings. He donated some to the church bazaars, but mainly sold them to a shop in Hereford, near the cathedral. The shop always took as many as he had to offer.

The baby moved inside her. "Your Daddy's a clever man," she told it.

The baby moved again and Katherine put her mind to choosing a name for it. "Let's see. Your Daddy says we must choose names which Oma and Opa can manage. What do you think of Richard? That's slightly different in German, I think. But not too much. I suppose I'd better think of a girl's name, just in case, but I'm sure you're a boy." Her eyes lifted to the beamed ceiling, above which was Siegfried's room. "I just hope you learn to love your Daddy better than his other son does."

*

Siegfried was thrilled when he heard Onkel Rudi was bringing a friend with him. Two more people he could speak German to! On the day they were due to arrive, Siegfried was reluctant to leave for school.

"They won't get here till later this afternoon." Katherine crammed his cap on his head. "Off you go, or you'll miss the bus!"

Katherine was relieved help was finally coming. She and Werner were finding the farm and family difficult to cope with on their own, despite Gertie Murdoch's constant stream of pies and cakes, and offers to babysit. After lunch she set off in the Land Rover for Penchurch to leave Sabina with Gertie, then drove on to Hereford station. She wondered what Rudi's friend, Gustav Halstrup, would be like. All Rudi had said was that Gustav wanted to improve his English. At least he would have been a help on the journey for Rudi, who spoke no English at all.

She was just in time for the train. It pulled into the station, disgorging a stream of passengers. Easy to spot amongst them was a tall figure she recognised, accompanied by a much shorter one she did not.

"Rudi!" she called from the ticket barrier.

He waved in acknowledgement as they queued to show their tickets. Finally they were through.

"Welcome to Hereford!" she said in German, kissing her brother-in-law warmly on the cheek. "I hope the journey was not too exhausting."

65

Rudi smiled appreciatively at her attempt to speak his language. He had thoroughly approved of Karl's English wife from the moment he first met her last May. "Once we reached Harwich it was very interesting," he replied, remembering the questioning by the customs official there. He cast his eyes over her bulging coat. "You are well?"

"Very well, thank you." The greetings over she turned towards the confidently smiling man next to him. "Welcome, Herr Halstrup. I hope your English is better than my German!"

Gustav reached for her hand and raised it to his narrow lips. "Gustav, please! I'm honoured to meet such a beautiful lady," he replied in English, handing her an expensive bunch of red roses which he had kept hidden behind his back.

Slightly embarrassed by the depth of his gaze, Katherine took the flowers and offered her thanks. "The car's over there." She pointed across the station forecourt. "Your luggage can go in the back of the Land Rover, and you can both squeeze in the front with me."

She was careful to engineer it so Rudi sat next to her. Gustav feigned disappointment that he was not allowed to sit in the middle.

It was Gustav who did most of the talking on the drive back to Penchurch to collect Sabina, although Katherine did manage to point out some of the sights on the way. Something about Gustav's manner was beginning to irritate her by the time they turned up the single-track lane leading to Lane Head Farm. He seemed rather full of himself, she decided, or perhaps he was simply trying too hard to be friendly. She hoped that was the reason as she pulled up in the yard and tooted the horn to let Werner know they had arrived.

Rudi looked around at his brother's home and understood at last why Karl had not come back to his family in Germany after his release. It was beautiful here; the black and white farmhouse, the pink stone farm buildings, the woods behind the farm now in their autumn colours, and the sweeping view westward across the sheep meadows and laden orchards, towards distant hills and the village further down the valley.

Katherine saw how entranced he was by the scenery and left him to enjoy it while Gustav made a fuss of Sabina. With the bunch of roses clutched in one hand, Sabina led Gustav by the other into the kitchen. Katherine followed, leaving Werner with Rudi.

Rudi finished admiring the scenery and turned round. "You must be Werner," he said, shaking the solid little man's hand. "Karl counts himself very lucky to have such a good friend and worker here."

Werner was dismissive of the praise. "I am the lucky one to work in such a paradise as this. We get on well together, all of us. Even little Siegfried calls me 'Uncle' Werner."

Warned by Werner's use of the word 'even', Rudi asked: "How are things between Karl and Siegfried now?"

Werner grimaced. "Not good. Karl tries to be patient with the boy, but I can see how hard he takes it every time Siegfried rebuffs him."

Katherine reappeared, having put her flowers in water. Gustav was paying her close attention and she decided to show the men their room and give them the chance to settle in.

"This is where you'll be staying, Gustav," she said, beckoning to Rudi too. She led them across the yard to the old feedstore. "It's not finished yet, as you can see, but I hope you will be comfortable. Werner has put in the plumbing but it's not yet connected to the mains water supply or the drainage system."

She showed them the compact living area and as yet unusable kitchen downstairs, then the bedroom and bathroom upstairs. "Karl plans to make all the cupboards and furniture himself eventually, but I got Werner to put in a few old pieces for you in the meantime. The new fodder store had to be finished first."

Although understanding nothing of what she said, Rudi looked round approvingly. "I would love to have a project like this to work on myself."

Gustav shook his head in amazement. "I wouldn't know where to start!"

Katherine smiled. "I'll leave you to unpack while I make us some tea."

She knew the two men would probably prefer beer or coffee, but she had made a point of fitting in with German customs whilst there, so they could do the same here. The whole point of visiting a foreign country was to experience all the customs and flavours it had to offer.

Siegfried arrived back from school while they were drinking their tea. The school bus dropped him off at the bottom of the lane, and knowing the visitors were due, he ran most of the way up the hill to the farm in the hope they had already arrived.

"Onkel Rudi!" he shrieked as he hurtled through the door.

The warmth of his welcome surprised them all. Stefan was the favourite uncle back in Medebach, but it seemed Siegfried was pleased to see any other German these days. Rudi stood and picked up his nephew, holding him high to have a good look at him.

"Look at you! Haven't you grown! You'll be catching your Dad up soon!" He put Siegfried down and pointed to a parcel waiting on the kitchen table. "That's from Oma and Opa. They sent you their love, as did Onkel Stefan, Tante Anna, Uwe, Monika and baby Lothar."

While Siegfried eagerly tore off the wrapping paper, Sabina tried to show him the toy bear which had been in her parcel.

"Go away!" Siegfried shouted at her as she invaded that precious moment of discovery. He pulled out a clockwork train, beautiful in its detail and paintwork, and ran his fingers lovingly over the present from Germany, as though it were a sacred object. Without a further word to anyone he ran off with it up to his bedroom.

Werner caught Katherine's eye in disapproval, but she did not want to cause a scene so soon after their guests' arrival. Siegfried could come and be more sociable once he had got over the excitement of his present. Instead she turned the subject back to her guests.

"So, Gustav, how is it that you can take three weeks off work? What is it that you do for a living?"

"I am actor, but at the moment I have no work. So it is a good time to come here to better my English."

Katherine was intrigued. She had never met a professional actor before. "Are you in films or on the stage?"

Gustav tried, not very hard Katherine thought, to look modest. "Mostly on the stage, but I had a small part in one film. I would really like to go to Hollywood one day."

The actor's eternal dream, Katherine supposed. "That's why you're so keen to improve your English, is it?" she asked, realising now why Gustav seemed so full of himself and eager to make a big impression on people.

"Yes indeed."

After tea Katherine decided to show the two visitors round the farm, allowing Werner to get on with his work. Sabina rode on her uncle's shoulders. They began by strolling down to the orchards to check on the progress of the apple pickers.

"Why do they use poles to knock down the apples?" Rudi asked. "Surely the apples will bruise."

"These apples are for a drink ... apple-beer," Katherine explained, not knowing the German word for cider. She pointed to a pile of apples, continuing in her pidgin German. "We leave them a week or two on the ground, covered with straw. Then they go to Hereford. Last year there were many apples; this year the same. We always get £14 a ton for them, but there are too many apples now. Perhaps we only get £10 a ton this year, and we can't sell them all."

"People must drink more cider," Gustav suggested. "I'd like to try some."

"Certainly. You'll have plenty of opportunity while you're here."

They moved on from the orchards back up the hill to Karl's new tree nursery, safely fenced off from the sheep. Rudi found himself once again envying his brother's total control over the farm. The Driesler sawmill was run as a family concern with their father still very much at the head of it.

After showing them the woods, Katherine led them back to the house. "I must cook dinner now, but you wander about and do what you like. Tomorrow we'll find some work for you."

*

Karl climbed stiffly out of the ambulance onto his crutches and braced himself to receive Sabina's hug. The children were not allowed to visit him in hospital. According to Katherine, Siegfried showed no inclination to go anyway, unlike Sabina. Karl balanced carefully on his good leg before bending over to kiss Sabina, who was already trying to show him her new bear.

"Has he got a name?" Karl asked her.

"Gustav," she replied with a broad grin on her freckly face.

Katherine hurried to explain. "He seems to have made a big impression on her," she informed Karl, after receiving her own kiss from him. "Gustav is very much a lady's man, I fear."

"I can see I'll have to keep an eye on him," he laughed good-humouredly, "in case he runs off with my daughter! Where are Rudi and this Gustav, anyway?"

"They're up in the woods with Werner, but I expect they'll be here in a minute. They must have heard the ambulance coming up the hill."

As she spoke there was a loud bark from behind a hedge and the two Border Collies came bounding up to welcome back their master. The three Germans were not far behind. Rudi hugged Karl warmly, slapping him on the back before he introduced Gustav.

"It's good to see you, Karl!" Gustav greeted him before Karl had a chance to speak. "What a wonderful place you've got here, and what a beautiful family! It makes a poor orphan like me realise just what I've missed in life."

Bemused by the effusive speech, Karl caught the twinkle of suppressed laughter in Katherine's eye. This was obviously Gustav's standard pattern of speech.

Sabina was most intrigued by her father's use of crutches as they all trooped inside.

"Don't get in Daddy's way," Katherine warned her. "You might trip him up."

As it was, Sabina was on his lap the moment he sat down on one of the kitchen chairs, his plastered leg stretched out in front of him. Katherine found a footstool for him to rest his leg on, and Karl sat back, enjoying the fuss being made of him.

Work was abandoned for the afternoon, at least by Rudi and Gustav. Werner retreated back to the woods, while Karl caught up on family news and Gustav chatted to Katherine, telling her of his exploits on the stage. The mixture of spoken English and German was not unusual to Sabina's ears. She soaked up both languages and had a reasonable vocabulary in both for a two-year-old, but showed a respectful preference for English.

Siegfried's appearance on the scene at four o'clock was predictable in its disruptive effect. Flinging his satchel on the floor, he stared coldly at his father, refusing to make any concessions to welcome him home, then greeted Rudi, and Gustav in particular. Making a grab for the jam tarts on the table he sat himself next to Gustav and regaled him with the graphic details of how a child at school had been sick over the back of another child that day.

Karl did not want his first words to Siegfried to be a reprimand, but the conversation was not a pleasant one, so he sought to change it. As was the custom at that time of day, he spoke in English.

"I hear Oma and Opa sent you a toy train. Would you like to show it to me?"

A withering look was Siegfried's response, then he carried on his conversation in German with Gustav.

Gustav realised such behaviour was not acceptable and made the point to Siegfried, in English. "Your father asked you a question. You must answer him."

Siegfried met each disapproving adult eye in turn. "*Nein. Ich hasse ihn! Und ihr seid alle so gleich wie ihn.*"

He jumped down from the table, spilling his milk in the process, and ran off upstairs to his room. He took the clockwork train from its position in pride of place on the shelf, and ran his fingers over the rough edges of the cog-wheels, feeling his anger burning inside him. He had told them they were all the same as his father. Gustav should not have taken sides against him. Now he felt his trust in Gustav was betrayed. They could all go to hell!

Down in the kitchen there was a moment's embarrassed silence before Karl spoke. "I'm sorry. You can see for yourselves what a difficult time we're having with Siegfried. It's taking much longer than I thought to get him to accept us as his parents. His life was brutally hard until recently and I'm afraid it still shows."

"I'd say he could do with a good thrashing," Rudi muttered in strong dialect so Katherine would not understand. He guessed she was opposed to such punishment.

Karl shrugged. "Maybe, but I feel I've lost the battle if I do that."

"Why does he hate you so much, Karl?" Gustav asked.

Katherine, recognising a long discussion in German in the offing, excused herself from the table to start preparations for Siegfried and Sabina's tea and their own dinner. The three men needed the chance to chat together.

"Why don't you all go down to the Walnut Tree this evening?" she suggested later, sitting Sabina up in her high-chair with a plate of egg sandwiches in front of her. "In any case, you'd better move on into the living room, or I'll never get Siegfried down to eat his tea."

"Let him go without his tea!" Karl snapped. "Why should I move because of him?" He instantly regretted his sharp tone. It was not Katherine he was cross with, after all. He quickly put his hand on hers and gave it a squeeze.

71

Gustav wondered whether to interfere or not. "Would it help if I went up and had a word with him, do you think? I had a sister who used to sulk and I was always the one sent to fetch her down."

Karl looked wistfully at his plaster cast. He ought to go himself but he did not fancy trying to get upstairs. "Thank you. You might find a way of getting to him that we've not discovered yet."

*

From his bed Siegfried heard Gustav's knock. "Go away."

"It's Gustav. I want a word. It's important."

Siegfried was curious. He had liked Gustav until now, so he went to open the door. Gustav came in and shut it behind him. He sat on the bed and indicated to Siegfried to do the same.

"Now, Siegfried. Listen to me. I know you are proud to be German, am I right?"

Siegfried nodded.

"So, a German boy does not sulk on his bed like a little girl. You must be strong and face your father, no matter how much you hate him. I feel as you do, that he has betrayed his country. He should work in Germany, helping the Fatherland grow strong again, not here making the enemy richer. It is up to you to make amends for him. But for the moment you must hide your anger, deceive him. The time will come one day when you are strong enough to punish him properly. That's what you want to do, isn't it?"

Siegfried was spellbound. "How do you know that?"

"I can feel it. Maybe because I hate the English as much as you. Their bombs killed my entire family. The others – Werner, Rudi, and of course Katherine – they all like Karl far too much to understand your feelings. I could see immediately how you felt. You may ask, why did I want to come to England? Well, I'll tell you if you promise not to tell anyone else." Gustav's hand held Siegfried's knee as he leaned forward to whisper: "I can spy on the English better if I know the language, can't I?"

Siegfried's eyes were as round as grenades. "You're a spy?"

Gustav put his forefinger to his lips. "Shh. Not yet. But I'm working on it."

"Cor!"

"Now spies have to be good actors. They must pretend they are different from who they really are. Do you understand?"

Siegfried could hardly believe his ears. Gustav a spy! He nodded eagerly.

"Right. So I want you to come downstairs with me now and we'll both pretend we like Karl and Katherine. Not too sudden a change from you, mind, or they'll be suspicious. Just gradually start being nicer to them. All right?"

"All right."

When Gustav reappeared with Siegfried in tow, nobody said anything. Siegfried sat down to eat his tea as if nothing had happened.

Later that evening Werner drove them down to the Walnut Tree to sample a few pints of English beer. The four Germans sat at a corner table and inevitably the conversation turned to the problem of Siegfried.

"So what did you say to him to persuade him to come down?" Karl asked Gustav.

Gustav finished his pint, giving himself time to think. "I told him he should be grateful to have a family, since I lost mine in the war. He shouldn't throw away a precious gift."

"But he's been told that before. Why did he listen to you?"

"Maybe because I'm not part of his family. Who knows?" Gustav tilted his empty glass. "Another beer, anyone?"

It was unusual for the other locals to hear German spoken. Karl and Werner kept to English when off the farm. As the evening drew on and Gustav became louder and more dramatic with every drink, some mutterings were audible to Karl from a group standing at the bar. He himself was drinking very little as he did not want to risk being unsteady on his feet, and Werner was keeping a reasonably clear head to drive them all back, but Rudi and Gustav were definitely the worse for drink.

Karl gave Werner a nudge under the table and looked pointedly at the clock. He was about to suggest to Rudi it was time to go when the door to the public bar opened and a couple stepped in. Karl immediately recognised them as his arch-enemy Pat Collins and her new boy-friend. Mrs Collins was a young war-widow who had always made her hatred of Germans clear to Karl, latterly to Werner too.

"We can't leave now, Karl," Werner whispered. "It'll look like we're trying to avoid her." They were both determined not to let Mrs Collins intimidate them.

"Another ten minutes then, but no more, otherwise Gustav is going to embarrass us, I think," Karl warned.

Gustav broke in, his speech beginning to slur. "What's this cider like then, that you grow the apples for? I'd like to try some."

"Another time, Gustav," Karl advised him. "The English have a saying: 'Beer on cider will stay inside yer, but cider on beer will reappear'. I've never tested the truth of it but I don't think we'd better start now. Finish your beer and we'll start back for home. We mustn't be too late as Werner has to get back to the village again after he's dropped us all off."

He noticed Mrs Collins and her beefy friend had sat near the group of regulars at the bar and seemed to be ignoring the foursome in the corner. Nevertheless he found himself on edge and growing increasingly anxious about Rudi and Gustav's loud voices. He hated his own oversensitivity to public opinion, but he had to live in the village, whereas Gustav did not.

Gathering together his crutches he stood up. Rudi and Gustav downed their last dregs and followed Karl past the bar towards the door. As Karl passed by Mrs Collins he seemed to trip over a bar stool and lost his balance. Gustav, who was right behind, made a grab for him and prevented him crashing to the floor. Having set Karl firmly back on his feet again, Gustav turned angrily to the poker-faced Englishwoman.

"You did that! You pushed that chair in front of him!" he accused her.

There was a hush at the bar and Karl saw Mrs Collins' boyfriend bristle protectively, but she was quite able to speak up for herself.

"How dare you come to our country and speak to me like that! Such behaviour might be normal in Germany but it's not acceptable here!"

Now it was Gustav's turn to bristle with rage. "You English think that because you have won the war you can do as you like!"

Karl stepped in quickly before the conflict escalated out of control. "Gustav! Outside, now!" he barked in a tone which brooked no argument.

Gustav hesitated briefly but Rudi grabbed his arm and pulled him towards the door. Karl turned slowly to face Mrs Collins. He hated what he had to do, particularly since he knew Gustav was correct in his accusation, but he knew better than to stir up ill-feelings.

"I'm sorry about that," he said coldly but civilly. "I think he has probably had too much to drink."

Pat Collins looked at him haughtily, saying nothing at first, as though it were beneath her dignity to speak to such a person as Karl. However, she could not resist a final fling.

"I see the SS are still used to getting their orders obeyed."

Karl heard the normally placid Werner grind his teeth. Ignoring the woman, Karl called to the landlord behind the bar.

"Goodnight, Alf."

"Goodnight, Mr Driesler," Alf Butler replied cheerily, glad that a potentially nasty rumpus had been avoided.

Outside, Karl hustled them towards the parked Land Rover, using one crutch like a shepherd's crook. Gustav looked over his shoulder toward the lighted doorway, obviously wanting to avoid an ignominious retreat, as he and Rudi helped Karl into the back of the Land Rover.

"Are they all like that around here?" Gustav asked once they were safely on their way.

"No, only her and Katherine's former fiancé, Andrew Kellett. Naturally enough he has no great love for me, but he is married now with two children of his own," Karl explained, hanging on tightly as Werner took a corner at speed. "Kellett and I stay a respectful distance from each other. Audrey, his wife, keeps him from my throat, and Katherine keeps me from his."

"Sounds wonderful," Rudi commented.

Karl laughed. "To set the balance straight you must meet the Murdochs. Oh, and Mrs Tucker from the village shop. She did a lot to influence people in my favour. For the most part, everyone here has been very friendly towards us, haven't they Werner? Especially Vera White, eh?"

Werner grunted. His landlady, a widow for many years, was proving to be most solicitous in her care of her lodger. The fact that Werner had great trouble in saying her name correctly did not seem to trouble her in the slightest, nor did the rumours circulating round the village that another Anglo-German wedding was in the offing.

Katherine was waiting for them when they trooped back into the house. They had managed to shake off the incident with Mrs Collins and were singing a rousing marching song in defiance of her.

"All right you lot! Quieten down, or you'll wake Sabina. Who wants a cup of coffee, tea or chocolate?"

Werner declined her offer, prefering to get back to his lodgings and Vera's company, but the others all opted for coffee.

"Let me help you," Gustav said, following her out to the kitchen. "You must not work so hard in your condition."

Katherine laughed but was grateful for his help. She was feeling tired, and her back was beginning to ache. She would have liked Karl to have rubbed it for her tonight, and wondered whether it would be possible, incapacitated as he was. She smiled as she thought of other matters which would be more awkward for the time being, but they knew of ways around that problem.

Gustav saw the smile. It was a shame Katherine was so obviously happily married, and pregnant with it. She was a beautiful woman.

CHAPTER SEVEN

Katherine brought Karl's mid-morning cup of coffee into the study. "Sarah just rang." She leaned over his shoulder, avoiding his plastered leg which stuck out to one side of the desk, and moved some paper so she could put the coffee down. "She and Perry want to come over this weekend to see us. I told her the house was rather full, so they're going to ask Donald and Gertie to put them up."

Karl looked up from his designs for cupboards. "About time too. How long have they been married? Two years? And they've only visited us once." His eyes narrowed in speculation. "I bet she asked to come as soon as she heard Rudi was here."

"Hole in one! She's never met any of your family, so you can hardly blame her."

"I'm not blaming her. I'm honoured she shows such an interest in them. I hope Perry can stand it, though."

"Stand what?"

"The German invasion. There are five of us here now. He'll be the only Englishman."

Katherine dismissed his flippant remark. "Perry's completely cosmopolitan. Anyway, you got on all right with him before."

"Let's just say we only have Sarah in common. I wouldn't choose him as a friend." He tried to explain himself better. "It's his job, Schatz. A London accountant. He seems only interested in money. Nothing else."

"You mean he's not interested in Sarah?" she goaded. "Why did he want to marry her then?"

He tilted his head in thought. "In my opinion, Sarah bulldozed him into marrying her so she would have somewhere nice to live when she was offered that job in London."

"Don't judge them so harshly!" She put her arms round his neck and pressed her nose pugnaciously against his ear. "Just because they don't show their affection in public, doesn't mean to say they don't love each other."

"I think she loves him because she can boss him around." He stared up into her bewitching green eyes. "Just like the way you boss me around. It must be a family habit."

For a moment she thought he was serious, then she pouted her lips so they reached his in a pecking kiss. "Do you know why I love you so much?" She did not wait for his reply. "It's because I know how much you love me. I know you would do anything for me."

"And I know you would never ask me for anything."

"Wouldn't I? Haven't I already?" She backed away so she could see him more easily. "What about exclusive rights to your body?" she said. Her twinkling eyes betrayed her otherwise serious expression.

Karl replied, equally straight-faced. "Well, you know. It's not always so easy for a handsome devil like me to keep the women away. I can't promise –" He saw the fear creep into her eyes and stopped his fooling. "Schatz, I was only joking. You know I would never –"

Her peal of laughter cut him short. "I'm a better actor than you are!"

She poked him in the ribs. In retaliation he lunged at her. She stepped aside, tripped over his outstretched leg and fell in a giggling heap on the floor.

"How undignified at my age and in my condition," she spluttered.

From his chair, Karl gave her a hand to help her up. "I wonder whether Sarah and Perry behave like children too, in private."

Katherine looked doubtful. "I somehow can't see Perry larking about. He's always so proper. I suppose we'll have a better idea when they visit us."

"Gustav will probably like him," Karl said. "He takes himself very seriously too."

Karl proved correct. When Sarah and Perry drove up from the Murdochs' house in Penchurch the following Saturday morning, Gustav was his usual forward self and dominated the visitors.

"I can see you are Katherine's sister," he greeted Sarah with a kiss of the hand. "You have the same beautiful hair and charming eyes."

Sarah was used to receiving men's attentions, but Gustav's continental forthrightness made even her blush. Gustav, however, was even-handed in his compliments and turned to the fair-haired young Englishman with the pale complexion and soft hands of an office worker.

"I hear you work in the City of London," Gustav declared, sounding suitably impressed.

Katherine and Karl watched in shared secret amusement as Perry responded, like Sarah, to Gustav's flattery. They continued to observe the couple over lunch. Sarah and Perry seemed happy enough together, although Sarah was definitely the dominant partner, butting in on her husband to correct him or explain things for him. Perry largely ignored his niece and Siegfried, declaring himself 'no good' with children, but Sarah was eager to be a good aunt to them both.

While washing up she gazed out over the yard. The overcast sky was brightening in the west and promised a fine afternoon.

"Who's for a walk on Hay Bluff?" Sarah asked. "I need to clear the London smog from my lungs. Siegfried? How about you coming and helping me show Gustav and Rudi the countryside."

Siegfried did not need persuading. "If Gustav goes, I go."

Gustav put Sarah's plan to Rudi, who seemed as keen as Siegfried. "I can carry Sabina when she gets tired," he suggested.

"That's five," Gustav announced. "Who also?"

"Count me out," Perry yawned. "I'm not one for walking. I'll stay here and keep Karl company. What about you, Katherine? I don't suppose you walk far with that bump of yours?"

"You'd be surprised," she said. "But I think I'll stay and have a rest, if you're all out. Take the chance while I can!"

Peace and quiet descended on the house after Sarah's expedition was packed off. Katherine felt her eyes closing as she sat back in the rocking chair. Karl was out in the toolshed showing Perry the start he had made on Sabina's playhouse, so hopefully she could doze for a few minutes.

Her mind drifted back pleasurably to the previous night when Karl was very restless in bed. She finally managed to get him to sleep after making love to him. She was glad her bump was no bigger than it was. Karl just lay there and let her do all the work. Being master of the situation for once had been an exciting novelty for her, and she knew she would repeat the exercise in the near future.

She woke with a start when the backdoor opened and Karl hobbled in.

"Where's Perry?" she asked, yawning widely.

"I left him in the toolshed. He seemed quite keen to have a go at woodcarving, once I'd shown him the basics. There is another side to Perry after all, apart from money."

"See, I told you!" she said, giving him a squeeze. She glanced at the clock. It was only three o'clock but her mouth felt dry after her sleep. "Want some tea?" she asked.

"It's all right. I'll make it." He stood behind her and slipped his arms round her neck and over her breasts. "It's a pity Perry's around or we could have done what we did last night," he breathed in her ear. "We don't often get the chance during the day now, do we?"

So he had been thinking about it too, Katherine smiled happily, as she watched him fill the kettle and carefully carry it over to the range.

"Was Perry really engrossed in what he was doing?" she asked tentatively.

Karl turned to glance through the window across the yard to the toolshed, then took the kettle off the hob. "I think so. Shall we?" He held out his hand to escort her upstairs.

*

As was customary after church on a Sunday, Katherine returned to Lane Head Farm to collect everyone to take them to the Murdochs' for lunch. A staunch supporter of Karl from his earliest days in the village, Gertie welcomed his brother with equal enthusiasm. Gustav received a slightly more reserved greeting from the petite woman, still as energetic as ever in her sixtieth year.

"You'll have to excuse Donald for a few minutes," she said. "He's gone off on a call, but he shouldn't be long."

Gertie organised them all with sherry in the sitting room. Katherine refrained from offering to help as she knew Gertie loved pampering them. It was partly why she and Karl continued to come for Sunday lunch, week after week. The Drieslers were a substitute family for the Murdochs, whose only surviving son, Robert, was in London studying medicine, seldom managing to return home. Donald and Gertie acted as English grandparents for Sabina. Siegfried had yet to accept them as such, but never complained about visiting them.

Once Donald returned, all ten of them sat down to roast beef and Yorkshire pudding.

"Gustav wants to get into films," Sarah announced to Donald and Gertie. "Isn't that right, Gustav?"

"Oh, really?" Gertie asked with great interest, her native Scots accent more marked than her husband's. "And how do you plan to set about doing that, Gustav?"

Gustav wiped his mouth on his napkin. "Perry knows people who find the money to make films. It is possible that he can find me a way in there."

Perry looked nonplussed at the suggestion. "It's not that easy, Gustav. The financial backers don't necessarily have any influence over casting."

"I know, but with some names and introductions I can make myself known to the right people," Gustav smiled confidently at Perry.

Perry felt himself persuaded to try. Gustav certainly had a way of getting what he wanted. "Perhaps there are people at Ealing I could introduce you to. I'll telephone a contact of mine on Monday morning and see if he has any suggestions," he promised the delighted Gustav.

Rudi and Siegfried sat silently eating their meal. Donald felt that the colourful Gustav was dominating the conversation, so tried to encourage Siegfried to join in the English conversation. The little boy's air of complete indifference to those around him worried him.

"Tell me, Siegfried. What do you want to be when you grow up? An actor like Gustav, a farmer like your father, or what?"

"A soldier," Siegfried declared with absolute certainty. "With a gun."

There was an awkward silence around the table. Katherine remembered a conversation between herself and her father soon after Karl's arrival on the farm. She had been obsessed by the thought that during the war Karl had killed people. To make her see sense, her father promptly suggested Karl should go out hunting with the shot-gun. She tried the same ploy now.

"We'll have to get Vati to teach you how to shoot, since he's an expert, won't we?"

Siegfried's response was instantaneous and enthusiastic. "Please, Vati, will you teach me?" he pleaded, his eager eyes shining.

Karl was utterly taken aback by the warmth of Siegfried's request. Not once had his son asked anything of him until now.

"Certainly. In a year or two when you are big enough to hold a shot-gun, then I will teach you," he promised.

Siegfried's impatience was evident to all.

"Finish your dinner, boy. It seems like you've got some more growing to do," Donald advised him.

Siegfried tucked in to the last of his greens with gusto.

When lunch was all cleared away and Sabina had been taken upstairs for her nap, Gertie sought out Karl to ask a favour.

"I wonder, Karl, if you and your brother would indulge me by singing for us. I remember hearing you say once that you and Rudi often sang together to entertain your visitors."

"I don't think you would like the politics of much of what we sang in those days," Karl remarked, "but I'm sure we can think of something more suitable. I'll ask Rudi."

Rudi was only too pleased to join Karl in song again, and since Siegfried knew a couple of the songs they sang, it was quite a family performance. Not to be outdone, Gustav proved to be an accomplished pianist and the spontaneous concert lasted most of the afternoon, with even a stumbling rendition of *Baa, Baa, Black Sheep* from Sabina, once she rejoined the proceedings.

Siegfried's sudden amiability towards Karl was seen through by everyone, but it was the general hope that the promise of shooting lessons would be the catalyst for an improvement in the relationship between father and son.

As they waved goodbye to their guests at the end of the day, Gertie could not help remarking on Siegfried's about-turn.

"How can a small boy, not yet seven, be so devious? I often find myself wondering what's going on in that head of his. Poor Karl has taken on more than he realises, I think." She led them all back into the warm house.

Sarah was more dismissive. "Siegfried won't keep up the pretence for long. He'll soon be back into his old ways, you wait and see."

Perry was keen to add his twopenn'orth. "Karl's going to have to teach that little blighter a bit of history sooner rather than later. He seems to have the idea that we started the war, and that Hitler was a great leader."

"Good Lord!" Gertie was horrified. "When did he tell you that?"

"Before lunch. I was trying to get him to talk to me, feeling sorry for him and all, but as soon as he began to praise Hitler I lost all sympathy for him. If his mother feels like that it's no wonder Karl lost interest in her."

Sarah corrected him. "One thing I do know about Karl's shady past, is that it was the other way around, darling. It was Ilse who found Karl's ideas intolerable. Siegfried thinks his father was a traitor to his country, because his mother always told him so."

"Hence Siegfried's excessive patriotism, trying to make up for his father's deficiencies in that respect," Perry deduced.

From his armchair by the fire, Donald blew out a swirl of pipe smoke. "That sounds plausible, Perry. So the more English Karl seems to Siegfried, the more he wants to make up for it by proving his loyalty to Germany." He tapped his pipe thoughtfully against his teeth. "You know, when they were all singing German folk songs together, I could have sworn Siegfried's enjoyment was genuine. I really don't see how such a small boy could be such a convincing actor."

"You obviously didn't see him flinch when Karl gave him a hug at the end," Perry remarked acidly. "Perhaps I was just unduly influenced by what I'd heard earlier, but to me, Siegfried's performance was one big charade."

"Don't be so hard on him!" Sarah scolded her husband. "We can't expect him to change overnight. Give him another year and he'll be fluent in English and reading the *Hotspur* like any other boy his age."

Perry laughed. "You're optimistic, my love. You've not seen boys' comics recently, by the sound of things. They're full of war stories with ugly Germans who can only shout '*Gott in Himmel!*' before being blown to pieces by British commandos."

"When did you become such an avid reader of comics, eh?" Sarah jibed, but she accepted his point. Siegfried would not take kindly to such stories, or to his schoolfriends being influenced in their perception of Germans by them. The comics reminded her of the war films being made. "You know, I don't know why Gustav wants to be in films which only show his countrymen as sadists or morons."

Perry was not so dubious. "He would if it was a stepping stone to better things. He's got great determination, has Gustav. I can see him doing well for himself eventually. In fact the more I think about it, the more interested I'm becoming in this film lark of his. I'm keen to see how he gets on."

"He's certainly very charming, isn't he?" Gertie commented. "I think young ladies would know what I mean, wouldn't they, Sarah?"

If her words were meant as a veiled warning to Perry, he missed it completely. "Star quality. That's what it's called, Mrs Murdoch."

*

On Monday evening there was a telephone call for Gustav from Perry. On re-entering the living room Gustav's face was wreathed in smiles.

"Rudi must go back to Germany alone," he declared triumphantly. "I stay in England with Sarah and Perry to work in films. He spoke to a friend of his who promises to help me. That's wonderful, isn't it?"

Katherine had to laugh at Gustav's boundless optimism, but nothing would shake his firm belief that a part in a film would be forthcoming.

Even Rudi, once Gustav translated, was pleased for his friend, but with some reservations. "I hope you'll stay on in Hereford to help out until Karl's out of plaster."

"Sorry, Rudi, but Perry has arranged a meeting for me with this friend of his for Thursday. I plan to leave here the day after tomorrow." He changed to English to address Katherine and to apologise for his abrupt departure.

"I change one delightful hostess for another," he flattered her. "But you surely understand, I hope. You and Sarah both like to act."

Katherine wondered how he came by that information, but she responded by playing down her interest. "I've had a few small parts in our local plays, but nowadays, with the children, it isn't so easy. Anyway, they have enough women in the Penchurch Players. It's men they're always short of."

"Then Karl must try it!" Gustav declared. "He seems to speak English so well. Surely he could help them out?"

"I've already offered to help backstage. If my leg wasn't broken I'd be down in the village hall this very moment."

Gustav's eyes twinkled in certainty. "Soon they will find a part for you. Wait and see!"

Katherine smiled. That was her hope too. A higher public profile would do wonders for Karl's sense of acceptance within the community. It might even begin to heal the rift between Lane Head Farm and Froxley Grange, which was proving very awkward at times. Andrew Kellett had never forgiven her for choosing to marry a German instead of himself.

Rudi made some comment which Katherine missed, and the conversation continued in rapid German. She got up from her chair by the fire and fetched her sewing box to patch the seat of yet another pair of Siegfried's short trousers. In a way she was glad Gustav was leaving so soon. She still felt uncomfortable in his presence, as though he were making a pass at her the whole time. Sarah had better watch out, if she was going to have him as a guest.

*

Karl gazed despondently at the accounts. The price for cider apples was as low as they had feared; demand was equally low. His plans to have the plumbing and sewerage connected to the guest flat, as they now called it, would have to wait. Most of his plans to diversify the farm's income would take time to come to fruition, although a gradually increasing revenue was being earned from the small forestry jobs performed for others. Rudi and Werner were out coppicing a neighbour's woodland at this very moment.

He looked at the watch inherited from Katherine's father. She ought to have dropped Gustav off at the station by now and be on her way home. Sabina was upstairs asleep. Karl hoped she would not wake up before Katherine returned.

He heard the telephone ring in the hall and cursed. Now Sabina would surely wake up. He reached for his crutches and hobbled out to the hall to answer the telephone.

"Mr Driesler? Good afternoon. It's Miss Smith here, from the school."

Karl recognised the headmistress's precise tones and returned her greeting warily, anticipating trouble. "Good afternoon, Miss Smith. Is there any problem?"

There was a brief pause from the other end of the line before Miss Smith spoke again. "I'm afraid so, but I would rather not discuss it over the telephone. Would it be possible for you to come straight down to the school to see me?"

The fact that she asked to see him personally rather than Katherine warned Karl of the seriousness of the situation. Siegfried was not simply ill and needing to be brought home.

"I'll have to wait until my wife returns to drive me," he told her. The whole village knew of his broken leg. "It might be another half an hour until I can come. Is that all right?"

It clearly was not, as Karl could hear by the impatience in Miss Smith's reply. "I would appreciate it if you could get here as soon as possible, Mr Driesler."

As he hauled himself up the stairs to answer Sabina's insistent demands to be lifted from her cot, Karl's imagination began to take over as he feared the worst. Siegfried had been unusually distraught that morning at the prospect of Gustav's departure. The pair of them seemed to have a secret understanding; Gustav could effect miraculous changes of mood from the surly Siegfried. Was this episode at school a response to losing Gustav?

Sabina clung tightly to him as he picked her up from her cot. She was soft and warm from sleep and he kissed the top of her head tenderly as he put her down on the floor. She reached up to him, wanting to be carried downstairs.

"No, Liebchen. Daddy can't carry you at the moment. You must walk."

He heard the Land Rover draw up outside "Listen! There's Mummy back. You run down and say hello."

Distracted from demanding to be carried, Sabina raced downstairs. Karl followed at a far more sedate pace, face sombre as he greeted Katherine.

"What's the matter, Schatz? Has Sabina been playing up?" Katherine asked, taking off her coat and hat.

"No, she's been fine. It's Siegfried. Something has happened at the school and Miss Smith wants to see me immediately."

Katherine halted in the process of hanging up her coat and put it on again instead. "We'd better get you down there then. I can drop Sabina off at Gertie's and come in with you, if you want."

"You don't have to, Schatz. If Miss Smith is going to reprimand me for Siegfried's behaviour then you don't have to sit and listen to it too."

"I don't mind, honestly. I feel I ought to be there. I am his stepmother after all."

Karl nodded his appreciation then reached for his own and Sabina's overcoats which were hanging by the back door.

When they arrived at Yew Tree Lodge to deposit Sabina, they sensed Gertie already knew something of what had happened, but she said nothing and quickly took Sabina off to the kitchen so they could get away.

It was a short drive back along the narrow valley road to the village school. Katherine parked outside the gates and waited for Karl to get himself settled on his feet. It was afternoon play time and the playground was filled with screaming children, but as they saw Siegfried's parents arrive an ominous hush descended over them, leaving Karl wondering what on earth Siegfried could have done to have affected the children so deeply.

Holding doors open for him, Katherine led Karl down the corridor to the school secretary's office to announce their arrival. Miss Biggins, a matronly figure who knew all the pupils and their parents, gave Karl an unusually frosty look as she showed them into Miss Smith's overheated office.

Siegfried was sitting on a chair at the side of the room. He stared defiantly at his father as he saw him enter the room, concealing the delight he felt at seeing his father brought before Miss Smith.

"Good afternoon, Mr and Mrs Driesler," the headmistress greeted them civilly. Miss Smith knew she had a delicate task on her hands. She always hated having to see a child's parents over a disciplinary matter, and this case was even more serious than usual. "Won't you sit down, please?"

Karl and Katherine sat on the upright chairs in front of the desk, upon which lay an open penknife. Miss Smith wasted no more time.

"This is the reason I asked you to see me, Mr Driesler," she said, indicating the penknife. "This afternoon, during the lunch break, your son not only threatened a child with this knife, but actually wounded that child. Fortunately it was not a deep cut, although Dr Murdoch was called to attend to it. When a member of my staff tried to take the knife off your son, Siegfried shouted what we can only presume was abuse in German at her. I have refrained from reporting this incident to the police only with the agreement of the other boy's parents, but as you can well imagine, I am reluctant to let your son continue at this school unless we can be sure that there will be no more incidents such as this." She paused, allowing her expression to soften behind her glasses. "I am aware of the problems Siegfried has with abuse from certain of the children here, which is why I am taking a more than leanient stance on this. Siegfried was not wholly to blame in the incident, but the possession of a penknife at school is strictly against the rules."

As he listened in horror to what Miss Smith had to say, Karl studied the pen-knife, baffled as to its origins. Turning to Siegfried for explanation he demanded angrily: "Where did this come from?"

Siegfried looked at first as though he would refuse to answer, but he caught Miss Smith's fearsome eye and grudgingly gave his reply. "Gustav."

Karl stared at him almost in disbelief and he heard Katherine's indrawn breath of dismay. "Why did you bring it to school?" he asked more gently.

Siegfried regarded him boldly, with no hint of remorse evident. "You have always a knife. Why then not I?"

Miss Smith seemed shocked. Karl strove to reassure her. "A penknife, Miss Smith. I use it often on the farm."

She nodded. "Siegfried has already been given a firm ticking off by me, but I expect you will have some words for him too, Mr Driesler. In the meantime, I think he had better stay away from school for the rest of this week, until tempers cool. The other boy's parents have assured me they will speak to him about his continual baiting of Siegfried. Let's hope we can put an end to this silliness. What do you say, Siegfried?" she said with a warmer smile at last in his direction.

"Yes, Miss Smith," he replied, meekly enough.

Miss Smith smiled even more fondly at him. She felt very sorry for the little boy and always wanted to laugh at his attempt to say her name, which came out as 'Miss Miss', but she would only be as bad as the children if she did laugh. "You had better take this," she said, handing the penknife over to Karl. She turned once more to Siegfried. "Now remember what I said, Siegfried, and we'll see you back at school on Monday."

As they led the boy back to the Land Rover they were all very quiet, each wrapped in his own thoughts, and glad to be out of Miss Smith's office. Karl considered her actions to have been very fair, and it was clear she held no malice against Siegfried. More the opposite in fact, he decided thankfully. He could feel the weight of the penknife in his coat pocket, and wondered why Gustav had given it to Siegfried without mentioning it either to himself or to Katherine.

Siegfried sat quietly on the front seat, wedged between the adults, considering his fate. So far his father had controlled his anger, but Siegfried wondered whether he would let it out once they got home. He rather hoped he would, and then Katherine would get cross, silly cow!

Katherine too was wondering whether Karl would stay calm about the episode. She noticed he neither apologised to Miss Smith for his son's behaviour, nor condemned it. They both knew John Winters must be the boy in question, as Miss Smith had warned them of the problem before. Could Karl secretly condone Siegfried's actions? Surely not!

They stopped off at Yew Tree Lodge for Sabina, and Gertie made them all a cup of tea. Katherine noticed she tactfully made no mention of Siegfried's leaving school so early. But when Karl and Siegfried sat in the Land Rover, ready to go, Gertie took Katherine by the arm for a quiet word.

"Don't let Karl be too hard on the boy. He needs support and understanding, not more violence and aggression."

"I know, and I'm sure Karl does too. He's been very restrained so far," Katherine reassured her, hoping she was right.

Karl's silence continued on the drive back to the farm. Only Sabina babbled away in ignorance. When they arrived back Karl took Siegfried with him into the study, closing the door behind them. He sat down, making Siegfried stand in front of him, the penknife laid on the desk as evidence, just as Miss Smith had done.

Siegfried calmly awaited the verdict.

"I am not going to say anything until I have heard the whole story from you." Karl spoke at last, after studying his son's complacency. "I know what it is like to be wrongly judged, and so I am giving you this chance to tell me honestly what happened. If it was your fault, I want you to tell me so. If it wasn't your fault, then I want to be able to believe you. Do you understand?"

"Yes." Siegfried thought quickly. Should he incriminate himself or not? He made his decision and began to speak.

"It was an accident. I was showing a boy my penknife, when John Winters came over and tried to snatch it from me. We were struggling with it and he got cut on the hand."

Karl let the story sink in. It sounded plausible enough, but he could not feel completely satisfied that it was the truth. With no other evidence, however, he had to take the story at face value. "So your only crime, apart from swearing at the teacher, was taking the penknife to school?"

"Yes; but I didn't swear. They just don't understand German," he lied.

Having said he would believe him, Karl had to keep his word. "All right. We'll say no more about it. But this knife stays locked in the drawer here for a month. When I give it back to you, it must stay on this farm. I don't intend searching you before you go off to school in the morning. That is humiliating and shows I don't trust you. I want to trust you, Siegfried, and I hope you will not abuse that trust. If you do, then you can expect severe consequences. Understood?"

"I understand," Siegfried assured him.

"Off you go then."

Siegfried left the study and ran through the kitchen out to his hideout in the woods. Katherine watched his carefree figure disappear behind the wall of the toolshed. So Karl had been lenient too. She sighed with relief.

CHAPTER EIGHT

Ilse tore open her son's letter. She could rely on five minutes privacy to read it, then she would hide it along with the others under the lining paper of a kitchen drawer. If Erich ever found them he would burn them just as he had the first. He had always been jealous of her love for Siegfried, demonstrating his jealousy by his violent abuse of the boy. She did not doubt she had done the only possible thing in letting Siegfried live with his father, but every letter reminded her of the son now lost to her, the mixture of English and German spellings demonstrating his sense of confusion.

> *Dear Mutti,*
>
> *the neu Baby is hier. his Name is Richard. I dont leik him he smels. Vatis leg is mutch better nau. I stil mis Gustav. I leikt Gustav. He torkt tu me. He wonts tu be a Fim Star. I hop you are happy. I mis you. Lots and lots of love from Siegfried.*

Already she sensed the antagonism her son felt towards the new Driesler baby. Not only that, there was his continuing isolation and loneliness. The only relief seemed to have been in October when Karl fell off a roof, according to Siegfried, and broke a leg. Siegfried's letters were full of Gustav at the time. Now it was February and he still mentioned the man. A film star.

The glamour of the film world began to overwhelm her as she gazed round her squalid kitchen; at her own new baby's nappies hanging up to dry, at the chipped and stained sink still with its single cold water tap, and at the smoking coal stove. She imagined a kind of Cinderella scene; herself bowed down with housework and children, cowed by her brutal, beer-swilling husband. There would be a knock at the door and in would walk ... She bit her lip at the all too clear image of Karl. Her meeting with him last May in Winterberg had reawakened all those feelings for him she thought she had long since lost. She had been a fool to leave Karl; even more of a fool to marry Erich. Their similar political outlook counted for nothing in everyday life, especially in a Germany which had turned its back on its former greatness. Now she was stuck with him.

Her five minutes were over. She heard Erich clumping up the stairs. Hurriedly she hid the letter. In her present mood she felt like confronting him yet again with all the inadequacies of the flat. She began as soon as he walked through the door.

"When are we going to get a hot water heater? I'm sick and tired of boiling up kettles every time I want to wash up or give the children a bath. Greta Klitzke's had one for months now."

"Bloody hell! I've only just got in and you're on at me. Why don't –"

"I have to nag and nag to get anything done around here. Instead of spending all the money on beer, you should do something to improve this dump."

"You know as well as I do, I don't spend it all on beer." He sat down heavily on the sofa and began to remove his shoes, ready for his afternoon nap. For once he was disinclined to argue. "We agreed to give money to help our friends who had their businesses confiscated by the British."

"I know, but I didn't know how much you were giving them! *We* need that money, Erich, just as much as they do. You shouldn't make your own family suffer –"

"Who's making them suffer?" Erich jumped up. Only just as tall as Ilse, he raised his voice to gain domination. "Are they hungry? Are they cold? No! Don't you dare complain again."

Ilse lowered her eyes in defeat. She noticed the holes in Erich's socks where his toe-nails poked through. Why didn't he cut them sooner? Did it give him a perverse pleasure to give her more darning to do? Probably, knowing him.

Baby Roslinde began to cry again, giving Ilse an excuse to escape from Erich. She went to the stove where a bottle of milk stood warming in a pan of water, then retreated to the bedroom to quieten the tiny infant so Erich could have his doze. She sat exhausted on the bed, cradling Roslinde in her arms, glad Margit and Heinrich were outside looking after Edeltraud in the pram. If only she could close her eyes. Just for a few minutes.

*

Katherine lay in bed and gazed fondly at the tiny dark head poking out of the bundle of white blanket in her arms. Richard had kept her up half the night, but now he was asleep he looked so angelic. Her delight at bearing a son for Karl was matched only by her relief that Sabina was showing signs of interest rather than jealousy in her baby brother. The new playhouse helped. Sabina was thrilled with it, showing every visitor and telling them her new brother gave it to her.

Karl put his foot round the door and pushed it open, his hands laden with her breakfast tray. He set it down on the chest of drawers then relieved her of the baby asleep at her breast, putting him back in the cradle. After settling the tray carefully on Katherine's lap he sat down on the edge of the bed to sort through that morning's post. An envelope addressed in a Germanic script caught his eye, and he opened it first.

"Good heavens! It's from Gustav!" he told her. He quickly scanned through the letter, whistling slowly in amazement as he reached the end. "Listen to this, Schatz. Gustav's not only landed himself a small part in a film, but he says they're looking for other German speakers. He suggested I would be ideal and asks whether I'm interested."

Katherine felt a chill stab at her heart. The thought of Karl being on stage with the Penchurch Players was one thing, but going away to make war films with Gustav was another matter altogether.

"I suppose you would end up getting killed in the film," she commented morbidly. "I don't think I would want to watch that."

Karl's smile faded. "Yes, I probably would. But it's only a film. You needn't see it if you don't want to, and besides, think how useful a bit of extra money would be."

"You sound as though you've already made up your mind." Katherine decided not to mention her qualms. If this was what he wanted then why should she hold him back?

Karl grinned. "It sounds exciting." He grew serious again. He must convince her that Gustav's suggestion hit a need in him. "Ever since I was fourteen, Schatz, my life has been talk of, or fighting in war. In 1945 I had had enough of it, and I am very happy in my life here with you. But sometimes I feel my life is too ... quiet."

He studied her eyes, hoping she would understand what he was trying to say. She herself had recognised that he ought to branch out into something outside the farm. This seemed the ideal answer, yet her eyes showed her unhappiness at the proposal. "You don't like the idea?"

Katherine turned her head away to hide her fears from him.

"Tell me, Schatz. What do you really think?" Karl persisted.

Katherine sighed with reluctance, but expressed her doubts. "It's stupid of me, I know, but I don't like the idea of you putting on that uniform again, or of friends of ours in the village seeing a film of you being a Nazi, even if you were only acting."

There. She had said it and she knew she had offended him. She tried to rectify matters. "It would remind me too much of how you were when you lost your memory, and I saw you how you used to be."

"When I was a Nazi, you mean," he said coldly. He picked up Gustav's letter and put it in his jacket pocket, preparing to leave the room, hurt by Katherine's reference to his past. His hand was already on the door handle when he heard her speak again.

"Karl! If it's what you want, then go ahead. I don't have to see the film."

"I'll think about it," he said.

Downstairs Siegfried was laughing at Sabina who had managed to tip her porridge onto the floor. Karl entered upon the scene, still unsettled from the episode with Katherine and promptly lost his temper.

"Stop laughing and help me clear up this mess!"

He saw Siegfried's smirk as the boy stooped to pick up Sabina's bowl. Karl took a grip on himself and made himself calm down. How Katherine coped with the children day in, day out, he could not imagine. At least Sabina would be starting nursery school after the summer holidays. School!

"Siegfried! Leave that. Hurry up and get ready or you'll miss the bus."

Karl finished wiping the floor, helped Siegfried on with his coat and satchel and hurried him out of the door. He breathed a sigh of relief as he saw Werner, reliable and trustworthy as ever, sorting out the tools for the day's hedging work. It would be good to escape the house when Gertie arrived and get on with some outdoor work. Perhaps that was what he needed. To have a break from the mundane daily grind and see some action again.

For how long would a part in a film take him away from the farm? It might only be a few days, or it could be weeks. During lambing it would be impossible to leave the farm, then there was the spraying of the orchards, and after that came hay-making, sheep-shearing and dipping. Could he really afford the time to indulge himself in such a madcap venture? Now that she had three children to care for, he could hardly expect Katherine and Werner to take over from him completely, unless they had help of some kind. But that would cost money and he hoped to bring in more from acting, not fork out.

Throughout the day's hedging with Werner, he vacillated in his decision, but each time he decided not to risk it, he felt the sense of disappointment which told him the decision was not the right one. Katherine was only too well aware of his dilemma, but made no more comments. He must decide for himself.

That evening at eight o'clock he made the call to London. Sarah answered the telephone.

"Hello, Karl. Gustav's out, I'm afraid, but he left a message for you. If you're interested you should be down here for Wednesday, March 28th, when they're casting. You should have got the lambing over and done with by then."

It might be a close thing with the latest lambs, Karl thought, but the temptation was too great to refuse. Werner and Katherine would have to manage on their own.

"Do you have room for me to stay a night or two?"

"Of course, if you don't mind sharing with Gustav. I'm out at work all day, of course, but Gustav knows his way around the flat. We'll see you on the 27th presumably?"

"Yes. I'll let you know nearer the day what time I'll arrive."

Katherine heard him replace the receiver. So he had decided to try for it after all. She was very surprised that with his experiences, he would want to become even remotely involved with any aspect of war again, especially knowing her own opinion too. He must feel the need for a bit of excitement in his life more strongly than she realised. Perhaps she did not know him as well as she thought.

*

Karl returned from his trip to London full of the interesting things he had done and been taken to see.

"The Festival of Britain site looks very impressive," he told Katherine whilst unpacking his bag. "It's being opened on May 4th. Perhaps we could manage a trip down there to visit it and see some of your relations at the same time. Most of them haven't seen our family yet, have they."

He was diverting her attention from the real purpose of his visit, Katherine knew, but his suggestion excited her nevertheless.

"We could see a musical," she said. "*Carousel* is supposed to be very good. Or there's that new one, *South Pacific*."

It was not until they were lying in bed that night that she asked him what the film was to be about. Karl had deliberately refrained from mentioning it until she asked.

"It's about the Royal Navy," he told her. "They need a number of Germans to be rescued from the water when their ship is sunk. Most of them will be played by English actors, but Gustav and I have speaking parts. I won't be in a recognisable uniform, and will be soaking wet and covered in oil or something, I expect. We don't die either, so there's no reason why you shouldn't see it."

Katherine was still not sure about that, but she could delay making that decision. "When do they need you?"

"They'll be letting us know soon. I should only be gone a few days. I'm only in one short scene, although Gustav appears more. I expect what I'm paid will hardly cover the train fare. Never mind. It's a start."

"I wonder what Siegfried will think of it all. He mightn't like seeing his father being taken prisoner by the British, even if only on film."

"He might think it very appropriate, seeing his cowardly father giving himself up."

Katherine caught her breath. "Is that how he sees you – as a coward?"

"I'm not sure how fully he understands the difference between a traitor and a coward. Ilse says I was a traitor, but I would say I was more of a coward. Only once I listened to my conscience."

"And you ended up at Dachau because of it," Katherine reminded him, running her fingers through his hair. "You still have bouts of depression because of that place. We don't want one now. I'm the one entitled to post-natal depression – not you. Besides," she added, cuddling up to him, "you'll always be a hero to me."

"I hope so," he replied more cheerfully.

*

Ilse lay under Erich's embrace and wished he would hurry up. He seemed to take a long time these days. Perhaps it was the beer or his age creeping up on him. Whatever it was, she was finding him more repellant as the years passed. He was only forty-three but looked a good ten years older. She could hardly talk, though. At only twenty-eight she felt an old woman, lifeless and careworn. Her once lovely blonde hair was dull and unkempt. She would have to ask her neighbour, Greta Klitzke, to try out her hairdressing skills on it, although she doubted whether Erich would notice any difference.

He climbed off her at last and she lay in the dark on the bed, watching the stars through the gap in the curtains where they did not quite meet. She remembered lying with Karl on a bed of pine needles in the forest around Medebach, watching the stars come out, happy, physically satisfied, and in love. Damn Karl for spoiling it all! She tried to ignore the insistent voice within her which proclaimed loudly how desperately she wanted him back.

Erich began to snore gently. More and more frequently Ilse's thoughts at night were turning to her former lover, remembering all their meetings together – their kisses and unions – in an attempt to fill the emptiness of her emotions.

The snores became intrusive. She prodded her husband, but he rolled over in his sleep, squeezing her off the bed. Easing herself carefully over the side, she stood up, wrapped a shawl around her and headed for the kitchen. She dared not turn on the light, in case she woke him. Instead she found the torch and went to the drawer in which she kept her little pile of letters, intending to read through them all again. Through Siegfried she learned news of Karl, antagonistic as it was. She knew now how much wrong she had done Karl, turning his son against him like that. She hoped he would forgive her some day. Did he ever think about her? She doubted it. Not with that attractive wife of his to keep him happy. He had chosen to ally himself with the victors, and was reaping the benefits accordingly.

She longed for a photograph of Siegfried. She must ask him to send one, but she would have to keep it hidden along with his letters. Damn Erich! She found a piece of paper and began to write carefully as usual, so Siegfried would be able to read it unaided. At the end of the letter she wanted to write the words: *Give your father my love.* She refrained.

*

The old-man's-beard was budding leaves, offering more cover now after its long winter of nudity. Siegfried took his mother's latest letter up to his hideout. These times alone with her were his most precious, savoured from the moment Katherine handed him the envelope with the German stamp and the beloved handwriting.

He always opened the letters slowly, prolonging the excitement, inhaling the German air escaping from inside the envelope. He settled himself comfortably on the mound of dried leaves and moss to read it.

> *My darling boy,*
>
> *I always love reading your letters, but it is hard for me to picture where you live. Could you ask Vati for a photo of Lane Head Farm to send to me? I would also love to have a photo of you, so I can see how big you are growing. One of you and your father would also be nice. Life for me is the same as ever. I am lucky Roslinde is very easy to look after. I expect she smells as much as Richard! In a small flat we can't get away from it. You are lucky to live in the fresh air of the countryside. You must be glad you don't live here still with all of us. Darling, I know now I was very wrong to make you hate Vati. You must learn to love him, like I used to. I was the traitor to leave him like that and not let him see his son. I hope you understand, Siegfried, and will do your very best to love him.*
>
> *My fondest love and kisses,*
> *from Mutti.*

When he reached the last paragraph of her letter, he read it again to make sure he understood. But reading it over and over left him feeling puzzled and uncertain. Suddenly she was going back on everything she ever told him about his father. Why? He could not understand her reasons. He liked hating his father and enjoyed plotting against him. It made his lonely existence here in England more interesting, and he did not want to change now, just because his mother told him to. He would just have to make her believe he was happy here.

Siegfried put the letter back in its envelope. Only Gustav really understood how much he hated being in England. Gustav's penknife was Siegfried's most treasured possession, and when his father took it, with only a vague promise to return it, Siegfried had not believed he ever would. Yet it was returned. Siegfried kept his promise to keep it on the farm only through fear of having it permanently confiscated. It was in his pocket now. He pulled it out, opening the bright blade which he kept shiny and sharp, using the whetstone from the toolshed. He hacked at a strand of old-man's-beard, then found a forked knobbly twig in the shape of a man. With intense satisfaction, Siegfried cut off its head.

*

The orchards were a haze of palest pink blossom, the sheep with their new lambs white dots on the green grass. It was a scene Katherine scarecely saw as she turned the Land Rover onto the valley road and drove towards Penchurch. She planned to visit the baby clinic to have Richard weighed, Mrs Tucker's General Store for a long list of items, followed by lunch with Gertie.

She knew she was foolish missing Karl so quickly, when he had only been away one day. Sabina could not understand where Daddy was, and now sat sucking her thumb and clutching hold of Teddy Gustav on the seat beside Katherine.

The baby clinic was held in the village hall. Katherine parked outside it, picked up the sleeping Richard in his carrycot, then helped Sabina out. Half a dozen other mothers with assorted babies and toddlers were already gathered, awaiting their turn at the scales. There was a chorus of greetings as she and Sabina walked in to the hall. They sat down but Sabina was soon off, showing her teddy to a little girl from a farm further up the valley.

Madge Crowthorne, the little girl's mother, spoke to Katherine. "Morning, Katherine. How's that new baby of yours? Sleeping well, is he?"

"Not too bad, thank you, Madge. It's Sabina who didn't sleep well last night. She's missing her Daddy."

"Oh yes. I hear he's gone to London to be in a film. Quite exciting for you all! Mind you, there's some folks round here surprised you let him go, him turning the ladies' heads the way he do. Now I know Karl better than that, but there's some here who reckon it's not wise letting him go off on his own and mixing with film people. I'm just warning you, mind, so you know what folks is thinking."

"Thank you, Madge, but like you, I've got no concerns about losing Karl to some starlet. He's always been a source of gossip for the rumour-mongers of Penchurch, so it's nothing new to me."

It was the closest Katherine could come to telling Madge Crowthorne to mind her own business, without being rude to her distant neighbour. Turning her back on Madge, she joined another conversation about sleepless nights until it was Richard's turn to be weighed.

Katherine reported Madge's gossip later to Gertie.

"Of course, Mrs Tucker warned me of exactly the same thing, when I was shopping," Katherine complained to her godmother and confidante. "They seem to think Karl will go off the rails without my control."

"Well I think people suspect you're the only thing that keeps Karl together," Gertie said, wiping a dollop of custard from Sabina's mouth. "After his mental breakdown they viewed him with considerable suspicion, despite their support for you both. They don't forget things like that easily, dear. Without your steadying influence they think he's liable to do anything."

"But that's ridiculous! Surely they know him better than that."

"Of course they do. They just love having someone so vulnerable to gossip about. But I sense you're not very happy about him going."

Sabina struggled to get down from her perch on several cushions, chanting: "I want play with hats."

Katherine lifted her down from the kitchen table and Sabina trotted off to the sitting room to play with a pile of dressing-up hats Gertie had collected from numerous jumble sales. Katherine watched her leave the kitchen and wanted to follow, but Gertie was awaiting an answer. She peered into Richard's carrycot, saw he was still asleep, exhausted by the indignities of being weighed, so she began to clear the dishes.

"You're right. I'm not happy about him going, but not because I don't trust him. I do. Completely." She piled the plates by the sink and ran the hot water, speaking over her shoulder. "It's for a different reason altogether. He was talking about wanting a bit of action in his life. After so many years fighting and seeing foreign places, he finds life rather quiet. I just don't want him developing a wanderlust or getting too used to the city's attractions."

Gertie paused in her task of wiping the table. "I'm surprised at you, Katherine! Karl's a countryman through and through. I can appreciate he's had trouble finding his feet living amongst foreigners, but I'm sure he wouldn't want to live anywhere else."

Katherine had to agree. "I suppose I'm just being foolish because I'm missing him so much. It wasn't so bad when he went the first time, but I think I'm a bit envious of him now, getting away and enjoying himself. He was out when I phoned last night."

Gertie put a consoling arm round her shoulders. "You've a case of the baby-blues, dear. Tell you what! When Karl gets back, I'll come and babysit for you one evening and you can go out on the town. You could leave a bottle for Richard, just the once, couldn't you?"

"I'm very tempted, I must say. I haven't been out for ages.

"There you are then. It's as good as arranged."

*

Karl was relaxing over a pint of beer with Gustav and half a dozen other extras who had spent the day immersed in a large tank of water at the film studios. As 'the Germans', they shared a cameraderie which was continuing off the set. A separate group of 'Royal Navy' extras was at the other end of the bar, both groups having their fair share of accompanying wardrobe and make-up girls. The pub's landlord was well used to having large numbers of film people at his bar, but was surprised to discover actual Germans amongst them this time. He was reluctant to serve them, and had only done so because they were buying drinks for the others.

Gustav noticed the man's reluctance and decided to pay him back for it by playing on his English companions' temporary affiliation to Germany. He began teaching them *Lili Marlene* in German, which went well until the rival 'Royal Navy' crowd set up an opposing version in English, both sides singing louder and louder in an attempt to drown out the other. With one of the wardrobe girls on his knee, Gustav waved his beer glass in the air, encouraging his side to even greater volume.

Karl felt another of the girls lean closer to shout in his ear: "Come on, Karl! You know the words. Sing louder!"

As she spoke, she slipped forwards off her chair and rested her chin on his shoulder, apparently to hear the words more clearly so she could join in. Reluctantly he responded. He knew why Gustav had engineered this, but was not so keen to make a nuisance of themselves to the prejudiced landlord.

When the song was over, jeers and hoots of derision took over as the sides tried to establish who had won the vocal contest. Gustav let loose a string of tongue in cheek verbal abuse about the pathetic English attempt, which was promptly countered by ribaldry about the German effort. When a beer mat missile was thrown by one of the 'Germans', the landlord decided he had had enough. There would be broken windows or worse soon. He approached the German group.

"Right you lot. Finish your drinks and get out of here or I'll call the police. I don't want your sort disturbing the peace in here."

"Why pick on us?" the red-head on Gustav's knee screeched in a hoarse voice. "They were singing too!" she objected, pointing to the grinning faces at the other end of the bar.

"Because you were singing in German. Simple enough? Now out!" The landlord stood with his arms folded, awaiting their departure. His wife looked on anxiously from across the bar, ready to call the police if things turned nasty.

Karl began to reach for his coat. Gustav and pubs seemed to spell trouble, and he wanted to keep out of it, but he sensed Gustav had other ideas.

"Come on, Gustav. It's time we were heading back for Chiswick," Karl muttered, edging out from beneath the arm draped across his shoulders. Barbara, the wardrobe girl, had become increasingly amorous as she downed her port and lemon. Karl was relieved to escape her clutches.

There was a giggle from Elsie, the red-head, as Gustav whispered something in her ear then stood up. Ignoring the landlord, the pair gathered up their belongings and sauntered outside into the street.

Karl followed, only to find Barbara hanging onto his arm, swaying gently on her high heels. For her own safety, he left her arm where it was. The other members of their group, feeling immune from the landlord's threat, decided to stay on in the pub and moved over to join their rivals at the other end of the bar.

"First we must walk Elsie and Barbara home," Gustav declared, as the cool night air brought another giggle from Elsie. "It is not far, is it Elsie?"

"No, not far," she squealed in mirth.

Barbara too was becoming infected with Elsie's laughter, as Elsie led them down several side streets and around a cemetary, before arriving at the front door of a Victorian terraced house. The giggles ceased abruptly as they neared the house, and both girls wore more sober, expectant expressions as Elsie asked their escorts in for a coffee.

"We must take Barbara home," Karl began, but she interrupted him.

"It's all right. I only live in the next street. We can have a coffee with Elsie first."

Gustav did not wait for Karl to agree, following Elsie in through the front door. It was only ten o'clock, so Karl had no grounds to urge leaving, but he felt unhappy about the way the situation was developing. Barbara was still possessively holding onto his arm as they were shown by Elsie into the tiny front room.

"Make yourselves comfortable, while I put the kettle on," she told them.

Karl was steered onto the faded and cat-clawed sofa by Barbara, but Gustav managed to grab a chair to himself. The owner of the claws, a fat tabby, occupied the other. Karl looked at the clutter of ornaments on the mantelpiece, representing the mementos of a whole life-span. Too dated to be Elsie's. He turned sideways on the sofa to face Barbara, distancing himself slightly from her in the process. "Do Elsie's parents live here?"

"Yes, but they both work night shifts, so she has the house to herself all night," she said with a sly smile. "Isn't that lucky?"

Her arm rested along his thigh, and her fingers gave it a light suggestive squeeze, leaving Karl in no doubt as to what was planned by the two girls.

"Perhaps Elsie wants some help in the kitchen," Karl said, abruptly standing up. He did not want to be rude to the girls, as it was obvious they had no idea he was married, but he had to extricate himself from this situation without offending them.

Barbara mistook his meaning. "I thought it was me you were with," she said, grabbing his arm so forcefully that she pulled him off balance and he sat down hard again on the sofa.

Gustav was watching Karl's growing plight with quiet amusement, as Elsie entered the room with a tray and four cups.

Karl decided enough was enough. "I'm not *with* anybody, Barbara. I'm simply walking you home, that is all. I am a married man with three children, and I do not spend my time with other women."

His brusque statement only resulted in a peal of laughter from both Barbara and Elsie.

"You won, Gustav!" Elsie screeched. "You said he wouldn't, but we didn't believe such a handsome man could really be tied to his wife's apron strings, just like you said. He's altogether too perfect."

So all this was Gustav's doing! Karl glared at him, but Gustav was impervious to his wrath.

"I thought you might like a bit of a change, Karl. That's all," he soothed, speaking for the first time in German. "What with your leg, and Katherine being pregnant, and then a new baby keeping everyone awake, I thought you might be in need of a bit of excitement. I was only trying to help."

Karl did not know whether to believe Gustav or not. The man was an accomplished actor, after all. He decided not to make too big an issue of it.

"You can stay if you want, Gustav, but I'm going."

"As you like," Gustav replied, not moving from his chair.

"I can see myself out," Karl told Elsie. He gave a polite nod of farewell to the two girls, then made for the door. Once out in the street he headed back in the direction of the pub, to find his way to the underground station. Gustav was certainly right about baby Richard keeping them awake at night. Poor Katherine was asleep as soon as her head hit the pillow these days, and their love-life was almost non-existant, yet neither Barbara nor any other woman held any attraction for him.

When he arrived back at the flat in Chiswick at a quarter past eleven, Sarah and Perry were just coming in from a visit to the reopened Old Vic theatre. With too much on his mind to sleep, Karl readily agreed to join them in the living room for a nightcap.

"No Gustav again?" Sarah asked.

"No. Does he often stay out all night?"

Perry sniggered. "Gustav's a bit of a bull, didn't you know, Karl? We've had to warn a few of our friends to keep their wives away from him."

"And their husbands," Sarah added with a conspiratorial wink at Karl.

"You mean he ...?"

Sarah laughed. "You didn't know? I thought since your brother brought him here, you would have known all about him. Gustav's game for anyone. How else do you think he got his work permit and his way into films so easily?"

Karl found it difficult to believe, especially since Rudi must have had an inkling as to Gustav's tendencies. The thought that Rudi might even have been a partner hit Karl like a hammer blow. Surely not Rudi!

"You look shocked, Karl," an amused Perry remarked. "These are modern times we're living in. All that old-fashioned morality went out with the outbreak of war."

"Are you saying you don't mind a man like that living in your house? His behaviour is illegal. You might have the police turning up here one day."

"We don't mind. In fact, we quite like having him here," Perry grinned intriguingly. "Don't we, Sarah?"

Sarah glared at him, as if he had said too much. Karl made his own incredible deductions from the remark.

Sarah was worried now, and cross with her husband for letting Karl know what was going on. "Karl, you won't tell Katherine will you?"

Karl felt numb with disbelief. "Tell her what, exactly?"

Sarah looked embarrassed at last. "What's going on here between Gustav and me ... and Perry."

Her confirmation, even if diffident, of his suspicions was almost too much for Karl. "All three of you? Together?"

Perry butted in. Karl was making a meal out of this and upsetting Sarah. "Yes, all three of us together, usually. Sometimes one or the other. There's nothing wrong in that, Karl. We're all consenting adults, and we enjoy it. You're welcome to try it with us, if you want."

Even Sarah knew that Perry had gone too far. Karl and Katherine were alike in their precious morality, but instead of Karl showing even more horror, she saw him actually smile.

"You like the idea?" Perry asked, hopefully.

Karl simply snorted with laughter and collapsed back into his chair, shaking helplessly in his mirth.

Sarah and Perry watched him in bewilderment until he gained control of himself again. Eventually, wiping the tears from his eyes, Karl managed to reply.

"That is the second time this evening I have had such a ... proposition," he coughed weakly, still spluttering with suppressed laughter. "Gustav tried to fix me up with one of the wardrobe girls, but I turned her down, only to be given an even better offer by you two!"

Perry was still not sure whether Karl was agreeing to his suggestion. Perhaps all three of them might be too much at first for Karl. "If you like, I'll just watch you and Sarah at first, and then you can watch Sarah and me."

Karl collapsed with laughter again, and Sarah spoke quietly to Perry. "I don't think Karl wants anything of the sort, darling. He's a country bumpkin like Katherine, and not used to our city ways. Just forget about it, all right? I wish to God you'd never mentioned it."

Perry looked disappointed but agreed to drop the subject. Leaving Karl to his laughter, they withdrew to their bedroom.

Half an hour later, after the angry shouting emanating from the main bedroom had died down, a more sober Karl crept along to the room he had shared the previous night with Gustav. There had been no hint of impropriety from Gustav then, and he was convinced now that Rudi could not have been involved with Gustav either. Gustav had a better idea who to approach than Perry, it seemed. He wondered how Gustav first managed to get into Sarah's bed, and then persuade Perry to join them. Sarah was always more liberally minded than Katherine, and it had been Sarah's friend Audrey Patterson – now Kellett – who, with Sarah's connivance, had released Karl from his long period of celibacy after the war. He could believe that Sarah might look favourably on Gustav, even though she was married, but he could not see why Perry had been persuaded to join them.

He shuddered as he began to undress. If Perry and Sarah knew what he had been through in Yugoslavia, they would never have made such a suggestion. Not even Katherine knew the full extent of his experiences with the Partisans. Only Robert Murdoch and Dr Goldberg, his psychiatrist, knew of the sexual assault on him by a band of Partisan men. The experience was still indelibly imprinted on his mind, despite Dr Goldberg's professional efforts to allow him to come to terms with it. His almost hysterical laughter that evening had been an escape, a method of avoiding having to face one of the issues which still occasionally haunted his dreams.

Karl got into bed with thoughts of Yugoslavia drifting uncomfortably close to the surface of his mind. If he had a nightmare tonight, he did not want Sarah, let alone Perry, running in to comfort him.

The following morning the atmosphere in the flat was oppressive. Eating his breakfast alone in the kitchen, Karl was aware of the silence reigning, until Sarah joined him, dark-eyed and still wrapped in her white satin dressing gown. Buttering a slice of toast she eventually spoke.

"I expect you heard us arguing last night. Perry was a damn fool talking like that in front of you. He should have known better than to think you were the same as Gustav. You must think us utterly depraved."

She waited for Karl to make some comment, but his silence only confirmed what she just said. He was staring directly into her eyes and she could read the disapproval for herself. She began to try to justify their behaviour.

"Strictly between you and me, Karl, Perry has always had ... trouble. In bed, I mean." Nervously she wrapped the belt of her dressing-gown around her index finger and avoided his eyes. "Much as I love him, I began to find this a bit frustrating, and Gustav provided me with what I wanted. Perry happened to come back early from golf one Saturday and found us in bed together. Instead of being shocked, he found he was ... well ... aroused by seeing us. Now, ever since Gustav joined us in bed, he's had no problems." She looked directly into his eyes at last. "It's marvellous for all three of us, do you understand?"

Karl felt awkward, hearing such intimate details from his sister-in-law. In the past Sarah always tried to hide the attraction she felt for him, but he knew last night she would have welcomed him into her bed had he chosen to accept Perry's offer.

"Yes, I do understand, Sarah." His gaze left hers for a moment. Should he say more? Would she think he was meddling in business which did not concern him? He decided to take the chance. He looked directly at her again, seeing the same green eyes as Katherine's. He must try to protect her. "I think you should know the risks you are taking."

The proximity of his wonderfully concerned face was exciting her, and she had to make herself concentrate on the matter at hand. "I'm quite aware of the risks, Karl. I know Gustav sleeps with all sorts of people and might catch something nasty, but there's treatment for that nowadays. That doesn't worry me in the slightest."

Karl rubbed his eyes wearily and tried again. "There are more risks than that, Sarah," he said firmly. He lowered his voice. "You may find Perry has changed more than you would like."

Sarah's eyes narrowed with anxiety. "What do you mean by that?"

Karl hesitated. He hoped he was not right in his suspicions about Perry, but he wanted Sarah to be forewarned. "Let's just say, he's been let off the leash. He may run off."

"Never!" Sarah scoffed. "You don't know Perry. He needs me."

Karl declined to argue the point. Sarah would only resent any further advice. She could still be very mulish in that respect. He stood up.

"Well, I'd better get off to work. I think a certain wardrobe girl will avoid me today. Thank God we should be finished by this afternoon, and then I can leave the place. I'm sick of being stared at by all the girls there."

"You shouldn't be so handsome," Sarah told him, glad to have dropped the previous topic of conversation.

"I can't help that. They shouldn't all think I'm some kind of Don Juan because of it."

"You could be though. Nobody would turn *you* down. Not even me," she laughed.

Karl managed to smile at her blatant invitation. At least she was in a better mood now. Hopefully she and Perry would have patched up their quarrel by the time he returned this evening. Tomorrow he would be safely home.

CHAPTER NINE

Siegfried blinked the drizzle out of his eyes as they left Hay cinema. Half the population of Penchurch seemed to be here. The other half would probably attend the evening performance of *White Ensign*. He spotted the portly post-mistress, Mrs Tucker, approaching him. His skin crawled with apprehension. She must have seen him steal the chocolate bar from her shop the other day after all! He tried to hide behind his father, without success. A strong smell of peppermint wafted onto him as she spoke.

"Did you enjoy the film, Siegfried? I think your father did ever so well. The Penchurch Players must make use of his talents."

"It was all right."

He released his breath when Mrs Tucker grabbed her chance to speak to the hero of the day. Siegfried had not enjoyed the film at all. Not only was there the indignity of seeing the British crowing over sinking a German ship, he also had to watch Gustav hauled out of the sea and taken captive as a surly and aggressive Jerry. Siegfried knew Gustav was not acting when he spat at the feet of his rescuers. It made the film that little bit more bearable. He didn't know why Mrs Tucker was making such a fuss about his father's acting. All he'd done was call for help, look wet and pathetic, and moan about his arm hurting. How feeble! Gustav's role was much more impressive.

He watched a progression of villagers approach his father and offer their congratulations on his performance. It was sickening! At least Vati had the grace to look embarrassed by all the praise. Siegfried noticed Katherine was standing back, avoiding attention. She didn't look too happy. Perhaps she didn't like the film either. They caught each other's eye and she moved over to his side.

"Come along, Siegfried. It's too wet to stand here." She took his hand and led him over to the Land Rover. "Jump in!" She got in next to him, pulling her damp coat collar up around her ears.

Siegfried thought she looked ill, but said nothing. It was none of his business. He made no comment either to his father when he finally joined them, glowing with the praise he had received. They drove in silence back to Yew Tree Lodge to collect Sabina and Richard.

Katherine perked up enough later to read Sabina's bedtime story. When she came down, Karl and Siegfried were just coming in from feeding the dogs and securing the chickens for the night. Karl took off his boots, finding his slippers in the log basket. "Richard again?" he laughed.

Katherine nodded. "Are you coming through to the living room now, or have you anything else to do first?"

"No, we're finished now." He pulled on the other slipper. "Well, Siegfried. Time for bed. Is his hot water bottle made, Schatz?"

"Yes. It's in his bed."

Siegfried felt he was being hustled out of the way. He dallied by the kitchen range. "What about my Ovaltine?"

Katherine pointed to the pan of milk waiting to be heated. "Go and get undressed first."

Siegfried sidled off upstairs. They definitely wanted him out of the way tonight. He took his time changing into his pyjamas and dressing gown, then hunted under the bed for his slippers. He found them and a copy of the *Dandy* which had slipped down the side of his bed. He read several pages before eventually returning downstairs. His steaming mug of Ovaltine stood waiting on the kitchen table. He took it through to the living room and plonked himself down on the flowery hearth rug. He did not intend moving for as long as possible. He sensed his father wanted to talk to Katherine. Let him wait. He began to trace the swirling blooms of the carpet with his finger. After only a couple of minutes his father was on at him.

"Drink up, Siegfried. It'll get cold."

"It's too hot."

"Well blow on it then."

Karl flicked through a few more pages of a tool supplier's catalogue then looked down at his son once more. The Ovaltine had still not been touched. "Come along. It's getting late. Time you were in bed."

"It's still too hot," Siegfried mumbled into the carpet.

Karl knew his patience was being tested. Well tonight he had no patience. He leaned across from his armchair to the stone hearth, picked up the mug and tasted the contents. "That's barely warm. Now drink it or I'll throw it away."

Slowly Siegfried sat up and drained the mug, then fixed his father with a stare.

"Goodnight," Karl said firmly.

Leaving the mug on the hearth, Siegfried sauntered out of the room and upstairs.

Karl breathed a sigh of relief when he heard the bathroom taps running. "I thought he would never go." He put down the catalogue. "Are you all right, Schatz? You were very quiet after the film."

Katherine put down her knitting and rested her hands on her lap. Karl thought she looked so calm and serene; not like he felt at all after the day's excitement then Siegfried's petulance.

She smiled. "I was feeling a little queasy, that's all. I'm better now." She was about to tell him more, then stopped. It was his birthday and their wedding anniversary next Thursday. She would tell him then, if he hadn't already guessed.

*

Katherine tried to take her mind off her nausea while icing Karl's cake by listening to the wireless news. Yesterday's informal cease-fire in Korea was still holding. The stumbling block to a more lasting peace was the question of the number of United Nations prisoners of war held by the Communists. Katherine felt deeply for all those men and their families. Both Karl and Robert Murdoch knew what it was like to be taken captive by the enemy. Poor Robert's time with the Japanese was especially harrowing. She only wished the fighting in the Suez Canal Zone would likewise come to a halt. It seemed incredible that, after all the horrors of the Second World War, countries would still be willing to risk lives over territorial squabbles, when the United Nations was supposedly there to act as a peace-keeping body. Still, with Mr Churchill back in office as Prime Minister there would be a firm hand at the helm to deal with it all.

Wiping the icing off her hands, she handed the spoon over to Sabina for her to lick, then stuck a single candle into the dark chocolate icing. Thirty-one. Karl's age was just about catching up with his looks. When she first met him he was so worn by his experiences it was difficult to believe he was only twenty-five. He had been through so much. Heaven help him if Siegfried proved too much for him to handle.

A crash of spoon on bowl brought Katherine out of her reverie. Sabina had licked clean every vestige of chocolate icing. Katherine looked at the clock. It would soon be time for *Listen With Mother*, after which Karl took Sabina off her hands for an hour or two. She wiped Sabina's sticky mouth and sat her on a chair ready for Julia Lang's voice to keep her amused for the next quarter of an hour. Richard was busy throwing toy bricks around the kitchen from his position under the kitchen table. He was going to be a devil, she realised wearily, but he could never be more devilish than Siegfried. If only Karl were not so conscientious about fatherhood and had decided to leave Siegfried in Medebach with Anna and Stefan. She was convinced he would have been far happier there.

What was done was done. She pushed aside her worries about Siegfried to concentrate on tidying up the kitchen. In addition to her baking bowls and tins there was a large pile of washing-up from lunch. She heaved a sigh and rolled up her sleeves. Scarcely had she wet her hands when there was a bump then a wail from Richard as he fell against a table leg. Katherine bent down to soothe him, but he wanted to be picked up. She pulled him out from under the table and sat with him on her lap to quieten him, so that Sabina could hear the wireless. Well, it was called *Listen With Mother*, so she might as well listen. The washing-up would have to wait a bit longer.

Apart from the gentle murmuring of the wireless, all was peace and quiet in the kitchen when Karl popped his head round the back door ten minutes later. Sabina jumped off her chair and ran to put on her coat and Wellington boots. Karl smiled to himself at the sight of his wife and son asleep together in the rocking chair, but then rebuked himself for his sentimentality. Katherine was exhausted. He would suggest again to her that she took on some help in the home. The finances would have to stretch that far, or her health would not. She often looked peaky these days. Perhaps she ought to pay a visit to Donald Murdoch. She could be anaemic or something. Or pregnant again.

He led Sabina out to the paddock to call Beth. The chestnut Welsh Cob served as the farm's work horse, although the Land Rover had taken over some of her work. Karl still used her when Sabina was helping him, as she liked to help harness Beth and ride on her back. Today Beth was needed to haul a load of logs down from the woods. As he held the girth in place for Sabina to try to buckle, Karl thought about Katherine's tiredness. He tried to remember when her period was due. The more he thought about it, the more convinced he was that she was late. She would not say anything until she was sure. Perhaps she intended announcing the fact tonight at their celebratory dinner.

He ruffled Sabina's thick auburn hair affectionately and gave her a passing kiss on the nose as he lifted her up onto Beth's back. They plodded leisurely up to the woods to rejoin Werner, Karl basking in the warm glow of family pride. Katherine gave him everything he wanted: peace, security, a loving family. She could have made a fuss about him going off filming so soon after Richard's birth, but she hadn't.

What did he give her in return? Love; plenty of that. Children; plenty of those, if his guess was correct. Anxiety; too much. She would never stop worrying about his happiness and state of mind. The drugs used on him at Dachau left him prone to depression, so his psychiatrist, Dr Goldberg, reckoned. Katherine knew this, watched for signs of it. Sometimes she saw it when it was not even there. When bad temper got the better of him, she blamed it on Goslar, the man responsible for sending him to Dachau. "A touch of the Goslars" she would say, lavishing extra love and understanding on him. What had he ever done to deserve a woman like her?

"*Schneller*, Daddy, *schneller!*" Sabina demanded, bored with the leisurely pace.

Karl made Beth trot on, keeping a wary eye on Sabina's precarious position on Beth's back. The next purchase would have to be a small pony, then Sabina could become initiated into the Pony Club. But that was Katherine's province. Karl preferred to stay well out of those circles. He was not welcome there.

*

Katherine waited until the attentive young waiter in Hereford's Green Dragon Hotel had poured their wine and left them before raising her glass.

114

"Happy Birthday to my Dashing White Sergeant!" She took a sip of the fruity white wine Karl had learned to order as Moselle rather than Mosel. "You're looking particularly dashing this evening in your dinner jacket. The woman at the table by the wall can't keep her eyes off you!"

Karl smiled at her flattery. "I might say the same about you, Schatz. You look very beautiful as always. And very happy."

She was wearing an off-the-shoulder evening gown of midnight blue satin, white gloves and a string of pearls which had been her mother's. The Arctic Fox stole, a Christmas present from Andrew Kellett in 1946, draped over the back of her chair.

"I'm happy because it's our fourth anniversary, and because I've another birthday present to give you. Three guesses as to what it is."

Karl slowly sipped his wine, almost certain what it was but wondering whether to let on that he knew.

"A course in acting?"

She laughed in delight at his foolishness. "No. Try again."

"A case of Moselle wine," he suggested, stressing the French pronunciation.

"No."

She looked so smug he had to do something about it. "A baby perhaps?"

The smugness transformed itself into pleased surprise. "You guessed right, Mr Smartypants. I can't keep anything a secret from you, can I?"

Karl raised his glass. "To the new baby and its very special mother." They chinked glasses. "So when do you reckon it's due?"

"June maybe. Donald will tell me more precisely when I go to see him."

The waiter arrived with their first course: delicately pink smoked salmon with cucumber garnish. The salmon was followed by tender local beef, nicely rare on the inside; for dessert came raspberry mousse.

"This meal's all pink!" Katherine laughed. "Perhaps that means the baby's a girl. I'm glad I usually feel better in the evenings and could enjoy it."

Throughout the meal, Katherine had noticed the increasingly curious glances at Karl from both the young woman and her partner at the table near the wall. As Katherine drank her coffee, there seemed to be much nudging and whispering going on. Eventually the young woman's partner stood up and approached Karl.

"I hope you don't think me incredibly rude." The man's voice caught in his throat and he coughed, betraying his nervousness. "My friend and I saw 'White Ensign' last week at the pictures, and Jane swears you were in it."

Karl smiled politely. "She's right. I was. She must have a good memory for faces. I had only a very small part."

The young man seemed flustered. "Oh. I'll tell her. Thank you. I'm frightfully sorry to have disturbed your meal." He backed away, hurrying to his table to divulge the information to his partner.

Katherine had difficulty smothering her desire to giggle, although Karl sat nonchalantly drinking his coffee.

On their way home, Katherine let her mirth escape. "I thought she was going to ask for your autograph when they left. I'm sure she would have if it hadn't been for her boyfriend."

"Maybe," Karl agreed. "But it's ridiculous making such a fuss because I was in a film. Just imagine how awful it must be for real film stars. It's people like Dr Goldberg who are important in this world, not me."

"Come on, Karl! You enjoyed the attention. Admit it!"

She saw the corners of his mouth gradually crease into a smile, and although he kept his eyes on the road, she knew she was right. They returned to the farm content but tired and listened to the babysitter's report.

"Your sister phoned, Mrs Driesler. She asked if you would phone her back when you got in, no matter what time it was."

"Thank you, Eileen."

Katherine was immediately concerned. It could have been Sarah simply wanting to wish Karl a happy birthday, but she would not have requested to be called back if that were the case.

While Karl drove Eileen back to Penchurch, Katherine called her sister.

"Sarah, it's Katherine. You wanted me to call back. Is anything the matter?"

Sarah's strained and tearful voice came back down the line to her. "Oh God, Katherine. I'm in such a state! Perry's walked out on me!"

"Oh Sarah! Do you know where he is? Are you sure he's gone for good?"

There was a strange hiccupping sound from the other end of the line, as though Sarah were swallowing her tears. "Yes to both questions," she gulped.

Katherine immediately took charge of her sister. "You must come and stay with us for a while. Take some sick leave or something and come up here tomorrow. Can you manage that?"

Sarah sounded relieved at the suggestion. "I'll try. Thanks – for being there."

"You know Donald and Gertie are always there too, if you need them," Katherine reminded her sister. "And Robert's not far from you."

"Yes, I know. But it's you I need right now." Sarah sniffed hard. "I'll pack my bags then, and catch the train tomorrow."

Katherine put down the receiver with a trembling hand, tasting the salt of tears on her lips. Poor Sarah! What on earth could have gone wrong?

When she told Karl the news he hardly seemed surprised, casually removing his bow tie and loosening his shirt collar as he spoke. "I had my suspicions when I was there."

"What suspicions? Why?" she demanded.

"Sarah must tell you for herself. She asked me not to say anything, and so I didn't."

Katherine felt a glimmer of enlightenment. "I do remember you saying something about Gustav ought to move out, and you were glad when he did. Surely she wasn't having an affair with him?"

Karl shrugged noncommittally. "She will tell you for herself what has happened. I can only guess. I think the best thing we can do right now is to get some sleep, so we can cope with Sarah tomorrow."

Reluctantly Katherine had to agree. As she turned out the kitchen light she reached for Karl's hand. How lucky she was to have him.

*

It was Karl who fetched Sarah from the station the following afternoon. When she saw him she flung herself into his arms and burst into fresh tears on his shoulder.

"You were right, Karl. You warned me and I didn't listen," she said through her tears.

He picked up her bags. "Let's get you back home, and you can tell us what you want to. Katherine knows nothing as yet," he assured her. "She only suspects Gustav has something to do with it, and she wouldn't be wrong, would she?"

Sarah lowered her eyes shamefully. "No."

Karl bustled her into the Land Rover and set off through the dismal mist which had refused to lift all day. Sarah let him concentrate on his driving as the mist became thicker along the valley floor. She felt better already to be home.

"Home has never been anywhere other than here where I was born and brought up. Perhaps I wasn't married long enough to feel established at Chiswick." She watched the grey wintery landscape pass by, each hedge and orchard, each cottage and barn so familiar after years of travelling that route. "You still call Medebach home, yet you also use the same term for Lane Head Farm. Do you still think of Germany as your home, Karl?"

Her question took him by surprise, unrelated as it seemed to her current problems. He had to think a moment about his reply.

"Although I think of myself as a German, my home is here with Katherine and the children. But I still feel I have another home; the house where I was born. For many years I had no proper home; only an address to write to or visit very occasionally. Home was where my heart lay, in Medebach. A part of my heart is still there."

Sarah nodded. "I know what you mean. When I was at university my lodgings were never my home, only the farm. But the flat in Chiswick has never felt like home to me for some reason."

Karl smiled. "That's because you never cared for it, or did anything to it. It was somewhere you used, to eat and sleep in, nothing more. You were out all day and most evenings. That is not a home. You must show a place that you love it, and it will love you and take care of you in return."

"So Lane Head Farm will take care of me now, when I need it most," she said slowly.

Karl heard the despair of failure in her voice. He tried to take some of the weight off her shoulders. "In a way it's my fault, all this. If I hadn't stupidly fallen off the ladder, Rudi would never have brought Gustav over here and you would never have met him."

"That's a long list of 'if onlys', Karl. It's my fault entirely, inviting Gustav to stay with us. I was attracted to him from the moment I first saw him. I let it go too far, that's all. Perry ran away with his freedom, as you said he would. How could you have known that then?"

They had reached the turn-off into the lane leading up to the farm. Karl dropped down into low gear to negotiate the sharp bend back on themselves and the beginning of the steep incline up to the farm, two-thirds of the way up the sheep-dotted hill. He was glad of the chance to choose his next words carefully, and just hoped his suspicions about Perry were true, otherwise he would be making an embarrassing mistake.

He cleared his throat. "When he made that ... offer to me, I felt what he really offered was himself. I'm right to think he's gone off with Gustav, aren't I?"

Sarah let out a tremulous sigh. "I knew that sometimes they slept together without me, but they began to exclude me more and more often. Finally, last night, he called me from Gustav's to say he wouldn't be coming home any more except to pack his things. He didn't even have the nerve to tell me to my face!" she stormed, at last giving vent to her anger. "What am I supposed to tell everyone – Katherine, the Murdochs, my colleagues? That my husband has left me for another man?" The tears of self-pity started again, and she blew her nose loudly in rage.

"Tell Katherine the truth and everyone else a different version of it," Karl advised as they drew up onto the muddy cobbles of the farm yard.

"But Katherine will be horrified and disgusted by it all, especially my part in it." Sarah visibly shuddered at the thought of revealing all to her staid and upright sister.

"You forget she's a married woman now, Sarah. Perhaps she would understand some of your desires, even if she would not approve of all of them."

Sarah shot Karl an agonised glance. "How come your marriage is so perfect? Almost every woman I know fancies you, me included as I'm quite sure you're well aware; and yet you never so much as look at another woman. Here am I discussing my innermost feelings and love life with you as if you were my own husband. I feel I can talk to

119

you, and I feel I want to share other comforts with you, but I know full well that can only be an impossible dream. What is it that holds you two so tightly together?"

"If you don't know, you should never have married Perry," he replied patiently, delaying getting out of the vehicle until he had said what was on his mind. "But you're wrong. Our marriage is not perfect. We have our problems and difficulties, we do not always see eye to eye on everything, but at least now we always make sure we are honest with each other."

He had deliberately brought the conversation back to Sarah's problems. "You must tell Katherine everything. Do you think it's a good idea to keep secrets from those you love best?" Karl pointed out. "Remember the trouble I had when I didn't tell all the truth. It seemed far worse to Katherine when she eventually found out I was in the SS. If I had told her in the first place she might have accepted it."

Sarah felt heartened by his words. He was right. She ought to make a clean breast of everything to Katherine, then try to start again with her life and her career.

"I'd better get inside and start facing the music, hadn't I?"

As they came through the back door Katherine was surprised how composed Sarah seemed, although the traces of fresh tears were still on her face. Karl must have done his best to cheer her up. She gave Sarah a long hug before helping her off with her chic wool coat.

"I am sorry the way things have turned out for you, Sarah."

Sarah nodded half-heartedly. "I'll tell you all about it later, when the children are in bed," she promised, ruffling Sabina's curls as her little niece begged to be kissed. She looked around the kitchen for the other children, but Richard was upstairs having a nap, and Siegfried was not yet home from school. She took a mirror from her handbag and cringed at the sight of her tear-streaked face. "I'll just go and tidy myself up a bit."

She set off upstairs to the bathroom, installed along with the kitchen in her mother's day as an extension to the old half-timbered part of the house. Her old bedroom was one of the originals, with beamed ceiling and creaking floorboards. Now it was Sabina and Richard's room, and a reminder that this was no longer her home. Since Siegfried occupied the room Katherine had slept in before her marriage, visitors such as herself had to make use of the converted feed store, but force of habit prompted Sarah to go upstairs, even though Karl had taken her bags out to the guest flat.

She washed her face carefully and retouched her make-up, hearing little snorts from Richard's room as he woke up. She entered her old room, transformed now by the Rupert Bear curtains she had sent from London upon her nephew's arrival. She looked down into the cot where Richard was hoisting himself up with his arms to stand and blink sleepily at her. Like Sabina he had his mother's thick auburn hair, perhaps a shade lighter, but there was more of Karl about his eyes. It was always so difficult to tell with babies. They seemed to change so much every time she saw them. His christening back in May was the last time she had seen him. She picked him up before realising he needed his nappy changed. Holding him at arms length she called down to Katherine, who came running up the stairs to sort him out.

"I've never felt like having children," Sarah said as she watched with distaste while Katherine cleaned him up. "My job's always come first, since I worked so hard to get it, but perhaps I never really thought Perry was the right father for my child."

Katherine looked over her shoulder in surprise while she held still Richard's struggling legs. "I've always wanted a child from Karl. Even before we were married and he was still a POW, I felt I wanted one, no matter what anybody thought."

"You never told me that before! I always thought you had strict morals about such things, which is why I was so dumbfounded when I suspected you were sleeping with him."

"Oh, I discovered how desirable a man could be when I met Karl," Katherine assured her. "It was Andrew's aloofness which held back my passion before that. I can understand why you fell for Gustav."

"Katherine, I ..." Sarah was about to try to explain the more sordid details of her marriage break-up when she was interrupted by the thudding of feet up the stairs and the crash of Siegfried's bedroom door. Richard was squirming hard as Katherine tried to pin his nappy, and Sarah realised that now was not the time. As they made their way downstairs again, Siegfried called after them from his bedroom doorway.

"I'm hungry. When's tea?"

It was as though Katherine stopped to count to ten before she turned round, replying in a restrained voice. "In a few minutes, Siegfried, but don't you think you ought to be more polite and say hello to your Aunty Sarah first?"

Siegfried appeared to think about what she had said. "Hello," was all he could manage before his head disappeared back inside his room.

Once they reached the kitchen, Sarah commented on Siegfried's surliness. "It's as though there's a war going on here, and everyone has to mind what they say to avoid a pitched battle!"

"That's exactly what it is. A war. And I think Siegfried is winning at the moment," Katherine said dispiritedly. "He's making our lives a misery, the trouble he gets into. A few days ago Mrs Tucker caught him stealing a bar of chocolate from her shop. She was very nice about it, knowing what problems we're having with him. She thinks his stealing has been going on for some time, but she's never managed to catch him at it before. Up until then I'd always thought Karl shouldn't hit him when he was naughty, but the thought of him cold-bloodedly stealing from dear Mrs Tucker made my blood boil, and I would have thrashed him if Karl hadn't got there first. Siegfried's been a bit better since then. He actually did as I asked him to just now on the stairs, but I wonder how long it's going to last. Gustav was the only one who's ever got through to him," she reflected. "Even Werner can't persuade him to cooperate."

Siegfried made a brief appearance for afternoon tea, then disappeared again until dinner time. Sarah helped Katherine with the dinner preparations. A rabbit stew was already in the oven, but the potatoes needed mashing. Sarah set to work while Katherine rescued Richard from the log basket before opening the oven door.

"Did you know Robert's got engaged?" Katherine put the casserole dish on a mat on the table and removed the lid. Pungent sage-scented steam coursed through the kitchen.

"No! When did you hear that?" Sarah was delighted. Both she and Katherine had always been close friends of Robert.

"Gertie told me at church last Sunday. Robert's going to bring Alice, his fiancée, up on a visit soon. It's a shame he's so far away in London. I still miss him, and I know Karl does."

"When are they planning on getting married?"

"When he's qualified next summer. Alice insists on only marrying a doctor, or so Gertie says." Katherine went to the back door to see where Karl had got to. "Why do men always disappear at mealtimes?" she moaned to Sarah, putting the lid back on the casserole dish.

"What about Werner's plans?" Sarah had just remembered that there had long been talk of another wedding between nations.

Katherine noticed Sabina was still busy painting in the corner of the kitchen. "Wash your hands, Sabina, and then go and find Daddy would you, and tell him dinner is ready." Katherine then went to the hall and shouted up the stairs for Siegfried to come down.

"Sorry, Sarah. What were you saying?" she asked, sitting down for a moment while the hordes assembled themselves to eat.

"I was asking about Werner," she reminded her sister with a small laugh. "Honestly, Katherine, it's no wonder you look worn out, with this lot to look after."

"I'm not worn out; just pregnant."

Sarah felt her stomach lurch in envy as it always did when she thought of her sister and Karl together.

"What, again? Sorry, congratulations, I mean. When's it due?"

"Not for ages yet. The end of June, I reckon. I must confess, I was a bit aghast at first. Richard's proving rather a handful at the moment, not to mention Siegfried; but I've quickly got used to the idea, especially when I saw how pleased Karl was."

"You're lucky he's so good with children. At least with yours," she managed to add before Siegfried arrived at the table. She quickly turned the conversation back to Werner. Katherine filled her in on the details of Werner's forthcoming marriage to Mrs White, planned for May of the following year.

"My word! Can Penchurch stand it, all these mixed marriages?" Sarah exclaimed as Karl entered the kitchen.

"You just watch. Mrs Collins will be the next to marry a German," Karl joked as he pushed Sabina's chair in for her.

"But she hates Germans," Siegfried said, his brow wrinkling in puzzlement. "Two days ago she hit me and called me a trouble-making Kraut." He did not add that she had also said "just like your father". He did not want any kind of association with him, even if it was only shared nationality.

123

Katherine paused in her serving out of stew, appalled by Siegfried's revelation. Karl too, was equally horrified. Knowing Mrs Collins' long-standing animosity towards his family, he did not automatically assume Siegfried had done anything to warrant the blow he received, but he had to make sure.

"Why did she hit you?"

Siegfried looked blank. "I don't know."

Sarah could see the dilemma written on Katherine and Karl's faces as to whether they should press Siegfried further. Assumption of guilt was a delicate subject in this household.

Katherine continued serving the food. Richard, restrained in his high chair, was growing impatient. Katherine mashed his food then blew on it, feeding him while she listened to Karl begin his interrogation of Siegfried.

"I'm sure Mrs Collins wouldn't hit you without a reason, Siegfried. Where were you when this happened?"

Siegfried picked up his knife and fork and began to eat. Through a mouthful of potato he replied sharply: "Ask her."

"Give me a chance to hear your story first. I know how unpleasant she can be, Siegfried," Karl reassured him. "I find it difficult sometimes not to be rude back to her, but I have learned that the best way is to ignore her, not to listen. Please try to keep out of her way, as I do, then things like this would not happen."

"If I live in Germany I need not to hide from people. I am still enemy here. Every day somebody calls me a rude name. I hate it here!"

Siegfried was working himself up into one of his regular impassioned outbursts against the English. He did not want to have to say why Mrs Collins hit him, and he knew this was a way of distracting his father from the cause of the upset. The fact that he let down the tyres on her bicycle the previous day, and she guessed who had done it, was neither here nor there as far as Siegfried was concerned.

Karl gritted his teeth, recognising the beginnings of a tantrum, and decided to let the matter rest for the moment. Getting the truth out of Siegfried was impossible. He was immune to any verbal threats of withholding pocket money or withdrawal of other privileges. No punishments Karl devised seemed to have any impact on the boy after whatever maltreatment his stepfather had inflicted on him.

Sarah watched the exchanges with interest. Siegfried was the image of his father, and as such she felt some affection for him, but his behaviour was outrageous. For the duration of the meal she could partially forget her own troubles and sympathise with Katherine and Karl in theirs.

Later that evening, after Karl had set off for a pantomime rehearsal and all the children were in bed, Katherine poured a glass of damson wine for them both, suspecting Sarah needed some help to unburden herself properly. The ash logs were burning warmly in the grate as Sarah raised the glass in a toast.

"Long may the home fires keep on burning!" She took a sip of the syrupy, dark wine and began her confession. "Karl said I should tell you everything, Katherine, even the bits I feel ashamed about. It's all rather sordid, you see, and I know you'll be shocked at what I'm going to tell you. When I see you and Karl together I realise just how much I've been missing in my marriage, which is why I was searching for something more."

She proceeded to tell Katherine about her rapid involvement with Gustav, about Perry's discovery of them, and his insistence he should join in. She could see Katherine's eyes widening in amazement at the thought of the three of them together, but when she revealed that Gustav and Perry were now excluding her totally, Katherine could not contain her horror.

"I can't believe what you're telling me! I can just about accept the three of you together, but for Gustav and Perry to ... It's against the law for a start. Aren't they likely to be found out if Perry's moved in with Gustav?"

"I thought about telling the police. After Perry's phone call to me, I was so angry," Sarah admitted. "But I decided against it. It was my fault he got involved with Gustav, and since I don't really want Perry back there's no point in my being vindictive about it. Let them get on with it. If they don't involve anyone else, they're not likely to get caught. It would shame me too, if the facts became public knowledge."

Katherine still could not believe what she had just been told. "And Karl knew all about this?"

It was now that Sarah had to hold back. She could never tell Katherine that she and Perry had wanted Karl to join in too. "He found out when he stayed with us. I asked him not to say anything to you about it, as I knew you would not approve, and at the time it was still great fun, before Perry and Gustav spoilt it all."

"Well, you have got yourselves into a mess," was all Katherine could find to say. She refilled their glasses and put another log on the fire, embarrassed by Sarah's disclosures, and slightly hurt that, despite his promise to Sarah, Karl had not mentioned an inkling of this to her.

"Are you going to divorce him? If so, what reason can you give?" she asked, swirling the wine around in her glass to avoid looking at Sarah.

"Yes. I'll divorce him. I'll ask Perry to fabricate some evidence of adultery. Get him to have a dirty weekend with one of the girls Gustav sometimes hangs around with."

Katherine's eyebrows raised. "Gustav seems to get around a lot."

"Yes, he's like that, as I expect you noticed from his stay here. I wonder what would happen if you put him and Audrey together?"

"A perfect match!" Katherine laughed, glad to see Sarah's spirits lifting again.

"Just like you and Karl," Sarah replied enviously.

CHAPTER TEN

Siegfried could not understand why Gustav's name was so suddenly out of favour. Aunty Sarah turned very quiet at any mention of Gustav, or even Uncle Perry for that matter. After lunch at the Murdochs' on Sunday, Siegfried hoped to draw the adults into a discussion of Gustav's acting merits. The adults were seated round the fire drinking coffee, Richard was asleep in Katherine's arms, while Sabina played with Richard's wooden train, driving it round the sitting room along the parallel lines of the carpet border, using chairs and peoples' legs as tunnels.

"Have you seen Gustav's film, Aunty Sarah?" he asked.

"Yes. I thought your Daddy was very good."

"What about Gustav? He was terrific!"

Just as Siegfried feared, there was silence from his aunt, follwed by a quick diversion from Gertie. "More coffee anyone? Karl? You look as though you could do with some. Pass your father's cup, dear," she told Siegfried.

Why did everyone refuse to talk about Gustav? Siegfried passed the cup to Gertie then wandered over to the padded window-seat to brood on his troubles. In the garden, two blackbirds, a male and a female, were sifting through a pile of dead leaves, throwing the leaves up into the air in search of the grubs and insects beneath. Siegfried watched the busy pair, feeling more isolated than ever. Gustav was his best friend, and now they were shutting him out. Was it a punishment for the recent trouble with Mrs Tucker and Mrs Collins? If so, it was really mean.

His fingers curled protectively round the penknife in his pocket. It was his only memento of Gustav. He would never let his father take it away from him again. Never! He kept hold of it the rest of the afternoon, put it under his pillow that night, and left it safely in his bedside drawer while he was at school. It began to take on an importance out of all proportion to its function, so that the discovery of its loss on December 20th, his eighth birthday, became a catastrophe for the entire household.

There was a pile of presents and cards on the hall table for him when he came downstairs that morning. It was the Christmas holidays so he had time after breakfast to open them all, apart from his mother's. He kept the tightly wrapped, brown-paper parcel from Germany to open by himself in his room. With it clutched under his arm he hurried upstairs, hearing a satisfying rattle from within, and shut his bedroom door on the rest of the household.

The wrapping was secured by tightly knotted string, so he looked in his bedside table for his penknife to cut it. Apart from his mother's letters, the drawer was empty. Leaving the parcel on his bed, Siegfried hunted about in his chest of drawers, under his pillow, under the bed, in the pockets of the shorts he'd worn the previous day, all to no avail. He could not find the penknife. Someone must have been in his room and taken it!

He stomped back downstairs to the kitchen to confront anyone in there, which happened to be Katherine and the children.

"Who has my penknife?" he demanded.

Katherine groaned. She sensed another commotion in the offing. "Most likely nobody, Siegfried. I certainly don't, and I doubt very much whether Sabina or Richard know where you keep it. You can look in their room, if you like, but I expect you've had it out somewhere and laid it down without thinking. I lost my kitchen scissors for days doing that, until I found them wrapped up in a pair of socks left out for darning."

Siegfried was unmoved. "It was in my room. Now it's not in my room. Someone must have it!"

Katherine sighed heavily. It was going to be one of those days. Siegfried had managed to summon up the names of two boys from his class he wanted to invite for a birthday tea. If the penknife was not found by then, Siegfried would be insufferable and the boys would never want to come to play with Siegfried again.

"Have you taken Siegfried's penknife?" she asked Sabina very circumspectly, not wanting to elicit an instant denial from the little girl.

"No," Sabina replied, her attention fully on her drawing of a house.

Katherine was satisfied she was telling the truth. She clearly had no interest in the missing penknife. Richard was only able to crawl about the house and hoist himself onto his feet hanging onto something. If he had by chance found the penknife and then stuffed it down the back of a chair, nobody would be any the wiser.

"Go and have a look in their room, just in case, Siegfried, but I really don't think it will be there. You must have left it somewhere else," she told him.

Siegfried slunk back upstairs and half-heartedly looked in Sabina and Richard's room. He knew as well as his step-mother did that the penknife would not be there. Five minutes later he was back in the kitchen again, his birthday present completely forgotten in the hunt for the penknife.

"I still can't find it," he whined. "I think my father has it."

"Why would he have it? You weren't doing anything you shouldn't with it, were you?"

"Of course not, but he never liked my penknife because Gustav gave it to me."

"Now you know that's not true, Siegfried. It was only because you took it to school and somebody got hurt that your father took it away from you before." Katherine thought of a means to distract him from his quest. "What about your present from your Mummy? Have you opened it yet?"

"That's why I need my penknife, *Dummkopf*."

There was silence as Katherine glared at him. "You won't get any more help from me, talking to me like that," she rebuked him. "Even if it is your birthday. I've got cakes to make for your tea party, so just run along and search the whole house if necessary. I don't know where the blessed thing is."

Siegfried recognised Katherine's temper was growing frayed and he wisely beat a retreat. No matter what she said, he was sure his father must have had a hand in his penknife's disappearance, so he went to search him out and confront him about it.

*

Karl had settled down in the toolshed to a morning's carving. He had been delegated by Vic Threadgold, the stage manager of the Penchurch Players, to carve an Aladdin's lamp for the post-Christmas pantomime. As a direct result of Karl's film experience, he was now a member of the cast in the role of the genie.

He marked out the shape of the lamp on a large block of balsawood and had begun to cut away the outline with a modelling knife, when the door to the toolshed opened with a crash and an angry-looking Siegfried marched in.

"Where's my penknife?" Siegfried demanded, eyeing the knife in his father's hand with suspicion.

"Not in here," Karl replied calmly, aware of the boy's aggression. "If you've lost it, go and look for it."

"I have, but I can't find it anywhere. *You've* taken it, haven't you?"

Karl laid down the knife on the workbench and turned on his stool to face his infuriatingly belligerent son. "I just said, you must have lost it somewhere. Why should I take it? I've got my own knives."

Undaunted, Siegfried persisted with his accusation. "You wanted to get rid of it, just like you got rid of Gustav."

His son's logic baffled Karl. "What are you talking about? Nobody's got rid of Gustav."

"Well why is no one allowed to talk about him now? I know you're not going to let him come back here ever again. I heard you saying so to Katherine."

So that was the cause of the problem! "That's Gustav's fault, not yours," Karl tried to explain, but Siegfried's limited self-control had run out. His hand darted forwards and made a grab for the sharp modelling knife on the workbench.

Karl had no time to debate with himself what Siegfried intended doing with the knife. Instinctively he punched Siegfried on the jaw in a blow equal to anything Erich Röbel ever dealt. Siegfried hurtled backwards, colliding with the doorframe with such force that the knife flew from his hand. Karl quickly stooped to retrieve it, but Siegfried was too winded to move and sat woefully rubbing his jaw until he realised his father was watching him intently.

"You pig! I'll never forgive you for that!" Siegfried shouted. He got unsteadily to his feet, spat at his father, then backed out through the doorway as though fearful of another blow.

Once outside he turned on his heel and ran out of the yard, past the house and on up to his hideout in the woods on the top of the hill. Pulling apart the creepers of old-man's-beard he crawled in and sat down heavily on the pile of dead leaves onto something uncomfortably hard. He searched amongst the leaves until he found the object. When his fingers recognised the shape of his penknife he swore vociferously. He could no longer accuse his father of anything. Suddenly he grinned. On the contrary! Just wait until Katherine saw the bruise on his jaw. She would be bound to shout at his tyrant of a father after this!

*

Karl sat quietly on his stool gazing morosely at the knife in his hands. Had Siegfried intended to threaten him with it, or had he merely wanted to run off with it? His own reflexive assault on the boy had prevented him from finding out. But not only that; it had frightened him. In that instant he had regarded Siegfried not as a small boy, but as a potentially lethal enemy. Karl felt at a loss as to how he came to hit Siegfried so hard. He deeply regretted his violent reaction, and knew that, despite the provocation, the boy was justified in feeling aggrieved. What little respect Siegfried had learned to accord him would be wiped out after this.

Taking the knife between finger and thumb, he flicked it down hard. The blade stuck into the scored and pitted surface of the workbench. Damn Gustav! His influence over everyone led to disaster.

He mulled over what he should do about Siegfried. He would have to apologise to him for punching him like that, but he must in no way condone Siegfried's own actions in the process. The boy had snatched up the knife, and Karl felt uncomfortably certain Siegfried would have used it against him, given the chance. He was no longer in any doubt that the incident at school with John Winters was apparent witness to that.

Leaving the balsawood lamp in its raw state, he went back to the house to discuss the situation with Katherine. She was busy beating a sponge cake mixture in an earthenware bowl, with Sabina hovering at her elbow, waiting to be allowed to 'scrape the bowl' as usual.

"Katherine. Can I have a word with you?"

Katherine looked up from her mixing. When Karl called her by her proper name, instead of his more usual 'Schatz', she knew something serious had happened. Quickly tipping the contents into two baking tins she passed the bowl and spoon to Sabina, picked up Richard from the floor and carried him out to the living room, Karl following at her heels.

"What is it?" she asked, settling Richard down by a pile of wooden bricks on the hearth rug.

Karl stood by his younger son and told Katherine of the recent events in the toolshed, including his own uncontrolled punch on Siegfried's jaw.

"I'm beginning to realise it was a mistake to bring him here," he concluded, "but it's too late now to send him back to Anna and Stefan. I can't expect them to cope with such monstrous behaviour. After today, I really believe he meant to injure John Winters with that penknife of his."

"Surely not?" Katherine gasped. "How can a boy of only seven do such a thing?"

"By example in his early years, and by having to defend himself against his stepfather, I suppose. But whatever the reason, I'm now worried about my own lack of control in dealing with him. Given a similar situation, I can see myself doing the same thing again, possibly hurting him more seriously next time."

"Like when Sarah and I only just stopped you from killing Andrew? But surely you could never do a thing like that to your own son?" One look at Karl's grim expression told her that he believed he could. She wrapped her arms around him, laying her head on his chest and spoke to his heart. "What on earth can we do with him? It will only get worse as he grows older. What if he suddenly turned on Sabina or Richard one day?"

Katherine had voiced Karl's own unspoken fears. He shook his head in despair. "Hopefully the worst of his anger is directed at me. But I think you're right. Once he reaches sixteen or so he'll be impossible to deal with."

Katherine stepped back and grasped his hands as if to gain strength from them. "He is now. I feel I have no control over him whatsoever. If he happens to do as I ask, I feel it's only because of some ulterior motive of his own."

Bored with the bricks, Richard began to wail for attention. Karl picked him up so that he could see his reflection in the mirror over the fireplace.

"Where is Siegfried, anyway?" Katherine asked.

"He ran off up to his hiding-place in the old-man's-beard. He'll probably stay there for the rest of the morning until the bruise on his

132

chin is a nice colour. Then he'll come in and show it to you. That's another thing he does, you realise, Schatz. He tries to make us fight each other, and he succeeds sometimes, doesn't he?"

His criticism sunk home but she wanted nevertheless to defend her stance on corporal punishment. "If you hadn't hit him just now, we might have been able to sort out this business with the penknife. As it is, it's all blown up in our faces."

"Would you rather I simply let him stab me?" Karl snapped back.

Katherine shut her eyes. When she eventually opened them again she managed an apologetic smile. "I'm sorry, Liebling. What with all the preparations for Christmas and Siegfried's birthday I've just got a bit overtired. You remember I asked you to take Sabina out to her nursery school Christmas party this afternoon? Could you possibly take Richard out too, so I can get on with Siegfried's tea party?"

Karl kissed her lightly on the forehead, and in the process Richard transferred himself across to his mother's arms. "Yes, of course. I'll take them over to Yew Tree Lodge first and say hello to Robert and Alice. They were due up from London yesterday, weren't they?"

"Yes. Why don't you invite them all up for Christmas Eve? You always complain we do nothing on that day."

"You just said you had enough work to do!"

"We can give them some of the *Stollen* and *Lebkuchen* your mother sent, and you can make up a big jug of your famous *Glühwein*. With a few mince pies we should have plenty to keep everyone happy."

Karl smiled. Her enthusiasm magically transformed his mood from depression to optimism.

"You're special. You know that, Schatz."

*

As predicted, Siegfried turned up just before lunch, the mark on his jaw now a satisfying dark blue. Seating himself at the kitchen table, he waited for Katherine to notice and comment upon the bruise.

"Did you find your penknife?" she asked him casually, hearing Karl's footsteps approaching the back door.

"Yes," he mumbled, as though speaking clearly were too painful.

"Where was it then?" Katherine asked, ladling chicken soup into his bowl. Karl sat down at the table, studiously ignored by Siegfried.

"In the woods."

"That's lucky you found it," Katherine continued brightly in her attempts to bridge the open feud between father and son. "So have you opened your mother's present yet?"

Siegfried scowled and slurped his soup. "No."

"Perhaps you'll get around to it after lunch, before your friends arrive at three o'clock."

"Perhaps."

Katherine rather hoped that Karl would help her out in this tedious conversation, but untypically he remained silent, making his continued censure of Siegfried only too plain.

Katherine frowned at him, and he remembered he had decided to apologise to Siegfried. Over the noise of Richard's screeching because his soup was too hot, Karl asked Siegfried: "How's your jaw?"

It was the best apology he could muster at the moment.

Siegfried glanced from Karl to Katherine and quickly reasoned that his father had already prejudiced the case in his own favour. Hence the lack of reaction from Katherine over the bruise. He continued drinking his soup and made no answer.

Reluctantly Karl decided to make an outright apology, using German to convey his sincerity. "Look, I'm very sorry I hit you so hard, Siegfried."

Siegfried simply stared defiantly back at Karl, blatantly refusing to accept the apology.

The look set Karl's blood boiling. "Just because it's your birthday, you seem to think you can behave as you like!" he shouted. "I'm not going to have my lunch spoilt by your insolence. Go and eat in your room!"

Silently Siegfried gathered together his soup bowl and plate of bread and marched out of the room, as though victory were his.

At Karl's sudden outburst, Sabina began to cry.

"Daddy's not shouting at you, Poppet," Katherine reassured her with a hug. "Siegfried's the one who's being naughty, not you."

Karl reached across the table and stroked his daughter's hair. "You've got your nursery school party this afternoon. Before we go I'll take you to see Aunty Gertie. Robert will be there too, with a nice lady called Alice he's going to marry."

"Ooo. Robert!" Sabina screeched in delight. "I like Robert. He makes me laugh."

134

"Yes, so just get on with eating your lunch and then we'll be off." Sabina's excitement dispelled some of Karl's anger, and he managed a smile at her.

From his room, Siegfried heard the sounds of departure a short while later. He had spent the time since opening his mother's present drawing a picture of his father. It was not a very good likeness, he had to admit, but it was adequate for his needs. Opening his penknife, he thrust the blade through the paper into the chest of the drawn man.

"That's what I wanted to do this morning, you traitor!" he snarled at the picture.

*

Sabina found the extrovert Alice quite delightful, and even Richard was entertained by her. Karl was a little surprised at Robert's choice of so flamboyant a future wife, but was very soon won over by her genuine charm.

"You're taking after your father, aren't you?" he joked to Robert from his armchair in the Murdochs' large but cosy sitting room.

"Why's that?"

"Marrying a nurse"

"Oh, I see! Yes, I suppose I am." Robert watched Alice and his mother helping Sabina with a jigsaw puzzle, while Richard bashed at a toy drum. He flipped a lock of his dark brown hair back to its side parting. Small of stature like his mother, his features still wore the half-starved look of the Far East POW he once was. Skipped and hurried meals at medical school only exacerbated his inherent slimness.

"I rather thought you'd be helping out with Siegfried's birthday today, instead of being banished down here for the afternoon. That's what's happened, isn't it, Karl? I sensed trouble when you telephoned earlier to arrange the visit." Karl had seemed tense then, and even now there was a shadow lurking behind the friendship in his eyes.

"You know me too well, Robert," Karl admitted. "I'm really supposed to be taking Sabina to her party and keeping Richard out from underneath Katherine's feet, but I was definitely not wanted up there by Siegfried. He and I had a ... well I can only describe it as a confrontation, but I ended up punching him hard on the jaw after he was about to threaten me with a knife. It's getting too serious, Robert. I don't know how to handle him."

Robert had always been Karl's confidant, almost from the first day Karl came to the valley. The two men understood each other as no one else could, Katherine included, but this was too incredible for words.

"But he's only ... eight now? And you say he threatened you with a knife? Good grief, Karl! You're telling me it's getting serious!"

Karl felt he ought to clarify the details. "He didn't get the chance to threaten me, but I know that's what he intended, after the John Winters incident."

Robert frowned. "Yes, I heard about that from Mum. You reckon he deliberately wounded the boy?"

"Yes, I'm almost certain he meant to."

"That's quite an accusation to make against your own son, Karl."

"I've almost given up thinking of him as my son," Karl said dejectedly. "He's certainly never looked on me as a father; only as a traitor to his country."

"I wish I could suggest something that would help, short of sending him back to his mother, but I don't suppose you would consider that."

"No. Not while his stepfather is still around."

"People like that never die," Robert said. "They only go on and on making others' lives a misery."

Karl broke the woeful silence. "Enough of my problems! I've scarcely spoken to Alice yet. I'd better take Sabina over to the village hall, then I'll come back here and get to meet her properly."

Robert looked sheepish. "I told her I wanted a quiet word with you first. I knew from your phone call that something was troubling you."

Karl got to his feet. "A problem shared is a problem halved. I remember you telling me that a long time ago. Don't you ever forget it, either."

*

Upon his return, Karl found Robert and Alice busy amusing Richard with some glove puppets. Alice seemed to dwarf Robert, not so much by her size but by her personality. Her mousey hair and rather

136

plain round features were amply overshadowed by her vivacity. Karl could well understand why Robert should want someone like Alice to brighten up his future for him. Gertie obviously thoroughly approved of her as a prospective daughter-in-law. While Richard played with some toy farm animals, the adults sat and chatted about Robert's coming finals and his plans for when he qualified. As a direct result of Karl's earlier problems, he had a keen interest in psychiatry, and was hoping to specialise in that field in due course.

At five-thirty it was time to collect Sabina again. Having made the invitation to all the Murdochs to come up on Christmas Eve, Karl gathered up the sleeping Richard, fetched an over-excited Sabina, then drove his family back up to the farm, to arrive near the end of the tea party. He did not want to be absent from the whole event, and Sabina very quickly helped to demolish the last of the fish paste sandwiches, before Katherine brought in Siegfried's cake with its eight candles burning brightly.

Such was Karl's improved mood that he gladly joined in singing 'Happy Birthday' and the party came to its end without incident. Karl drove the two boys back home and returned to find most of the tidying up already done.

It was difficult packing the younger children off to bed after the excitement and Richard's rather late sleep at the Murdochs', but finally Katherine and Karl had the downstairs to themselves and Katherine collapsed into one of the living room chairs.

"Did Siegfried open Ilse's present eventually?" Karl asked her before she could fall asleep.

"Yes."

"Well, what was in it?" he prompted.

Katherine opened her eyes again. "A toy gun," she replied wearily, "which actually fires rubber suckers. I've already warned him not to shoot it at anyone," she said, anticipating his next comment.

"Hmph. Ilse certainly seems to know what will make him happy. He's growing so fast I'm going to have to keep my promise to him soon and teach him how to shoot a real gun."

"Not just yet though, will you?" she pleaded.

Her voice was leaden with fatigue and Karl brushed a strand of hair from her eyes, caressing her cheek in the process. "No, not yet.

You shut your eyes, Schatz, and I'll switch the wireless on for you. You've had a busy day. I'm off out to the shed to finish that Aladdin's lamp. I can't afford to take another day off work."

Katherine hardly heard him leave the room and did not hear the back door open a second time five minutes later.

CHAPTER ELEVEN

"Siegfried! Siegfried!"

Werner learned of Siegfried's disappearance within seconds of arriving for work. From the barn he could hear Karl calling Siegfried's name with increasing urgency. He hurried into its dark recesses where Karl was rummaging behind a pile of empty apple crates.

"Gone missing, has he?" Werner was still the only person on the farm to whom Siegfried had shown no animosity. He felt considerable affection for the young scoundrel, despite the way he treated his father.

Karl abandoned the crates. "Yes, and we've no idea how long he's been gone. His bed was cold when Katherine found it empty this morning. We were both pretty tired last night and neither of us bothered to look in on him before we went to bed. He could have been gone all night."

"At least it was mild last night for the time of year. He should have been all right," Werner consoled him as they left the barn and moved on to the stable. "But there's colder weather on its way. Has he taken anything with him, that you know of?"

"Katherine's checking at the moment. I'm just doing a quick search of his usual haunts, just in case he's only camping out for the night to frighten us, but I doubt it."

Katherine came scurrying towards them, her face grim. "As far as I can tell, he's taken the rucksack, a torch, some food and warm clothing, and he's raided the money from the biscuit jar. There was about five pounds in there, I reckon." She paused to collect her breath. "He's also taken his penknife, his new toy gun, his mother's letters and ... his passport."

"Blow me! He's going to Germany," Werner muttered.

Karl glanced at Katherine and let out a deep sigh of defeat. "We'd better telephone the police and let them know. I guess he's heading for Harwich. He's travelled that route, so has at least some idea how to go to Germany."

"I can't believe he thought to take his passport. He must have been planning this for some time," Katherine said to Werner as Karl disappeared indoors. "He'll never make it. They'll pick him up at the port, if he ever gets that far."

Having made his report to the local police Karl set about organising a search of the local area. He ought to be seen to be doing something. He must not let anyone see the disturbing sense of relief he felt at Siegfried's absence. He summoned Robert and Alice to help in the search. Katherine was to stay with the younger children at home to man the telephone should the police call.

Katherine's first meeting with Alice was brief. An exchange of hellos was all they had time for before Robert whisked Alice away to search the riverbank. Karl and Werner were tackling the woods. With the house empty once more, Katherine sat down with Sabina in the kitchen to make paperchains. Holding a red strip of paper flat for Sabina to glue, Katherine's eyes wandered towards the window which looked out over the valley and away towards the mist-shrouded escarpment of Hay Bluff, just across the Welsh border. It was to Hay Bluff that Karl had fled back in the spring of 1947, when Andrew Kellett informed her that Karl was in the SS. Shortly after that he suffered a mental breakdown. Katherine just hoped that Siegfried, after his dismal childhood experiences so far, was not going to echo his father's history as faithfully as he mirrored his appearance. She remembered at one time frequently praying for Karl to find tranquillity of soul. It might be as well now to utter that same prayer for Siegfried's benefit.

"Mummy, what do I do now?" Sabina held up her efforts for inspection.

"Oh, sorry, sweetheart. Let's have a look."

Sabina had managed to smear glue over the entire length of the paper strip. Katherine gave her another strip.

"Just put the glue on one end," she said, demonstrating again. She watched Sabina successfully complete two links of the chain before her thoughts wandered back to the search party.

She thought she detected a certain lack of enthusiasm from Karl about organising a search party. Yesterday's incident in the tool shed seemed to have shattered all Karl's illusions about having Siegfried to live with them. She suspected it was not only Siegfried's behaviour which hurt him, but also his own violent response to it. Karl had been trained from childhood to fight, and that training seemed effective in its permanence. It was a part of his personality, his aggressive streak. Normally it was kept well under wraps, but she knew it could break out, given sufficient provocation. And Siegfried knew how to provoke.

The telephone remained silent as the paper chain grew in length. At ten o'clock the searchers returned, despondent and muddy, anxious to hear whether Katherine had any news yet. Their despondency continued over cups of coffee and scones, although Alice tried her best to cheer everyone up.

Pushing away his scone virtually untouched, Karl picked up Richard and sat him on his lap. Katherine watched him, her heart going out to him in his search, physically and emotionally, for his elder son. If Richard ever ran away from home, Karl would stop at nothing to find him. But Richard should never feel the need to leave his loving family. Siegfried, it seemed, had yet to find his true home. It was not here at Lane Head Farm.

*

Siegfried crouched behind a thick hedge next to a road junction, listening and waiting for the heavier engine noise of a delivery lorry or van. It was his intention to climb into the back of the first likely-looking vehicle to come along, and see where it took him. Overnight he had walked towards Hereford, reaching the outskirts just as the sun was rising through the early morning mist. Now he was in danger of falling asleep. Since his arrival at the road junction nothing had passed by except for an old man on a bicycle. Siegfried's legs ached from his long walk and his clothing was damp through to the skin. Wearily he shifted his position slightly, then noticed the faint rumbling of an approaching vehicle.

Peering through the gap in the hedge he spotted a post van coming up the lane towards the junction. That was no good. It would probably only be delivering locally. He fished around in the rucksack and ate a hunk of bread.

A short time later, another vehicle approached, larger by the sound of it. Quickly Siegfried assessed its usefulness. Above the driver's cab was written the legend *A.G.Glover & Sons, Gloucester*. As the van drew up, Siegfried was already half out of the hedge. He threw himself over the tailboard as the van pulled out onto the main road towards Ross-on-Wye and Gloucester. Not even the clanking of the cider bottles in their crates could then keep Siegfried awake.

It was the hubbub of Gloucester's busy streets which woke him in time before he could be discovered. The van turned off the main road into a quieter back street on the edge of the city. Siegfried guessed the van must be near its destination, and jumped down from the back as it negotiated a sharp turn. Now all he had to do was find a similar van heading for London.

The difficulty of his task, finding his way all alone to Germany, did not daunt Siegfried in the slightest. He was finally doing what he had dreamed of doing ever since he was forcibly taken from Germany – going home. He was satisfied he could now deal with his stepfather. Gustav's gift might well come in useful if Erich threatened him again.

Siegfried sauntered down the pavement, wishing the rucksack did not make him look quite so conspicuous. He stopped outside a baker's shop, where the warm, yeasty smell was so evocative of the flat over the bakery in Dortmund. A woman with two small children entered the shop. Making use of the distraction they caused, Siegfried sneaked behind the counter and stole a large loaf off the shelf. Once outside he tucked the loaf into the rucksack and headed towards the spires of Gloucester Cathedral.

He guessed the time was about ten o'clock by now, but the day felt cooler rather than warmer. The clouds which had blanketed the earth overnight were being cleared by a biting easterly wind. Siegfried shivered, despite his coat and gloves. He pulled his navy Balaclava further forward over his ears, unconsciously hiding his distinctive blond hair from the eyes of alerted policemen.

It was the rucksack which gave him away. A policeman on traffic duty spotted the lone figure and remembered his briefing an hour earlier to be on the alert for a runaway boy from Herefordshire. He reported his sighting to the beat constable, who hurried off in the boy's tracks.

Siegfried was studying the potential of a removal van parked outside a house, when he felt a hand clamp down on his shoulder.

142

He ducked down to try to escape the grasp but the hand followed him, biting into his coat with deft precision.

"Were you thinking of going somewhere, sonny?"

Siegfried screwed his neck around and peered up at the tall young policeman. "I wasn't doing anything. What do you want with me?" He remembered the loaf of bread. Perhaps the shopkeeper had seen him after all.

The boy's German accent confirmed the police constable's suspicions. "The name's Siegfried, isn't it? Couldn't forget a name like that, could I now? Well, Siegfried," he went on, still with a firm grip but a friendly enough tone of voice, "you'd better come with me and we'll get you home. Your parents are worried about you."

"My home is in Germany, so you'd better take me there," Siegfried retorted, unafraid of the man who clearly thought small boys posed no threat to him.

The constable's expression promptly darkened. "I see. Like that, is it?" This boy certainly knew how to lose friends. "Come along, get moving!"

Siegfried found himself propelled along the street, observed by the removal men from behind a large Edwardian wardrobe. So his father had set the police after him, like a criminal, Siegfried fumed. Well, he had no qualms about behaving like a criminal when he wanted to.

He had kept his penknife in his coat pocket rather than inaccessible in the rucksack. He felt in his pocket, opened the blade of the penknife then whirled round suddenly on his captor, his right hand flashing upwards towards the policeman's neck.

The high collar of his uniform and heavy duty strap of his helmet saved the policeman from serious injury. He ducked aside as he saw what was coming, the sharp blade only catching the side of his neck before being deflected off the chin strap onto his collar. A small nick in his flesh was all he suffered.

"You little bugger!" he stormed, swiftly disarming his juvenile attacker. He pocketed the penknife himself then, with an even tighter grip on Siegfried's arm and shoulder, marched him off to the police station.

The duty desk sergeant was surprised at the force one of his constables was using to bring in a young lad. The boy was struggling wildly, and had been doing so for some time, judging by the red glow on PC Warburton's face. Sergeant MacFarlane then noticed the trickle of blood on his junior's neck.

"Bloody hell, Warburton! What's he been up to?"

"It's that runaway Jerry boy from Hereford, Sarge," he puffed. "He didn't want to come quietly."

"I can see that."

Siegfried ceased his struggles abruptly when faced with two policemen. He suddenly felt very tired and stood sulkily, eyes cast down to the floor.

The desk sergeant opened his report book. "I thought we'd given up having to recapture escaped Jerries," he joked as he unscrewed the top of his fountain pen. "Now. What's his name again? Siegfried something, isn't it?"

"Yes, Sarge. I can't remember the surname. Typically German, though."

Aware that Siegfried was not going to help out by supplying his surname, Sgt MacFarlane leafed through the briefing notes of that morning. "Ah, here we are. Siegfried Driesler. Aged eight, blond hair, grey eyes ..." The sergeant pulled back the Balaclava to reveal Siegfried's blond hair. "Seems to fit the description all right, Warburton, but how are you certain it's him?"

"He speaks with a foreign accent and he told me his home was in Germany. It's him, I'm sure of it, Sarge."

"Right. We'd better inform the Herefordshire police who can contact his parents. In the meantime we'll have to find somewhere to put him. Stick him in the interview room and lock the door. I'll get WPC Rose to come and sit with him until we know what to do with him."

Warburton seemed to be debating with himself about something, deciding finally to speak. "I won't mention it in my report, but the blighter attacked me with a penknife." He took the offending item out of his pocket and laid it on the counter next to Siegfried's rucksack.

MacFarlane's eyes narrowed. "So that's how you got that nick on your neck, is it?"

"Yes, Sarge, but I'm damned lucky it wasn't worse than it is."

"God save us from these infernal Germans!" MacFarlane implored, his eyes raised heavenward. "Whatever must the father be like?"

Siegfried broke his silence at last. "He's a coward and a traitor! Not like me!"

MacFarlane was taken aback by the boy's ferocity. "That's enough now, lad. I don't want to hear any more from you. I'm having second thoughts about leaving you alone with WPC Rose. You'd better stay too, Warburton. Oh ... and get him something to eat."

Siegfried was led off through a doorway into a short corridor. Warburton opened the first door on the left and steered Siegfried inside, sitting him down on a chair by an empty table.

"Stay there while I get you some food."

When Warburton returned with a tray he also had a fresh piece of sticking plaster on his neck. He noticed that Siegfried was still sitting with his coat and Balaclava on.

"Take your things off and make yourself more comfortable," Warburton told him, putting down the tray of bacon, egg, bread and mug of milk in front of the boy.

Siegfried did not move.

"Look, I'm trying my best to be friendly with you," Warburton went on. "Can't you understand that?" He was a young man, too young to have fought in the war, and it was the first time he had come face to face with a German, albeit an eight-year-old one.

Still Siegfried made no move.

"Suit yourself, but I'm staying here with you, so you'd better get on and eat that before it's cold. By the way, where did you get that bread in the rucksack from? It's fresh today. I bet you didn't buy it, did you?"

Without apparently hearing the question Siegfried took off his Balaclava, but left his coat on, and began to eat. Ten minutes later the door was opened and a motherly-looking woman police constable walked in, smiling at Siegfried as she did so.

"Don't be fooled by his age, Vi," Warburton warned her. "He's a violent bugger is this one."

"Language!" Violet Rose scolded him. She was always called in for juvenile offenders and was convinced that a good example should always be set to them. "Sgt MacFarlane did give me the details before I came in."

Siegfried scowled at her by way of welcome, wondering what a namby-pambying woman was wanted for.

WPC Rose sat at the table opposite him. "Your father is driving down here to collect you. He should be here in about forty minutes."

Her chatty manner was designed to put the boy at ease, but Warburton's assertion that he was a hard-bitten case proved correct as he stared resolutely past her. In her experience such boys only went on to commit worse crimes, no matter what was done for them. They had irrevocably crossed the line into the criminal world, and she judged this lad to be one of them. Nevertheless, there were such things as miracles, and she never gave up hope completely on a child.

Siegfried sat in silence while they waited, Warburton and Vi Rose exchanging the occasional word, Siegfried trying to maintain a scowl until his eyelids drooped and his head fell forwards onto the table. Warburton decided it was safe to leave Vi alone with the boy, and took the tray out.

As he returned to the lobby an adult replica of the German boy walked through the outer door. So this was the so-called coward and traitor, he thought with interest. He exchanged a glance with MacFarlane and loitered in the vicinity of the desk.

"Can I help you, sir?" Sgt MacFarlane asked in his mildly supercilious air, designed to intimidate those members of the public he considered to be of dubious quality.

"You have my son, Siegfried Driesler here, I believe," Karl said firmly, having no reason to be intimidated by the man or the uniform. There was only one uniform he had learned to fear, and that was now obsolete.

Sgt MacFarlane eyed the tall man warily for signs of trouble so evident in the son, but the man seemed amenable enough.

"That's right, sir. PC Warburton here found him trying to cadge a ride on a removal van."

Karl turned to the young policeman. "I'm most grateful to you for finding him, constable."

You don't sound it, mate, Warburton thought. Perhaps young Siegfried had good reason to run away from home after all. "It's all part of my job, Mr Driesler," he explained modestly, fingering the sticking plaster on his neck.

"Bring the lad out here, Warburton," the sergeant told him officiously.

PC Warburton disappeared to do the sergeant's bidding while MacFarlane brought out the rucksack and penknife from behind the desk.

"I must mention, sir, that your son attacked PC Warburton with this penknife, inflicting a wound which, but for Warburton's prompt evasive action, could have been very serious. In view of the boy's age we are not taking any action other than to point out the fact to your local police and to recommend to you, sir, that the penknife be removed from his possession."

MacFarlane noted that the father did not seem in the least surprised by this revelation.

"I most certainly will, sergeant," Karl told him, declining to mention Siegfried's two previous knife attacks.

"If I were you, sir, I'd keep a jolly strict eye on that lad in future. We don't want to have to press serious charges against him one of these days."

"Don't worry. It won't happen again."

MacFarlane wondered how he could be so sure. Warburton appeared with a sleepy Siegfried in tow. Neither father nor son spoke and it was left to Sgt MacFarlane to bridge the gap between them.

"Off you go now, sonny. But don't let me hear you've been using that knife on anyone again or you'll be in a whole packet of trouble."

The threat bounced off Siegfried. He did not intend remaining in England long enough to get into any more trouble here.

Karl picked up the rucksack, pocketed the infernal penknife and laid his hand on Siegfried's shoulder, just as Warburton had done a couple of hours earlier. "Come on then. Let's get home."

Reluctantly Siegfried headed for the door.

"'Bye, Siegfried!" WPC Rose called to him cheerily from the door to the corridor.

He turned his head and scowled, before setting off outside with his father.

"I wouldn't like to be in his shoes," MacFarlane muttered when they were gone.

147

"Whose? The boy's?" Warburton asked.

"No, the father's. That boy's trouble, if you ask me."

"With looks like that they're both trouble," Vi Rose murmured almost inaudibly, her eyes fixed glassily on the street door.

Warburton nudged MacFarlane in the ribs before addressing the vacant-faced Violet. "Wishing you were ten years younger, eh, Vi? Or even thirty?"

"Get away with you!" she laughed to cover up her more than professional interest in the pair.

*

Robert sat patiently waiting in the Land Rover outside the police station. When he saw the door open and Karl walk out with Siegfried firmly in his grasp, he groaned inwardly, got out of the vehicle and held the door open wide for Siegfried to get in. He then followed the boy in, so that Siegfried sat between the two men on the front seat.

Karl drove in silence until they reached the outskirts of the city and were back on the main A40 to Ross-on-Wye. "You got off lightly there, Siegfried. Yet again I might add. Why is it that people always try to be kind to you, do you think?" he asked without taking his eyes off the road.

"I don't know," Siegfried replied disinterestedly.

"Tell Robert what you did to the policeman, and see whether he thinks you got off too lightly or not," Karl continued, stonily.

Siegfried was really rather proud of himself, so answered readily: "I attacked him with my penknife."

"No serious damage done," Karl hastened to explain, as he heard Robert's gasp of horror. "But you could easily have seriously injured him, Siegfried, couldn't you? Just like you wanted to hurt me yesterday."

This time Siegfried wisely kept his mouth shut. He did not like the unpleasant iciness in his father's voice. There was no hint of familiarity in it, and Siegfried became suddenly aware of a significant change in their relationship.

"What do you think of my son's behaviour, Robert? What do you think I should do with him now?"

Robert, too, did not like his friend's tone, even though he well appreciated the difficult situation Karl was in. He did not want to interfere in a family matter, however. "Well, he's gone too far, that goes without saying, Karl. He'll end up killing someone at this rate. But how you stop him, I haven't a clue." He turned his attention to Siegfried.

"Why do you keep attacking people, Siegfried? Do you want to hurt them, or can't you stop yourself from doing it?"

It was not a question Siegfried could easily answer. He did his best, however. "I hate it here," he said quite calmly. "I hate England. So I fight to get away."

"You can go then," Karl said slowly, his voice leaden and emotionless.

Siegfried was taken aback at the suddenness of his father's decision. "You mean it?"

"Yes. I will write to your mother and tell her that, just like her husband, I refuse to have you in my house any longer. It was she who turned you against me, so she can sort out this mess. You will not act like my son, so I refuse to act like your father any more."

The bitterness of his words left Robert in no doubt that Karl meant what he said. He was giving up responsibility for Siegfried permanently.

"Until you go, though, Siegfried," Karl continued, "you must stop this war with me, or I can't promise that I won't beat you even worse than your stepfather ever did. I accept that you have won this battle, so play fair now that it's over."

"But what if his mother can't or won't have him back?" Robert objected. "If this Röbel fellow threw Siegfried out, he's not going to let him come back now, is he?"

"That's for Ilse to sort out. I'm not asking my family to take in the little monster."

Siegfried felt the deep pain of total rejection for the first time. His father was talking about him as though he was not there to hear, and more to the point, he was implying that he would never again let Siegfried stay with Oma and Opa. With this threat in mind, Siegfried decided he could afford to be more generous to his father.

"I promise I'll behave from now on, until I go back to Germany," he said solemnly. "You can keep my penknife until then, Vater."

Karl was surprised at his son's promise, but was equally determined not to give an inch. "You're dead right I'm keeping it! You can have it back on your twenty-first birthday, if you still want it then. By that time I hope you'll have learned a sense of responsibility."

"Easy, Karl!" Robert intervened gently. He was beginning to wonder what had got into Karl since yesterday. "You're in danger of flouting the truce even before it's begun."

"Hmph," was Karl's only reply.

*

Predictably, Katherine and the newly-introduced Alice made a big fuss over Siegfried when he arrived back at the farm. Karl left them to it and went to join Werner who was pruning the orchards. His abrupt return to work, with hardly a word spoken to anybody, least of all to Siegfried, disturbed both Katherine and Robert.

"I rather think Karl's got something he wants to tell you this evening, once the children are in bed," he advised her, as he and Alice bade their farewells.

"Well, it will have to be after his pantomime rehearsal. It's the last one before the Christmas break."

"Oh gosh, yes. I'd forgotten. Mum's out at that too."

"What's it about, Robert? Do you know?" she asked fearfully.

Robert hedged her question. "It's for Karl to tell you, not me."

Katherine's anxious face almost made him relent. Instead he laid his hand on her shoulder and gave her a quick brotherly kiss on the cheek. "See you on Monday, then."

"Monday?" she asked, forgetting for a moment the Christmas festivities amidst all the troubles with Siegfried.

"Christmas Eve," he reminded her gently.

*

The old village hall was still festooned with paper chains and balloons from the nursery school Christmas party. Gertie watched the stage hands manhandle a table for a scene change. It was a tribute to the enthusiasm of a few that a scattered farming community could provide sufficient members for the Penchurch Players. Activity noticeably subsided over the summer months,

150

when everyone was busy in the fields, but the long winter evenings drew them back to the village hall. Next year, hopefully, they would be able to use the new Memorial Hall for their productions. Gertie turned over the next page of the script. As prompt she was having to work hard this evening. Karl's mind was not on his words, and Dennis Hobday, the producer, was growing impatient with him.

"Someone give him the script to read, for God's sake, or we'll be here all night!" he yelled, after the genie had missed yet another cue.

Karl fumed inwardly and refused the script. "I'm sorry, Dennis. I'll try to concentrate more. I know the lines really."

"OK, OK," the producer conceded. "You're excused this once. We all know about your son's exploits. Perhaps when we pick up again after Christmas we'll all be raring to go. It'll only be three weeks to curtain-up by then."

The remainder of the rehearsal passed more smoothly but with an unusually lacklustre performance from the genie. As they were packing up to leave the village hall, Gertie approached Karl for a quiet word.

"Robert told me what happened in Gloucester today, Karl. I hope you won't think I'm interfering but I do hope you'll reconsider sending Siegfried back to live with that stepfather of his. The damage that man's done to the boy already shouldn't be added to. I'm sure there must be a better way to deal with Siegfried."

"So long as Siegfried is in England rather than Germany, his behaviour is going to stay aggressive and disruptive," he insisted. "At the moment we have a truce, as he believes he's going home. But if I go back on my word now, he'll be worse than ever. We have no kind of a relationship any more, if we ever did have one. There is no point in him staying here."

"You seriously mean you're going to wash your hands of him?"

The hall was more or less empty of cast by now; only Dennis Hobday remained, noisily haranguing the stage manager about the set, so Gertie felt she was in no danger of being overheard. Which was just as well, she thought, when she heard Karl's reply.

"Yes," he said grimly. "Otherwise I fear I'll kill him one of these days."

"You're not serious, are you? Does he really drive you that far?"

"Yes, I'm afraid he does."

The resignation in his voice told Gertie she was powerless to interfere. "I see. Well you must do as you think fit, of course. I'm so sorry it has turned out like this for you both."

"So am I, Gertie. So am I."

CHAPTER TWELVE

"What? You've told him he can go back to Germany?" Katherine slammed the *Radio Times* onto the table beside her chair. "Whether it's the right decision or not makes no difference," she blazed, rising to her feet to face Karl. "The fact that you went and told him without even consulting me is what's so galling! I think I have some right to a say in such matters, after all the trouble I've taken to –"

"If you'd been with me and seen him there, you'd have felt the same. The police told me he'd be in bigger trouble one of these days, and I believe it." His voice rose angrily. "I'm not prepared to let him ruin all our lives. I shall write to Ilse tomorrow to see if she can find a home for him somewhere. At least in Germany he might feel obliged to behave."

Katherine stood, hands on hips in frustration. She could see that Karl had dug his heels in and would not be budged from his decision. Pig-headed. Stubborn. Call it what you will. She recognised the signs only too well after a childhood spent battling with Sarah's mulishness. She had to ease off to get anywhere. She sat down again in the armchair.

"You can't send a boy that age back to such uncertainty," she said in more moderate tones. "It's obvious there's nowhere else to send him or she would have done that before, rather than hand him over to you."

It was always the same when they argued. Katherine regained control first and Karl invariably followed her lead. He did so now. "Circumstances change, Schatz. We can only try. But as I said to Gertie this evening, I'm genuinely frightened I might kill him. When I try to talk to that boy now I find my fists start to clench and my teeth grit. I just don't know whether I can stay in control of myself at times like that."

A lurking suspicion crossed Katherine's mind. "You're not using your breakdown as an excuse to get rid of him, are you?"

"Excuse?" Her total lack of comprehension infuriated him. He stooped to lean on the arms of her chair, imprisoning her within it. "You don't know what I feel when I hear my own son condemning me as a traitor to the Nazis. I never talk about those times with you, but that must show you how difficult it still is for me. I live in fear of returning to the nightmare."

He stood up and turned to the mantelpiece, grasping it as though determined not to let go. He stared at his reflection in the mirror, at the fine lines engraved on his weatherbeaten face; lines which spoke all too clearly to him of past ordeals. He looked past his reflection at Katherine, sitting shocked but attentive in her chair. He could not face her directly for what he was about to say.

"I think that is partly why I want to be in these war films," he told the mirror. "To help me see the past as something which stops when the director says 'cut'; something I can walk away from at the end of the day; to help me see an SS uniform and not feel panic since the person inside it is only an actor and not ..." He ground to a halt, hands clutching his head.

Katherine felt scared. The pressure of having to cope with Siegfried's behaviour seemed to have released in Karl all his old turmoil and anxieties.

"Not Goslar, you mean, Liebchen?" she said softly, getting up to put her arms around him, all idea of discussing Siegfried abandoned. His body felt rigid within her embrace, but gradually she felt him begin to relax.

"I need you, Schatz!" he murmured eventually into her hair. "My God, how I need you!"

*

She found him first thing next morning in the study writing to Ilse. She looked over his shoulder at the words on the page.

"Shall I read you what I've written?" he asked, sensing her discomfort at him communicating with Ilse.

"If you like."

He cleared his throat and read from his letter, translating from the German. "Dear Frau Röbel, you have so successfully turned my son against me, that I find I am no longer able to find a place for him in my home. Since he still regards you as his mother I consider it your

154

duty to fulfill your parental obligations and find a home for him, whether in your own home or elsewhere. I shall, of course, bring him over to Germany just as soon as I hear from you. Yours, Karl Driesler."

He looked up at her. "Well, what do you think? Do I make my feelings clear?"

"Abundantly," Katherine said in astonishment. "But isn't it a bit too ... brutal? She used to be your fiancée, after all!"

"I think I have a right to be brutal. She's got to see how serious the situation is here."

"I suppose you're right." A shriek came from the kitchen. "I'd better go. That's Richard yelling for his breakfast."

She hurried off to find Richard squirming in his high chair. As she made the porridge she thought about Siegfried's mother receiving such a letter. Poor woman! What on earth would she do?

*

Siegfried kept to his word and behaved impeccably throughout the Christmas holidays. He did not want his father to have any excuse to change his mind about sending him back to Germany. He only lived for that day, but his mother's reply was slow in coming. Each morning Siegfried hunted through the post, and still there was nothing from her. By the time of the pantomime he was burning with impatience, his self-control wearing thin.

In the village hall he watched his father's performance incredulously. How could he demean himself by appearing in such rubbish? Wisely, the pantomime dame, Widow Twankie, refrained from calling upon Siegfried's help for the audience participation joke-telling. Siegfried sat in silent disgust at the sheer silliness of it all, as Sabina stood on stage and in a clear, confident voice told the joke about crossing a sheep with a kangaroo. However, when the show was over he remembered Gustav's instructions for deception, and ostentatiously joined in with the applause, even when the genie, dressed in baggy, blue satin pantaloons, turban and sparkling waistcoat, came to take his bow.

*

A few days later the long-awaited letter from Ilse finally arrived. It was addressed to Karl so Siegfried had to wait by his elbow in a frenzy of impatience. At last his father finished reading. He stood

155

looking at it a moment then showed it to Siegfried without a word. Siegfried struggled to read it.

Dear Karl,   *Dortmund. 22.1.52*

It has taken me a long time to reply to your letter. I am deeply sorry for the way things have turned out, and I have been trying my utmost to find a solution, but it is hopeless. Erich refuses outright to have Siegfried back, and I have no other relatives to turn to. My only hope is that you and he can sort this problem out between you. I have written to him to explain how wrong I was to make him hate you, and that he must come to love you as a father. Whether this will make any difference, I don't know. You didn't give any details in your letter, but it was so distant and unfriendly that I assume Siegfried is causing a lot of trouble.

Please accept my sincerest apologies to you and your wife, but I dare not have Siegfried back for his own safety's sake. It may be presumptive of me to suggest this, but couldn't you ask your family in Medebach to have him? It seems the only possible alternative. Please tell me what you decide.

Yours in friendship,
Ilse.

Karl spoke first. "I did my best to get her to have you, Siegfried, but that husband of hers refuses to give in. I expect you remember how difficult it is for her, living with him. It's not really her fault she can't have you."

"I know," Siegfried replied in a small voice, deep with disappointment.

Despite himself, Karl was moved by Siegfried's plight – cast out by both parents. He could not be totally cruel. He must compromise somehow. Maybe Ilse's alternative was possible.

"Since you've managed to behave so well over Christmas, and have shown us you're perfectly able to behave properly when you want to, I'm inclined to ask Tante Anna and Onkel Stefan whether they're still willing to look after you. If they are, then I'll take you over to Germany as soon as possible, before we're too busy here with lambing. We might get some skiing in while we're there, if we're lucky."

156

Siegfried recognised the effort his father was making once again to establish some kind of a rapport between them, but he let the opportunity pass. He had no further need of his father now. He was going to Germany and that was all that mattered. With a whoop of victory he ran out of the kitchen to the sheepsheds to tell Werner the news.

*

Siegfried's goodbyes two weeks later were restricted to the dog, Meg and to the Murdochs, who gave him a parting gift of a German/English dictionary, just like the one they once gave his father. Siegfried put it in his case with hardly a thought that he would ever use it. He would never have to speak English again.

There were no schoolfriends who would particularly miss him, whilst his farewell to Katherine and the children was perfunctory in the extreme. He neither waved nor turned his head for a last look at his former home as Werner drove them to the station. England was in mourning for her dead king, but Siegfried was jubilant as he left her shores.

Haus Fichtenblick was exactly as Siegfried remembered it. Oma's welcoming hug still smelled of cinnamon and Opa's of pipe tobacco. The only difference was the presence of baby Lothar. All four children, Uwe, Monika, Lothar and Siegfried, were temporarily crammed into the one bedroom, but Siegfried did not mind in the least. He could chat and make jokes to his heart's content with his cousins.

Rudi was out on business in Kassel when they first arrived, but came home in time for the evening meal of noodles with hard-boiled egg and gherkins. Siegfried blissfully tucked into the vinegar-sharp gherkins. The lost two years he could have spent here so happily seemed like an eternity to him now.

For Karl it was a strange experience being in his former home without Katherine and the children around. He was completely free to visit all his old haunts with Rudi, although Rudi was now always accompanied by the delightful Adele Bierling. A lively girl with a wicked sense of fun which often got her into trouble with her police chief father, Adele was intrigued to hear that Karl had been in a film, and was even more so when, over a few beers in the Zum Österntor, he told her it was on the cards that he would be picked for a larger role in another film to be made in the spring.

"Is Gustav likely to be in it too?" Rudi asked, aware of the disruption Gustav had caused to Sarah's life.

"I've no idea. We have no communication with him now. But if he is there, I won't be talking to him," Karl said emphatically.

"Why? What's he done?" she asked, suspecting dark secrets. What she heard shocked her to the core. "And it was you who took him over to England, Rudi?" she asked in amazement. "Didn't you know what he was like?"

"No, I had no idea. I'm really sorry, for poor Sarah's sake."

"If you ask me, she's far better off without Perry," Karl told them. "She has a good career, a hectic social life and no husband to wonder where she's got to at midnight. That kind of life suits her down to the ground. She has no interest in domestic issues or having children."

"We want lots of children, don't we, Rudi?" Adele said, cuddling up to her partner with a gleam in her eye.

For a moment Rudi looked bashful, but on remembering that his brother already had three children with a fourth on its way, he entered into the spirit of domesticity. "You've probably gathered from all this, Karl, that Adele and I intend to get married. We've not announced it formally yet, but everyone seems to assume it anyway."

"Well, my congratulations to both of you!" Karl said, shaking Rudi by the hand and leaning over the table to give Adele a kiss on the cheek. "You're going to have to build an extension on the house to cope with you all."

"Oh, we don't intend to live with your parents, Karl," Adele corrected him. "Rudi has found an old house here in town for us, which he's going to do up. It's rather derelict at the moment. It was Frau Raspe's; she lost all her family and there's no one to inherit it now she's dead."

Karl remembered the Raspes. Six of them in all: the parents and four boys. All dead now. He set the thought aside. "So it's only going to be Lipinskis at Haus Fichtenblick from now on; no Drieslers apart from mother and father," he remarked in dismay.

"And a Schwerte. Don't forget Uwe," Rudi reminded him. "But does it matter, Karl? Katherine's home in England has no Carters in it any more, only Drieslers, so what's the difference?"

Unaccountably it did make a difference to Karl. His own family home would be devoid of Drieslers, once his parents died. Apart from Siegfried, of course! He had completely forgotten Siegfried's part in the family. Would the boy ever consider Haus Fichtenblick his home?

*

Before returning to England, Karl took Siegfried to Dortmund to see his mother. Dortmund was almost unrecognisable as the city he once knew. Even Siegfried had trouble finding his old home now that the ruins were gradually being bulldozed and new apartment blocks built in their place.

"That's it!" he called at last, as he spotted the entrance to the courtyard with its shabby bakery, pockmarked and crumbling plaster evidence of the war waged round it.

Karl parked opposite the courtyard entrance. They left the car and walked over the cobbled courtyard. Ilse had asked them to come when Erich Röbel would still be at work in the bakery. A shadow crossing one of the upper storey windows told them Ilse was at home. By the entrance door to the upstairs flat was a push-button bell. Above it a tattered label bore the name "Röbel".

"Go ahead, Siegfried. Ring the bell," Karl told the feverishly excited boy.

Without having to be told twice, Siegfried pushed the doorbell. They soon heard footsteps coming slowly down the stairs and into the narrow entrance hall.

Karl stood back as the door opened. This was Siegfried's business, not his. From his vantage point he was well able to discern the kaleidoscope of expressions which crossed Ilse's face. Joy was rapidly displaced by fear as she quickly pulled them both into the hallway and shut the door, before enveloping Siegfried in a smothering but silent embrace.

"I didn't tell Erich you were coming!" she whispered fearfully. "If he finds out he'll ..." Her hand automatically rubbed her jaw, leaving Karl in no doubt that Erich Röbel was in the habit of beating his wife as well as Siegfried. "Let me just get the children ready and I'll meet you up in the ruined church in about ten minutes. We can talk there."

Having only just met his mother, Siegfried was reluctant to leave but Karl dragged him out so that Ilse could sort out her family.

"Come along, Siegfried," he chivvied the boy along. "Show me where this church is."

Siegfried managed to find his way through his old haunts to where the roofless and fire-gutted church stood. No attempt had yet been made to rebuild it. Housing still took priority here. They stood together in the ruins, the soot-blackened stonework darkening the interior even more than the dull February day warranted. Siegfried fidgeted about, throwing lumps of rubble through an empty window arch until they heard Ilse's and two childrens' footsteps. Siegfried ran to the empty doorway to meet her, but halted stiffly when he saw Heinrich and Edeltraud by her side, and his new half-sister, Roslinde, in her pram.

Dropping hold of her two rather plain-faced childrens' hands, Ilse bent down to hug her handsome Siegfried. "I couldn't leave them alone in the flat, could I now?" she explained.

Siegfried shook his head slowly, then put his arms around her waist and clung to her with all the desperation of two years of maternal deprivation.

As Ilse stood there holding him she looked over towards Karl. He noticed she had the decency to look contrite.

"I'm truly sorry I turned him against you so, Karl. When I got your letter I realised how disappointed in him and me you felt. It's hopeless is it, between you and Siegfried I mean?"

Karl nodded. "As far as Siegfried is concerned, yes, I think so. I did everything I could to make him accept me, but nothing seemed to break through the hatred you instilled into him. He seems incapable of loving me. I now consider it too dangerous for us both to occupy the same house."

"Dangerous?"

Karl touched Siegfried on the shoulder. "You tell her what happened, go on, if you haven't already in one of your letters."

Siegfried shrugged off his father's hand. "No, I didn't tell her. Once you said I could leave there was no point."

Ilse was waiting for the explanation, but with half an eye on little Heinrich and Edeltraud, who were now playing on the rubble of the altar. "Tell me what?"

Looking his mother boldly in the eye, Siegfried re-opened the war on his father, vitriol thick in his words. "He punched me so hard on the jaw that I crashed into a doorway and was nearly knocked out."

"The *whole* story," Karl growled, already beginning to lose his temper with the scheming boy who was endeavouring to set his own parents against each other.

With a toss of his head, Siegfried continued. "Well, then I ran away because I was afraid he would do it again."

Karl shook his head in despair. "He's like this the whole time, Ilse," he told her. "He makes himself out to be blameless in everything. In fact he threatened me with a knife, and actually wounded a boy at his school, as well as a policeman, with his penknife. And that's just the tip of the iceberg when you consider all the trouble he's been in over the past year. He is aggressive, immoral and immune to punishment. I presume we have your husband to thank for that last difficulty. It has meant I can't control him. He has no respect for me and no punishment is effective. I can do nothing more for him."

Ilse listened to the catalogue of complaint with shock but no disbelief. "Is that true, Siegfried?" She had no doubt that it was. He had been a little demon whilst still in her own care. He had only gone from bad to worse as he grew older.

"Yes," he replied haughtily. "He knew I never wanted to live in England, but he forced me there. I'll be good now I'm back in Germany. I like it with Oma and Opa. I don't want to upset anyone there, so I won't."

Ilse stared in amazement at such words from her eight-year-old son.

"See what I mean?" Karl said. "He knows exactly what he wants and how to get it, no matter how much trouble he causes in the process. He has no concept of morality."

"And you think that's my fault?" Ilse asked, remembering Karl's frosty letter to her.

"Not entirely. But you must admit that you are solely to blame for making him hate me so. I might have been able to do something with him, otherwise."

"Oh, Karl! Yes, I know," she melted. "I tried to tell him in my letters that I was wrong about you, but it was too late by then." She licked her pale lips as she contemplated the man who had once made her so happy. "Can I show him now how wrong I was?"

Pushing the still clinging Siegfried gently aside, Ilse stepped forward closer to Karl, reached up with her lips and gave him a kiss that was a passionate cry from the depths of her heart to be released from her prison in Röbel's flat. Recognising the cry, Karl answered it. He knew how desperately she needed to be shown some love, and allowed her her moment of pleasure.

Siegfried was apparently unmoved by the event, although he rapidly sought back possession of his mother before his father could dominate her affection.

"Karl ..." Ilse began hesitantly. "Could we get together again –"

"No, Ilse," he interrupted firmly. "I know what you want, but the answer has to be no. Find yourself another man to take you away from all of this." He gestured at the ruined church, as ruined as Ilse's life.

"How can I?" she blurted out, close to tears. "I have four children, not counting Siegfried. Please, Karl, do me a favour, I beg you. It used to be so good between us. I lie awake often now, remembering how it was. Can't you refresh my memory, just the once?"

"No, Ilse," he repeated more gently. "Even if I wanted to, we have no opportunity. You must try to get out and meet some different people, perhaps find a job if you can. Your eldest daughter is already at school, is she?"

"Kindergarten," she corrected him. Reluctantly she abandoned her desire. He was right. It would be impossible with the children around. "I'll never meet anyone like you, Karl," she whispered pathetically.

Siegfried was beginning to feel embarrassed by the stupid talk from his mother. "I could get rid of Erich for you, Mutti, then I could live with you and look after you."

Ilse winced visibly at his words, but Karl was used to Siegfried's ways. "See? No morals at all."

She nodded slightly in agreement then cast her eyes about for her other children, calling them back from the far end of the church. "I'll have to be getting back to make lunch. Erich and Monika will be in soon." She turned once more to Siegfried, stroked his hair and gave him a kiss. "I'll try to come over to Medebach to visit you, or perhaps you can ask your uncle to bring you here to meet me, like this, not at the flat."

Her fingers lighted on Siegfried's serious mouth, lingering there tenderly, absorbing and radiating their mutual love. Then it was time to say goodbye to Karl.

She was acutely aware of how derelict she must appear to him, how insignificant and lowly, with her once graceful elegance beaten out of her. She would show him she was not completely bowed down. Resolutely she straightened her back, raised her chin and felt her lost dignity begin to return. She knew she wanted one more thing of him to complete the process of recovery.

"Would you mind kissing me one last time?"

He gave her what she wanted; a kiss such as they used to share under the stars in the forest at Medebach.

She was crying when they drew apart. Hurriedly she wiped her tears, grabbed a wide-eyed Heinrich and Edeltraud by the hand, kissed Siegfried once more on the forehead and left the church through the shattered doorway.

"Why did you kiss her like that?" Siegfried demanded, once she was gone.

"Because she wanted me too. She's a very lonely woman in search of some love."

"Oh," Siegfried said, as if he fully understood.

*

Ilse flung herself down on the sofa in the living area of her flat and burst into tears, leaving Heinrich and Edeltraud to take off their own coats. She allowed herself ten minutes' wallowing in self-pity before washing her face in the cracked sink and setting about making ready the family's lunch. A neighbour brought Margit back from Kindergarten, so she did not have to worry about that, but Erich would be in soon and would wonder why his food was not on the table.

As she heard his heavy tread on the stairs her heart sank even lower than usual. She made no pretence of loving him these days. He took what he wanted from her, providing food and shelter in return, as had always been the case. Love had never come into their marriage, and he did not seem to notice its absence, but for Ilse, her re-awakened urges had suddenly become unbearable. She must do something to get away from this man.

Margit was in a tearful mood when she returned from Kindergarten. Ilse did her best to cheer her up, but would really have preferred to sit down too and join in with the tears. As she served out the potato and sausage stew she heard four-year-old Heinrich telling his father of their morning's activities.

163

"We went up to the church, and Mummy kissed a man," Heinrich's unsuspecting treble voice said clearly.

Ilse stiffened, quickly putting down the hot dish in preparation for the onslaught she knew was inevitable. She was just in time as Erich grasped her shoulder and spun her round.

"You cheating bitch!" he swore, his right fist crashing into her lips. She staggered and fell against the stove, burning her hand on the edge of it. "Who was it? I'll kill the bastard," he raged, hurling her now onto the rough wooden floor, kicking her ribs as she fell.

Through years of bitter experience Ilse knew that to submit was her safest bet. Erich liked to see her grovel and it usually softened his anger.

"It was Siegfried's father," she said through swelling lips. She knew Karl would be well away by now, and soon back in England. He would be safe.

Erich was momentarily stunned by her reply. "That traitor? You kissed *him*?" He bent down and grasped her hair, pulling her head up off the floor. "Then you're a traitor yourself! Get out of my house and don't ever come back!" So saying he dragged her across to the stairs, stood her up and pushed her down them.

Ilse missed the first three stairs, managing by sheer luck to find her footing on the fourth. She crashed into the door at the bottom, clinging onto the door handle to try to stop her head spinning.

"Get out!" Erich thundered from above, throwing a boot at her. Ilse ducked as it hit the door above her, then she quickly opened the door and fled out into the icy cold street, with no hat, coat or any other possessions.

The first thing she did was to run to her neighbour's flat across the courtyard. At her urgent pounding the door opened and Greta Klitzke let her in.

"Ilse! What's happened to you? Has he been beating you again?" the dumpy woman asked. She was older than Ilse, and tended to mother the poor young woman who had the misfortune to marry the infamously aggressive Erich Röbel.

"He's thrown me out, Greta."

She was shivering with terror and cold, so Greta quickly led her into her warm and homely kitchen. Running some warm water into a basin, she set about wiping away the blood from Ilse's face.

"You're well out of it, is all I can say, pet," she commented angrily.

"But what about the children? They're still there with him!" Ilse moaned.

"Then they're best left with him," Greta said brutally. "I know he cares for those children in his own strange way. He won't let them come to any harm. But you'll manage far easier without four little ones to look out for. You'll find it hard enough on your own. Have you anywhere to go? You can stay here, of course, but I expect you feel it's too close to him for comfort."

Ilse nodded, her mind frantically trying to come to terms with her new situation. "I don't know where to go yet. I have no money, no clothes ..." her voice trailed off as the full horror of her predicament dawned on her. "I'm as badly off as when I first came here at the end of the war. Worse, in fact. I've no longer got my youth to offer."

Greta Klitzke tut-tutted in disagreement. "Don't go looking for another man to help you. Stand on your own two feet. Go out and find a job. A good job, not barmaiding or whatever. You're an intelligent girl, I know."

Suddenly, to Greta's surprise, Ilse smiled. "You're the second person to tell me to get a job today, you know."

"Perhaps I'd better not ask who the first was, but I think he may have been Siegfried's father?" Greta asked slyly.

"You saw them!"

Greta nodded. "Presumably you can't go to him?" she enquired hesitantly.

Ilse sniffed and swallowed hard. "No. If only I could."

Suddenly she knew what she wanted to do. Karl was still in Medebach. She would go there and ask him to help her. He would not refuse; not now, she realised, feeling the touch of his lips on hers.

CHAPTER THIRTEEN

Uwe and Siegfried hid behind a tall stack of planks in the sawmill. They were not supposed to play anywhere near the place, but Siegfried had bet Uwe they could creep up to the office in one corner and take some biscuits from the tin there without anyone seeing them. No one would hear them, because of the screeching band saws. It would be a cinch.

Determined not to look a coward in front of his cousin, Uwe put aside his qualms about disobeying such a strict rule, and followed Siegfried between the stacks of snow- and sawdust-coated timber. At the end of the line they had to cross a more open area of log piles. Siegfried crouched low and darted across, diving between a bark stripper and its pile of bark. He stopped and beckoned to Uwe to follow, then suddenly put up his hand to halt him. An empty timber lorry was driving into the mill.

The lorry parked by a loading hoist and both cab doors opened. Siegfried gaped in astonishment.

"Mutti!" he yelled.

Ilse could not hear him above the noise of the saws, and began to follow the driver towards the interior of the mill. Siegfried left his hideyhole and ran across the yard, throwing himself exuberantly on her back.

"Mutti!" he yelled again.

Ilse turned round to face her son. Siegfried immediately noticed the bruises on her face and he felt a protective anger surge up within him.

"Siegfried!" Ilse cried, bending to enfold her son in her arms. She clung onto him, as all that was left to her in such a cruel world.

The driver went off to summon one of his employers. A minute later Rudi Driesler announced his presence by tapping Ilse on the shoulder.

"Let's go outside," he shouted, pointing his intention.

Ilse nodded and was led by Rudi away from the din, to a quieter corner of the yard where they were joined by Uwe. When they could speak without shouting, Rudi began to question her.

"What are you doing here, Ilse? And what's happened to your face?"

Ilse was trembling. She felt emotionally exhausted and only wanted to explain everything once.

"Where's Karl? I must speak to him."

Rudi looked apologetic. "He's not here. He's gone with Anna and Stefan to see a solicitor about them being legal guardians for Siegfried. I don't suppose they'll be too long," he added, seeing her dismay. "Why don't I take you up to the house? My mother can get you a drink. And something to eat perhaps. You don't look as if you've eaten anything recently."

Ilse smiled. It was years since she had seen Rudi, yet he spoke as though it were only yesterday.

"Thank you, Rudi."

She was hatless, her coat too short, and her shoes were too flimsy to stand the walk through snow and mud up to the house. Rudi led her to a truck.

"You boys can ride in the back," he told Uwe and Siegfried. "I'll ask you what you were doing down here later."

Siegfried was loath to leave his mother's side, but when she gave him a gentle nudge he acquiesced and climbed up into the back of the truck with Uwe.

"That's your mother?" Uwe asked, incredulously. "What's she doing here? And why does she look such a mess?"

"I don't know, but I can guess my stepfather hit her. He was always hitting her ... and me."

The truck bounced over a rut, and the boys grabbed hold of the edge rail.

"I wish I could go to Dortmund and beat the living daylights out of Erich myself," Siegfried declared. "Then I'd go and do the same to my father."

Aghast, Uwe stared at his cousin. "Why on earth would you want to do that?"

I've said too much, Siegfried thought. I mustn't reveal my thoughts to anyone like that ever again.

"Why?" Uwe persisted. "Come on. Tell me!"

He had to say something. "Because he let her down and she ended up having to marry Erich. Isn't that a good enough reason?"

"Oh." Uwe still did not quite understand why Siegfried wanted to hit Onkel Karl, but they had arrived at the house and he let the matter drop.

The boys followed the adults through the back door into the kitchen. Gisela was preparing meatballs but stopped dead when she saw the woman.

"Ilse? Is that really you? My goodness, girl, just look at you! Whatever's happened?"

Rudi guided Ilse to a chair and took the borrowed coat, while Gisela sat down in front of her grandson's mother. "I never thought I'd be seeing you again, Ilse, and certainly not in a state like this. Did that husband of yours do this to you?"

Ilse nodded, beginning to relax at last in the warmth and safety of the familiar kitchen. It had been modernised slightly since she last saw it, with new cooker and refrigerator, but the wooden cupboards, table and chairs remained the same, built to last generations.

Gisela took charge. "Siegfried, get some cherry tart from the larder while I make us some coffee. Uwe, you get the cups and some plates out, please."

Ilse watched them bustling about. It was all so welcoming here. Why ever did she spurn such a sanctuary during the war? What misery she would have saved herself and Siegfried. She heard a voice from the hall.

"Smells like coffee! We're just in time."

It was Karl. Her heart pounded with relief and excitement. He would sort out everything! She stood up and ran to him as he came through the door, tears of self-pity springing readily to her eyes.

Without any warning Karl found a weeping Ilse in his arms. He looked over the top of her head to his mother, who nodded as if to say 'let Ilse indulge herself a moment'. Karl stood and held her while she clung tightly to him, ignoring Siegfried's jealous scowl. He began to push her gently away when her clinging carried on beyond acceptable limits, but she resisted. He had to use more force to extricate himself from her grasp.

"Come on, Ilse. Sit down. It's all right," he soothed her. She responded enough to be led back to her chair. Karl noticed her face then. So that's what it was all about. Erich had beaten her up again. But why had she come running to him?

"Tell me what happened," he urged, as his mother put a cup of coffee in Ilse's hands.

Ilse wiped her eyes on the back of her hand. She did not even have a handkerchief.

"Heinrich told him you came. He was very angry and threw me out. For good." Her blue eyes swam with more tears. "Help me, please, Karl. I've nowhere to go. No clothes. No money. Nothing except Siegfried and you."

There were murmurs of sympathy from Rudi, Anna and Stefan, who had come in with Karl.

"What about your other children?" Karl asked her.

Ilse's voice trembled with grief. "He'll look after them. I c..can't."

"To abandon her children like that she must be desperate indeed," Gisela muttered to no one in particular.

Karl let out a long sigh. "Well, for the moment, I'm sure you can stay here," he said with an inquiring look at his mother, who nodded. "But it may not be the best thing for you in the long run. As I said yesterday, you need to make a new life for yourself. Perhaps you could get a job locally, then find somewhere of your own to rent."

He could not allow her to presume Driesler hospitality indefinitely.

Ilse sobbed loudly. "I want to be with you, Karl. Don't go back to England. I need you too much."

Anna and Stefan exchanged glances with Rudi and quietly left the room, taking Uwe and the protesting Siegfried with them. Gisela stayed to help calm Ilse in her present near-hysterical state. She was crying freely now, her streaming eyes pleading with Karl. She reached towards him, grabbing the lapels of his jacket.

"Don't leave me, Karl. I can't go on without you. I was a fool to leave you before, but I'm sorry. I'll make it up to you," she blubbered. "Remember all the good times we had? It could be like that again, just you and me and Siegfried."

"Ilse!" Karl said sharply. "Calm down, please. You don't know what you're saying. You know I can't stay with you."

"You must," she pleaded. "I feel so helpless. My life's in ruins. I don't think I can go on anymore."

Her heartbreak moved him. How could he leave her in such a state? Grasping her arms he sought to control her floundering emotions. "I'll stay an extra day here to help you get sorted out, find some clothes and suchlike, but then I must go back to England. You know that."

Gisela put her arms around the lonely woman's heaving shoulders. "We'll all help you, Ilse. You're one of the family, you know. You can stay here with us, until you find your feet again."

Sandwiched between Karl and his mother, Ilse felt the strength of their protection. Her sobs began to lessen, and presently she sat down again and reached for her cup of coffee.

"There. That's better," Gisela said, pushing a slice of tart over to her. "I'll go and find you a clean hanky."

While his mother was gone, Karl got Ilse to talk about more mundane matters, like how she managed to reach Medebach with no money.

"My neighbour, Greta Klitzke, lent me a coat and some money," she explained, her voice a little steadier now as she tucked in to the tart. "I caught the train, and was waiting for the bus in Winterberg when one of your lorries approached. Peter Witter, Margit's husband, was driving it and he stopped when I flagged him down. He knew of me and gave me a lift the rest of the way."

"So you have other friends in Medebach who can help you," Karl reminded her. "I'm sure Margit will want to do what she can for you. Tomorrow I'll drive you to her house. No doubt she'll be pleased to see you."

At last Ilse smiled. "Yes. You're all so kind. I'd forgotten what it's like to have so many people willing to help. Greta was my only real friend in Dortmund."

"Well you'll soon find many more here, I'm sure. There are still plenty of people who remember Siegfried's mother."

"And Karl Driesler's fiancée," Ilse said wistfully. She looked long and hard into his eyes, and for a moment thought she saw the love that was once there. If she could only capture it for ever. She leaned forward, wanting to rediscover what was lost, but Karl drew back.

"No more kisses, Ilse. I told you. You must find someone else."

She could not bear thinking about it. She tried to tighten the bond with him. "You know, Karl, I'll always think of your mother as my mother-in-law. She's so kind to me. I haven't seen your father yet, but I always liked him too."

Gisela appeared with a handkerchief and gave it to Ilse, giving Karl the chance to escape for a moment. He stood up.

"I'd better try booking a call to England. I hope Katherine won't mind me getting back a day late."

Ilse watched him leave the room with a heavy heart. If only she had never left him and lost him to an Englishwoman!

*

Three children would be quite enough, Katherine decided. She was already beginning to find bending over awkward. She stooped to pick up a trail of socks, cardigan and dungarees around Sabina's bedroom. Richard decided to help her by rifling through the open chest of drawers pulling out yet more clothing onto the floor.

"Richard! No! Now we'll have to put them all back," she scolded him.

He looked up at her with a mischievous grin, then draped a pair of Sabina's knickers over his head, so tufts of dark hair stuck through the legholes. Katherine laughed at his antics.

"Yes, I know you're a funny boy, but we still have to put all these clothes away."

She finished tidying the childrens' bedroom and moved on to her own. She settled Richard by her slippers. He always liked stroking the fluffy lining and stuffing toy cars down inside them. Katherine pulled the bottom sheet straight and shook out her pillow. The pillow on the other side of the bed lay uncrumpled and unused.

"Five days Daddy's been gone," she told Richard, who was too intent on dropping his toy car into the wastepaper basket to listen. "Which means five days without Siegfried too. What a difference it's been without him. Just you and Sabina to harass me!"

She retrieved the car as Richard turned his attention to a loose thread on the ageing carpet. She let him pick at it. The carpet was so worn it hardly mattered. This whole room needed redecorating. She had wanted to do it in 1948, before Karl came home from the prison camp, but had not been able to find any decent wallpaper. Then

171

there always seemed to be other priorities. Now the rose-patterned wallpaper over the wardrobe was peeling off, and she decided the room must be redecorated before the new baby was born. Her eye caught the bag of material perched on top of the wardrobe.

"This afternoon, Richard, I must start cutting out that new dress. I'm sick of all my old maternity dresses, and I wanted this new one ready to wear for when Daddy gets back, though I don't suppose it will be. Not if you have anything to do with it, you little monkey," she said, removing a pair of stockings from his grasp. "Come along now. It's time to fetch Sabina."

She picked him up off the floor, and with her other arm cradled the basket of washing to take downstairs. As she reached the top of the stairs the telephone began to ring.

The washing basket and Richard between them obscured her view of the stairs. The wooden train left there by Richard skidded from under her right foot, pitching her forwards. Desperately she tried to rid her right hand of the washing basket to grab the handrail, but the basket was too cumbersome. It bounced her off the banisters, against the wall and out into space. The grandfather clock at the foot of the stairs came hurtling towards her, as she crashed into the telephone table, sending the still ringing apparatus flying. It was only when her head hit the stone-flagged floor in front of the clock that her left arm released its hold on Richard, and he began to cry.

*

Werner noticed the Land Rover still in the yard at a quarter to twelve. Katherine should have been off to collect Sabina from nursery school by now. He looked at his watch again. Perhaps he'd better go and remind her of the time, although how she could have forgotten was difficult to imagine. He shut the meadow gate behind Meg and hurried up to the house. From outside he could hear Richard crying loudly. Kicking off his boots at the back door he strode through the deserted kitchen to the hall where Richard was crying. The baby looked up at him and howled even louder, but Werner ignored him. Beside Richard on the hall floor lay the prostrate figure of Katherine.

"*Gott in Himmel!*"

Werner rushed over to the motionless body and bent down to check for signs of life. He thought she was breathing but was not sure. It was difficult to tell at the angle she was lying. He dared not move her in case of serious injury. The buzz of the telephone off its hook prompted him into action. He jiggled the cradle rest to call the operator's attention.

"Hello! Emergency," he said as soon as he heard her voice.

"Who's speaking?" the operator asked anxiously.

"Werner Gimpel at Lane Head Farm. I must speak with Dr Murdoch immediately!"

"He's on his way, Mr Gimpel. Mrs Murdoch tried to call your number earlier and got through but could only hear the baby crying. She was worried and asked me to listen out in case anyone came back on the line, while she called her husband. He's out up the valley, but is coming straight over to you."

Werner released his held breath. "Please call Mrs Murdoch. She must get Sabina from *Kindergarten*," he said, forgetting the English word in his anxiety, "and come to look after the baby."

Richard was still howling, and had begun to crawl over Katherine's back. Werner whipped him off her, trying to comfort the struggling boy. He quickly replaced the receiver on the cradle and stood the telephone back on its table. He turned back to Katherine. She was still unconscious. He felt helpless, unable to do anything for her or to soothe Richard. He sat on the bottom stair, trying to rock Richard gently in his arms, but the baby screamed and wriggled hard, struggling to get to his mother.

"Please hurry, Dr Murdoch," Werner begged.

*

Karl's call to England was finally connected at twenty past five. Expecting Katherine to answer he was surprised to hear Gertie's muted Scottish voice.

"Lane Head Farm."

"Gertie? It's Karl. Where's Katherine? Busy with Richard's nappy or something?"

"Oh, Karl. Thank heavens you phoned. I've been trying to contact you. Now listen, dear," she said calmly, so as not to panic him. "Katherine has had a fall down the stairs."

"What? Is she all right?"

"She's in hospital and has regained consciousness. They're worried about the baby, though. She might lose it. I think you ought to try to get home as quickly as possible." Gertie knew her words would distress him, but she could not hide the seriousness of the situation from him.

Finding his legs trembling, Karl leaned against the wooden panelling of the hall. "I'll get the first flight. Even so it will take far too long to get there. God! Why am I so far away when I'm needed?"

"It can't be helped. She's in good hands, Karl. But there's something else you ought to know. Richard hurt his arm in the fall, and they've kept him in hospital too. I'm here with Werner looking after Sabina and the animals, so don't you worry about any of that. Sabina's coming back to stay with us tonight, so there'll be no one here. I hung on here as I was waiting for my call to you to be connected. It took longer than I thought."

His initial shock was wearing off but Karl still felt devastated by her news. "Thank you, Gertie. I'm on my way."

He hung up and closed his eyes in misery. "Oh, Schatz, I'm sorry I'm not there," he whispered to Katherine in her hospital bed, far away.

Anna came through the hall and saw her brother's troubled face. "What is it, Karl? Bad news?"

He nodded. "I must go home immediately. Katherine fell down the stairs and is in hospital."

Anna knew his unspoken fear. "The baby?"

"She might lose it." The horror of those words spurred Karl into action. "Anna, would you telephone Düsseldorf and get me on the first flight back to England. I'll break the news to the others."

"Of course. I'm so sorry. I hope Katherine's all right."

Karl hardly heard her as he headed back to the kitchen. He could only picture Katherine lying all alone, wanting him at her side and he was not there.

His mother hugged him in sympathy when she heard what had happened, but Ilse was furious.

"You can't go!" she wailed at him. "You promised you would help me. I need you more than she does. You've got to stay! You've got to!"

She was becoming hysterical, shoving aside Gisela and clinging on to Karl in her desperation not to let him leave. As he tried to push her away, her demented screams rose in anguish, bringing Siegfried running into the kitchen to see what was happening to his mother. He arrived just as Karl slapped her across the face.

Siegfried let out a howl of rage and forced himself between his distraught mother and her apparent attacker. "Leave her alone!" he yelled, punching his father in the midriff.

Ilse backed off at her son's onslaught, giving Karl the room to deal with him. He caught both Siegfried's wrists and pinioned his arms behind him, avoiding some of the boy's kicks, but not all. Siegfried was like an eel, and Karl had trouble using the minimum of force to hold him still. They were both breathless by the time Stefan appeared to help deal with him.

"Stop it, Siegfried!" Ilse finally demanded, frightened out of her selfish hysteria. "It's not your father's fault. It's mine."

Siegfried stopped his struggling and stood still. Karl and Stefan let go their grip on him.

"He hit you. I saw him!" he protested, still angry.

"It was nothing. I was being foolish." Ilse stood awkwardly in front of Karl. "I'm very sorry. Of course your wife needs you. I don't know what got into me. It's all been too much, I think. Perhaps I'll go and ask Margit if I may stay with her. It might be better, as you said."

"That's all right, Ilse. I know what it's been like for you. Don't worry about it." To show there were no hard feelings, he kissed her on the cheek.

Siegfried ground his teeth.

Anna came in, finally able to tell him details of his flight. "There isn't one today but you're booked on tomorrow morning's."

"Blast! Perhaps I'd get there quicker by train, if I left tonight."

"The weather's not too good, Karl," Stefan told him. "The ferries might be delayed if the wind gets up any more. Besides, you don't want to arrive looking green."

Karl remembered his journey out with Siegfried. It had not been pleasant. "You're right. I'll fly. It's probably quicker after all."

He went upstairs to pack his bags, ready for a very early start. He would have to say goodbye to Siegfried tonight. He could not leave their relationship so stormy.

As expected, it proved an almost impossible task. Only Ilse's urging made Siegfried accept a farewell handshake. His eyes remained fixed on the floor throughout and he said nothing. The ordeal over, Siegfried kissed his mother and grandparents goodnight and followed his cousins to bed.

"I'll try to win him around to you, Karl," Ilse promised, once he was gone.

"Thank you, Ilse. I think you'll have a tough job. I hate having to admit defeat, but it's a relief knowing you'll be with him now. Good luck yourself in finding a new life."

"We'll make sure she finds a job and somewhere to live," Dieter reassured his son. "It might be easier all round if Siegfried stays on with us, then Ilse doesn't have to worry about fitting in his schooling with her work. What do you say, Ilse?"

"It sounds perfect. Siegfried likes it here and I'm sure he'd be happy with an arrangement like that. Thank you. All of you." She looked around her adopted family, feeling exhausted beyond belief by all that had happened. "If you don't mind, I think I'll go to bed too."

Anna rose immediately. "Let me show you your room. I'll lend you a nightie."

In front of his family, Ilse bid Karl a more friendly goodbye than her son. He had risen to his feet and she sensed his reserve. She offered him her hand. He shook it, hung onto it for a moment, then relented, giving her a swift kiss on the cheek.

"Goodbye, Ilse. No doubt we'll meet again soon."

Ilse followed Anna upstairs and soon lay snugly in a bed of her own under a feather quilt. Once a frequent guest at Haus Fichtenblick she knew the layout well. Karl would be in the other guest room, next to hers, tantalisingly close. She groaned in frustration and tried to put him out of her mind. She had almost succeeded when she heard him and Rudi climb the staircase and walk along the landing to their own rooms. Muffled footsteps came through the intervening wall, finally the thud of the wooden bedhead against the wall as he settled down for the night to attempt sleep. It was a long time coming for them both.

*

The bell rang for the end of visiting time. Katherine watched the other women on the ward waving goodbye to their visitors. She felt sick and lonely. She folded her hands over her empty belly. She did not even have that small presence any more to comfort her.

176

What a stupid thing to do! What must Werner think of them? First Karl with his ladder, now her with the stairs. And to have hurt Richard too! And the baby. A life that would never be. A son or daughter denied to her.

Hot tears flowed down her cheeks onto the starched pillowcase.

"Are you all right, Mrs Driesler?" a gentle voice asked.

Katherine could only see a blur. "Could you find me a hanky please."

The nurse handed her one, then sought the cause of the tears. "Your husband not here yet?"

"No. He's in Germany. I don't know whether he knows what's happened."

The nurse gave her hand a squeeze. "He'll come as soon as he can. Dr Murdoch told me his wife contacted him."

Katherine felt a wave of relief wash over her. He would be on his way. But how could she tell him she had killed their baby? A gush of tears spilled over and the nurse mopped them up for her.

"There, there. You've had a nasty experience, but it's all over now. You just try and rest. You'll feel better in the morning."

Katherine looked away in disbelief. How could she possibly know what losing a baby felt like?

The nurse was called away by another patient, leaving Katherine alone. If only Karl were here.

*

The ward sister came to see her the following afternoon. "Well, Mrs Driesler. Mrs Murdoch has just telephoned to say your husband will be in to collect you this evening."

"What about my little boy?"

Sister Markham's plump face smiled. "He can go too. He's none the worse for bouncing down the stairs. Just a few bruises that's all. They kept him in overnight just to be sure, but you're both fit enough to go home. You must just remember to rest for a few days. I'll have a word with your husband when he gets here. I remember him from when I was on men's orthopaedics. He broke his leg, didn't he?"

Katherine smiled. "Yes. We seem to be making good use of the hospital."

"Not as good as some people, I assure you, Mrs Driesler," she said with a sigh. "I'll leave you to your lunch, then."

177

Katherine sank against the pillow and fought back the tears of relief.

Later that evening, when she saw the familiar figure walk onto the ward, she felt the tears start to flow again. Angry with herself for being so emotional in public she tried to quell them. As Karl reached her bed he put his arms around her and she clung on as though she would never let go.

"We'd better go and get Richard," he said at last.

He held her arm as they walked slowly to the children's ward. Richard was in a cot near the sister's office and she showed the parents to their son. He was standing up, rattling the bars like a caged gorilla.

"There's nothing much wrong with him now," Sister King laughed, her eyes switching from son to father and hastily back again, before her thoughts gave her away. She let down the cot-side and scooped up the baby. "He'll be walking soon," she commented, handing him over to Karl.

"It's his birthday this week," Katherine told her. "I don't suppose he'll mind not having a party this year."

"No. I'm sure he won't," Sister King agreed, with a final pat on the head for the boy.

Katherine thanked the nurses for their care of Richard, then set off down the corridor. Once outside and heading for the car park she smiled broadly. "I felt so depressed until you came along, and then watching all the nurses fawning over you was so funny, it cheered me up no end!"

"Glad to be of service," he said without a smile. He unlocked the Land Rover, helped Katherine in, then passed over Richard to her. He got in the other side, started the engine and headed off around the city.

Once on the Hay road he began to speak. "I was so worried about you both. I'd never have forgiven myself if I lost you. Damn Siegfried! I won't ever go away and leave you again."

Katherine was taken completely by surprise by his outburst. "But Schatz, it wasn't your fault. It could have happened when you were at market, or anytime. You can't tie yourself to me for the rest of your life."

She noticed his knuckles were white against the steering wheel. He was more upset than he was showing yet.

It soon came out. "I don't know what I'd do if I lost you. You are so precious to me ..."

"You're not going to lose me, Karl. Don't upset yourself over nothing. It's the baby we've lost, and I've still got to get used to that fact."

"Yes, of course. I'm sorry. I've just had a rather difficult time these last couple of days dealing with Ilse."

"Ilse?" Mention of that name always brought fear to Katherine's heart. "You saw her?"

"Yes. I took Siegfried to see her the day before yesterday. Apparently one of her children told her husband I'd been there, so he beat her up then threw her out without a penny." He briefly told her the details of how she came to Medebach.

Katherine was appalled. "Poor woman. What a life she's had! It rather puts my problems into perspective, doesn't it?"

She hugged Richard close to her. The prospect of having to leave her children was unimaginable. The loss of this baby was bad enough, but at least she had never known it. How infinitely more terrible it must be to hand over the care of your children to a brute like Erich Röbel. She shuddered.

"Don't ever throw me out, Schatz," she said, trying to raise a smile from Karl.

She did not succeed.

"I won't," he solemnly promised.

CHAPTER FOURTEEN

Within a few weeks Ilse's life began to blossom. She had not experienced such freedom since her courting days with Karl. Leaving Siegfried with the Drieslers as agreed, she moved in briefly with Margit and Peter Witter, found a temporary job in the grocery store until something better turned up, then rented a room of her own in Kapellenstrasse. She had a roof over her head, a bed, a wardrobe but no clothes except what Anna and Margit between them could give or lend. But at least she was free of Erich's brutality and the wretched flat. Here she had room to move, and peace and quiet.

It would have been impossible to cope with her other four children. She was too busy fending for herself to worry about them. The empty space they left was surprisingly easily filled by Siegfried. He had always been her favourite, despite his waywardness, and she had two years of his childhood to catch up on. She wanted to discover what influence, if any, Karl had managed to exert over him. In addition it would be interesting to see what effect living with the Medebach Drieslers would have on him. Karl's father had moulded his sons into likenesses of himself – disciplined, responsible, caring men, thorough in whatever job was undertaken. If Dieter's influence extended to Siegfried she would have cause to be thankful. Gisela's influence was not so marked in her sons as in Anna, but Ilse was confident that the two women would provide all the loving warmth Siegfried so desperately needed when she was not there.

After a day spent stacking tins and weighing out cheese, she sat on her bed to change her stockings for an unladdered pair, in preparation for a meal with Margit, Peter and a few other friends. How good it felt to wear nylon stockings after years of ankle socks and thick woollen stockings. She rolled the delicate tube up her leg, fastening the suspender with a satisfying snap. She felt more elegant already. Her legs were still in good shape, at least; no thickened ankles or varicose veins. With her newly washed and shining hair, she was beginning to feel more like her old self – her self before she left Karl.

All her misfortune started the moment she deserted Karl. Instead of staying in Medebach she went to Mannheim, was bombed out and fled east to Dresden. She shook her head in shame. She may not have Karl back, but at least she had Siegfried.

"I won't desert you ever again, Siegfried. I promise. Not for anyone! If I do find anyone to love me, he's going to have to learn to love you too." She pulled on the other stocking, slipped on her not so elegant working shoes then studied her reflection in the wardrobe mirror. "There's hope for you yet, Ilse Brünninghaus."

*

She wrote to Erich to ask for a divorce. To her surprise he readily agreed, provided she admitted she was guilty of desertion and laid no claim to the children. She had thought Erich would be obstructive and oppose divorce just to be awkward. As it was, Ilse decided to accept Greta Klitzke's advice to become self-sufficient. Erich could have all the worry of custody. Strangely enough, now that she had Siegfried back, Erich's children faded into insignificance for her. She put them to the back of her mind as she had once tried to do with Siegfried.

Weekends were invariably spent at Haus Fichtenblick. Siegfried's family became her own. To all intents and purposes she was Dieter and Gisela's daughter-in-law, even if her supposed husband was married to someone else. Through them she heard of Karl's wife's miscarriage and then, on the 12th April 1953, of the birth of their second son, Paul.

In the spring sunshine of a Sunday afternoon Dieter poured glasses of Sekt to wet the new baby's head. Ilse saw the pride in his still clear, grey eyes as he welcomed his latest grandson. "To baby Paul. May God give him wisdom and strength."

Ilse mouthed the words. "To Paul!"

Her words were to prove prophetic.

*

A sleek black Mercedes drew up outside Haus Fichtenblick shortly after Ilse's own arrival one Saturday afternoon in June. She immediately recognised the equally sleek, dark-haired man and his air of self-confidence.

"That's Paul Zopf!" She grabbed hold of Anna to come to the window to look.

They saw Dieter Driesler already outside welcoming the man, preparing to shake the man's right hand before realising he did not have one.

"So it is! They must have let him out of prison. We heard he got seven years for war crimes."

Anna's information hardly surprised Ilse. Paul was always an ardent Nazi, joining the SS, rather than Wehrmacht like Karl.

"I wonder why he's here?"

Anna noticed Ilse's interest and smiled to herself.

Paul's explanation filtered through the open front door to them as he entered with Dieter. His clipped and business-like voice echoed off the wooden panels of the hall.

"I thought I'd do the rounds of my old friends and let them know I'm back in circulation. I know Karl's not here, but I thought you could fill me in on a few details, like whether he ever found ..."

He broke off in astonishment as his eyes fell on the person he was about to mention.

"Like whether he ever found the famous Ilse Brünninghaus!" Paul Zopf finished, bending his dark head over Ilse's hand in formal greeting. "Well I never, Ilse! Still as beautiful as ever, if I might be permitted to say so."

Ilse stared back at the man who had paid her such an undeserved compliment. Her disconcertion was momentary. Gathering her wits she smiled brightly at him.

"Thank you, Paul." She felt suddenly emboldened by the magnetism of his brown eyes to add meaningfully: "It seems that you and I both have new futures ahead of us. We must make sure we both do our bit to make Germany prosperous again."

"Indeed we must, Ilse," he replied, still holding onto her hand. He gave it a light squeeze to show he fully understood her meaning, before following his hosts into the living room.

Dieter and Gisela Driesler tactfully withdrew a short while later, under the pretence of fetching some beers and a snack. Even a simpleton could not have missed noticing the instant attraction between the pair. They returned with the refreshments to find their suspicions confirmed. Paul and Ilse were oblivious to anything other than each other, as she told him all the details of her life with Siegfried and subsequent purgatory with Erich Röbel.

When Siegfried joined them all later, after returning from a swim in the nearby lake with his uncles and cousins, Paul remarked on the boy's striking resemblance to Karl.

Siegfried banged his fist on the wooden arm of his chair. "I'm not like him! He's a traitor to Germany, and I'm not!"

Paul Zopf's eyebrows raised at such fervent nationalism in one so young. Ilse must have taught him well. She was going to be a fine catch. The boy's outspoken comment caused an immediate rumpus, however.

"Siegfried! How dare you talk about your father like that!" Dieter demanded icily. "I want an apology from you."

Siegfried looked suitably contrite and hung his head. "Sorry, Opa," he said dutifully, casting a wicked grin in the direction of the former SS man.

Like his mother, Siegfried took an instant liking to Herr Zopf. The man exuded power and authority, which not even the years in prison could suppress. Siegfried knew the man must be a true German if the Americans had imprisoned him. His mother approved of him, so he began to make his own interest felt by paying rapt attention to everything Herr Zopf said.

Paul noticed the boy's attentiveness and his duplicity towards his grandfather. He seemed to be a master of deception. What wonders could be done with a boy like that! When he finally took his leave, Paul shook Siegfried's hand like a man, then kissed Ilse's.

"I very much hope that I can see you again, Ilse," he told her. "If I called at your lodgings next weekend, would you be in?"

A satisfied smile rose to her lips. "I shall make certain I'm there, Paul."

*

He called her during the week to warn her to be ready bright and early on Saturday morning. She did not dare face him again dressed in Margit's cast-off clothing, so dug deep into her meagre savings and bought herself a lilac, cotton print dress. She hoped the day would stay warm, as she had no jacket, and wanted to avoid having to wear the baggy-elbowed cardigan Anna had donated to her wardrobe.

She washed and dried her hair, applied make-up and was watching out of the window over-looking Kapellenstrasse by seven-thirty. Paul's Mercedes drew up ten minutes later. She wondered how he could drive with his right arm missing, but as she sat down in the passenger seat she saw the modifications made to the car for its disabled driver. She also wondered how a man so recently released from prison could afford a car such as this. There were a wealth of questions she wanted to ask him, but he took the lead as they drove through the forested hills towards Dortmund.

"I'm puzzled, Ilse, as to why you did not return to Medebach when you found yourself homeless during the war. Apart from Karl's parents, you seem to have had friends here who would surely have helped you and Siegfried, didn't you?"

The same old question! It was not casually asked, despite its pretence to be so. Knowing Paul's Nazi background, Ilse gave the answer she knew would impress him. The true answer.

"I had to visibly distance myself from Karl. I didn't want his disgrace to reflect on me or Siegfried in any way. It was foolish of me, I know, to be so high-minded, but I had no idea then that the war would be lost. I assumed that my devotion to the Führer would see me through the hard times. Instead I ruined my life and Siegfried's because of my principles."

Paul's immaculately shaved cheeks hollowed as he digested her words. "Karl never realised that, you know. The last time I saw him, his only concern was to survive so he could find you and Siegfried. I tried to help him achieve that. No doubt my action saved his life, although he was extremely lucky to survive those final months of the war. Most of my former unit ended up dead or prisoners of the Russians and have never returned. Such is the price we pay for our loyalty."

The warm, mystical scent of pine trees wafted in through the car windows. Ilse felt reckless with happiness. Here was a man she could love! She wanted to please him any way she could. For the moment it would be with information. "I think Karl remembers your loyalty to him. He's called his third son Paul."

"Has he now? That's very gratifying to know. What's his second son called? I never did get to hear about Karl once I saw you!"

Ilse began to fill him in on all the details she knew about Karl and his English family, before coming to the difficulties he experienced with Siegfried.

"I just wish Siegfried could have adored Karl as much as he plainly adores you. I've never seen him behave like that before. He recognises you as someone special." She let her voice tail off, her own views implicit in her silence.

Paul glanced across at her, his calculating eyes measuring up this woman who had fallen on hard times to preserve her loyalty to the Führer. She would be suitably rewarded now, and he would have great pleasure in so doing.

"You are a beautiful woman, Ilse. Someone special in your own right. I should like very much to show you just how special you are. I think a little shopping is called for." He gave a meaningful glance at her new dress.

So what if he thinks the dress cheap, Ilse thought happily. She had fallen on her feet at last. There was nothing she would not do for Paul Zopf!

As they passed the last of the sawmills, and the hills of the Sauerland began to level out, Ilse knew she would be looking towards Dortmund again as the focus of her future.

They parked in a street within the former city walls, outside a newly built ladies' outfitters. Signs of reconstruction were everywhere, and Ilse remembered that the Zopf family business was a construction company. So that was where the money for the Mercedes came from. She soon learned there was much more money besides, as she emerged an hour later from the outfitters, alongside a shop assistant laden down with boxes and bags containing everything from underwear, shoes and hats to day dresses, cocktail dresses and casual wear. She had entered wearing a cotton frock, and left in a navy and white linen suit, with a white silk blouse, shoes, handbag and pillbox hat.

Paul opened the Mercedes' boot but let the assistant load the purchases into it. "Next stop a beautician, then coffee and cakes!" he declared with satisfaction at his transformation of the pauper into the princess.

The next stop, however, proved to be a jeweller's, where Paul presented her with a string of pearls. Ilse began to feel overwhelmed by her sudden riches.

"Really, Paul. You're spending far too much on me. I'm not used to such extravagance."

"Then you're going to have to get used to it!" He dismissed her protest with a penetrating smile. "That is, if you want to be seen in my company."

She dutifully accepted the pearls. "I do," she replied.

That day, Ilse saw a side to Dortmund she had never experienced before, even in those idyllic days with Karl in the early years of the war. Everywhere they went, Paul Zopf was known and respected. Ilse was not deceived by the fact that he only took her to places where his family were regular patrons, but she enjoyed the attention nevertheless. Coffee and cakes were taken in a small establishment on the banks of the Lippe, lunch at a smart restaurant. Afterwards they drove back to his apartment in a new, luxury block to the south of the city centre.

Ilse marvelled at the layout of the apartment; its open-plan living areas, kitchen fitted with every conceivable modern convenience, the gleaming tiled and mirrored bathroom. Paul's taste for modern architecture was not reflected in the furnishings, however, which were more traditional. The highly polished floors were adorned with Persian rugs, upon which stood an ornately carved wooden dresser, tables and a black leather three-piece suite.

Fresh white roses graced the centre of the dining table. Paul plucked a bud from the bowl, wiped it dry, then placed it carefully with his single hand in her lapel, his lips close to but not quite touching hers.

"Shall I show you the bedroom now?"

Ilse had earned her bread like this before. This time the task would not be a chore.

The bedroom was lavishly furnished with a thick pile white carpet and a king-size double bed, whose black silk sheets and blood red counterpane stirred her passion as the flag they represented had once done.

"You like it?" Paul asked, his lips on the back of her neck.

"Oh, yes," she breathed. "Most impressive."

He was deft at undoing buttons with his single hand. Ilse gave a moan of pleasure as she felt his fingers reach inside her blouse and cup her breast. She turned slowly round to face him, dropping her handbag on a nearby chair.

"I want you, Ilse," he said. His left hand was on her skirt fastenings. As it slipped gently to the floor she stepped out of it. He had not yet kissed her on the lips. He seemed to want her undressed first. Whatever he wanted, he could have.

His hand moved to her slip. He stood slowly tracing the outlines of her nipples through the silk. Ilse waited in an agony of suspense and desire. When he pulled the straps over her arms and added the slip to the clothing on the floor, Ilse stood erect, shoulder's back, displaying herself for his admiration. Erich never gave her a second look during his fumblings under the bedclothes. She relished now this chance to be admired, despite the ravages of five pregnancies. Paul seemed pleased with what he saw. He began to undress himself.

Ilse stood and watched, hoping she would not be put off by his stump, but there was not one. The arm was lost from the shoulder and left a smooth outline to his upper torso. She reached towards him and caressed him from shoulder to waist in a lingering motion which held the promise of an experienced lover.

He took his time undressing as she continued to feel his smooth skin, so different from Erich's matted pelt. She could worship this man.

Paul smiled at his enslavement of her. If she only knew, he was captured by her himself. Waiting a while to enjoy her attention, he pulled her hand to his mouth, his tongue washing over its back, up her forearm to her shoulder, then down over her breast. He lingered a while, transferred his attention to her left nipple, then his tongue continued its downward passage.

Her pleasure almost overwhelmed her. There had been a few lovers since Erich, but she had felt nothing like the intensity of longing as she did now. Paul read her mounting passion and moved her onto the blood-red bed.

"We are of like mind, you and I, Ilse," he said, finally kissing her on the mouth.

Over his mutilated shoulder she saw a framed picture of Adolf Hitler looking down at her. With a victorious moan she offered herself to him and the man who still served him.

*

Paul had a surprise in store for her the following morning. "Pack a cocktail dress and wear one of your new outfits, the red blouse with the black and white spotted skirt, perhaps," he told her over a late breakfast. "We're invited for the day to some friends of mine out at Soest."

Ilse was becoming used to Paul's authoritarian manner. What else could you expect from a former SS officer? She donned the clothing he suggested with a wry smile at his choice of colour scheme. It seemed to be a favourite with him.

Seated alongside Paul in the Mercedes on the road east to Soest, her former life seemed a million miles away, her four children by Erich insignificant details of history. Siegfried on the other hand was different. Paul showed an interest in him which could not simply be due to his parentage. For the first time Ilse found herself proud of her firstborn child, instead of embarrassed by his unruly behaviour. With Paul, Siegfried had been attentive and instantly obedient. Paul would be able to make something of Siegfried; something she could be proud of.

Promptly at midday they drew into a gated driveway which led up to one of the most impressive houses Ilse had ever seen. The grey, multi-turreted roof, worked in complex patterns of slates, overhung a facade of yellow-ochre broken by three rows of green painted shutters. They parked alongside a selection of Mercedes and Opels, then climbed the stone staircase leading up to the massive front door. A manservant answered their knock and led them through to a gilded and tapestried room whose large french windows opened onto a terrace already thronged with elegantly dressed guests sipping champagne.

They were immediately spotted by an expensively coiffured and bejewelled lady, somewhat older than themselves, whose impressive girth put many of her guests to shame.

"Paul, my dear! We're so glad you could come, and with such a charming companion too. Please introduce me to her!"

Paul clicked his heels and bent over her heavily ringed hand. "Bertha, this is Ilse Brünninghaus, an old acquaintance of mine. I've recently had the very good fortune to meet up with her again. Ilse, meet Frau Bertha Altenried. Her husband, Otto, was a former superior of mine, and a good friend besides."

The two women shook hands cordially, and Frau Altenried made sure they were supplied with glasses of champagne before gently propelling Ilse over to a couple of young women at the edge of the terrace. They had the devoted attention of an elderly man easily mistaken for a banker, but who was in fact a professor of biochemistry. Paul took himself off to join Otto Altenried amongst a huddle of men who were indeed financiers.

They did not meet up again until luncheon was served in the dining room. Paul whispered in passing to reach his seat: "You seem to be in your element here."

"I'm loving it!" Ilse grinned back, sitting down beside one of the financiers. Her poverty-stricken life of the last ten years had been an aberration. Her parents' home in Hamburg before the war had hosted many a formal gathering, and Ilse was equally at ease with intellectuals or government officials. Over lunch she noticed Paul watching her conversation with the financier, apparently pleased at her social graces. She seemed to be passing all the tests he was setting her.

Coffee was served on the terrace. Bertha Altenried led Ilse to a low table where a nondescript, middle-aged man sat alone. Ilse had not noticed him amongst the luncheon guests, but assumed his mediocrity in appearance made her pass him by.

"Ilse, may I introduce you to Peter Fuchs, who seems to be all alone. I'm sure you can provide him with some pleasant company." Frau Altenried nodded at Peter Fuchs, before departing to attend to the needs of other guests.

Ilse sat down on a wickerwork chair opposite the silent man. No title had been given or indication of the man's occupation. She supposed she would have to find out for herself.

"Do you know many people here, Herr Fuchs?"

"Yes, I know all of them," came the measured reply. "So, tell me something about yourself, since you are new to me. How long have you known Paul?"

It was not long before Ilse was launched into her life story. Peter Fuchs seemed particularly interested in her association with Erich Röbel.

"So it was your mutual political interests which attracted you to him in the first place?"

Ilse could not lie about so important an issue. "I needed food and shelter first and foremost, but after that, yes, we found we had ... ideas and allegiances in common. I confess I never was attracted to him as a person though. It was, shall we say, a marriage of convenience."

"Yes, I can understand that. Röbel is rather a brutish specimen, I must admit."

"You know him then?"

"Indeed."

"You seem to know a lot of people," Ilse said hesitantly. She was beginning to have some idea as to what Herr Fuchs's function was. Why else had she been left alone with him, than to satisfy himself as to her loyalty to the Party?

"Indeed I do," he answered gravely. "Your former husband prides himself on his support for a certain cause. I do remember him saying some years ago his wife shared his support of that cause. Would I be right?"

It was out in the open at last. Ilse smiled with relief. "Yes. Although we had precious little money, and I did sometimes begrudge what he gave away. But it was the amount he spent on beer that annoyed me!"

Peter Fuchs suddenly leaned forwards and put his pale hands on hers. "Welcome to our group, Ilse. What help you gave our comrades during those dark days will be repaid, I assure you."

As if he had been watching the whole episode and was awaiting the official approval, Paul came over and sat beside her, giving her hand a congratulatory squeeze.

"So, Peter, what do you think of my Ilse? A stunner isn't she? Beautiful and intelligent with it," he proclaimed.

He had called her 'my Ilse' and they had only met again a week ago, Ilse thought without rancour. In a way she was 'his'. She was certainly dressed with his money, and her heart was most definitely his.

Paul dropped her off in Medebach late that night. All her new clothes remained at his apartment in Dortmund, but he assured her that he would be down the following weekend to collect her.

"We'll go dancing, go to the theatre, whatever you like, Ilse my sweet," he told her before she left his car.

She had one reservation, however. "Siegfried will miss the time I usually spend with him," she mentioned casually.

"Then next time you must bring him along too! I'll arrange for us to meet some other friends of mine who have children of his age. Perhaps he'll enjoy himself so much that he'll want to stay the night with them. Who knows?"

Ilse was happy to comply with his suggestion. She could foresee many happy weekends in store, and Siegfried would not be excluded.

Siegfried's response to her news was ecstatic and after his first weekend back in Dortmund could talk to his grandparents of nothing else except Paul Zopf.

"We went to an ice cream parlour, Oma, and Herr Zopf let me try five different flavours! Mutti was worried I would be sick but I promised Herr Zopf I wouldn't. The waiter patted me on the head when we left and told Herr Zopf what a fine son he had! I wish I was his son. I really do. Do you think Mutti will marry him soon? They kiss each other a lot."

His grandparents smiled at his uncharacteristic exuberance. "Perhaps she will sometime," Gisela replied. "But she's still married to that Röbel man. You like Herr Zopf then?"

"Yes. Very much. He's a father I could be proud of!"

Gisela and Dieter thought this sentiment odd for such a small boy. Fathers were kind or fun or jolly. They weren't usually primarily someone to be proud of.

Gisela mentioned her impressions to her eldest son in one of her regular letters.

Paul seems to exert a charismatic influence over both Ilse and Siegfried, she wrote. *Ilse is besotted with him and can't believe her luck at last. We're all pleased for her, of course. She deserves someone better than Röbel, and Paul seems well able to look after her. I'm not so sure why Siegfried treats him as a god, however. We rather fear it's because he was in the SS. Siegfried began to worship him the moment they first met. The good thing is that Siegfried will do whatever Paul asks, so when Paul told him to work hard at school, Siegfried began to excel at his lessons. I remember you telling us Siegfried was coping remarkably well in his English school, so he is obviously a bright lad. He is determined to get top marks to please Paul.*

Karl's expression, as he read it over lunch a few days later, prompted Katherine to comment: "It must be something to do with Siegfried."

"Mmm," Karl muttered noncomitally, reading on to the end of the letter whereupon he put it down by his plate. "He seems to have found a father at long last."

"He's really taken to this friend of yours then? Well, that must be a big relief for Ilse."

"Yes, I suppose so," he replied, unwilling to commit himself to any further opinion on the matter.

*

Erich Röbel sat with his friends at their customary table in the Gasthof *Zum alten Tor*. Swirling the white foam round his glass, he drained it in a gulp then looked at his watch. Time to return to the flat and the sleeping children.

Since throwing Ilse out, his drinking was seriously curtailed unless he could persuade Frau Klitzke to come and watch over the children for the evening. The woman he employed during the day to care for them left at six promptly. At first, Erich had relinquished his socialising, but as time passed and frustration set in, he got into the habit of leaving them asleep while he popped out to meet his friends.

"I'd best be off," he sighed, belching deeply as he rose.

His companions did not try to detain him. Erich's family problems were well-known to them. An unfaithful wife was a natural hazard when you married someone as attractive as Ilse.

Erich stumbled against the edge of the table, spilling foam from his companions' glasses onto the table. He had only had four beers. He should not have been drunk, yet the room was swaying gently before his eyes. He crammed his hat onto his head, lurched around his chair and made for the street door. Once outside his head cleared temporarily with the first blast of fresh air, but after a minute's careful walking along the canal bank he felt increasingly unsteady on his feet. Not wanting to appear drunk to the two men who were walking close behind him, Erich stopped to light a cigarette and let them pass. In the act of striking a match, he felt himself knocked off

192

his feet and shoved towards the canal. A strategically placed foot tripped him headlong into the dark, oily waters of the Dortmund-Ems Canal.

*

The telegram was waiting for Ilse as they returned to her lodgings in Medebach after another exhilarating weekend together. Paul picked it up off the hall-stand and passed it to her. She took it silently, eyebrows raised in surprise, then hurried upstairs to her room, followed by Paul.

Ripping open the envelope, Ilse scanned the few words on the sheet inside. A broad grin flowered on her face and Paul breathed a sigh of relief.

"Erich's dead!" she whispered in glee, then flung the telegram down and ran into Paul's single-armed embrace. "I'm free! We can marry whenever we want. We don't have to wait for the divorce any longer!"

Ilse was like a schoolgirl, bouncing up and down with excitement. Paul smiled indulgently, relishing the ecstacy of power he held over her emotions and fate. Drunken soaks could be made to fall into canals any day of the week; capturing a woman's heart was just as easy when your name was Paul Zopf.

He sensed reality striking Ilse as she pulled away from him. "What about my children, Paul? The telegram was from my old neighbour, Greta Klitzke. They're staying with her at the moment, but I'll have to take them off her hands as soon as possible."

"What a fool I am, wanting to marry a woman with five children," Paul groaned, rolling his eyes in mock despair. Then he laughed. "It seems I shall have to invest in a larger property in the country somewhere, where there's room for all your brood to run around in their nanny's care."

He hoped it sounded spontaneous. In fact he had already instructed an agent to seek out just such a property for him to buy. Ilse could organise hiring a nanny though. It would give her something to do when she gave up her pathetic little job in Medebach. She no longer needed a pretence at being independent.

"And we'll have a cook too," he went on, adding fuel to her growing excitement. "No *Kinder, Kuche, Kirche* for you, Ilse my darling. I want you to be with me, to accompany me on business trips and on social engagements. You'll prove a great asset to me, I fancy."

Ilse gazed up at him with rapturous eyes. She adored the man and she did not mind in the least him knowing it. "Paul! I do so love you. You'll be the perfect father for Siegfried ... and the other four."

"Yes, we mustn't forget them, must we? What are they called again?"

"Margit, Heinrich, Edeltraud, and Roslinde," she softly reminded him, beginning to slip off his coat, which, in their haste to read the telegram, he still wore. "You don't have to go back just yet, do you, Schatz?"

CHAPTER FIFTEEN

The waves lapping gently under the boathouse floor were drowned by the sound of Lotti's increasingly frantic gasps. Ever since Siegfried's sixteenth birthday last December she had craved his attention. Her only way to get it was to teach him all she knew about making love. When she was not cleaning or making beds she was occupying one with Siegfried. Here in her employers' hunting lodge in the Bavarian Forest it was easier to find privacy for frequent moments of passion. Siegfried was young and hungry. Lotti was young and besotted.

The floorboards squeaked under pressure, but Siegfried was oblivious to distractions. Lotti was almost there and he knew they would share this one together. He bit on her ear lobe, hard enough to make her squeal. His excitement peaked at her cry. As he began to pound harder into her, a cascade of icy water showered over them from the rafters above, making Siegfried gasp in both ecstacy and surprise. By the time he had recovered enough to peer up at the rafters there was nothing to be seen save a dangling bucket and an open window in the roof.

"Heinrich!" Siegfried growled, but Lotti was giggling as she brushed aside dripping curls from her eyes.

"Leave him, Siegfried. It's not worth chasing him now. Anyway, I thought it added to the fun."

"I didn't." Siegfried did not like being caught in an unguarded moment. This time it was one up to Heinrich. "I'll get even with him tomorrow!"

Lotti smiled. This constant battle between the two boys caused many an excitement in the Zopf household. So far no serious trouble had resulted, the boys keeping within certain rules of combat. Only once had injury resulted, when Heinrich fell off a wall while pursuing Siegfried. It was acknowledged that Siegfried was bigger and stronger than his younger half-brother, so attacks were usually achieved by surprise and stealth. Heinrich certainly won this time.

Her smile annoyed Siegfried. Lotti had seen Heinrich get the upper hand. It would never happen again! Siegfried shook the water from his hair, grabbed his clothes and began to dress hurriedly.

Lotti retrieved her underwear from inside a derelict rowing boat. Siegfried was cross with her for smiling. The subject needed changing, urgently. "Are you looking forward to seeing your father and his family tomorrow? I suppose it's years since you last saw them."

Siegfried tucked his shirt in. "That's none of your business," he scowled, and left her to finish dressing.

Lotti watched the door close behind him. What a strange reaction to an innocent question!

*

The Wire-haired Pointer froze, docked tail extended, its nostrils quivering at the scent of quail. Siegfried raised the shotgun and took aim, allowing for the startled creature to fly into his line of fire. He squeezed the trigger. The plump bird appeared to explode in a puff of feathers as it cartwheeled into a clump of grass. The liver and white dog went to retrieve it.

"Good shot," Paul Zopf congratulated him. "Mind you, you ought to be good; hunting's in your blood."

So you keep reminding me, Siegfried thought, although he would never dream of saying such a thing out loud. This unrelenting pressure from his mother and Paul to make him accept his father only had the opposite effect. Nothing could eradicate from his memory the pain and indignity inflicted on him by Erich Röbel. For that predicament Siegfried solidly blamed his father; no one else.

"So when do they get here?" he asked, taking the quail from the dog.

Paul looked at his watch. "I've arranged for a taxi to fetch them from town. Assuming all their rail connections have gone to plan, they should arrive here about half past four." He looked at the full game bag. "All done? We've done well without Heinrich's help. I can't think why he didn't want to come with us today. Anyway, Ilse should be happy." Paul prodded the game bag. "She's had Frau Neumann in endlessly to discuss the meals for this week."

He fell into step beside Siegfried and the Pointer. The lad was almost as tall as he was now, and so like Karl. It was like stepping back in time over twenty years and seeing Karl beside him. If only

Siegfried didn't harbour such a grudge against his father. It could make the coming visit very awkward.

"Ilse wants everything to be perfect for your father's family, Siegfried, as I do," he said firmly. "I haven't seen Karl for sixteen years, and as I said before, I don't want any unpleasantness from you to spoil it for any of us. Is that understood?"

"Yes, sir." Siegfried knew better than to wilfully disobey, but he wondered how easy it would be to keep his promise.

The day was hot, and they walked leisurely down through the forest clearings and trails back to the lodge, whereupon Paul withdrew to his study. Siegfried handed over the birds to Lotti with a sly wink and a blown kiss, then sauntered down to the lake. It was here that Margit, Edeltraud and Roslinde spent most of their time, idling away the hot summer days when they were not out riding through the forest. Heinrich was there too, fishing from a rowing boat in the middle of the lake.

Silently, Siegfried crept through the reed beds around the lake's edge until the boat was between him and the girls, and Heinrich's back was towards him. Slipping off his clothes and shoes, he slunk into the lake with scarcely a splash or a ripple. The last few metres he swam underwater to lessen any warning of his approach to the boat. Grabbing the gunwale, he pulled himself over the side of the boat, tilting it so violently that Heinrich toppled overboard with a yelp.

Once aboard, Siegfried quickly fitted the oars in the rowlocks and pulled away from the spluttering and furious Heinrich.

"You swine! I'll get you for that!" the twelve-year-old gasped as he trod water, unable to catch up with the receding boat.

"That's for yesterday!" Siegfried shouted gleefully. He slowed the boat as he neared the landing stage, and drifted in for a silent mooring. Whatever he was doing, Siegfried made a point of practising commando-type skills.

"That was a mean trick," Margit scolded him.

She considered that, at sixteen, Siegfried should have grown out of playing pranks. She herself had been the butt of many of them in their early days of living together, but Siegfried seemed to recognise at last that he should leave her alone, now she was a young lady of fourteen.

"I was only paying him back for something he did to me," he grunted, securing the boat's painter through a mooring ring.

He could not be bothered with high and mighty Margit these days. Her precious dignity was a wall around her, shutting out all the fun she had once shared. She was trying even now to intimidate him with one of her self-righteous glares.

"And so it goes on, endlessly," she criticised. "Just like your feud with your father. I hope you're going to remember what Paul told you about your behaviour while they're here," she added piously. "You ought to wear a swimming costume. You know how prudish the English are supposed to be."

Edeltraud and Roslinde sat on their towels listening raptly to the exchange. Sibling rivalry was their chief source of interest, apart from horses. Naturally enough they sided with Heinrich, their full brother, but they both had a deep respect for Siegfried's talents. They watched his reaction to Margit's goading.

"I hope you remember what Paul told you ..." he mimicked in a prissy voice.

He edged closer to Margit, who was dangling her feet over the edge of the landing stage. She sensed his intentions too late as he seized a handful of her long, brown curls, dragged her to her feet, then pushed her into the clear, green water.

Edeltraud and Roslinde did not join in with Siegfried's laughter. It was no use telling tales on Siegfried to their mother or stepfather. He was the favourite: the golden boy. The Röbel children had long since learned to accept that fact.

Margit swam back to the shore as gracefully as she could. She refused to let Siegfried see and enjoy her wrath. She wrapped her towel round her, picked up her watch and looked at it.

"Time for lunch," she declared imperiously.

*

Katherine gazed out of the train window wishing they were already at Regensburg. They had broken their journey from England with a few days at Medebach, but it only seemed to have made the whole trip longer. Once at Regensburg they would have a bus ride to the town of Cham, where a taxi would be waiting for them.

They had all been invited to Ilse and Paul's wedding, but decided against travelling to Germany again so soon after Rudi and Adele's wedding. On subsequent visits to Medebach, Ilse had reluctantly advised against Karl seeing Siegfried, but the day finally came when Paul and Ilse considered Siegfried responsible enough to contemplate a meeting with his father again, and so the invitation from the Zopfs was made.

The long bus journey was lightened by a group of students on their way to camp in the forest, who were keen to practise their English. They kept the children amused, teaching them hiking songs, congratulating them on their knowledge of German. Katherine felt her own ability was put to shame by her children, but she had been making a real effort to brush up on her spoken German ready for the holiday, since Ilse spoke no English. It could be a difficult holiday. Sabina, Richard and Paul were used to staying with their German cousins, having common blood to unite them. Ilse's children might be very different, and as for Siegfried ... Blood ties meant nothing to him. She voiced her fears to Karl, who was sitting across the aisle next to Richard.

"I just hope Ilse's children are as good with ours as Trevor and Shirley were. I wasn't too sure about having Evelyn's family to stay at first, but it worked. I suppose it will again. It just seems rather a big age range, from seven to sixteen. I hope Paul's not left out too much, being the youngest."

Karl did his best to reassure her. "I expect they'll split up into two groups. Four boys and four girls should get on all right."

Katherine's eyebrows raised in disbelief. "You're an optimist!"

She knew he did in fact share her concern. It would be a difficult time for him too, seeing Siegfried again, considering how volatile their relationship had been. Likewise there was Ilse to consider. Katherine had noticed how both Ilse's marriages had saved her at difficult times in her life, and hoped Ilse's match with Paul Zopf was a lasting one. She was in no doubt that eight years ago in Dortmund Ilse cast her eye upon Karl as a replacement for Erich. She hoped Ilse's invitation now would not turn out to be a continuation of the same. Sarah, when consulted, was dubious about the wisdom of the families staying together, but then Sarah tended to have a jaundiced view of marriage anyway.

Karl noticed her furrowed brow. "It's a holiday, Schatz. Enjoy it! There'll be riding, swimming, no cooking. What more could you want?"

Katherine gave a slight shrug and mouthed the words so the children would not hear. "No Siegfried."

It would not do to prejudice the children against their half-brother. She spent the remainder of the journey convincing herself she had nothing to worry about.

As arranged, a large Mercedes taxi was waiting at Cham to drive them the last few miles through thick, coniferous forest to the hunting lodge. In her mind's eye, Katherine had pictured a simple, Canadian-style log-cabin; but she was grossly mistaken. This wooden edifice had two floors, with a veranda or balcony around each. Every available surface was elaborately carved and adorned either with window boxes of pink and orange geraniums, or with the antlers of unfortunate deer. Beside the lodge was a courtyard with a complex of stables, outhouses, garage, and servants' accommodation, all built to the same rustic, but ornate design.

"Wow!" Sabina's eyes were alight with awe. "What a place!"

Until that moment, Katherine had no idea of how wealthy Paul Zopf was. She realised Karl had given her hints as to his friend's fortune, but she had not fully appreciated the scale of it.

"And this is only their holiday home!" she gasped.

She had no further time for reflection as the drive filled up with milling children. Paul and Ilse came forward, hands outstretched, and the welcomes and introductions began. Katherine scarcely noticed an elderly man taking their luggage inside, or the departure of the taxi, apparently already paid for. She almost offered her right hand for Paul to shake, remembering at the last moment his lack of a right arm. His tailored sports jacket had no right sleeve at all. She found herself immediately impressed by Paul's dynamism and dark, rather intense face, which she recognised from the Driesler family photo album. Ilse too was far more like the attractive young woman of the photos than when Katherine had last seen her, ten years ago in Winterberg. She now had the vitality and sparkle so lacking before, embodying her new happiness and helping to restore her lost youth.

She could not help but watch closely from the corner of her eye, as Ilse greeted Karl with a kiss on the cheek. There was the slightest delay in her withdrawal. Simply recognition of their once close relationship, Katherine hoped.

Karl spent a moment complimenting Ilse on her appearance, before turning to face his childhood friend. Here again there was a lingering handshake as the two men re-established contact after an interval of sixteen years.

"You've hardly changed a bit, Paul," Karl greeted him. "Just a few grey hairs, and bit of a paunch. The sign of success, eh?"

Paul laughed as he surveyed his friend. "*You're* commenting on *my* waistline? You must be almost twice as heavy as when I last saw you!" He put his hand on Karl's back. "Come along in for some refreshment. You still look as though you need to put on some weight. Does Katherine not feed you?"

Katherine understood his remark for the joke that it was. "Yes. But he doesn't drink enough German beer to make him fat."

"*Touché!*" Paul laughed, guiding her and the children up the veranda steps to the side of the lodge overlooking a large lake. Comfortably upholstered seats were arranged on the veranda around a table laden with cream cakes and fruit tarts.

"We thought an English afternoon tea would be appreciated after your long journey from Medebach," Ilse declared. "We also have coffee or lemonade if you prefer."

Despite her intentions when abroad to eat like a native, a cup of tea sounded irresistible to Katherine, but Karl chose coffee. His German upbringing still dominated over the years spent drinking tea in England. The children all opted for lemonade, and eagerly eyed the cakes, awaiting the signal to dive in and help themselves, which Ilse duly gave.

Spurning the chairs in favour of swinging their legs over the side of the veranda, the children made a good start at getting to know each other.

Above the hubbub Ilse finally mentioned her missing elder son. "You're probably wondering where Siegfried has got to."

"Yes, I was," Karl admitted. He had not liked to comment on Siegfried's notable absence from the family throng.

Ilse smiled reassuringly. "We all rather felt that your meeting with him shouldn't be overshadowed by this lot," she said, indicating the seven children with cream-smeared mouths.

"We suggested he waited until things settled down a bit before he appeared. Younger children do tend to steal the scene, don't they?"

Karl became aware as she spoke, that Siegfried was indeed loitering in the shadows of the doorway. He felt his pulse rate rise expectantly as Siegfried silently stepped out onto the veranda.

"Hello, Siegfried," Karl said quietly, looking up into the expressionless eyes.

"Hello, Vater." The broken voice of adolescence was flat too. Siegfried turned to Katherine and summoned a smile. "Hello, Katherine."

Unlike her husband, Katherine stood up on Siegfried's arrival. She felt some sign of affection must be made, since Karl seemed so unwilling. She stepped over to Siegfried and kissed him lightly on the cheek, smelling the dank, algal odour of lake water in his close-cropped hair. He did not return the kiss, but did not flinch away either.

"My goodness! What a difference! You're quite a man now, aren't you?" she told him, making a point of speaking in German so as not to alienate him immediately.

There was a suppressed smirk on Siegfried's lips as he recognised the ruse to flatter him. "I have grown a bit," he agreed, pleasantly enough. With a pointed look at his father he went on: "Enough to show you how well I can shoot."

It was a direct reference to Karl's unfulfilled promise of long ago, but Karl let it pass without comment.

"Certainly! I'm sure you can show me where the best game is to be found," he replied, injecting some enthusiasm into the statement.

There had been no physical contact between them; no handshake or embrace, but as far as it went, their reunion was sufficiently cordial. Ilse sensed enough had been made of it and deftly opened the conversation up to include everyone again.

"During your week with us we've got a hunt lined up, which some of our friends are joining us for. We also have horses and ponies for riding. Do you hunt at all, Katherine?"

"With a gun, no. I leave that to Karl. But I ride on fox hunts."

"Really? Do tell me all about it. I've seen an English hunt in films, and it always looks so exciting."

As Katherine battled on manfully in German to Ilse, Paul explained to Karl, with Siegfried's help, what other entertainments were planned for their guests during their visit. After an hour's conversation and reminiscing, during which time the younger children all disappeared to the lake, Ilse called a halt. "I expect you'd like to see your rooms and have a wander round the place, wouldn't you? I can see Paul is just itching to show you the gun room, Karl, but we'll take you upstairs first. The view from the balconies across the forest is rather fine."

Siegfried detached himself from the party and hurried off in search of the other children, to sniff out possible fun and games for himself. He had noticed that the youngest son, Paul, most resembled their father, and should therefore bear the brunt of any practical jokes. The fact that he was the youngest, and so probably the most easily upset, did not trouble Siegfried, who felt even less for these other half-siblings than he did for the Röbel children. Only Sabina, whom he vaguely remembered as a toddler, held any interest for him; Richard had been a squealing baby, whilst Paul was just a name to a face he had not seen until now.

His father's face. The discovery irritated him, as much as his own reflection when he saw those same grey eyes staring back at him. There could be no escape from his father's shame, not when he was made in his father's image. And now there was another image to taunt him – Paul Driesler's.

Siegfried felt the hatred burning once more inside him. He remembered how much he enjoyed the sensation. Gustav's doctrine he also remembered. He would lull them into a false sense of security. Then the fun could begin.

*

Margit helped little Paul into the boat. She had made certain from Sabina that he could swim, before suggesting going on the water. Heinrich was the self-appointed head oarsman, although he condescended to let Richard have a go once they reached the centre of the lake.

The children felt safe from adult intervention here, and quickly opened up to each other about their various parents. Richard was keen to hear how Herr Zopf had lost his arm, while Sabina was fascinated by the fact that the Röbel childrens' real father had drowned in a canal.

Edeltraud suddenly decided to join the conversation with a question that had long puzzled her. "Why didn't our Mummy marry your Daddy, if Siegfried is their son?"

There was total silence for a moment apart from the lapping of the water under the hull. Sabina was the first to speak.

"I've no idea. I've never thought about it before. Have you, Richard?"

He shook his head. "No. I never really thought of him as Dad's son. He was just a troublemaker they got rid of." He turned to Heinrich. "Is he as bad as we've heard from our schoolfriends' parents? They say he was always in trouble for something – stealing and suchlike – and once he attacked a boy with a knife. He even ran away from home on his eighth birthday. Is he like that now?"

The Röbel children were astonished at his outline of Siegfried.

"Good heavens, no!" Margit spluttered. "He wouldn't do a thing wrong to upset Paul – big Paul," she clarified. She pronounced little Paul's name in the German fashion – as 'Powl' rather than 'Porl' – so that some confusion was inevitable. "It's only with us that he's a pain in the neck!"

"Why's that?" Sabina asked.

Heinrich wanted a moan. "Oh, he's always playing tricks on us, or getting us into trouble for things we haven't done. And because he's the favourite, he always gets away with it."

"Yeterday he tipped Heinrich out of the boat, and threw me in the lake too!" Margit informed them angrily. "You'd better watch him, as he's bound to start on you too! He really fancies himself as a commando, and likes to play his little war games all the time."

Richard found himself warming to Siegfried. He might learn a thing or two from his half-brother. His own father had taught him how to shoot, but Richard was sure there was plenty more he could learn from Siegfried.

"He certainly fancies himself," Heinrich muttered cryptically, but would not be persuaded to expand on details in front of the younger children.

Sabina felt she ought to make some move in defence of Siegfried, even if it was only by changing the subject. "I fancy a swim!" she declared. "I'm sure it's long enough since we ate. Let's go back and see if we can find our swimming costumes."

Heinrich helped Richard turn the rowing boat towards the landing-stage, and the children were soon running into the lodge to find their rooms and their suitcases. Lotti had already unpacked for them, and they quickly clattered back down the polished stairs and ran back to the lake.

"My God! A herd of elephants just went by," Paul Zopf joked to Karl, as they stood admiring the antique contents of the gun room.

"Siegfried wasn't with them, though," Karl remarked. "I wonder where he's got to?"

"He's got his own interests. He doesn't often mix with the others. Between you and me, Karl," he said, lowering his voice, "he considers himself rather superior to the others, and I must confess, I encourage him in that belief. There's no mistaking your blood in him, no matter how much he resents the fact."

Karl tutted. "Blood isn't everything, Paul. Upbringing has a lot to do with it, and Siegfried's early years left a lot to be desired. The violence in him stems from those times, and has nothing to do with me."

"Violence? Come now, Karl, you mean fighting spirit, don't you? Every time I look at him, I see you and me at the same age."

"Yes, but we were being deliberately prepared for war then. Hopefully, Siegfried will never have to fight in a war."

"But there's no harm in being prepared, is there? The Soviets are a real threat we can't ignore. Wouldn't it be foolish not to have our young men trained to fight?"

Karl could only shrug. He stared at the ornate weaponry displayed on the walls of the gun room. He was not a pacifist, despite his experience of war. As an invader of other nations, he had seen for himself how their populations fought to defend their land. Germany had been no different either, once the tables were turned. He had fought at the end for Germany, not Nazism, and would have done so again, except that he now carried a British passport.

"Aggression is all very well so long as it's controlled," Karl said eventually.

"Oh, I think you'll find he's very controlled now, Karl. I think I've managed to instil some self-discipline into him at last."

"If you have, I'll be very impressed."

Paul grinned smugly. "Then let's go and open a bottle of schnapps and drink to your son's future."

*

"Can I come with you? I can shoot too."

Karl almost did not hear Margit's softly-spoken request. He was on the veranda checking that he and Siegfried had everything they needed for their day together: hunting rifles, game bags, lunch. He hesitated long enough before answering so that Margit knew what his reply would be.

"Another day, Margit, please. I rather wanted to have Siegfried to myself for a few hours. I'm sure you understand why," he said as gently as he could. She hid her disappointment well, he noticed with surprise.

"I understand," Margit said, but she did not go away. "He is your son, and you haven't seen him for years." She picked up a bottle of water and handed it to Karl to put in the rucksack. "He looks very like you, doesn't he?"

Margit seemed determined to make conversation and be friendly. Perhaps she was unconsciously trying to make up for Siegfried's reticence towards him, Karl thought. She was certainly a helpful and thoughtful girl, the way she was looking after Paul so well.

"Yes, I suppose he does."

"Little Paul does too." As if suddenly fearing she had outstayed her welcome, she flicked a stray lock of hair from her face and half turned away. "I think I'll go for a ride instead. The others are busy making a raft, but perhaps Sabina would like to come with me."

From the doorway Siegfried watched her go. So young Margit was growing into a woman. Her interest in his father was possibly worth exploiting. Nobody could blame him for Margit's emotional entanglements, and it might prove amusingly awkward for his father. On second thoughts, he decided, it was not worth bothering with. Margit was probably too sensible to do anything stupid and his father would never encourage her. It would just be amusing to watch her infatuation and see how long it took his father, and Katherine, to catch on to it.

"Are you ready then, Siegfried?"

Siegfried stepped out onto the veranda. "Yes." He nodded towards the retreating girl. "Margit wanting to come too?"

"Yes, but I told her it was just you and me today. I thought it important we try to get to know each other."

"Suppose so."

"You don't have to come with me if you don't want to."

Siegfried remembered Paul's instructions. "Oh, I want to come," he lied.

They set off with the Pointer at a stiff pace through the open woodland around the lodge, moderating the pace slightly as they branched off up a narrower track, where low branches impeded their progress.

"This reminds me of the day when you ran away at Medebach, Siegfried, and I had to carry you back down through the trees because you'd hurt your ankle. Do you remember?"

"Yes, of course I do. How could I forget such a humiliating experience?"

"Speaking of humiliating experiences, there was that time I fell off the ladder and broke my leg. I seem to remember you hovering over me as I lay there, having a good look and a gloat no doubt, eh?" Karl said with a friendly grin, not intending to be critical.

"Yes," Siegfried replied eagerly. "It was because of that Gustav came to stay." There was a significant pause. "Do you still have the knife he gave me?"

So he still remembers it, Karl sighed. "You'll get it back when you're twenty-one, as I promised."

"And not before?"

"I didn't bring it with me. But if you were to come over to England to visit us soon, perhaps I might be persuaded to let you have it back."

There was no response from Siegfried, and Karl took it to mean a refusal of the invitation. They scrambled up a steep hill and Karl sat down on a rock at the top for a breather. Siegfried too was blowing hard with the exertion, but did not deign to rest. He had something else on his mind.

"I never did understand why Gustav fell so suddenly out of favour."

Karl decided that, at sixteen, Siegfried could be told, and what was more important, would probably enjoy hearing the full story.

There was a hoot of laughter from Siegfried when Karl came to the end of the story, with Perry's moving in with Gustav.

"I can just imagine Gustav getting up to something like that!" he roared.

"Can you?"

"Yes! You don't imagine I'm still innocent in such matters do you? Just ask Lotti!" Siegfried boasted.

Karl suppressed a smile. "Does your mother know about such goings on? And what about Lotti? I hope you're –"

"Oh, don't worry about that. Lotti's always prepared. We're not stupid." Siegfried suddenly dropped the frivolity. "My mother doesn't know about it, but Paul does."

"He encourages it, I presume."

Siegfried smiled again. "Yes. Would you?"

Karl was taken aback by the directness of Siegfried's question. "Well ... I don't think I would actively encourage such a thing, but as long as you're being sensible about it, I can't say I would discourage it. I think you're going to find in future years, Siegfried, that you'll have to learn restraint at some time. Women will find you attractive. It's not always the man who does the chasing, you know."

Siegfried stared at him astutely. "You have that problem, don't you? I bet women are falling over themselves in the rush to get at you! Have you got a mistress?"

Karl was horrified by the assumption made by his son. Siegfried's long-standing lack of moral principles seemed to have continued into adolescence. "Just a moment, Siegfried! Who do you think I am? Why is it that because I'm supposedly good-looking, people, including you, think I'm prepared to betray my wife? This is what I was trying to warn you about just now. Temptation is often put in your path, but it's not usually in your best interests to succumb."

Siegfried would not be sidetracked from the original question. "But wouldn't it be fun, just once in a while? Don't you get bored with Katherine all the time? I bet you'd like another go with my mother. You didn't have such inhibitions and petty morals when I was conceived, did you?" he taunted.

Karl felt uncomfortable. "I think the conversation has gone far enough, Siegfried. Those were different times. Let's press on, shall we?"

He stood up and began to walk away. Siegfried followed, grinning to himself. He had forgotten how much he enjoyed baiting his father.

When they reached a rocky plateau, Siegfried pointed down to a grassy area at the forest's edge. "This is a good place for deer and hares. We could stay here and wait a bit. See what turns up."

"Fine. Whatever you say."

They settled the dog and themselves down behind a rock to wait in silence, loaded rifles at the ready. Siegfried positioned himself slightly behind his father, whose attention was already riveted on the scene below. All Siegfried could look at was the back of his father's head. Such a tempting target. It would be so simple to fulfill his dream. As if of its own accord, his body began to turn infinitesimally slowly, until the gun aimed directly at the man in front of him.

CHAPTER SIXTEEN

Such a feeling of power! Siegfried's fingers curled expectantly around the trigger. A gentle squeeze was all it would take to exact the retribution his heart demanded.

He saw his father tilt his head a fraction and raise his rifle to his line of sight. Swinging his own rifle rapidly through ninety degrees, Siegfried saw and fired at the deer in almost the same second, killing it cleanly with a shot through the head. He lowered the rifle in satisfaction, and smugly prepared to receive his father's congratulations.

"Why was your rifle pointing at me, Siegfried?" Karl's voice was level, not accusing or menacing, simply politely enquiring. He had seen the shadow of Siegfried's rifle career over the rock in front of him and knew without a doubt that his son had been aiming a loaded gun at him.

Boldly, Siegfried met his father's eyes ... his own eyes. No apology came to Siegfried's lips. "I wanted to see what it felt like."

Karl slowly raised his own rifle. Siegfried was at point blank range. "Shall I see what it feels like? Then perhaps we can compare notes."

He stood there for ten long seconds, his eyes never leaving his son's. Siegfried's cocksure grin revealed his absolute conviction that his father would never fire.

The shot hit the ground by his left foot, sending Siegfried leaping backwards in fright.

"You were watching my eyes, not the rifle, weren't you, Siegfried? And my eyes told you nothing, as yours tell me nothing." Karl lowered the rifle as he spoke, declaring a formal end to the duel of nerves. "You're hiding your hatred well, but it's still there, isn't it?"

"Of course it's still there!" Siegfried retorted viciously. "Why should it have gone? You've done nothing to redeem yourself. You're still as stupidly proud as ever that you betrayed your country and changed to the winning side. You can't even take a mistress like any normal man, in case it gets you into trouble with your precious Katherine. She's turned you into even more of a coward than you were before!"

Stunned by his son's immature outburst, Karl felt his anger fade, leaving him intensely saddened. "I only hope that one day, Siegfried, you will find a woman to love as much as I love Katherine. Perhaps then you will understand what it means to consider someone else's feelings more than your own."

"I do already. I would do nothing to bring shame on Paul. That is why I didn't pull the trigger when I had the gun aimed at you, tempted as I was. Consider yourself safe from me, Vater, for as long as you retain Paul's approval."

Siegfried saw the fury on his father's face and laughed out loud. "And don't think I'm frightened of what you might do to me. You would never risk disgracing yourself. Never!"

How can you be so sure?, Karl thought unhappily, but kept his doubts to himself. Instead he abandoned the confrontation. "Well, since we've both agreed we're not going to hurt each other, we'd better go down and do something with that deer."

There seemed no point in prolonging the day's hunting. Neither wanted to share the other's company for any longer than was absolutely necessary. They ate a quick lunch, strung the deer by the hooves onto a pole and carried it back on their shoulders without another word spoken until they met up with Sabina and Margit returning from their ride.

Siegfried immediately noticed Margit's blush. Silly fool. What on earth can she see in him?

"Hello, girls. Had a nice ride?" Karl asked.

"Great. We've been out for ages," Sabina replied from the back of a sweating bay gelding. "We took a picnic with us. It was lovely to be able to ride for miles without having to open any gates or cross any roads!"

Margit was eyeing the deer. "That's a big one. I bet that's heavy."

You might as well say: "Gosh, aren't you strong!" Siegfried thought in disgust, forgetting it applied to him too.

"We'll be glad to get back, I think," Karl said with feeling and a glance at Siegfried.

"We'll ride on and tell Lotti to have a cold beer waiting," Margit said, nudging her horse into a more active walk.

Father and son dropped the pretence at amicability as soon as the riders were out of sight.

*

Little Paul sidled up to his father and tapped him on the knee for attention. "When are you coming to see our raft, Daddy?"

Karl put down his empty beer glass. "How about now? Even better, I shall try it out, but I think I'd better get changed into my swimming trunks first, don't you? Who else is coming swimming?"

"Me!" came the unanimous chorus, and there followed a general exodus to go and change.

Karl's inspection of the raft was thorough, which pleased the children immensely. He got them to tighten one or two of the lashings, as he did not want their hard work to disintegrate ignominiously in front of everyone. When he was satisfied he helped them launch it onto the lake. It was big enough to carry the three boys and Karl, but the girls quickly made it clear they wanted a turn on it too. Karl dived off it, to allow room for Roslinde and Edeltraud to join the boys, Sabina and Margit agreeing to wait their turn.

Katherine rowed alongside in the boat, in case of any difficulties, as Paul was not yet a very strong swimmer. Siegfried too was on hand, acting as a human outboard motor, helping to push the raft out into the lake as the children paddled.

She watched the sparkling drops from the oars fall and blend into the cloud-mirrored surface. The effect was almost hypnotic. The gentle surge of the boat forwards, followed by a glide; surge, glide, surge, glide. Like life itself, she thought. Times of hectic activity, then lulls. Moments when one could reflect on life before the next maelstrom arrived.

The hunting expedition seemed to have done both Karl and Siegfried the world of good. Whatever had troubled Siegfried in the past, he must have grown out of. No, it was Margit she might have to watch now. She had begun to notice the previous day that the poor thing could not keep her eyes off Karl, and today she could not keep her hands off him either. She and Sabina were endeavouring to be towed along by him as he swam, by hanging onto his shoulders.

Karl was good-naturedly putting up with the assault, only trying to rid himself of the limpets by tickling them, but it was Margit who was the most determined to cling on. At fourteen she was at the age of schoolgirl crushes, and was doing her utmost to be noticed by Karl.

Katherine was inclined to be tolerant of the situation. Karl did not seem aware of anything, and Margit would find some other, more appropriately aged young man to focus her attentions upon, once they returned to England. There was no need to worry Karl about it.

The raft reached the diving platform in the centre of the lake. Heinrich tied the raft to it and the passengers disembarked to begin a session of jumping in unison into the water to see how big a splash they could make. Katherine stayed in the rowing boat, perfectly happy to potter about, peering into the depths to look for fish or other wildlife. A family of coot sped across the lake, away from the rumpus of the children. Katherine lay across the thwart, with her chin resting on the gunwale, and watched the clouds skim gently across the water. Karl was right. What more could she want than this? No meals to plan and prepare, just a week's idleness.

Shrieks of laughter made her raise her head. The children had grabbed hold of Karl by all four limbs and were about to hurl him into the water. As he went in he held onto the wrists of Richard and Margit, pulling them in with him. Richard and Margit surfaced, but Karl did not.

Katherine smiled to herself, scanning the surface to see where he would pop up, like a great-crested grebe after a prolonged dive. Paul, Edeltraud and Roslinde were peering anxiously over the edge of the diving platform as Margit and Richard climbed aboard the raft. Siegfried and Heinrich stood nonchalantly by. They knew it was a game.

Sure enough, less than a minute later she saw him emerge behind the diving platform.

"Repel all boarders!" Heinrich yelled, alerting the other children.

Karl's repeated attempts to climb aboard the diving platform only resulted in him being pushed back in. Eventually he gave up and swam over to join Katherine in the rowing boat.

"Permission to board?" he asked, his arms resting on the gunwale.

"Permission granted," Katherine laughed. She moved back to balance the boat as he hauled himself in. His body was already well tanned, unlike hers, which was sensitive to the sun and tended to burn if she was not careful. His cold, wet back brushed against her warm flesh and she flinched.

"You've been in the water too long, Schatz. You're frozen."

"I'll soon warm up," he said, enfolding himself within her arms.

She felt his wetness permeate her swimming costume. "Now you've made me all wet, you rotter."

Nevertheless, she did not move away, but rested her cheek on the top of his head as he sat on the bottomboards of the boat.

"Where are Ilse and Paul?" he asked.

"Ilse's gone into town to do some shopping and Paul's in his study, working. He's got some tender or other for a brewery extension to prepare, and it wouldn't wait, he said. He's as bad as you, Schatz. Always working!"

He turned his head to look up at her. "We'd better invite them over to us for a return visit. That should force him to forget work for a bit."

"Where on earth would we put them all? We haven't got half a dozen spare rooms like they have. Or a cook," she added meaningfully.

Karl patted her thigh. "Don't worry. I don't think they'll come to England anyway. It's not their favourite country. I'm not even sure if Paul's allowed, being a war criminal and all. I've already mentioned a visit to Siegfried and he wasn't keen."

"I thought you two were getting on better now. You seemed to be talking quite happily when you got back from hunting this afternoon."

She felt his fingers involuntarily dig into her leg.

"All an illusion, I'm afraid. He hates my guts and I –"

"Daddy!" Sabina's panic-stricken voice carried across the water to them. "Daddy! We can't see Paul!"

Karl sat bolt upright in an instant. Together he and Katherine searched the water's surface for the blond head of their youngest son. It was nowhere to be seen.

"Oh, God!" Katherine whispered, clutching onto Karl's arm in terror.

Pushing her aside, Karl grabbed the oars and rowed the fifty yards to the diving platform at top speed. He leaped out of the boat onto the platform and joined the frantic children in peering into the water. Directly below them, deep down, they could see dark, beckoning weeds, but further away from them the surface was like a mirror, with only blue sky and white clouds to be seen. Without further delay Karl dived in.

He swam down ten feet then spun on the spot, staring through the green water for a glimpse of a white body caught in the weed. Just before his breath gave out, he kicked back up to the surface again.

He saw Katherine's terrified face looking down at him from the diving platform and shook his head, too short of breath to speak.

Katherine was about to jump in to help in the search, when she noticed Siegfried. He was a much better swimmer than she was, and her eyes might be of more use on the surface.

"Don't just stand there, Siegfried!" she shrieked at him. "Jump in and help!"

Siegfried did as he was told, leaving Katherine and the other children holding their breath in sympathy for the divers. The wait was agonising. Roslinde began to cry, but Katherine could do nothing to comfort her, her own fears too urgent to ignore.

The two blond heads bobbed up again, still without a third. It was more than Katherine could bear.

"Paul, Paul!" she screamed. Her voice echoed emptily back from the cliff across the lake and she sank down on her knees in despair.

"I'm here," a small voice said, from the direction of the raft.

There was a swirling of water then Paul's head appeared beside the barrels which kept the raft afloat.

"Thank God you're safe!" Katherine felt faint with relief. Her hands were shaking as she helped Paul up onto the diving platform just as Karl and Siegfried re-emerged.

"You've got him!" Karl gasped. "Where was he?"

Paul stood up proudly. "I was in the space under the raft all the time. I was watching you look for me. It was funny. You all looked so worried, I could hardly stop myself from laughing."

His remarks were met with dead silence, and the smile faded from his face, as he saw both his parents' relief switch to anger. He quickly tried to explain.

"Siegfried said it would be a good joke to play after Daddy made us all worried earlier," Paul said pitifully. "He bet me I could disappear for much longer."

There was a splash as Siegfried struck out for the shore. "See you all later," he called back to them.

Karl swam up to the platform and climbed on. "Are you telling me he knew where you were all the time?" he asked the now miserable and teeth-chattering Paul.

"Yes."

Karl spun to face the disappearing Siegfried, but Katherine put a restraining hand on him.

"Leave him. It's not worth making his victory any greater by letting him see you lose your temper. Let's just get everyone back on dry land and warmed up. We can tell Ilse and Paul about this later. I think they can deal with it better than we can."

She could tell Karl was reluctant to leave the chase, but Paul's chattering teeth made him relent.

"All right. You row him back and I'll help the others with the raft."

"Big Paul told Siegfried to behave himself while you were here," Margit said as she swam alongside Karl, pushing the raft ashore. "I don't know what he'll do to Siegfried for disobeying him. He's never had to punish him before. Unlike us," she added darkly.

"Really? You mean Siegfried's never done anything wrong before?" Karl asked in astonishment.

"Of course he has, but he always sees to it that we get the blame. He's very devious."

"You don't like him, I take it."

"No. None of us does, except Mutti, Paul and Lotti." Her reproving tone told him she knew of Siegfried's exploits with the maid. "I once heard old Wilhelm, who taught him to shoot, complaining to Frau Neumann how ruthless Siegfried was about getting what he wanted. Of course, he has Lotti to help him. She would do anything for him. And I mean anything!"

The raft grounded on the shore. Margit positioned herself to lift the same corner as Karl as they all hauled it further out of the water.

"You just watch. I bet Paul won't believe Siegfried was to blame."

Karl considered what Margit had said as he went upstairs to change. If she were right, it would not be worth even mentioning the incident to Paul and Ilse. But he could not simply ignore it. Siegfried would think he could get away with anything. No. He would have to say something to them, and hope they took appropriate action to prevent a repetition.

The opportunity did not present itself until late that evening. Some friends of the Zopfs were invited for a formal dinner, and it was well past midnight when they finally left. Karl loitered downstairs after Katherine and Ilse went up to bed, their dresses brushing companionably together.

"A nightcap, Paul?" Karl suggested, as his friend put his hand on the bannisters.

Paul paused in the act of ascending the first step and turned curiously towards Karl. "You want to drink me under the table? You could never do it before."

"No. I'm just not tired. Fancied a chat. We haven't had much of a chance to talk alone."

Paul grinned. "Come on then. Let's attack a bottle of *Jägermeister*."

They returned to the living room, and Paul produced a bottle of the herbal schnapps from the corner bar's refrigerator. He poured a generous measure into two glasses.

"*Zum Wohl!*" they toasted each other, downing the drink in one. Paul refilled the glasses and they sat down in easy chairs on opposite sides of the marble-topped coffee table, still cluttered with cups and glasses from earlier. Lotti would see to them in the morning.

Paul stretched out his legs, the pressed creases in his black trousers as sharp as glacial mountain ridges. "So. You wanted to talk to me about Siegfried."

Karl's surprise showed. "Has he spoken to you about what happened today?"

"Yes. He said little Paul played a practical joke on you, and when it backfired he got scared and tried to suggest it was Siegfried's idea."

"I see." Karl kept his face impassive and downed his drink. So Margit was right. Paul would not hear ill of Siegfried. Since there was no proof of Siegfried's involvement, it was pointless trying to convince Paul. "It's a sixteen-year-old's word against a seven-year-old's."

"Exactly."

Reluctantly Karl decided to let the matter drop in favour of something else which had been on his mind. "What are Siegfried's plans for when he leaves school?"

Paul smiled at Karl's capitulation. "After his national service he'll join me in the family business. He's already taking a keen interest in the building trade. He'll be good at it, I think. He won't let anyone get the better of him."

"No. I can see that." Karl held Paul's gaze intently. "You think of him as your own son, don't you, Paul?"

"Yes, I suppose I do. I'm very proud of him. So should you be."

Karl felt Paul was challenging him to deny it. "All I've seen so far is his hunting ability. I can't judge him solely on that."

"He's a perfectionist, Karl. And if he sets his mind to something, he'll do it," Paul said proudly.

"As long as it's in his own best interests and no one else's."

Paul waved aside the criticism. "He's still young. All children are self-centred. But no, I believe he can act unselfishly when he has to. He's very loyal to me. I can ask things of him he doesn't like to do."

"Like being polite to me?"

Paul grimaced. "Yes. It's unfortunate, his attitude, but he doesn't understand. He's got it into his head that you deserted him and his mother, and they both suffered terribly because of it."

"*I* deserted? You know full well that's not true! Why have you never told him what really happened?"

Paul reached for a cigar from the box on the coffee table and lit it carefully. "It seemed pointless to try until he was old enough to understand." He paused, giving emphasis to his next remark. "Do your other children know what you went through?"

A swirl of cigar smoke wafted across to Karl. "No," he admitted. "They don't."

"There you are then. Perhaps you ought to sit down and tell them."

There was a silence which Paul found disconcerting. "You ought to, you know," he repeated.

"I know. But it's not that easy for me to talk about it."

"I guess not," Paul conceded. He decided not to pressure Karl further and took a big puff of his cigar. "Don't you think Ilse looks beautiful?"

"Yes," Karl replied cautiously, wondering what Paul was driving at now. "You've done her the world of good. She must be very grateful to you."

"She is. She would do anything for me."

It was strange, Karl reflected, that he had heard that same phrase already today in connection with Siegfried. Between them, Paul and Siegfried held a considerable degree of power over people.

"What about you and Katherine?" Paul probed.

"Us? Oh, I would do anything for her."

"Like you gave up your acting? Didn't she like you away so much?"

"It proved incompatible with full-time farming. It wasn't anything to do with Katherine."

"Oh no?" Paul asked doubtfully. "But what about her. Would she do anything for you?"

"I don't expect it of her." As you seem to of Ilse, Karl thought.

"That's where we differ, Karl, you and I. I do expect it of Ilse." He grinned suddenly. "She knows I like a little bit on the side, every now and then. She doesn't object."

Karl bit his lower lip in distaste. "So that's where Siegfried gets his ideas from."

"What ideas?"

"He asked me whether I have a mistress."

"And do you?"

"Siegfried truly is your son," Karl declared contemptuously. "Your attitudes are his. No, I don't have a mistress, Paul. I don't need one."

There was a laugh from across the table. "I'm sorry, Karl. I've ruffled your feathers. I agree we see differently about things, but don't let that come between us. We're old friends, eh? Let's have a last drink to that." He refilled their empty glasses. "To us, Karl. Long may we continue to be friends."

Karl raised his glass but was straight-faced as he repeated the toast. "To us!"

*

Katherine was still awake when he entered their bedroom, although the light was off.

219

"Well?" she whispered. "Any joy?"

"No. None whatsoever. They're totally loyal to each other. Paul won't hear a bad word about him."

He sat down on the bed next to her and turned on the bedside light. "Siegfried's more Paul's son than mine now. I told him so. I don't consider I have any more responsibility for him."

Katherine sat up and loosened Karl's tie, then smoothed the frown off his brow with her fingertips. "Isn't that a weight off your mind?"

She eased his jacket off his shoulders, throwing it carefully over to a nearby chair, then proceeded to unbutton his shirt.

"I suppose so," he replied. "But it doesn't stop me worrying about him."

"Come closer," she breathed, pulling him towards her.

His mouth sought hers, the taste of her so reassuringly familiar. "Who needs a mistress, when I've got you?" he said.

His comment alarmed her and she backed off suddenly. "What do you mean?"

Karl nuzzled her ear and immediately felt her body begin to relax once more against his. "Paul apparently does. But Ilse accepts it."

At that moment, the last person Katherine wanted to hear about was Ilse. She stretched languorously as Karl's warm breath moved across her neck and down her throat. She could not contemplate making love with anyone other than Karl. His hands on her breasts worked a magic only he had the right to invoke. Likewise she knew those hands were kept for her, and her alone. She would never share him with anyone.

He sat up briefly to finish undressing, and as always she admired the smooth, muscular leanness of his body. She could not help remembering Paul Zopf's comment on their arrival. Karl had been scarecrow-thin when she first knew him, but it seemed Paul had seen him in a far worse state.

"I love it when you look at me like that," he said, turning back to her and deftly removing her cotton nightdress. "It's almost as though you've never seen me before."

"I never tire of looking at you." The night was warm, and she lay back naked against the pillow allowing him to admire her equally trim body. "I'd do anything for you, Schatz," she told him.

His hands froze in mid-caress.

"What's the matter? Did I say something wrong?" With relief she saw he was smiling.

"No. But today different people keep saying the same things to me. It's ... strange, that's all."

Katherine misunderstood. "Who else said they'd do anything for you? Not Margit, surely?"

"No, no. She was talking about Lotti doing anything for Siegfried. And Paul said Ilse would do anything for him."

"Ah." Katherine smiled wickedly. "Siegfried's a bit of a lad, isn't he? I can understand just how Lotti feels." She reached up and put her arms around his neck, pulling his mouth down to hers, effectively ending the conversation.

*

Siegfried stood on the lake edge feeling frustrated. He cursed his impotence to hurt his father. It was hopeless. While Paul still looked on Karl as a comrade, there seemed little Siegfried could do at the moment to harm him, without causing unwelcome problems for Paul as a result. Although Paul had not mentioned the incident on the lake, there had been a studied look from him over breakfast which warned Siegfried to tread carefully. Paul was suspicious, if unwilling to condemn outright.

Idly he bent down and picked up a flat pebble. With a flick of his wrist he sent it skimming across the water. The stone bounced four times, then sank. It gave Siegfried hope. He might need time and patience to destroy his father, but somehow he would succeed. The chief obstacle in his path was Paul's protection. If he could only get that withdrawn, he would have a free hand.

He saw his mother on a deckchair by the veranda, reading a novel. Paul must be in his study. The Drieslers had taken the Röbel children on a boat trip on the Danube. Now might be a good time to do some investigative groundwork. He sidled up to her.

"Good book?"

Ilse laid it on the table beside her. "Not especially. I can't seem to get into it."

Siegfried sat down on the daisy-covered lawn by her feet and pulled the heads off several flowers. He allowed a decent length of time to pass before broaching the subject on his mind.

"It must be strange having my father here to stay; especially since you were once so close to him," he said, staring out over the lake to avoid her eye.

"Not really. It was a long time ago."

"Eight years is not so very long," he said artfully.

"Eight? More like ... oh, I see what you're referring to. That day in the burnt-out church in Dortmund." She smiled ruefully at the memory. "I suppose I did want him back then. But I've got Paul now, haven't I, Schatz?"

Now Siegfried looked calculatingly at her. "Did you call my father 'Schatz' first, or him you? He uses the same for Katherine, you know?"

"Yes, I know. I've heard him."

Siegfried tried to decide whether she sounded jealous or not, but he could not tell. "Well?" he asked. "Was it him or you?"

Ilse leaned back in her deckchair, remembering her youth with Karl. "It was him."

"How did you meet?" Siegfried prompted. While his mother was in reflective mood he would pump her for all the information he could get. Something might prove useful. He noticed his mother's eyes glaze in dreamy recollection.

"It was outside a butcher's shop." Ilse paused to look at her son. His sudden interest in Karl was welcome. Perhaps he finally wanted to get to know his father better. She would tell him everything there was to know.

"So did he ask you out, or what?" Siegfried asked impatiently.

"Well, we got talking. He remarked I was a stranger to Medebach, and I told him I'd come from Hamburg to help in the kindergarten. He asked me if I had time for a coffee, so off we went. We spent every afternoon of Karl's leave together before he was sent to Norway. Then after that we wrote to each other. It was months before we saw each other again, but when we did, we both knew we had fallen in love through our letters."

Siegfried did not interrupt her again. Hard facts were what he wanted, not sickly-sweet reminiscing, but he let her take her own pace now.

In her eagerness to convey her feelings, Ilse suddenly grasped her son's arm. "You can't imagine how proud I was when he was made an officer, Siegfried. Shortly after that he was awarded the Iron

222

Cross, First Class for rescuing about fifty men pinned-down by a Russian machine-gun post somewhere on the Russian Front. All Medebach congratulated me when we heard the news, even though we were also told he'd been wounded. I was thrilled when he was sent home for convalescence and an officer-training course. We had a few days together then, over the Easter of 1943. He looked wonderful in his officer's uniform. I paraded him up and down the length of Medebach. I'll never forget that Easter." A smile spread over her face, and she lowered her eyes decorously. "That's when you were conceived. We planned to marry when he next came home on leave."

Her voice dropped wistfully, and Siegfried felt threatened by her emotion. So far he had heard nothing he could foreseeably use against his father.

"I didn't see him again," she continued. "Not until I handed you over to his care in Winterberg."

It seemed she had come to the end of her reminiscing, but Siegfried was impatient to hear more. "So what exactly did he do to end up in the labour camp?" he demanded. "You've never told me."

"You never asked!" Ilse laughed, but instantly grew more sombre. She reached for the lemon juice on the table but did not drink, simply holding the cool glass in her hand while she struggled to answer his question in a manner least damaging to Karl.

"Paul found out all this while arranging Karl's release from the labour camp. Basically it was because Karl fell foul of a particular SS officer when he was serving in Yugoslavia. He refused to obey the man's order."

This was more like it, Siegfried thought eagerly. "What was the order?"

Ilse looked uncomfortable. "To torture a Partisan woman for information, apparently. He obeyed the first time the order was given, but refused the second. Paul says he'd been seriously injured and maltreated by some Partisans who captured him and was too weak to obey the order a second time. He should have still been in hospital, not being made to torture people. If I'd known that I wouldn't have been so quick to condemn him. Anyway, as a result, he was dishonourably discharged by the Wehrmacht – under pressure from the SS – then was promptly re-arrested and taken to Dachau."

Ilse finally took a sip of her drink. Siegfried saw her tension. There was more to tell.

"What happened to him at Dachau was terrible, Siegfried. I can hardly bear to tell you about it, but Paul assures me it's true."

Ilse's voice was breaking with emotion. She cleared her throat. "Standartenführer Goslar, the man whose order Karl refused to obey, sent Karl to be used in certain experiments at Dachau. He was given injections of various drugs, all of which had nasty or painful effects. Even after the experiments were complete, Goslar's interest in Karl did not stop. He wanted to ensure Karl would obey any order, so he had a doctor there give Karl an addictive drug for a week or two. While on leave himself from Yugoslavia, Goslar called at Dachau to test his own experiment."

She took another sip of her drink and swallowed hard. She was finding this very painful to recount even though she was so remote from it all herself. For Siegfried's sake she persevered in her narrative.

"Karl was then deprived of the drug he craved. When Goslar told him he could only have some more if he did exactly as he was told, Karl complied."

Siegfried saw her clasp her hands so tightly, the knuckles whitened. Here it comes, he thought.

Totally unaware of her son's relish, Ilse forced herself to reveal the worst. "He was made to assault and mutilate a number of Jewish inmates. Goslar seemed to relish the power he had over Karl, because he could see how bitterly Karl struggled to resist obeying the orders. Karl was a slave to his own body, so Paul says. The addiction was so strong, Karl would do anything to be allowed another injection."

Siegfried was enthralled. His own father a drug-addict and torturer of women and Jews! Yet he made himself out to have such high moral values! What a hypocrite!

Ilse did not notice his excitement, and continued in her efforts to win Siegfried's sympathy for his father. "When Goslar left, Karl was given no more drugs. He suffered terrible withdrawal symptoms as he gradually shook off his addiction. In poor physical and mental health by now, he was sent to the labour camp. Paul says it's a measure of how supremely fit Karl was to start with that he survived the whole experience – from being captured and tortured by the Partisans, the experiments at Dachau, to the deprivations of the labour camp. He would certainly have died in that camp if Paul had not found out the truth and got him out."

Siegfried was hardly listening any more. Ideas were tumbling into his mind.

CHAPTER SEVENTEEN

The strut of the folding table would not budge. Margit hit it with the flat of her hand but still it would not shift.

"Here. Let me help you," Karl offered.

Siegfried saw Margit's usual blush when his father spoke to her, but he knew she would do nothing. She was too young and shy. Useless. But tonight at the farewell party something would happen; something that would make his father wish they'd never come!

He set another chair in position by a table on the lawn as his mother called across to Karl.

"Those lights need hanging from the veranda." Ilse pointed to an untidy heap of coloured glass lanterns and tangled flex, like a mass of spaghetti with peppers and tomatoes thrown in. "Siegfried will help you with them."

Without a word Siegfried joined his father in the task of unravelling the spaghetti to find the end with the plug.

"Whoever took this down last ought to be shot," Siegfried said after finally finding the plug deep within a knot of flex.

"A bit extreme, maybe, but you can make a better job of stowing it away tomorrow." Karl stretched the flex along the veranda as Siegfried eased the fragile lanterns from the pile. "We'd better test the bulbs before we hang them up. Where's the nearest socket?"

"Dining room. We usually put an extension lead through the window."

Karl waited for Siegfried to offer to find it, but he made no move.

"Where is it?"

"What?"

"The extension lead."

Siegfried shrugged. "Ask Paul," he said and walked off to help his mother who was struggling with a hamper full of tablecloths and napkins.

Karl smothered his frustration at his son's lack of help and went inside to Paul's study. It was at the front of the lodge, away from the noise and distractions of the garden. Paul was on the phone when Karl entered.

"You'll phone back with those figures this evening, or you're fired, Reimann. I need them today!" Paul slammed down the receiver, then noticed Karl hovering by the door. "Come on in, Karl."

"Sorry to disturb you, Paul." He approached Paul's desk.

"No problem. I'll be with you in a tick. Just let me jot something down before I forget." He scribbled notes from his phone call. Karl picked up a glass paperweight with a view of the Brandenburg Gate in its base. He had walked through the Gate once while passing through Berlin. He wondered if he ever would again.

Paul put down his pen. "Right! I can't do anything now until that idiot rings back." He held up a heavy file of architect's drawings and building specifications. "This tender for a new sports hall has to be in by next Tuesday. That moron I was just speaking to was supposed to have prepared the estimated materials requirements, but he claims everyone's on holiday and he can't get the figures. If he hadn't put off doing it until after his own holiday, there'd have been no problem." He dropped the file with a thud onto papers spattered with calculations. "I've been working flat out today doing half his job as well as my own. I told him to get off his arse and make a nuisance of himself until he has the information we need."

Karl put down the paperweight and sat on the edge of Paul's desk. "I know what you mean. I remember trying to get hold of a mechanic on Cup Final day."

"It's tough at the top, isn't it? Oh for the simple life when all we had to do was obey orders."

"And survive frostbite one day so we could be incinerated by flame-throwers the next. Yes. Those were the days. Do you still miss them, Paul?"

Paul ignored the sarcasm. "To be quite honest: yes. But I know your views so I'll not bore you with further reminiscing. How are the preparations going? I'm sorry I can't be of much use out there."

"Don't worry. Ilse's got us all under control. I came to ask you where the extension lead for the party lights was kept."

"Wonderful woman, isn't she? I'm so grateful she never married you. I suppose I have to be thankful to Katherine for getting in there first. Is she enjoying herself here? She seems very quiet."

"She usually is."

"Each to his own, I suppose."

Karl idly ran his forefinger over the paperweight. "She's what I need. She keeps me sane."

Paul thought Karl was joking. "Sane! I would go mad with someone as quiet as that! Ilse's certainly no shrinking violet."

Karl smiled, keeping his eyes on the paperweight. "I'm perfectly happy with Katherine as she is. In fact I wouldn't want her any different. She's like the horizon – usually level and always there. I know exactly where I am with her. That way she keeps me level too." He looked back at his friend. "Now, where's that extension lead, Paul?"

Paul was surprised by Karl's comments, so unlike the man he once knew. He had never been one for wanting to keep level before. Even more startling was Karl's reference to his sanity. It betrayed a vulnerability not evident from casual conversation. Interesting. Worth probing further. While these thoughts raced through Paul's head, he answered Karl's question.

"There's a store room next to the garage. It's probably in there. Get Siegfried to find it."

"He sent me to you."

Definite antipathy there still, Paul observed. He decided to delve deeper. "How are things going between you two now? Any better?"

"No."

"Ilse told me she'd explained all about Dachau and the rest to Siegfried. That hasn't made any difference?"

Karl made to speak then closed his mouth again. He studied his fingers then finally spoke. "I know I agreed he should be told, but I wasn't expecting it to be so soon. He certainly hasn't let on he knows. No sympathy or lessening of antagonism."

"Old habits die hard. Give him time. He may mellow."

"I doubt it." Karl stood up abruptly. "I'd better go and find that lead or Ilse will think I'm skiving. I hope your figures come through."

"Thanks. So do I, or I won't enjoy the party." Paul sat staring at the closed door after Karl had gone. He had the distinct impression Karl had problems with Dachau. A pity.

*

Paul's threat to Reimann paid off and he was able to complete the tender before the guests arrived at eight. About thirty were expected, mostly from the nearby town. For the first time ever Siegfried was allowed to attend, but the other children were obliged to remain upstairs, having been promised a midnight feast in recompense. They could watch the party from the balconies.

From the lawn Katherine waved up to Richard in his pyjamas, then sipped at her champagne. It was a perfect evening. The light breeze of earlier had died down, and the ducks on the lake were giving a few desultory quacks before settling down for the night. The veranda lights gave a warm glow over the dozen guests standing there, as Lotti dispensed cocktails. Katherine breathed in deeply, relishing the scents of expensive perfumes, flowers and the natural freshness of the forest around the lodge. Her tranquillity was soon disturbed by Ilse laughing loudly amongst a group she remembered as comprising a local wine merchant, his wife, an artist whose landscapes were dotted around the lodge, and a couple whose occupation she had not understood. Ilse saw her loitering and beckoned her in to join the circle, but Katherine found the conversation impossible to follow. The Bavarian dialect was just too broad. Even Ilse had trouble occasionally. After a while Katherine drifted off to find Karl. She didn't like to seem an inseparable part of him, but at least he could translate when necessary.

As she moved across the grass in search of him, a young man approached her from the shadows of the unlit garden.

"You seem alone," he said in English.

Katherine paused. He was a bit older than Siegfried. Nearer twenty, she guessed, although probably invited as company for him. His mid-brown hair fell in a sweeping curve over his forehead, while luminous blue eyes reflected the rays of the setting sun. The contrasting depths of his pupils drew Katherine closer, like a whirlpool. She blinked to break the spell.

"Yes. I was just looking for my husband. I'm afraid I don't speak very good German. It's a relief to find someone who speaks my language."

"Let me introduce myself then, Frau Driesler, and hopefully I can entertain you for a while. I'm Ulrich Waiger, student of law when I finish my national service."

"I'm pleased to meet you, Herr Waiger. Are you a friend of Siegfried?"

"Yes. I always see him when his family comes here for the summer. He's told me about his English family." His words gave no hint to Katherine of what exactly he had been told. He pointed to her empty glass. "Can I get you another?"

"Thank you. That's very kind."

Ulrich Waiger took her glass and hurried to the veranda where Lotti manned the drinks. He gave a wink as he handed the glass over and she nodded in reply. Turning her back on the garden she poured a generous measure of vodka into the glass before topping it up with champagne. Ulrich smiled, had his own glass refilled with champagne only, then returned to the lawn, where Katherine stood waiting.

"Cheers."

Katherine raised her glass in reply. "Cheers. So you want to study law," she prompted.

Ulrich launched into details of his career plans and followed it up with amusing anecdotes from his national service. He was a lively and entertaining speaker but took care not to dominate the conversation. He gradually drew Katherine out, getting her to reveal what life in England was like. As she emptied her glass, Katherine ceased worrying that Karl was not with her. He was in the middle of a group on the veranda, which included Siegfried, and seemed well ensconced in the conversation. She was content to leave him in peace so he could chat freely without having to translate every so often. Ulrich was a charming companion, and had not bored her yet.

While he was away fetching a refill, Katherine realised the champagne was going to her head rather too quickly, and she decided she must slow down. The food, a cold buffet, was just being brought out onto the tables so guests could help themselves when they felt like it. Katherine knew she ought to eat something as soon as possible to soak up the alcohol.

Ulrich arrived back with her glass. "I must tell you about the poor chap in my platoon whose mother keeps sending him strange parcels."

Ulrich launched into his narrative, and Katherine took an unintentionally large sip of her drink.

"But then we all realised it was only a sausage!"

Katherine burst out laughing, then choked. Ulrich began to thump her on the back. His hand lingered there, even after her coughing had subsided.

"Would you like to sit down?" he asked.

Katherine's head was starting to spin rather worryingly. "Yes. That's a good idea." She did not fancy walking over to the buffet now. She had a horrible suspicion she would stagger. She stepped cautiously over to one of the chairs she and Sabina had positioned under the sweet chestnut tree. As she sat, the chair legs dug into the grass and she nearly fell off. Ulrich lunged forward and steadied her, his hands gently gripping her shoulders even after she had regained her balance.

*

Siegfried kept his father engaged in conversation with the group on the veranda while keeping an eye on Ulrich's performance. He saw Katherine nearly fall off her chair, and later, when they were joined by Ilse and the artist, he heard their raucous laughter. So far so good, he thought, blocking Karl's movement towards his wife with a suggestion that it was time they ate. As he loaded his plate with cold cuts of venison and boar, potato salad and gherkins, Siegfried stole another glance at the group by the sweet chestnut. The wine was flowing freely. Katherine was giggling uncontrollably.

"Keep it up, Ulrich," he murmured.

At midnight Lotti took some food upstairs for the children, then wandered round the grounds, topping up guests' drinks. Frau Driesler seemed to be enjoying herself at last. It had taken the whole week for her to lose her prim and proper English ways. Lotti grinned as she heard Frau Zopf suggest a swim in the lake. This was the usual climax to the Zopfs' parties.

The shaggy-haired artist was the first to strip off. He was a regular guest each year and knew the form. His gleaming white buttocks disappeared into the dark water, closely followed by Ilse, whose sinuous black dress had slipped off her shoulders and over her hips as if by a single shrug. She wore nothing underneath to hinder her progress into the water.

"Coming?" Ulrich asked Katherine.

Katherine hesitated. She felt rather hot from all the wine, and the water looked inviting, but to strip off down to the flesh ...

Ulrich had taken off his tie and was busy unbuttoning his shirt. More and more guests were discarding their clothing, though by no means everyone. Paul Zopf remained on the shore, watching his wife cavorting with the artist. A few ladies also refrained.

"Come on. You English are so shy!" Ulrich taunted, stepping out of his underpants.

That decided her. "When in Rome ..." she giggled, reaching behind her neck to unzip her dress. The zip caught half way down. "Bother! Can you help me, Ulrich?" She turned her back on him. In front of her stood Karl. "Oh! You made me jump. Can you help me, Schatz?" She turned again. Ulrich was already making off towards the lake.

Karl tugged the zip back up. "I don't think you should swim, Katherine. You've had more to drink than you realise."

Katherine spun round, stumbling as she did so. "Don't be a spoil sport!" She brushed away Karl's steadying arm, as if to prove she was sober, but her slurred speech betrayed her further. "Everyone else is having fun, so why can't I?"

"Because they're not as ... tipsy as you are." He hesitated to use the word 'drunk', but Katherine picked up on it.

"What makes you think I'm drunk? When have you ever seen me drunk?" she demanded.

"Now. I'm serious, Katherine. I don't want you to swim." He tried to lead her away from the lake but she gaily flung aside his hand.

"Try and stop me!" Katherine made a dash for the lake. If she couldn't take her dress off, she would jolly well swim with it on.

Karl easily caught her. "Don't be stupid," he hissed, trying not to create a disturbance. "You'll drown in that dress."

"Well help me off with it, then!"

Karl had never seen her on such a high. Usually after a drink or two she just grew sleepy. Short of throwing her over his shoulder and locking her in their room, there was nothing he could do. She was too far gone to reason with. Perhaps the cold water would sober her up. Angrily he spun her round to undo the zip.

"Your watch!" he reminded her as she cast off her underwear.

Karl stuffed her watch into his pocket, then hurried to remove his own clothing. He did not intend leaving her alone in the water.

*

From the balcony the Driesler children watched the scene below in amazement. The Zopf children had seen the water frolics before.

"Why's Siegfried not swimming yet?" Margit asked. "I'd have thought he would be first in."

"He's too busy watching Frau Driesler," Heinrich answered without removing his head from between the balcony rails.

All eyes swung to the chestnut tree.

"Daddy's trying to stop her undressing!" Sabina gasped. "He looks really angry."

"Your mother's won," Heinrich said, as if commenting on a boxing match.

The children watched open-mouthed as first Katherine, then Karl undressed and disappeared into the water.

"Why's no one wearing a bathing costume?" Paul asked.

Heinrich sniggered, but Margit tried to explain. "It's the tradition at my mother's parties. They wear masks for Carnival, nothing at all for summer swimming."

"Oh." He seemed satisfied with that explanation, but Sabina was worried by all the nudity. Her parents, especially her father, had a relaxed attitude towards it at home, but seeing so many people naked she found a little disturbing.

"I think we ought to go to bed," she said. "It's very late."

"Not on your nelly!" Richard objected. "I want to watch what happens."

"Well I think Paul should certainly be in bed. Come on, Paul. I'll tuck you in."

"Ohhhh. I want Mummy to."

"Mummy's busy."

"And drunk," Richard added with a smirk.

Sabina scowled at him, then grabbed Paul's hand and led him off to bed. If Mummy and Daddy are going to make fools of themselves, I don't want to see it, she thought, as she pulled the covers over Paul. To her surprise, Margit came through with her younger sisters.

"You're right, Sabina. We all ought to be in bed. Sleep well."

"What about Richard and Heinrich?"

"They said they're just coming. There's not much to see, now everyone's in the water."

Nevertheless, Sabina went out to the balcony again. The two boys were watching intently.

*

Karl trod water ten metres off shore. The water was cool and under other circumstances he would have enjoyed a midnight swim in the nude. He could not allow his thoughts to wander, however, and kept a sharp eye on Katherine. She was swimming just within her depth at the moment, but Ulrich was edging further out and she seemed eager to follow. Karl noticed Siegfried in the water at last, and immediately felt doubly anxious. His fears were soon justified.

"Let's swim out to the diving platform," Siegfried suggested to Ulrich. "Coming, Katherine?"

In her present euphoric state, Karl knew she would not refuse. Sure enough she began to follow.

"Damn!" He trailed behind, keeping out of her vision, but able to hear her breathing become more and more ragged, with the occasional splutter as she swallowed a mouthful. To a strong swimmer, the distance of a hundred and fifty metres was nothing, but Katherine was not a strong swimmer, and she was drunk. As Karl expected, a race was on between Siegfried and Ulrich. Katherine was left far behind. Karl cast a glance behind him. No one else was attempting to swim out this far. No. He was wrong. Another head bobbed along some distance behind, swimming smoothly and evenly. It was too dark out here to see who it was, apart from the glint of moonlight on wet hair. Karl concentrated back on Katherine. Her speed had dropped right down. She was hardly moving. He surged forward and drew alongside.

"All right, Schatz?"

She turned her head and he saw she was in an unreal world, unaware of her danger. Her mouth filled with water as she ceased swimming. Karl made a grab for her and kicked hard to keep them both above water.

"Float on your back," he commanded, but she only swallowed more water and began to choke. Karl grabbed her shoulders, flipped her over and cupped his right hand under her chin so she floated. "Relax, Schatz, I've got you."

She was still choking, but his reassurance seemed to do the trick. She coughed, gulped, then breathed freely. He felt her let herself float. Karl was now facing the shore. It was further away than the diving platform. They had better carry on. He began to tow her towards it. Katherine lay quite happily. It was unnatural.

They reached the diving platform at last. Ulrich leaned over the edge to pull Katherine out of the water. She lay on the canvas surface a moment, a beached white whale, then slowly sat up. As she did so, Karl hoisted himself up beside her. Their eyes met, hers dreamy and full of stars.

Karl looked menacingly up at Ulrich and Siegfried. The platform bobbed unsteadily beneath his feet as he stood to confront the two young men. "You nearly drowned my wife. *You*," he pointed accusingly at Ulrich, "have spent the whole evening deliberately getting her drunk. I think you doctored her drinks, just to make sure." He then jabbed a finger in Siegfried's chest. "And it was *your* idea."

Siegfried grinned insolently, then turned to Ulrich. "My father has this complex. He thinks I'm out to harm people all the time. I don't know where he gets that idea from! It's his wife's fault if she doesn't know her limitations."

Karl was furious. "You deliberately led her on, then left her swimming on her own while you showed off in front of her."

Siegfried just laughed." We're not her keepers. She's old enough to look after herself."

His refusal to accept responsibility enraged Karl. Still taller than his son by half a head, he stepped right up close. "You're evil," he said through gritted teeth. "You enjoy hurting other people. Don't you."

Siegfried stood his ground, head tilted back arrogantly meeting his father's blazing eyes. A smile curved his lips. "Me? Hurt other people? That's rich coming from you, the torturer of women!"

The accusation struck home. As if in reflex, Karl's fist shot up and caught Siegfried under the jaw. Siegfried went sprawling across the canvas and almost over the edge of the platform. Before he could recover, Karl was over him, hauling him up to deliver another blow, but Ulrich went to Siegfried's aid. He slammed a fist into Karl's back, then pulled his right arm into an arm lock while Siegfried scrambled to his feet. Realising the double threat, Karl tried to kick Siegfried over the edge. Siegfried stumbled again, but saved himself. He saw Ulrich had his father pinioned, but Karl's free hand was groping for Ulrich's genitals. Ulrich let out a yell and bent double, hands over his groin.

"If you can fight dirty, I can too!" Siegfried growled. Side-stepping his father, he jumped down hard on the rocking platform. Katherine, who was sitting oblivious to the fighting, toppled over the edge with a splash. Karl rushed to the side to haul her out, but Siegfried blocked him. They both fell on the canvas, wrestling to gain supremacy, fighting with every portion of their bodies. Knees, elbows, teeth and feet made contact as Siegfried tried to hold his father down, while Karl fought madly for release to rescue Katherine. Although Karl had age against him, he had physique, experience and fear for Katherine on his side. His fingers reached for Siegfried's windpipe, digging deep into his throat. Siegfried faltered as he realised his danger. His father would kill him. Where was Ulrich? His arms began to flail in desperation, but he could not get a grip on his father's wet skin. His eyes bulged and blackness was creeping in around the edges of his vision until he saw Ulrich's face over his father's shoulder. Suddenly the grip on his throat lessened and air poured into his lungs. Giving himself only a moment to recover, he got to his haunches then lunged at his father.

"Siegfried! Stop!"

Dimly Siegfried heard his mother's voice, but it did not penetrate his rage. He kneed his father in the kidneys, only vaguely aware of his mother's insistent screams. Ulrich began to back off, enabling Karl to shove Siegfried aside.

"Stop it! All of you!" Ilse shouted again.

Through his gasping breath, Siegfried finally heard her. He went down on one knee to catch his breath, keeping an eye on his father who seemed to be doing the same.

"Ulrich, help me with Frau Driesler," Ilse commanded.

Ulrich shuffled over to where Ilse was supporting Katherine in the water. Once again he hauled her onto the platform. Ilse followed, scowling first at Siegfried, then at Karl. To Siegfried she looked like a

Rhine Maiden, her heaving breasts shrouded by her dripping blonde hair. He smiled fondly.

"Wipe that silly grin off your face and go and get the boat," Ilse said. "Quickly!" she snapped, seeing Siegfried's reluctance.

He shrugged and dived into the water without a backward glance at his father or Katherine.

Ilse watched him swim powerfully back to the shore while Karl went to Katherine's side. She seemed lethargic still, and he put his arms round her, holding her cold body close to his to warm her. Ulrich kept a safe distance.

Satisfied Siegfried was returning with the boat, Ilse knelt down by Karl. "So why were you two trying to kill each other?"

"It's obvious, isn't it? Look what he's done to Katherine. She's drugged and he intended her to drown."

"Drugged? What makes you say that? She's drunk. Purely and simply drunk. You can't blame Siegfried. No wonder he wanted a go at you!"

He guessed there was no point in arguing. He had no proof Katherine was drugged, unless Ulrich cared to confess. "It's just as well we're leaving tomorrow. I couldn't have stayed any longer after tonight. I'm sorry, but I don't think we'll be coming back, Ilse. Not the way things are."

Ilse grasped his shoulder. "But what about the children? Margit and Sabina are getting on so well together. They're good friends now."

He nodded. "True. It would be a shame to break them up. Margit's welcome to visit us in England whenever she likes."

Ilse smiled her relief. She couldn't bear to break all links with Karl. Sitting naked with him in the moonlight, even though his arms held his wife, not her, Ilse could dream of what might have been. She had noticed the long scars on his back, which told of events since Siegfried's conception. She ran her fingers lightly over the raised lines.

"Yugoslavia?"

He nodded slightly, wary of her touch. In his arms, Katherine stirred. Thankful for the distraction, Karl spoke to her. "Katherine. Can you hear me?"

She smiled, her eyes still half-closed. She wriggled, turning to nestle more comfortably against his chest. There was a clattering of oars in rowlocks as Siegfried arrived by the platform.

"All ashore!" he called cheerily.

Karl was astonished. How could Siegfried be so flippant? He was acting as though nothing had happened. To cap it all, he had even brought towels for them all. Karl wrapped Katherine in one and carefully lowered her into the boat. Siegfried tried to help but Karl would have none of it, not trusting him an inch.

Once on dry ground, Karl carried Katherine through the watchful guests into the lodge and upstairs. Richard and Sabina were anxiously waiting on the landing and followed him into the bedroom.

"Is Mummy all right?" they demanded simultaneously, as he laid her on the bed.

Karl tucked his own towel more securely round his waist as he began to dry Katherine's hair with another. "She's fine. Just overtired. She tried to swim to the raft and couldn't make it. You go on back to bed."

"But you were fighting with Siegfried and another man, Daddy," Sabina said. "Look, you're bleeding." She pointed to his elbow.

"It's only a graze. Now go on. Off you go. Mummy needs to sleep. I'll explain in the morning." He could see the burning questions on their faces, but they did as they were told. As they shut the door he sighed. Now Siegfried knew his history there was nothing to stop him blathering a distorted version of it to the others. He would have to tell the children everything, sooner than he would have liked.

There was a knock at the door.

"Who is it?"

"Lotti, Herr Driesler. Frau Zopf sent me up with some hot chocolate for you. And your clothes."

He was tempted to tell her to go away. He had no doubts she was part of Siegfried's scheme, but the chocolate would be welcome. He opened the door, not allowing her in, and took the clothing and mug from her without a word.

As he drank his chocolate, Karl sat on the bed watching over Katherine. She seemed to be asleep now. There was no point in him returning to the party. Sounds of car engines told him the guests were leaving. He exchanged the towel for a dressing gown and stepped out onto the landing, heading for the bathroom.

On his way back he met Siegfried, now fully clothed, making his way to his room. They both stopped, blocking each other's paths.

"I could happily kill you right now, Siegfried," Karl whispered, fists involuntarily clenched.

"That makes two of us," Siegfried smiled back. He took a step back and bowed. "After you, Vater."

"Do you mean shall I kill you first, or are you just letting me past?" Karl's voice was low but menacing.

"Take it as you will."

Siegfried's cocksure self-control allowed Karl to regain a measure of his. Without another word he stepped past his son and into his room, shutting the door quietly behind him. He took off his dressing gown and got into bed beside Katherine. She did not stir, despite his restless tossing and turning the remainder of the night.

*

Katherine opened her eyes slowly. She quickly shut them again. Her head felt like it had been hit with a lump of lead. She lay still a while, feeling her pulse pound inside her skull. There was a click as the door opened and someone sat on the bed beside her. She opened one eye. Karl was there, fully dressed.

"Oh, it's you, Schatz. What time is it?"

"Ten o'clock. I thought you might like some aspirin."

"Please." She saw he had some ready and waiting. He must have known she would have a hangover. "I think I drank too much last night," she said, swallowing the tablets down with large gulps of water.

"You could say that," he replied. "Do you remember what happened?"

Katherine blinked as both eyes opened. "That sounds ominous." She rubbed her forehead gingerly. "No. I don't. What happened?"

"You went swimming. Remember?"

"No." She struggled to sit up, but her head persuaded her to abandon the attempt.

"Then I'd better tell you before you hear it all from the children."

Katherine's eyes grew round with horror as he related the events of the night to her. "But I don't remember a thing! How could I have swum out there and nearly drowned without remembering. I can't have drunk that much! Schatz, whatever must everyone think of me. The children!"

"They've got more on their minds than last night, I'm afraid. I've spent the last half hour with the children telling them the horrors of my past to forestall any more attempts by Siegfried to shatter my family. The sooner we leave here, the better," he added, "before I do kill him."

Katherine's head was not ready to cope with such dramas. "So you've told our lot everything. Even little Paul?"

"Even little Paul." He pulled her dressing gown over the bed towards her. "Come on, Schatz. I'm afraid you'll have to make a move. We've got a train to catch."

*

The train puffed steadily north towards Frankfurt, past acre upon acre of vineyards. Sabina stared past her reflection, eyes fixed on the alien landscape, her mind elsewhere. Richard too had his mind on other matters.

"I bet Siegfried and Lotti are already at it in the boathouse," he whispered to his sister from behind his hand.

Sabina was shocked. "Richard! Who told you that?"

"Heinrich. He said Siegfried and Lotti often –"

"Shut up, idiot. Paul's listening."

"No he's not. He's asleep."

Sabina looked beside her. Sure enough, Paul was curled up with his head on his mother's lap. She too was fast asleep, her head lolling to the rhythm of the train. Not wanting to disturb them, Sabina refrained from further conversation. Besides, she wanted to think about what their father had told them that morning. It had all bounced off Richard and Paul. They were too young to fully understand the horror of their father's shame. They had found the tales of torture exciting rather than nauseating as she had.

Poor Daddy! She noticed his reflection beyond hers and focused on it. He had found it very difficult to tell them about his past, and she sensed he had held back on some details. Perhaps they were just too awful to talk about. Now his mind seemed far away and he looked so sad. She remembered other occasions when he'd had the same doleful expression. She would know why in future, and would make sure she tried to cheer him up. In fact she would do it now. She moved across to the corner where he sat and cuddled up to him.

"I love you, Daddy."

He turned in surprise at her sudden display of affection and smiled. "I love you too, treasure."

They sat with their arms round each other, Sabina watching his reflection. The sadness was gone.

CHAPTER EIGHTEEN

There was to be no return to normal upon their return from holiday. Robert, Alice and their two boys were staying another week at Lane Head Farm rather than burden themselves on Gertie, who was beginning to suffer from arthritis. She and Donald came up to the farm most days to see their grandsons, making the most of Donald's recent retirement from general practice.

Shortly after their arrival home, Karl sought out Robert to go for a stroll through the fruit-laden orchards, accompanied by the ageing Meg and the latest dog, Fly. Ostensibly it was to check all was well with the farm, but Robert suspected Karl needed to talk. He waited patiently until the right moment to discover what was on his mind.

They had already passed through one orchard and exchanged news before the moment came.

"I don't know what we'd do without you lot," Karl told Robert. "I doubt we'd ever get to Germany if you didn't farm-sit for us."

"I keep telling you, Karl. We love it. It's a cheap holiday for us. I spend all my time in my office seeing patients, hardly ever getting out into the fresh air; and with only a small garden in Edinburgh to run around in, the boys think this place is heaven. Helping with the animals gives them a sense of responsibility, and we all get plenty of exercise into the bargain. It's perfect!"

"Well, as long as you're happy, I know we are." Karl reached out and cradled a James Grieves apple in his palm. It would not be ripe for another month or so yet.

"Are you? Happy, I mean?" Robert paused to lean his elbows on a gate to the adjacent meadow, where a flock of black-faced sheep stood like giant shaggy ink-caps.

Karl came over and leaned on the gate next to him. "It's no wonder you're a psychiatrist, Robert. You've got a great nose for sniffing out problems."

"Well, I do try to keep a special nose out for you. I smell trouble and it begins with an 'S', I think."

The sheep began to bleat at the sight of the dogs, anticipating activity of some kind. Karl's eyes roved over them, checking for signs of ill-health or lameness. "He always has been trouble," he replied distractedly.

"Come on, Karl. Open up. I shouldn't need to tell you that."

Karl turned his back on the flock, satisfied with their condition, and leaned against the gate. He looked sideways at Robert. "He frightens me. I can't understand his mentality. Sometimes he's friendly enough, as though nothing were wrong. Other times he's close to killing me with his bare hands, and yet a few minutes later he's all politeness again. I don't know how he switches so quickly from one to the other. I certainly can't."

"You mean you're close to killing him all the time?"

"Very perceptive."

"Well, it's not difficult to see. Just talking about him your fists are clenching."

Karl relaxed his hands. "I had hoped, now he's older and wiser, things would be better between us. I was wrong. There is a menace to him. He plots and schemes, always in control, taking things just far enough not to annoy his stepfather. I think that keeps the lid on him and prevents him from murdering me outright." He kicked at a clod of earth almost as if it were Siegfried's head, Robert thought. Karl ground the earth with his boot until he was satisfied with its consistency, then, without looking up he continued his report. "Siegfried actually threatened me with a gun, you know? But he said he'd do nothing while I have Paul's protection. Do nothing! He tried to make Katherine drown!"

"Good Lord! Are you sure?"

"More or less, but it would be difficult to prove. When I confronted him about it, he just claimed I had a complex about him trying to harm people."

"Perhaps you do. Have you considered that?"

Karl turned back to the sheep. "I said, he threatened me with a gun. I didn't imagine that."

"No, but perhaps it's your attitude to him that made him do that."

Karl was silent. Robert laid a hand on his shoulder. "I know. I can't make any comments unless I've seen him myself. He was only young when I last saw him, and I must admit he was a scheming blighter then. We could all see it. You're probably correct in your assessment of him."

"I'm glad you agree. I wouldn't want you to think I was cracking up again."

"Katherine would soon tell me if you were. How are the nightmares these days? Under control?"

Karl nodded. "Reasonably. How about yours?"

"Fair." Robert grinned. "We're like two old women discussing our health." He grew more serious. "No, it's stomach problems I suffer with. The Japanese diet didn't agree with me."

Fly yawned with a loud squeak, making both men laugh. "I think he's telling us he's bored," Karl said. "Let's move on up to the rest of the flock." He opened the gate and they set off up the hill to the next gate leading into Steps Meadow. They began to hear the shrieks of children as they neared the house.

"They're certainly growing up quickly, aren't they?" Robert said. "Richard and Paul will be a great help to you. They seem interested in the farm."

"Yes. I'm very lucky. I've no problem getting them to work. Sabina too. She helped out with the lambing this year. I know I can depend on her to keep her eyes open. She's a poppet, she really is. Ever since I had to tell her about ... events of the past, she's been making a special effort to cheer me up. It's wonderful! She's just like her mother in that respect."

"She's quite a young lady now. Coming up to twelve next month, isn't she?" Robert had noticed Karl's dropped hint and casually asked: "What made you tell her?"

They had reached the top of the meadow and the last gate before the farm buildings. Before Karl could answer, five-year-old Stewart saw his father and raced over to him, whooping like a Red Indian. He was brandishing a plastic tomahawk, which he tried to bury in Robert's chest. Little Douglas was close behind, adorned by a pheasant's tail feather stuck in a corrugated card headband.

"We've caught you!" Stewart yelled. "We're taking you back to our camp to join our other prisoners."

"Well I hope the Lone Ranger comes to rescue us," Robert laughed, as he and Karl were hustled up to Siegfried's old camp in the old-man's-beard. There they found Sabina, the squaw, dressed in several chamois leathers, guarding two cowboy-hatted prisoners.

"You know, I usually feel sorry for the Indians in cowboy films," Karl whispered to Robert. "They're always the baddies."

"Except Tonto."

"No talking!" Douglas piped up, rapping his father's knees with a stick.

Richard and Paul grinned as the grown-ups had their hands inexpertly tied by Stewart. They had both already worked their hands loose, but kept them hidden behind them to play along with their young friends. Richard noticed the two dogs slumped down in the shade. "Wolves!" he yelled.

Stewart and Douglas went into a pretend panic, while Sabina single-handedly drove them off.

"Let's call a truce and smoke the pipe of peace," she suggested to her tribe.

Stewart stood with arms folded and scowled. "Quiet, squaw! Tonto and the Lone Ranger approach."

Everyone turned to see Katherine and Alice bearing trays of lemonade and biscuits up to the woods.

"Reinforcements at last!" Robert called to them.

"What was that about three and fourpence?" Alice called back.

Sabina set about freeing her father's hands, while Richard freed Robert. The game was over for the moment. They all sat in the sun at the edge of the woods overlooking the farm. Sabina had never felt so happy as she did now. Since their visit to the Zopfs, she had discovered a purpose in life: to protect her father from any more pain. Over the years she had heard him cry out in the night with his occasional nightmares. Now she understood and would do all she could to keep him happy. She reached over to the tray and passed him a glass of lemonade. Then she sat with her head on his arm, a smile of contentment on her face.

She caught Robert watching her. He had always been Daddy's protector, she realised. She smiled her thanks to him, hoping he would not mind her taking over the duty.

*

It was the first time Sabina had had to move out of her room for visitors. In the past, all the boys had crammed in together, Douglas still in a cot. Now it was easier and less chaotic at night to give

Stewart and Douglas Sabina's room. Sabina was to sleep on a camp bed in her parents' room. She changed into her nightdress and eased herself carefully into the new sleeping bag before reaching for her book. From the boys' rooms came the sounds of high jinx: tapping on the walls and creaking floorboards as one of the boys crept along the landing. Stewart, she guessed.

Five minutes later her mother came up to sort the boys out. Sabina heard the Murdoch boys being told to go back to their own room, then her mother's head popped round the door.

"All right, Bina? Are you comfortable?"

"Just about. I wouldn't want to always sleep on it." She wriggled further into the sleeping bag. "I can't imagine Daddy trying to fit on it when he first lived here. Is that why he went to sleep at Uncle Donald and Aunty Gertie's?"

Katherine sat on her own bed. "No. It was because your Grandad died and Daddy wasn't allowed to live up here after that."

"Why?"

Katherine cursed herself for not thinking before she spoke. She had made it sound as though Karl was responsible for her father's death. A proper explanation was required.

"We weren't married then. It's not considered proper for a man and woman to live alone together if they're not married."

Sabina thought about this for a moment. It seemed daft that her father had to walk for miles each day, when there was a bed for him at the farm.

"But why?"

Katherine sighed. Sabina was obviously not going to be fobbed off with make-do answers. The time had come to tell her the facts.

"We loved each other; and when a man and a woman love each other, they like to sleep together and make love. This is the way babies are made, and although you've seen the rams tupping the ewes often enough, for people there's far more to it than that. Or should be." She studied Sabina's face. Rapt attention. Good. "With people," she continued, "there must be the commitment of love and marriage before a child can be considered. There must be a loving home, food on the table. That is why people should not sleep together, or even live together, until they are married. We weren't allowed to get married then. Do you see?"

246

Sabina smiled, grateful that her mother had been so honest with her. "Yes. Thank you, Mummy."

"Right. Well it's late enough now, so no more reading. Good night, treasure."

After her mother had given her a kiss and turned off the light, Sabina lay awake, turning over in her mind all her mother had said. Fleetingly, her thoughts turned to herself. She could never do *that* with anyone. She tried to imagine her parents together in the double bed beside her. No image would come, but she did not feel the revulsion she had at the thought of herself with someone. Her parents loved each other, and that made it all right.

She had learned a lot in the last week about what it meant to be an adult. The revelations about her father's past had come as a shock. She also now understood what Heinrich had been hinting about between Siegfried and Lotti. And *they* weren't married! It only confirmed what a bad lot Siegfried was. But it also told her love was not necessary, only preferable. Siegfried loved nobody but himself.

When her parents crept into bed later that evening, Sabina pretended to be asleep. She waited, listening for sounds of activity, but apart from a whispered 'goodnight' and the sound of a quick kiss, there was silence.

Each subsequent night she lay awake, awaiting evidence of what her mother had told her went on between a man and his wife. To no avail. It was not until she was back in her own room, after the Murdochs' departure, that she heard, or thought she heard what she wanted to hear. Tiptoeing across the landing she stood listening outside their bedroom door. What she heard astonished her. At first she thought her father must be having one of his nightmares, but when her mother's muffled cries joined his, Sabina knew for sure. When all was quiet once more, she crept back to her own room, carefully avoiding the creaking floorboards.

Still the image of what had occurred eluded her. She lay in bed, pondering how different adults were from how she had always envisaged them. Especially her father.

He had killed people. Tortured them. How was it she could love him so much, knowing that?

Because he had been punished enough. He had gone mad with guilt. She shuddered at the thought. She must make life easier for him. Even mend his relationship with Siegfried, if she could.

The grandfather clock struck eleven. She was competing in a gymkhana tomorrow and really ought to be asleep. With a secret smile, she rolled over and closed her eyes.

*

Rain clouds shrouded Hay Bluff, but the sky remained blue over the paddocks at Froxley Grange. Sabina squinted against the sun as her mother tugged at her hair. "Why couldn't Daddy come with us? He comes to all the other gymkhanas."

Katherine finished plaiting Sabina's hair. Dressed in full riding kit of white shirt, tweed jacket, jodhpurs and boots, Sabina was eagerly following in her mother's footsteps.

"He's busy today." Katherine slipped an elastic band over the end of the plait and hoped it put an end to Sabina's questions.

"How is it he's always busy when the gymkhana's at Froxley Grange?"

Katherine turned her daughter round and straightened her tie. "If you've noticed the connection, then I think you know the answer, Bina."

"Because you married Daddy, not Mr Kellett?"

"More or less. Now off you go and check Sally's all ready, while I sort out the boys. You know Paul can't keep tidy from one moment to the next!"

Sabina ambled off to where her pony was tethered to a rail fence. The bay mare glistened, her tack spotless, tail and mane neatly plaited. She was as ready as she ever would be. Sabina stroked Sally's nose and thought about her father's exclusion from Froxley Grange. Only now did Sabina realise why she and her brothers were not invited to the Grange Christmas parties, when all the other village children were. It seemed particularly unfair since she had known Alex Kellett, the eldest child, ever since they both started competing in gymkhanas.

"I'll sort this out for Daddy," she told Sally. "I'll get the two families together somehow. They'll all see how childish they've been, then Daddy won't have to hide away from the Kelletts any more."

An announcement came over the public address system for her class to report. She fastened her riding hat and picked up her crop. Her mother hurried over to help her mount and check the girth, then

248

Sabina walked Sally over to the warm-up ring. Alex Kellett was already there on his powerful mount, Paris. Alex was no lightweight himself. Sabina smiled at him as they passed at a trot.

"Good luck, Alex!"

He was startled by her sudden greeting and had no chance to reply. She smiled as they passed again. Alex chose to ignore her. He had always been told to avoid the Drieslers because they were German. Their paths only crossed at gymkhanas anyway. Alex boarded at public school, while Sabina Driesler was due to start at the local grammar. He only knew that because he remembered hearing his father comment about it to his mother, when Alex's end of term report was so poor. "We spend all that money on his education, and where's it getting us? Nowhere!" his father had said. "And we're paying rates to educate the likes of that Driesler girl at grammar school. It's not on!"

 Alex had to smile. If Sabina could make his father annoyed, then she couldn't be all bad.

The dressage event was not Alex's best, and he knew Sabina had scored better. When she left the ring he rode over to congratulate her. "Well done. You beat me as usual. You'll have to give me some tips before I go back to school. By the way, congratulations on getting your eleven plus. Are you looking forward to starting at the Grammar?"

Sabina grinned. "Yes, thanks. I can give you your first tip now, if you like. Paris is anticipating the canter. You've got to check him more. You started off before the mark."

"Right." Alex dismounted and he and Sabina were soon in deep discussion about riding. Neither noticed Alex's father approach as Alex was saying: "You'll have to come over here when I'm back for half-term. You can have a go of Paris and see if you do any better with him!"

"I don't think so, Alex."

They both spun round. Sabina looked up at the stocky, balding man who would have been her father, if it weren't for the Second World War. She did not like what she saw. His aversion to her was obvious. He did not look more kindly at his own son.

Alex shrugged and led Paris away without another word, but Sabina knew she had found an ally in the Kellett camp.

Alex decided to work on his mother. He suspected she only played along with his father's animosity towards the Drieslers. It would be fun to see if he could get her to intervene between the two families. It wasn't fair that he couldn't invite whoever he wanted over, just because of some stupid reason of his father's. The war was over years ago.

Alex went to seek her out, but she was busy judging. It was not until after he had competed in the show-jumping that he had the chance to speak to her. "Sabina Driesler beat me this time, Mother. She told me she'd been given some tips in Germany over the summer, and she's willing to come over here and pass them on to me. But you know what Father's like. Can't you speak to him and get him to make friends with them? They seem a nice family. I can't see what he has against them."

Audrey Kellett ruffled her son's brown wavy hair. "I know, darling. It is silly, isn't it? It's gone on too long. I promise I'll have a word with him."

Audrey watched her son run off. So he had an interest in Sabina, did he? He was only young yet, but things might develop and she did not fancy a repetition of the Montague/Capulet situation. She had no objections whatever to a close link with the Driesler family. Andrew on the other hand ...

"Good Lord! I don't believe it!" Katherine read through the invitation once again to make sure there was no mistake.

"What's that, Mummy." Sabina was polishing her shoes before dashing for the school bus. Living so far from school had its disadvantages, but she was used to early starts.

"It's an invitation to dinner at Froxley Grange."

Sabina smiled. She had not expected Alex to take up the cause so steadfastly. "That's nice. When is it?"

"30th September. I don't know what Daddy's going to say. He and Mr Kellett ..."

"Make him go, Mummy. It's about time they patched things up."

"It might not be so simple, Bina, but I think you're right. If they've bothered to invite us, we ought to go. I'll tell him before he and

Werner set off for 'The Beeches' this morning." She caught sight of Richard at the back door. "Richard, have you polished your shoes?"

"Not yet. Give me a chance, Mum."

"Well, hurry up. You've got to get changed yet, and it's nearly time for school. Here's your dinner money." She put three envelopes on the kitchen table, then went outside to see what Paul was up to. She found him in the toolshed with Werner, selecting saws and axes for the day's tree-felling. "Really, Paul! It'll be the day when I don't have to chase you up each morning. Come along!"

"Sorry, Katherine," Werner said with a wink at Paul.

Once the children were off to school, Katherine caught up with Karl loading equipment into the Land Rover.

"Something for you to think about today, Schatz. We've had an invitation to dinner from the Kelletts."

His reaction echoed her own. "My God. What's made them do that?"

"I've no idea. Except ... It's probably nothing, but I did see Sabina talking to Alex Kellett at the gymkhana last week."

"So?"

"Well, when I told Sabina about the invitation, she seemed very keen for us to accept. I rather think she and Alex want to get together, and are trying to build bridges between us."

"Sabina and Alex Kellett? They're a bit young to be –"

Katherine laughed. "Horses, Schatz. That's what they're interested in."

"It could lead further eventually." He lifted a crate of tools and stowed it carefully in the Land Rover.

"And if it does, would that be such a bad thing?" she said to his back

He whirled round. "If he turns out like his father, yes!"

"Well, I don't see that we can refuse the invitation. Shall I accept?"

Karl threw a coil of rope over the tools. "If you think so," he said grudgingly.

Katherine returned to the house and wrote their reply.

CHAPTER NINETEEN

"When I bought this dinner jacket I never thought I'd wear it so often," Karl said, as he steered the Land Rover between the gateposts of the long drive up to Froxley Grange. "Heavens! This brings back memories. I haven't been here since that Boxing Day Hunt, when you were still engaged to him."

Katherine's eyebrows arched. "Thanks for reminding me. I hope you're not going to mention what happened that day."

"Would I be so stupid?" He put his hand on hers. "I promise to be on my best behaviour this evening."

"I expect Audrey's making Andrew promise the very same thing," Katherine said with a laugh. "For our childrens' sakes, this evening's got to be a success. Agreed?"

"Agreed."

The stately cedar tree still stood near the Georgian mansion house and Karl parked beneath it, as Katherine's father had on that Boxing Day, almost fourteen years before. Karl had felt out of place in his POW garb amongst all the hunting pink then, and he felt no less uncomfortable now. Katherine, however, was more familiar with the house, having been a frequent guest in the past, and led him up the stone steps to the front door.

Audrey herself answered their ring of the bell. Her long black dress and blonde hair reminded them rather of Ilse, although Ilse's blonde was natural and straight, while Audrey's curls looked distinctly bleached these days. She kissed Katherine warmly in welcome. "I heard your Land Rover, Katherine, and simply had to let you in personally. It's been too long, it really has!"

A maid stood by to take their coats. Karl handed his over, then stooped to accept and reciprocate Audrey's kiss of the cheek, allowing no hint of past liaisons. First Ilse, now Audrey, he thought, as she led them through to the drawing room. What Katherine has to try to ignore! He braced himself to meet Andrew Kellett.

The drawing room already held a number of guests standing about on the plush Chinese carpet, drinks clutched to their chests. Andrew stood beside a large oil-painting in a gilded frame, depicting a Victorian hunting scene outside Froxley Grange itself. He stopped chatting when he saw the new arrivals, and excused himself from his guests. A hush descended over the room, until politeness forced conversation to resume. Even so, all eyes were watching as the two renowned foes met.

"Good evening, Katherine. Karl." There was a touch of frost to the last name, but Andrew held out his hand and Karl shook it. An almost audible sigh of relief carried about the room. "So glad you could come. Can I get you a drink?"

The formal pleasantries carried them over the awkwardness. Andrew made sure they were given a dry martini each, then retired to his other guests, leaving Audrey to lead them to a group by the porcelain cabinet. The two couples there knew Katherine from former times, but Karl was known only by reputation.

"It's been such a long time, Katherine," gushed Margaret Wilkinson, a former gymkhana participant, and school-friend of Audrey. "I couldn't believe it when I read about your wedding in the paper." She cast an anxious glance up at Katherine's husband, described then as 'SS man'. "Of course, when Audrey told me you would be here, I couldn't resist meeting you again."

Katherine decided the 'you' was definitely intended to be plural. Deflecting attention from Karl, she greeted Margaret's husband. "Edward! You're looking well. Business booming, is it?"

The small talk began. Another couple arrived, were introduced, more drinks dispensed, then Audrey called them all to the dining room. Karl found himself seated at Andrew's end of the table with Margaret Wilkinson separating them. To his left was the wife of a landowner from Leominster. The flabby-jowled man seated next to Andrew, opposite Mrs Wilkinson, was the family solicitor, Edgar Hanfield-Payne. He seemed determined to glean Karl's opinion on matters German.

"What do you make of the East Germans closing the border last month, Mr Driesler? Surely the people won't have it? There'll be an uprising!"

Karl shook his head. "You must remember, it is the Soviets talking, not East Germany. They occupy the country with a powerful army. How can ordinary Germans object?"

"Isn't that just the mentality of a people accepting what their leaders tell them? That could never happen in England."

"How do you know? England is not occupied."

"No, thank God and the RAF. But you must have had experience of occupying countries. Didn't you come across instances of rebellion and resistance?"

Karl knew the solicitor wanted to hear him admit to brutally repressing any such resistance. He obliged. "Yes. And the people generally paid a high price for it." He looked to Andrew for help in ending the uncomfortable conversation, but Andrew was highly entertained by it, keen for once to let someone else do the arguing. It was Mrs Wilkinson who came to Karl's aid.

"I think it's wonderful how we can all get together at the Olympics and show there doesn't have to be hatred between nations. I would have loved to have been in Rome to see it all."

"Could you have stood the heat?" the Leominster landowner's haughty wife asked. "I gather it was simply stifling."

Karl relaxed as the ladies skillfully turned the conversation away from warfare, drawing Andrew in for comments on Britain's single bronze medal in the equestrian events. Karl tactfully avoided mentioning Germany's team gold in the Grand Prix Jumping. Down the other end of the table Katherine was happily immersed in conversation. Karl concentrated on eating the smoked trout in front of him, while Andrew spouted on about horsemanship. He had the ladies' attention, but Hanfield-Payne preferred meatier topics.

"I understand you were in the SS, Mr Driesler. Does that pose a problem for you still?"

Karl took a deep breath. "Only when people make a point of mentioning it."

"You misunderstand me. I meant a problem for yourself. Your conscience."

"No. Why should it?"

Hanfield-Payne smiled smugly. "Surely you have the consequences of your actions to consider."

"What actions?"

"Your actions as a member of the SS. Do I have to elaborate?"

Karl laid down his knife and fork with a clatter. "Yes, you do. Because I seem to be misunderstanding you. Are you saying that just because I was a soldier I am guilty of a crime? Someone in your profession should know better than that!"

There was dead silence round the table and Karl knew he had been set up. Andrew gave an indulgent smile to Audrey, as if to say, that if she would invite a German, conflict was inevitable.

Audrey took control. "I can't wait for the outcome of the Lady Chatterley debate. What's your opinion, Edgar? Is it literature?"

Hanfield-Payne willingly accepted the spotlight. "Not having read the book in question, of course, I am unable to comment fully. But my understanding of its content is that it is pure filth and not fit for publication. No wonder standards are declining in this country when such things can even be considered!"

Audrey smiled at Karl as Hanfield-Payne continued his diatribe against the evils of modern society. They both knew Lady Chatterley was nothing compared with Audrey Kellett. She was more discreet than formerly, before her marriage, but Karl recognised the gleam in her eye. He broke off eye-contact with her and sipped his wine, then engaged the Leominster lady in innocent conversation for the remainder of the meal. The solicitor refrained from further attack.

They gathered in the drawing room for coffee, and this time Audrey was careful to seat herself near Karl. "I'm sorry about Edgar," she whispered, passing a dish of petits fours. "Andrew would only agree to you being invited if Edgar came too. It was also at Andrew's insistence that Edgar was seated near you at table. I think he hoped for more of a ding-dong than there was. You seemed to handle Edgar well."

Karl took a marzipan apple. "I've learned to stand up for myself, and make no apologies for my nationality. It was impossible just after the war, but now ..."

"Now you're a respected and well-established member of the community. I know. I hear all about you. Your son, Siegfried, gave you a tough time, by all accounts. Fancy you of all people having an illegitimate son! I always thought you had such high morals."

"Compared with you, I did." Karl bit into the marzipan.

A wicked smile touched Audrey's lips. "Enforced celibacy didn't suit you. I was doing you a favour." She noticed Margaret Wilkinson heading towards the chesterfield where they were sitting and muttered: "Bother!" She just had time to add: "I'm not a reformed woman, you know," before Mrs Wilkinson sat on an adjacent Queen Anne chair and took over the conversation.

"What lovely soap you have in the cloakroom, Audrey. Do tell me where you buy it."

Mrs Wilkinson was soon joined by Mrs Hanfield-Payne. After five minutes Karl stifled a yawn. His thoughts began to wander. Audrey had hinted at infidelity. If Audrey was seeking passion elsewhere, was Andrew doing the same? Probably. Would he look in Katherine's direction? Possibly. If this resumption of friendship between the households meant Andrew pestering Katherine, then the Kelletts could forget it. Karl observed the party. Sure enough Andrew was sitting next to Katherine, although they were part of a larger group. His suspicions were not yet justified, but he decided to make his presence felt.

"Excuse me," he said to Audrey and the other ladies, and went over to join Katherine. Andrew did not seem pleased at the intrusion, but room was made for Karl to pull a chair into the circle. After a couple of minutes he caught Katherine's eye and gave her the slight nod they both understood as meaning it was time to go.

Katherine decided she ought to be the one to make their excuses. She drained her coffee cup. "Well, it's getting late and some of us have to be up early in the morning." She rose to her feet, and all the men rose with her.

Andrew called across to Audrey. "Darling, Katherine and Karl are leaving."

"So soon?"

Katherine bade hasty goodbyes to the other guests, then turned to her hosts. "If you're ever riding you must come by our way sometime. We'd be pleased to see you."

"Thank you," Andrew said enthusiastically. "We'll do that."

The Kelletts saw their guests to the door, where the maid returned their coats. Polite thanks and waves of farewell concluded the evening in an amicable vein, but it was with distinct relief that Karl sat once again behind the steering wheel.

"Phew! I'm glad that's over."

Katherine looked askance at him. "It wasn't that bad, surely?"

"You weren't down my end of the table. I've been fending off attacks all evening, both hostile and amorous."

Katherine giggled. She had taken care not to drink too much, but was pleasantly animated. "Men hate you, and women love you. It's the story of your life, Schatz."

"Yes, but everybody loves *you*! Why did you have to invite the Kelletts over? Andrew seemed to leap at the chance. No doubt he'll choose a time when I'm out."

She was silent. Significantly so, Karl thought. "Have I touched on something I shouldn't? Has he been over before?"

"No," Katherine denied, a shade too quickly. "Not since we were married."

From experience, Karl knew she was uneasy. "There's something you've not told me?"

Katherine gulped. A policy of total honesty and openness was all very well, if you had nothing to hide. If she told Karl that Andrew had raped her back in 1947 when she had finally sent him packing, Karl would feel more like killing Andrew than entertaining him.

"He's never been over uninvited," she explained, truthfully.

Karl seemed unconvinced, but did not press her to explain further. They were nearing home. Katherine spotted the lights of the farmhouse on the hillside above. Was Sabina's wish really worth the risk of reopening old wounds?

*

At October half-term, Sabina rode over to Froxley Grange on Sally. Alex was waiting for her on Paris at the beginning of the drive.

"So we managed it, eh?" he said by way of greeting, nudging Paris into step beside Sally.

"Yep. We sure did. My Dad still hates your Dad's guts, but at least he allowed me to come here."

They trotted briskly up the drive, to the paddock set out with jumps and dressage ring from the gymkhana. They spent the next hour perfecting techniques and swapping mounts, until a rest was called for. They walked their ponies to the stables, leaving them in the hands of a groom, then went inside the house for a drink.

"We'll have to stay in the kitchen, I'm afraid," Alex said. "Riding clobber's not allowed in the rest of the house."

"That's OK. I'm used to the kitchen. We spend most of our time in there at home." Sabina accepted a glass of squash from the cook and swigged it down in one draft. "My German friend Margit's coming to stay next Easter. You'll have to come over and meet her. She can give us both some more tips. She was taught to ride by a champion dressager."

"Gosh! Lucky her. But you said friend. Isn't she a relation? I thought she was something to do with your half-brother."

Sabina giggled. "Oh, my family's so complicated! Siegfried's my half-brother, and Margit's Siegfried's half-sister, but Margit and I aren't related. Got it?"

Alex looked blank. "Not really, but never mind. Does she speak English?"

"Only a little. She's keen to learn more so she can understand what Elvis Presley's singing about. She's a great fan of his. I prefer Johnny Mathis and Matt Munro myself. Who do you like?"

"I don't know. I'm not allowed to listen to that kind of music, although Mother's a secret admirer of Frank Sinatra."

Audrey walked in. "Are my ears burning? Did I hear you mention me and Frank Sinatra?" She smiled warmly at Alex's guest. "Hello, Sabina. Had a good ride?"

"Yes, thank you, Mrs Kellett."

"Sabina was just telling me about her German friend, Margit," Alex said. "The one who gave Sabina tips on riding. She's coming here next Easter."

"That will be nice," his mother said. "You'll have to invite her and Sabina over. We'll all have to brush up on our German, won't we? Although I expect you speak it quite well, don't you, Sabina?"

Sabina looked modest. "Yes, pretty well. My school says I can take German O' Level without having any lessons, when the time comes."

Audrey was impressed. "My word. Isn't that useful."

Alex looked uncomfortable at talk of O' Levels. They were four years off yet, but his parents were pressurising him already about them. "Can we have some cake, Mother?"

"Ask Mrs Jones for some, darling. Well, I'd better get back to Angelina and Alan before they wreck the rose garden with their over-zealous pruning. See you again, I hope, Sabina."

"Yes. Thank you, Mrs Kellett."

She watched in amazement as the cook, with a face to match her bread dough, produced a selection of chocolate and cream cakes for them to choose from. The extravagance was like at the Zopfs'. At home it was scones, fruit cake or jam sponge, never anything like this except on birthdays. No wonder Alex was so chubby.

She licked her fingers clean of chocolate and looked at her watch. "I suppose I'd better head for home. It'll be getting dark soon. It's been fun today. Do you want to come up to my house tomorrow?"

"Yes. What time? After lunch?"

"Fine. Thank you for the cake, Mrs Jones," she said as she left the kitchen.

Mrs Jones beamed. "That's all right, miss." What a nice young lady. The Driesler girl was welcome in her kitchen any day!

*

Alex arrived at Lane Head Farm on Paris promptly at two o'clock. The first person he saw was Sabina's father. He was unloading crates of apples from the back of the Land Rover with another older and much smaller man. Alex caught the sound of spoken German as he dismounted. Werner Gimpel, Alex assumed correctly. From the nearby shed came the sound of boys' voices. Richard and Paul must be helping stack the crates inside. Alex felt wary at first of addressing the German, but told himself the man was only Sabina's father.

"Good afternoon, Mr Driesler."

"Afternoon, Alex. Sabina's in the stable with Sally." He nodded across the yard to where Alex could see a stable door.

Alex smiled his thanks and led Paris over to the stable. Mr Driesler had hardly a trace of a German accent; certainly not what Alex was expecting. He seemed friendly enough too. Sabina popped her head out of the doorway when she heard Paris's hooves on the cobbled yard.

"Be ready in a tick," she said. "I had to do the washing up, and Mummy had been baking. There was tons of the stuff!"

259

It was another world to Alex, helping with chores. "Fancy Richard and Paul working with your father! He must be a patient man. Mine wouldn't want me helping him. He'd shout at me all the time."

Sabina finished threading the throat lash on Sally's bridle. "We're expected to help. It's necessary, but it's also interesting learning all about the farm. The boys know they'll be running it one day, and I just enjoy being with Daddy."

"So you help with the farmwork too?" he asked incredulously.

"Of course! My mother always helped her father."

Alex could not imagine his younger sister, Angelina, wanting to dirty her hands with anything more strenuous than pruning roses.

Sally was ready at last and the two set off for the meadow set aside for jumping. Richard and Paul appeared after half an hour to help replace the dislodged poles. Alex had no time for his own younger siblings, but found Sabina's brothers knew how to be useful as well as fun. When Katherine called everyone in for tea, Alex was surrounded by a mass of humanity, all talking at once, frequently with their mouths full, in a family atmosphere so relaxed he could not believe it was possible.

"Can I come up again tomorrow?" he begged Sabina when it was time for him to leave.

"Sure. Whenever you like. Come for lunch, then we can go for a hack afterwards, all of us."

"Will that be all right, Mrs Driesler?"

"Of course, Alex! I'll phone your mother, just so she knows it's a proper invitation."

As he rode home down the country lanes, Alex's spirits began to sink rapidly. For all its magnificence, Froxley Grange was a cold and lonely house.

*

It was not until Friday evening, when Alex had spent the whole of the previous three days at Lane Head Farm, that his father asked what he had been up to. Andrew Kellett had called his son into the study after the childrens' supper to test him on his Latin verbs and found them non-existant.

"What have you been doing all week? You were supposed to have the third and fourth conjugations off pat by now."

Alex wriggled his toes inside his shoes. If he said where he had been, then Lane Head Farm would instantly be put out of bounds.

"I forgot. Sorry, Father."

"Sorry?" Andrew reached behind him to the bookcase for the riding crop he kept for such occasions. "This will make you sorry! I'm not having my son grow up a dolt! Now bend over."

Alex knew he would not feel like riding tomorrow. He positioned himself in front of his father and bravely took what was coming. Somehow he could not imagine Mr Driesler doing such a thing to Richard or Paul. Or even having to. Everyone there worked for love and mutual respect. Jobs were done because they had to be done and everyone mucked in accordingly. But what was the point of Latin verbs?

Andrew put the warm crop back on the shelf, impressed by his son's self-control. The boy had learned something from school at least. "Tomorrow you spend in your room learning that list of verbs. Do you hear?"

"Yes, Father. May I go now?"

Andrew impatiently signalled his son to leave. Alex walked carefully out to the parlour where his mother had the radio on quietly. She was reading *Country Life*, but put it down when she saw Alex's face.

"What is it, darling? You look like you want to cry."

Alex tried to put on a brave face, but it was hard in front of his mother. He did want to cry, but he was too old for that sort of nonsense. "Father says I must stay in my room tomorrow and learn my Latin, but I had arranged to go up to Bina's again."

Audrey noted with satisfaction the use of the familiar form of Sabina. "Can't you learn the verbs tonight? If I test you on them in the morning, I'm sure you can still go. Your father's out, anyway, so he won't know where you are."

"Really? Thank you, Mother!" Alex gave her a spontaneous hug, the first since he was a toddler.

Audrey clung to him for a moment. Perhaps Alex wasn't so like Andrew after all. "You go off now, and start learning that Latin. You don't want to disappoint Sabina, do you?"

"No!"

"Perhaps I'll come with you even. I quite fancy a ride over the hills."

"Just you and me? Not Angelina and Alan?"

"Just you and me. They can stay with Nanny."

Alex was thrilled. Now his mother would see what wonderful people the Drieslers were. His sore behind was totally forgotten as he ran upstairs.

*

Two sets of hooves were entering the yard. Over the garden hedge Audrey's head appeared alongside Alex's. Katherine abandoned the washing basket in the garden and hurried to the yard.

"Audrey! You finally made it up here. I was beginning to think you'd forgotten us. You're just in time for coffee. You will have some, won't you?"

"That would be lovely." Audrey dismounted, handing the reins to Alex who led both animals to the paddock, thoroughly at home, she noted. She followed Katherine to the kitchen, and, in a moment of sentimental indulgence, sat on the rocking chair she knew only too well from her brief fling with Karl.

"Alex has been a different boy since he's been coming up here," she told Katherine, who was busy preparing coffee. "He was always a bit of a loner, but he seems to fit in so well here."

"Yes. He does seem to get on well with Sabina and the boys."

"Karl too. I gather he's been showing Alex how to lay a hedge this week. It's funny. I never imagined Alex would enjoy being a farm labourer."

Katherine was worried Audrey was politely voicing an objection to such activities for Alex. "You don't mind, do you?"

"Good gracious, no! It's good for Alex to work alongside a man. He never gets the chance at home. I'm afraid Andrew just doesn't have any patience with him."

"That's a shame." Katherine set out four mugs on the table. She had thought of using the best china, in view of Audrey's status, but decided Audrey would appreciate being treated as the old friend she was. Nevertheless she opened a packet of chocolate biscuits rather than plain. Pouring glasses of milk for the children, she then summoned the family with a loud call from the back door. The kitchen quickly filled with bodies, Werner and Karl being the last to appear.

Karl felt his heart lurch when he saw Audrey sitting as bold as brass in the rocking chair. He greeted her with a casual nod. "Morning, Audrey."

"Good morning, Karl. I thought I'd finally take you up on your invitation to ride over, since Alex was coming."

Karl made no reply, feeling none was necessary or possible above the chattering children. Milk and biscuits were swiftly consumed, however, and the children departed for the paddock, leaving the adults in peace once more. But not for long.

A car drew up in the lane outside. The car door slammed.

"Sounds like ours," Audrey said, puzzled. "But Andrew's supposed to be in Hereford today."

They expected to hear a knock at the front door, and Katherine rose to go to it, but was diverted by the sound of angry shouting from the paddock.

Audrey jumped up in alarm. "It *is* Andrew!"

They all rushed outside only to see a furious Andrew dragging Alex by the arm back to the car.

"Andrew! Stop that!" Audrey protested. "I said he could come here."

"And I said he couldn't. You've deliberately gone against my express orders."

"But he learned his Latin. I tested him on it last night."

Retaining his firm grip on Alex, Andrew approached the onlookers. "I don't expect my wife to go behind my back. His not coming here was a punishment whether he learned his Latin or not!"

By this time Alex was finding it difficult not to wince at the pain inflicted on his arm. He looked imploringly at his mother to intervene. Audrey knew the quickest way to let Alex out of his misery was to get him on his way home.

"Into the car, Alex. I'll bring Paris home." Ignoring her husband she turned to her hosts. "I'm very sorry about this. I can see it's upset your children."

Andrew gave a tug at Alex and marched off to the car without another word. Once they were safely out of sight, Audrey gave vent to her fury.

"Beast!"

Katherine tried to console her, but Karl had noticed Sabina's distress. He strode over to the paddock gate where she stood in bewilderment, her face streaked with tears. Richard and Paul looked equally shocked.

"He called us German yobs and said we were a bad influence," Richard protested to his father. "And he was especially rude to Bina."

"Oh yes? What did he say, Bina?" Karl asked gently.

She flung her arms round him and sobbed heartily, unable to talk.

Richard helped her out. "He said she was a forward young hussy, and wasn't going to corrupt *his* son."

Karl's anger had to wait. His children came first. "He's blinkered by his old hatred of me, and I'm afraid it affects you too. He didn't mean what he said. He was angry with Alex, not you. You know how it is when you're angry. You sometimes say things you know aren't true, don't you?" They all nodded. "Well then. Let's try to forget about it, and feel sorry for poor Alex instead."

Audrey watched him with his children, saw them begin to cheer up, and the hug Sabina gave him. Jealousy flared within her breast and she hurriedly turned to Katherine.

"I'd better get back and try to sort Andrew out. He's no right coming here, upsetting you all like this. Thank you for the coffee and for having Alex. But don't be surprised if he's not allowed up here again."

Katherine patted her shoulder. "Don't worry about us. You just do what you can for Alex." She called over to Sabina. "Bina! Can you get Paris ready on a leading rein? Mrs Kellett's going now."

Audrey left the farm knowing she would never return. Not only did it hurt too much to see their happiness, but Andrew had scuppered all hopes of an end to the feud.

CHAPTER TWENTY

The daffodils in the garden at Iserlohn were fading fast. Siegfried watched his mother pottering about amongst them, pretending to do something useful in the extensive garden. She hasn't enough to keep her occupied, he thought. He strolled up to her and received her usual smile at the sight of him.

"Back so soon?" she asked. "I thought Paul said you'd be out till late tonight."

"The meeting was postponed. Herr Altenried called for a security check on one of the members before we meet again."

"Oh? Anyone I know?"

"No. Somebody new. You ought to come along to the meetings again, Mutter. People are beginning to wonder where you've got to."

"I might. I just tend to find them a bit ... heavy these days. I'm a bit out of my depth, I suppose."

Was she turning against the Party? Siegfried carefully studied her expression. He decided not. "I can't blame you. For the most part it's beer drinking and singing the old songs. We do make some plans though. Herr Altenried sees to that. He makes sure we younger ones feel involved." He stooped to pick up the basket of daffodils as his mother moved along the border. "Margit ought to come along too. She's old enough now to join in the fun. She'd like it, I'm sure."

Ilse reached for the basket and threw in a handful of withered flowers. "Maybe she would. You'd better ask her. She's just arrived back with all her luggage. Goodness knows what she's bought. Half of Hereford by the looks of it!"

Mention of Hereford momentarily wiped the smile from Siegfried's face before he rapidly re-established it. "Where is she? It'll be good to catch up on all the news."

"In her room, sorting things out with Lotti."

"I'll go and say hello."

He left his mother to the daffodils and ran into the grand house Paul had bought to contain his large family. Skidding across the marble hall floor, Siegfried bounded up the stairs to Margit's room. He gave a cursory knock on her door, then marched in. Margit and Lotti were busy hanging armfuls of clothes in the wardrobe.

"Welcome back. Enjoy England did you?"

Margit looked at him in surprise. It was unlike Siegfried to be civil. "Yes. Very much actually."

Siegfried sat down next to one of the open suitcases on her bed. "So. Are you fluent in English now?"

"Don't be daft. Anyway, we spoke German most of the time. Except when Alex was around, of course."

"Alex? Who's he?"

Margit decided to leave the rest of the unpacking to Lotti, since Siegfried seemed keen to hear all her news. She sat down on the bed opposite him. "He's one of Bina's friends. Except his parents won't let him see her, because she's half-German or something silly like that. So they have to meet secretly. It's all quite exciting really."

"So Sabina's interested in boys now?"

Margit giggled. "We talked quite a lot about ... boys ... and things."

Siegfried could not resist the opportunity to have some fun at Margit's expense. "What about you and my father? Do you still fancy him?"

The question caught her unawares and she blushed deeply. From the wardrobe came a snigger. "No! I never did!"

"Oh yes you did. Last summer you couldn't keep your eyes off him. Could she, Lotti?"

There was a noncommittal grunt from Lotti. Siegfried realised she was not going to back him up so directed his questioning elsewhere. "How were they all? Katherine didn't get drunk again, I take it?"

"Of course not! The Drieslers hardly ever drink at home, and when they do it's only home-made elderberry or damson wine." As Siegfried pulled a face of disgust, she added: "It's nicer than it sounds, actually."

Siegfried asked a few more questions, hoping to hear something he could use to his advantage, but Sabina's liaisons with Alex seemed in the end to be most promising. With a wink at Lotti, he rose to his feet and was about to leave the room when he remembered his earlier conversation with his mother.

"There's a meeting soon, organised by Herr Altenried. You ought to start coming. I'll take you with me next time." Without waiting for her acquiescence, he left the room.

"Cheek!" Margit said, before realising Siegfried's ally, Lotti, was still present.

But Lotti only shook her head in despair. "He takes people for granted, if you don't mind me saying, miss. Me included." She hung the last skirt back on the rail, trying to summon the courage to speak. It only took a moment, such was her need to sort out her relationship with Siegfried. "I happen to have found a nice young man of my own, and don't want to be at *his* beck and call any more, but he won't listen. I'd appreciate it, miss, if you could have a word with him, or your step-father. I'm not his personal whore – excuse my language – so he must stop treating me like one."

Margit felt honoured by the confidence. "I'll do my best, Lotti, but I don't think he'll listen to me. If there's nothing doing, I can certainly try having a word with Herr Zopf; see if he can help."

"Thank you, miss." She looked about the room for any more full bags, but everything had been tidied away apart from a big pile of washing. Gathering this up in her arms she begged leave to go. "Will that be all, miss?"

"Yes, thank you, Lotti."

On her way to the laundry room, Lotti caught sight of Siegfried lurking by the kitchen door. He grabbed her arm as she passed.

"Tonight. Eleven o'clock," he whispered.

His self-assurance infuriated her. She could not wait for Margit to intervene. "No!" she hissed. "I don't want to anymore. You're getting too rough for me."

There was silence. Lotti saw his lips narrow and knew she was in trouble. For a moment she thought he was going to hit her, but the moment passed.

"Well. So the worm has turned." His voice was calm yet sharp as a knife. "Why this, all of a sudden? What's Margit been saying?"

"Nothing! It's not her. I've got my own boyfriend now, and I don't –"

"I see." Letting go of her arm, he walked away.

Lotti breathed a sigh of relief and hurried into the laundry-room.

*

At eleven o'clock Siegfried opened Lotti's door. She was unpinning her hair ready for bed. She caught his reflection in the dressing table mirror and whirled round.

"I told you not to come!"

Siegfried closed the door carefully behind him. "I don't take orders from you. I give them. So shut up and take off your clothes!"

Lotti stared at the unblinking grey eyes of the seventeen-year-old boy. She knew only too well to what depths he could sink to get his own way. Hadn't she even helped him on occasions? Reluctantly her fingers began to unbutton her blouse.

"I'm handing in my notice after this!"

"I told you to be quiet." Siegfried grinned. This was the perfect moment to try something he had always wanted to do. Something Erich had taught him. Reaching for the dresser drawer, he pulled out several pairs of Lotti's stockings. As Lotti's bra fell to the floor he grabbed her wrists and pulled them in front of her, wrapping a stocking tightly round them.

Realising his intent to bind and gag her, Lotti screamed.

Siegfried slapped her so hard she fell across the bed. "Bitch!" He made to leave the room, but it was too late. He could already hear footsteps running up the stairs to the servants' quarters. Along the corridor a door opened. He stuffed the stockings back into the drawer just as Paul burst into the room.

Paul took one look at Lotti sprawled sobbing and half dressed on the bed then glared at his stepson. Siegfried had never seen such ferocity in Paul's dark eyes.

"My study. Now!"

So as not to lose face in front of Lotti or the cook, who had just arrived on the scene, Siegfried gave a careless shrug and sauntered out. He heard Paul say something to comfort Lotti, but was soon out of earshot. Whatever Lotti told Paul could easily be denied.

He wandered down to the hall and waited in Paul's study, grinning to himself as he remembered previous tongue-lashings from his father in England. None had ever done any good. He stood at the bookcase, studying the covers of Paul's numerous books on construction and building methods, alongside the obligatory dictionaries and works of Goethe, Schiller and Shakespeare. He reached for the edition of *Faust* and flicked through the pages, remembering passages studied at school. In another year he would be sitting the *Abitur* then heading for national service. That would be fun!

Paul came in at last and caught him grinning. "Wipe that smile off your face!"

Carefully closing the copy of *Faust*, Siegfried returned it to its place on the shelf then sat down.

"I didn't tell you to sit," Paul snapped.

Siegfried shot to attention. This was going to be worse than he thought.

"Lotti's been telling me a few things about you. Like what you did to your stepmother last summer. Having seen it with my own eyes, I believe her, and there is nothing you can say to redeem yourself. Lotti has resigned, and unfortunately I couldn't persuade her to stay even the rest of the week. We are losing a thoroughly good worker because of your arrogant stupidity." Paul paused only to draw breath before continuing his tirade. "You must learn to respect people who have earned that respect. I have given Lotti a gratuity in return for her silence. You will repay me by complete and utter obedience to what I say. Understood?"

"Yes, sir."

"Firstly, you will never, ever treat a woman like that again. You have sullied this entire household with your dishonourable behaviour. Do you hear?"

"Yes, sir," Siegfried mumbled.

"I didn't hear!"

"YES, SIR."

"Secondly, you will come with me now, back to Lotti's room and apologise to her, face to face. Knowing your sense of pride, that is the most appropriate punishment I can devise."

Siegfried scowled. It certainly was!

"Right. Upstairs."

Siegfried led the way back across the hall to the back staircase and boldly marched upstairs, determined to complete his punishment with dignity. When he got to Lotti's door he knocked and waited.

Lotti was expecting them. "Come in."

She had tidied herself up, but her left cheek was still red from where Siegfried had hit her. Siegfried stood in front of her, a respectful distance away, and looked her straight in the eye.

"I offer my sincerest apologies for the way I have treated you, Lotti. Not only this evening, but in the past. I hope your memories of working for the Zopf family will not be overshadowed by my shortcomings, and that you will find a suitable new appointment as soon as possible. I also hope you find long-term happiness with your boyfriend, whoever he is."

"He's the grocery-van driver," Lotti said proudly, completely taken in by the model of repentence in front of her. "Thanks for your good wishes, Siegfried. I enjoyed my time here for the most part. I never wanted it to end like this." To show there were no hard feelings, she stepped forward and gave him a light kiss on the mouth. "That's for my happier memories."

Siegfried's lips twitched into a smile. "Goodbye, Lotti," he said, and left the room.

Paul followed him, knowing Siegfried had not meant one word of what he just said. But he could not fault the performance. Despite himself, Paul felt immensely proud.

*

It took Siegfried half an hour to find out the name of the grocery-van driver, his daily round and where he lived. It took him a day to reconnoitre the route thoroughly and choose the spot.

A week after Lotti's departure from the household, Paul summoned Siegfried once again to his study. The local newspaper was open in front of him. He stabbed a finger at a report on the second page. "Have you seen this?"

Siegfried went round his desk and quickly scanned the short report. "Why do you ask?"

"I thought you might know something about it."

Siegfried snorted. "Why should I? Lotti's boyfriend takes it into his head to drive his van into a stone wall and smash his face in. What's that got to do with me?"

"How do you know it's Lotti's boyfriend?"

"Self-evident. It says he's a grocery-van driver. You wouldn't be asking me otherwise."

"Even so, a curious coincidence, wouldn't you agree?" Paul smiled at last. "And very cleverly done, I might add. There's not a hint of suspicion it wasn't an accident."

"Even from Lotti?"

"Ah." Paul frowned. "If she does suspect anything, she's too clever to speak up. She knows what we can do. Her boyfriend was lucky to survive, wasn't he?"

"He was. I mightn't feel so lenient next time."

Paul looked up from his chair at the youth beside him. "This kind of thing seems to be your forte. So long as you continue to make sure there is no possible link with our organisation, I'm sure we can find some more victims for you to practise on ... in due course. I just hope you're devoting as much time to your studies as you seem to on planning your revenge."

"I'm working hard. I won't disappoint you, Paul."

"Good. Count yourself lucky you have brains as well as brawn." He waved his hand at the door. "That's all."

As Siegfried made his way out, Paul recalled him. "One more thing. Ilse says you're taking Margit to the next meeting. Make sure you introduce her to Herr Garisch's son, Wolfgang. I know she's only young yet, but these things can develop in time."

Siegfried nodded, his eyes twinkling with amusement. "And who have you got lined up for me?"

Paul's single hand raised in denial. "I wouldn't presume to choose someone for you." His hand lowered and he added in jest: "I'll leave that to your mother!"

Siegfried left the study feeling totally satisfied with events. It was so easy planning accidents for people. Thoughts of his father gave him all the inspiration he needed. As he passed the hall mirror he stopped a moment, looking at the reflected grey eyes. His father's eyes.

"One of these days, it's going to be you," he promised.

*

Now he no longer had Lotti to satisfy him, Siegfried set about finding a replacement. Most of the girls he knew were too young and well brought up to contemplate such antics, but some older women found his youth and looks irresistible. Over the next few months he became an ever more popular guest amongst the Zopfs' friends. Ilse never liked to enquire too deeply where Siegfried got to of an evening or weekend.

For his eighteenth birthday, Paul bought him a Volkswagen Beetle to run around in. Siegfried could blend in quite happily amongst fellow students or on any street for surveillance work for Paul or Herr Altenried. Unconstrained by the needs of a full-time girl-friend, he was able to divide his time sensibly between his studies, his lady-friends, and the needs of the Party.

Once he had passed his *Abitur* with flying colours, Siegfried prepared himself for the military life he had been anticipating with relish for so long. His Party activities were necessarily subordinated to avoid suspicion while living in such close quarters with other young men. He even found months going by without him giving a thought to his father. His entire purpose was to embrace the military lifestyle to the best of his ability. The Cuban missile crisis and threat of nuclear war did not tempt him to reveal his extreme right-wing views, despite ample opportunity during discussions at the barracks. In July 1963 he enthused along with the rest of them over President Kennedy's visit to West Berlin.

Paul had been insistent on the need for secrecy. There was to be no hint of Fascist leanings in Siegfried's military record.

CHAPTER TWENTY-ONE

"Liebling!" Ilse cried, hugging her tallest and favourite son. "At last! I've been watching out for you for the past hour."

Siegfried put down his luggage on the hall floor then stooped to kiss his mother on the cheek. "I told you when I'd be leaving the barracks. You couldn't have expected me any earlier than this."

"No, but you know how much I've been looking forward to you finishing there. It's good to have you home at last."

He took off his overcoat and looked around for the maid, Renate, to hand it to. He winked covertly at her over his mother's head. It was unfortunate she was not as comely or intelligent as the delectable Lotti. Releasing himself from his mother's embrace, he asked: "Is Paul in?"

"Due back any moment. He had a meeting in Dortmund, but he promised to get back early for you." She ushered him into the furnace-hot living room. "Sit down, Liebling, and I'll get Renate to bring us some coffee."

Siegfried sat on an armchair upholstered in pale blue watered silk. The dove-grey carpet and white marble occasional tables were new since his last trip home. Very tasteful, he thought. He was glad his mother had not succumbed to the gaudy plastic trash of modern fashion.

After giving her orders to Renate, Ilse rummaged amongst some papers on the table by her chair. She handed a sheet of paper to her son.

"This is the guest list for your birthday. I've added the names of people Paul and I want to invite. There's quite a few, but you know them all." Her finger paused by the names heading the latter list. "You're very honoured that Otto and Bertha Altenried have said they can come."

Siegfried took the list from her and scanned it quickly. "What's *he* on here for?" he asked testily, seeing his father's name on the list.

Ilse sat on the arm of his chair and stroked his cropped hair. "He has the right to be on the list. See it as your last duty to him, and his

273

to you. Once you're twenty-one he'll have no rights over you. You'll be free of him."

"With any luck he won't accept the invitation."

"He already has."

"Why?"

Ilse's scarlet-painted finger-nails came to rest on her charcoal grey skirt, glowing embers on a bed of ashes, just like the fire of resentment still burning in Siegfried. "You're his son. Isn't that reason enough?"

Siegfried's eyes flashed in anger. "You never give up hope, do you?"

"Of you coming to love and respect him? No. I –" Her pleading was cut short by Renate entering the room carrying a tray of coffee and cakes.

While Renate poured the coffee, Siegfried brooded on the prospect of seeing his father again. Out of sight was not exactly out of mind, but while Karl was far away in England Siegfried had got on with life and ignored him. It was his father's own fault if he chose to come over and reopen the wounds. Siegfried felt the familiar old, gnawing anger settle in his guts; familiar as an old friend returning after a long absence. He welcomed its vigour, thriving after the years of dormancy. He drank his coffee, only half listening to his mother's gentle chatter.

After coffee he escaped upstairs. Renate was busy unpacking his bags. He left her to it and wandered along to Margit's room, knowing full well she was out at school. He rifled through her drawers, searching for the latest letter from Sabina. Finding what he was after in Margit's dresser, he took the letter out of its envelope and read its fluent German intently.

Dear Margit,   *Lane Head Farm, 10.10.64*

How's things? Sorry I haven't written for so long, but I seem to have so much homework for my O'Levels, and I've been helping with the apple picking.

Alex got into real trouble for spending so much time with us over the summer. His father's just as obstinate as ever about not letting us meet. He's even hired a tutor to keep an eye on Alex over half-term and to try cramming some work into him. I rather think it's a lost cause as Alex is only interested in sport. Rather boring these days, really.

The Harvest Supper was terrific this year. There was a jolly good band and I got to dance with some of the other local boys. I wore that dress I bought in Chelsea. Do you remember the one? Sea-green, pink and turqoise, really short. Daddy was a bit dubious about me wearing it, but I managed to twist his arm. Have you worn your plastic outfit yet? What did Paul say when he saw it? I bet he was mad! I'm really looking forward to seeing you again in December at Siegfried's 21st. Daddy was determined to do the right thing and accept your Mum's invitation. I can't think why, but he says he has one last duty to perform, whatever that is! There'll be quite a crowd from Medebach there, as you probably know, since my grandparents and cousins are invited too.

Christmas in Medebach! I can't believe we're finally managing it! You must put in an order for masses of snow, as Daddy's promised to teach us to ski. I wish I was as good as you must be.

Please pass on my best wishes to the rest of your family.

Love,

Sabina.

Siegfried refolded the letter and replaced it in the dresser. It told him much about his English half-sister. She was maturing into a young lady with an interest in fashion – and boys. He would have to fix up someone for her in December. Someone her father would learn to detest.

*

At the next Party meeting of senior officials, Siegfried cornered his quarry. As ever the event was held in the utmost secrecy, in the guise of a family anniversary party in a private room of a restaurant. He found Wolfgang Garisch entertaining a gaggle of admiring girls while Wolfgang's father, Josef Garisch, huddled in a corner with the Altenrieds and Paul. Siegfried ordered a couple of beers from the bar then took them over to Wolfgang's table. At his nod, the girls obediently got up and went off to find alternative amusement.

"I have a favour to ask, Wolf," Siegfried said, setting a beer in front of him.

Wolf grinned. "I know your favours, Siegfried. Tests of loyalty, more like. Come on, out with it! What do you want me to do this time?"

True to his name, Wolf was very much a member of the pack. He regarded his own father as pack leader, but Siegfried as the dominant male of the younger generation. Siegfried knew this, exploiting his year's seniority to the full.

"You know I have family in England."

"Yes. The unfortunate skeletons in your cupboard. Margit's told me about them. Not the sort of people the likes of us associate with!"

Siegfried scowled. "She can talk! She gets on well enough with them. She's even visited them three times. But it's not Margit I want to talk about. You've finished with her, haven't you?"

"Ye-es," Wolf said cautiously. "What's this all about?"

Siegfried lowered his voice and shuffled closer. "A long-term project. I want you to get friendly with my half-sister, Sabina. *Really* friendly. Her family's coming over for my twenty-first in December, but you won't have much time to get to know her before they go home after Christmas. You'll have to get in quick – pay her lots of attention, flatter her, that sort of thing. She'll fall for you sure enough."

"But why?" A cold stare greeted his question. Wolf knew better than to question an order. "Sorry. But it might help if I knew what you hoped to gain."

"Revenge. On her father."

Wolf's green eyes looked puzzled. "But isn't her father your father too? And how are you going to get –"

A nudge from Siegfried shut him up. Margit was approaching.

"Siegfried! You're hogging Wolf. There's others here want to talk with him, you know."

Ignoring Margit, Siegfried looked questioningly at Wolf, who, after a brief pause to consider, nodded. Satisfied, Siegfried rose to his feet. "I'll tell you more details later," he said, skirting round Margit. "There's more to it than you think!"

*

On his birthday, Siegfried welcomed his first guests. Otto and Bertha Altenried placed a large, gaily wrapped present on the reception table in the spacious hall. The table was soon covered as more guests arrived, shivering as they came in from the frosty, night air. Paul had suggested a formal black tie party, and Siegfried was only too happy to agree, despising the frivolities of many of his contempories. He greeted his parents' friends with deference and courtesy as befitted their rank and past histories. He stepped forwards as the door opened to admit the latest guests.

"Frau Garisch! Wolfgang! Delighted you could come." He bowed over the spindly woman's frail hand, then shook that of her son.

Claudia Garisch handed over a small parcel, an apologetic smile creasing her thin face. Her voice was as brittle as her bones. "My husband sends his utmost apologies, Siegfried, but sudden business called him away. You know what it's like with these politicians."

"I quite understand. I'm glad you were still able to come, both of you."

Ilse moved in to greet them, leading Frau Garisch over to the open doors of the reception room. Wolf stopped for a few words with Siegfried.

"Is she here yet?"

Siegfried looked down into Wolf's anxious eyes. "No. Don't worry. You know exactly what the plan is. It's in your hands. I know you'll do your best."

Wolf nodded, then gave a wicked smile, his uneven white teeth lighting up his weatherbeaten features. "If she's as pretty as you say, I might even enjoy this!"

"Yes, well don't get carried away. Just remember your instructions. Now go and join the others in the music room. I'll bring her along to you later."

"Right."

Siegfried maintained his position in the hall. About half the expected guests had arrived. Another seven soon turned up, thickly swathed in overcoats, which were quickly discarded. Siegfried took a deep breath, then bowed formally as he greeted the newcomers.

"Vater. Katherine. Welcome." He quickly turned to his grandparents. This time there was more warmth in his voice. "Oma, Opa." Lastly he greeted the younger members of the group. "Uwe, Monika, Sabina. Welcome."

"Happy Birthday, Siegfried," they all wished him in turn. Ilse and Paul quickly joined the group.

"I expect you're all frozen after that long drive," Ilse said.

"We stopped off at a nearby hotel to book in for the night and get changed," Karl explained. "We didn't fancy such a long drive home tonight."

"Come on through to the warm anyway." Ilse fussed over Gisela and Dieter, taking one on each arm through to the blazing log fire of the reception room. Paul accompanied Karl and Katherine.

"The youngsters are congregating in the music room," Paul said. "Ilse's other children are there, although Roslinde and Edeltraud will be banished upstairs at ten. I hope you don't mind us not inviting your two boys, but we didn't think this sort of party would interest them."

"No, of course not," Katherine assured him in careful German. "They're with Lothar tonight – Uwe and Monika's younger brother. Sabina was so pleased to come with us. This is her first really formal party. We had so much trouble to find an evening dress she liked!"

Paul laughed. "I know just what you mean. With three young women in this house, half my earnings seem to go on clothes!"

Karl let Katherine dominate Paul's attention as he looked to see where Siegfried was leading the others. To the right of the sweeping central staircase was another room, where a band played dance music. The Zopfs' Iserlohn residence was as impressive as their hunting lodge had hinted at. An inlaid mother-of-pearl grandmother clock graced the festively ivy-clad hall. The table stacked high with presents was antique too, possibly French. Karl smiled. Ilse had really fallen on her feet.

The reception room was certainly warm. Karl and Katherine were introduced to various guests, then left to their own devices as Paul and Ilse returned to the hall to continue their greeting of new arrivals.

"However many more are coming?" Karl whispered to Katherine, running his fingertips round his shirt collar.

"Goodness knows! It's a good idea letting the youngsters have a room to themselves, though I expect we'll all be dancing in there later."

Karl was approached by a frail lady in her late forties, who grasped his elbow to gain attention. "I can see you're Siegfried's father. My word, what a likeness! My Wolfgang doesn't look a bit like either of his parents." Realising she had not yet introduced herself, she put a hand to her mouth. "Oh, excuse me! I'm Claudia Garisch, wife of the FDP politician, Josef Garisch. You may have heard of him?"

"No. I'm sorry, Frau Garisch. I'm afraid I don't know much about German politics these days."

"Oh, that's right. You live in England, don't you? I remember Wolfgang telling me now." She rambled on, relating how her husband and Paul first met at the Altenrieds'. "They're here too. Have you met them? Charming couple. They absolutely dote on Siegfried. Lost their sons, you see."

"Oh. No, I haven't met them."

Frau Garisch pointed across the room. "That's them by the door. The lady in the turqoise dress, and the man on her left with his hands behind his back. I must introduce you. They would love to meet Siegfried's father."

Karl shuddered. Altenried bore all the hallmarks of a military man: straight back, chest thrust out to display the medals no longer worn. And a military man in Paul's company most likely meant SS. Karl wondered just how many of Paul's guests still clung to their old beliefs. Impossible to tell. The financial backbone of the neo-Nazi movement of Nordrhein-Westfalia could be gathered here, for all he knew, but he refrained from commenting as such to Katherine. No need to worry her. He could cope with meeting any Nazi, old or new. Any Nazi except one, he corrected himself, as Claudia Garisch led them over to meet the Altenrieds.

To his relief, Karl was not subjected to the usual barrage of questions about why he chose to stay in England after the war. Instead, Otto Altenried enthused at length on Siegfried's qualities and achievements.

"Paul tells me he takes after you in many respects: competitive, ambitious, tough. He's going to do well in the family business, you mark my words!"

"I'm sure he will."

Karl managed to sustain a few more minutes of stifling conversation with the Altenrieds before suggesting to Katherine they should go and dance in the other room. Katherine took the hint and agreed. They smiled as they saw Sabina swirling round the floor in the arms of an athletic-looking young man.

"Her dancing lessons have paid off," Katherine said, stepping out in a foxtrot with Karl.

"Yes. She seems very smitten with him, whoever he is."

Sabina passed them, a broad smile on her face. When the music ended, they noticed she stayed with her partner for the next dance.

"Perhaps I'd better make some enquiries as to who he is," Karl said, after Sabina's third dance with the attentive young man. "I think we might be seeing more of him. Look at them. They're in a world of their own now."

"Oh, what it is to be sixteen," Katherine laughed, as the dance came to an end.

"Talking of ages," Karl muttered, "there's something I must do. I'd better catch Siegfried while he's not busy."

He broke away from her and pushed his way through the throng of dancers to where Siegfried stood talking to a group which included Margit, Uwe and Monika.

"Not dancing, Siegfried?" Karl asked lightheartedly.

Siegfried turned, cancelled the scowl which momentarily appeared and replaced it with a faint smile.

"Later."

Karl put his hand in his pocket. "I have something I promised to give you when you were twenty-one. I expect you've forgotten about it, but I try to keep my promises." He pulled out a small bundle of brown paper. "Here. This is yours."

Siegfried hesitated, not daring to believe what he hoped. Slowly he took the bundle and carefully removed the brown paper to reveal a black-handled penknife. "Gustav's knife!" he murmured, reverently opening the blade to find it well-oiled and sharpened. He ran his finger over the blade then snapped it shut. He looked his father boldly in the eye. "I'd not forgotten about it."

As tall as each other now, Katherine noticed from across the room. Their body symmetry near perfect, like two sides of the same coin. Old and young. Good and evil. Recognising Siegfried's veiled hostility only too well, she hurried over to intervene with a tug at Karl's elbow.

"Let's dance. It's a waltz."

Karl hesitated. His mission was accomplished but now it came to the crunch, he was strangely reluctant to leave his son's side and relinquish all claims to him, despite everything Siegfried had done to wreck their relationship. But Siegfried had already turned away. Karl did likewise and resumed dancing with Katherine. He noticed Sabina once more in the arms of her young man. After the waltz was over and the band stopped for a pause, Karl led Katherine over to where Sabina stood, eyes only for the slick and sophisticated young man with her.

"Having fun, Bina?"

Sabina smiled up at her father. "You could say that!"

Karl looked expectantly at her partner, who obligingly introduced himself.

"Wolfgang Garisch at your service." He clicked his heels and bowed to both Sabina's parents. "Your daughter is paying me a great honour, gracing me with her company for so long."

It was said with just the right amount of humour not to sound pretentious. Katherine beamed at Wolfgang. First impressions were important and Wolfgang instantly won her approval. Karl too was impressed – enough to begin finding out more about the young man.

"I believe I met your mother earlier. She told me your father is a politician."

"That's right. Free Democratic Party. He has a seat in the state parliament in Düsseldorf. He was supposed to be here this evening, but was called back there suddenly for an urgent meeting."

"Do you have an interest in politics yourself?"

Wolfgang laughed. "All that hot air and endless debate? No! When I finish national service I'm going to study electronic engineering. The army's taught me that's where the future lies. Not only in military hardware. Everybody's going to own a television and hi-fi soon, you'll see. I intend having my own business one day."

"A man of vision," Karl said.

Sabina was overwhelmed by her parents' favourable response to Wolfgang. She had known there was something special about him from the moment he first came up and asked her to dance. He was intelligent, charming, not bad-looking and she felt herself smitten. Hard luck, Alex, she thought. You're not a patch on Wolfgang.

The evening passed all too quickly. The food was lavish and appetising, the wine and soft drinks flowed. Sabina knew not to make a fool of herself in front of Wolfgang by drinking too much.

She had learned that from her mother's mistake. Fortunately Wolfgang respected her wishes and did not ply her with wine. Instead they stepped outside onto the terrace to cool off. Wolfgang offered her a cigarette.

Sabina waved the packet aside. "No, thanks. I don't smoke."

"No?" He lit one for himself then drew a tin from inside his jacket. "Perhaps you'd like one of these, then. They're not tobacco." Inside the tin were what looked like hand-rolled cigarettes. "Go on, try one. They're herbal. More pleasant than tobacco."

"Really, I don't know how to."

He took one from the tin, lit it from his own cigarette and popped it between her lips. "Draw air in and inhale," he told her.

To please Wolfgang, Sabina did as she was told. As smoke entered her lungs she began to cough, her eyes watering profusely.

"Have another go. You'll get the hang of it."

Sabina doubted it, but took another, smaller drag. This time she coped better, eventually managing to smoke to the end.

"How was that?" Wolfgang asked.

"Weird!" She shivered. "Time to go back in. It's cold out here."

Back inside, hush was being called by Paul who stood on the band's podium above the milling guests. Waiters were swiftly dispensing glasses of sparkling Sekt.

"Honoured guests," Paul began. "It is my great pleasure to see so many good friends here on the occasion of my stepson's twenty-first birthday. I say stepson, but I regard Siegfried as the son I never had. I know Karl, his true father, won't mind me saying that." There were furtive glances in Karl's direction, but he made no comment or sign of disagreement. Paul continued speaking. "Siegfried was a boy I could be proud of, and now, as a young man, I know he will continue to justify my faith in him. I would ask you all to raise your glasses and drink a toast to Siegfried."

The room echoed the toast.

"To Siegfried", Karl murmured, glad Paul had not asked him to say a few words. There was nothing favourable he could have said.

As the voices died down, the lights in the room were dimmed. Through the uncurtained windows a shower of fireworks streaked up into the night sky, exploding in a cacophony of sound and stars.

The display lasted ten minutes, climaxing in a static, golden figure 21. As the "oohs" and "ahs" subsided, Karl decided it was time to go. He had done his duty in attending; his paternal responsibilities to Siegfried were over, but his filial duties remained. His parents were beginning to flag. He cast his eyes about for Sabina. Monika and Uwe he found immediately, but Sabina proved elusive. Wolfgang was nowhere to be seen either.

"Have you seen Sabina?" he asked Monika.

"Probably with Wolfgang somewhere," she suggested.

"I rather guessed she would be!"

Katherine eventually found them on the terrace, after discovering a french window open. The smell of cigarette smoke accompanied them, as well as a slightly sweeter smell she could not identify.

"Ah, there you are, Sabina. We're thinking about going now. Oma and Opa are tired."

"Can't they drive back to the hotel on their own? Uwe and Monika could squeeze in with us."

"No. We'll all go back together. The roads are icy and Daddy would rather we followed behind Opa."

"Oh. All right, then." Sabina turned to Wolfgang. "It looks like I've got to go."

"I hope very much I'll see you again, while you're over here," he said chivalrously. "Perhaps I could get in touch with you?"

"I'll give you our phone number in Medebach."

Katherine left them to their fond farewells and hurriedly sought the warmth of the music room. Wolfgang had made a big hit with Sabina.

Karl's farewell to Siegfried was, predictably, not so fond. Ilse more than made up for their coolness.

"We're so pleased you came all this way for Siegfried's benefit. It wouldn't have been the same without you all here. We don't like Siegfried to forget the other half of his family."

Margit approached Sabina. "I don't seem to have seen much of you this evening, Bina. Still, I can't blame you. Wolf is rather sweet."

Siegfried looked towards Wolfgang and received a surreptitious nod. The stone had been cast into the pool.

CHAPTER TWENTY-TWO

Oblivious to the commanding view over the snow-clad hills, Siegfried paused for breath. He had managed to detach Wolf from the rest of the skiers by forging ahead up the hill. Settling his skis back on the snow he stepped into them. "Progress report?" he demanded.

Wolf raised his ski goggles and wiped the sweat off his brow. "Reasonably good. I've had four letters from her so far – not too intense, but getting there. She's asked me about the cigarettes I gave her. Says she liked them, but doesn't know where to get them in England. I said I'd send her some more."

"She's no idea what they are?"

"No. She's totally naïve about drugs."

"Not totally. She's just not heard of cannabis. Doesn't know you can smoke it."

"She's bound to find out sooner or later. Then what will she think of me?"

"Do you care?"

Wolf made no answer.

"You're not falling for her, are you?"

"Of course not. But I thought the whole idea was for her to fall out with her father, not with me."

"That's right. I want her dependent on you – for cannabis, love, sex if and when the time comes. I suppose it's too early for that yet."

"Too right! I'd screw my chances if I suggested anything like that. She's not naïve in *that* department. Knows full well what's on and what isn't!"

"Give her time."

"What! Like two more years you mean? You must be joking!"

"I said this was a long-term project. You agreed."

Wolf looked away down the slope to where the rest of the Zopfs were still struggling up the hill. Heinrich was delayed by having to carry his mother's as well as his own skis, otherwise he would have been up already.

"It's just more of a commitment than I anticipated, Siegfried," he complained.

"Your whole life is a commitment to our cause! Just think of this as an extension to that."

"This is *your* cause, not mine."

"And now I've made it yours too. I expect your full support, Wolf."

Behind the goggles Wolf saw the determination in his friend's eyes. Siegfried would not let him give up now. "All right. You've got it. Just be patient."

"I've been patient for the last twenty-one years. I'm in no hurry."

In demonstration of his statement, Siegfried launched himself back down the slope, not at his usual full tilt, but in a series of curves, passing close to the others who were nearing the top. Wolf decided to wait for them. He wanted Margit's advice. While they all finished puffing and blowing from the climb, he manoeuvred himself next to her.

"Bina will be jealous when she hears how much snow we've had. She really enjoyed the bit of skiing she did over Christmas."

"You're lucky to get leave this weekend," Margit replied in short gasps. "I'm surprised you didn't plan a quick trip to England to see her. You two seem very hot on each other."

"She's a smashing girl. In fact I want to send her a small gift, but I'm stuck for ideas. You know her better than I do. What do you think she'd like?"

"How small is small? I know she has a passion for marzipan."

"Perfect! Thanks."

*

Her hands trembling, Sabina opened Wolf's parcel. Inside the layers of tissue paper she found a tin containing a chocolate-covered marzipan log. There seemed to be something else under the log. Lifting it out of the box she discovered another bundle of tissue paper. Carefully pulling the paper away she revealed twenty herbal cigarettes. She smiled. He hadn't forgotten. She quickly re-wrapped them and hid them behind a book on her shelf where her mother wouldn't find them. These would not be smoked anywhere near the house!

She wasn't sure why she liked Wolf's cigarettes so much. Probably because they reminded her of him, giving her a warm, cosy glow of happiness. When she particularly missed him, she would go up to the woods and smoke one, just to be close to him again. By the Easter holidays she had needed to ask Wolf for several more consignments of cigarettes.

She was sitting smoking one in her favourite spot in the woods when Alex rode up on Paris. She did not notice him in her dreamy state, until he called out to her.

"Hello! I didn't know you smoked." He dismounted, leaving Paris to munch on the budding foliage. He sat on the log beside her. "Haven't seen much of you for ages. Did you enjoy your trip to Germany at Christmas?"

"Mmm." Sabina did not want him here. He was disturbing her peace and tranquillity.

Alex felt rebuffed by her brevity. She no longer seemed interested in him. "Can I have one?" She looked blankly at him, so he pointed to the cigarette.

"They're special. I've only got a few."

He sniffed. The smoke certainly wasn't tobacco, but he had smelled something like it before. "I know someone who smokes those. I'm sure I could get you some more, if you want."

Sabina's eyes lit up, raising Alex's hopes. "Could you?"

"Sure. When I get back to school. Some of the sixth formers have them. Perhaps I'll try some myself. They all seem to think they're rather special."

"They are," Sabina murmured. With the prospect of a ready supply, she felt generous enough to offer Alex one. She opened the tin she kept them in. "Here. Try one."

Unlike Sabina, Alex had already tried smoking so was able to enjoy the reefer without any trouble. They smoked in silence until both reefers were no more than stubs.

"That's amazing! I'm definitely going to get hold of some of those," Alex declared, stretching lazily in the Spring sunshine. "Where did you get those from, Bina?"

"Someone I met at Christmas. No one you know." She did not want to tell him about Wolf. He was far too special to share with the likes of Alex.

Alex, however, was hardly listening. "I feel as though I want to sit here with you for ever and ever," he said, laying his arm across Sabina's shoulders.

If her mind had not been on Wolf, Sabina might have left it there. Instead she slipped out from underneath it and stood up. "Aren't you worried your father will catch you up here?"

"He can go stuff himself. He can't stop me riding." He stood up, feeling randy as hell. His eyes focused on the outlines of Sabina's breasts. Breathing heavily he drew nearer to kiss her. She had let him last summer, so he wondered why she seemed to hesitate now. But her hesitation was momentary and her lips met his.

As they drew apart, Sabina felt awful. She knew she was using Alex, that she had only allowed the kiss so he would bring her more cigarettes from his school. But she had enjoyed the kiss, despite it not matching up to Wolf's. She even allowed him another, but when his hand reached for her blouse she recoiled. Pleasant though the sensation was, she was not allowing Alex any more liberties.

"I must be getting back now, Alex. I'm supposed to be helping Mummy clear out the hen house. I only came up here for a few minutes."

Alex looked at his watch. "I suppose I'd better get back too. The tutor will be wondering where I've got to, damn him. I'm only allowed an hour's lunch break, even though it's the hols."

"Bad luck," Sabina sympathised. "Still. Not long till the exams, eh?"

"You sound as though you're looking forward to them!"

"I am, I think. Funny, isn't it?"

"You're telling me! I wish I had your brains. And your parents," he added, reaching for Paris' reins.

Sabina watched him ride off, then headed down the hill towards the farm. The new lambs were bleating loudly in the meadows, and she could see her father with Richard and Paul loading drums of chemicals onto the trailer, ready for spraying the blossoming orchards. Everyone was busy except her, so she hurried to join them.

*

In his Easter gift, Wolf sent more of the cigarettes. With the knowledge that Alex too could supply her, she felt able to smoke them more frequently. She wished she was able to go to Germany for Easter, but with the O' Levels looming, she had known better than to ask. In recompense, Wolf managed a surprise telephone call early on Easter Sunday. Sabina glowed with happiness for the remainder of the day. That evening she missed him more than ever, and in a fit of reckless abandon, she opened her bedroom window wide and leaned out to smoke one of his gifts.

She did not know her father was in the yard.

Their eyes met. In guilty haste, Sabina put the reefer behind her back, but she knew he had seen it. And smelled it.

"Sabina," he said softly. She knew instantly she was in deep trouble. "What's that you're smoking?"

"A ... cigarette."

"No it's not. I want a word with you. Wait there."

While she waited, Sabina stubbed out the offending article. She felt scared. Daddy looked more angry than she remembered seeing him for a long time. Too quickly she heard his feet on the stairs and the creak of the landing floorboards. He knocked, but did not wait for a reply.

"Where is it?" he asked.

Sabina handed him the stub. He sniffed it cautiously, satisfying himself that it was not tobacco.

"Do you know what this is?"

Dumbly she shook her head.

"Who gave it to you?"

Instinctively Sabina knew she must protect Wolf. She hesitated, eyes downcast.

Karl took both her hands in his and made her look at him. "I think this is cannabis. Who gave it to you, Sabina?" he repeated more firmly.

Sabina was devastated. "I hadn't realised. Honest. Else I'd never have smoked it. I know how strongly you feel about drugs, Daddy." She was in tears now. She dared not implicate Wolf. If Daddy were to ban her from seeing him again ... "It was Alex. He gets them from school." Her lies tripped lightly off her lips. The fear of losing Wolf seemed all that mattered.

"Alex? Does he know what they are?"

Now Sabina had to back-pedal to protect Alex. "I don't think so. They're just something passed around at school. I don't think he had any idea."

Karl liked Alex and did not want to get him into even more trouble with his father, but if there was cannabis at the school, someone ought to be told.

Sabina could see his train of thought. "You won't tell Mr Kellett, will you, Daddy? Honestly, Alex just thought they were a kind of cigarette. I'll tell him what they are. I'm sure he won't try any more."

"How can you be sure? Was this the only one?"

She nodded but unwittingly glanced at the bookshelf where her tin was usually hidden. She had left it clearly visible on the shelf. Karl spotted it, reached over and picked it up. He opened the tin.

"You were going to keep these, weren't you?" he thundered. "You see where drugs lead you? Lies, deception, dishonesty. I can't believe it of you, Sabina, I really can't. I thought I'd made my own experiences perfectly plain, and yet you continue hiding these so you can smoke them later!"

Shame and fear disguised themselves as aggression."They weren't hidden!" she yelled at him. "You spotted them easily."

"Then why deny they were there?" he yelled back.

Sabina could not tell him she wanted to keep them because Wolf had given them to her. In her frustration she snatched the tin from him and hurled it at the door. "Just leave me alone, can't you?" she wailed, flinging herself on the bed.

Karl stood looking down at her, his hands trembling – with fright, he realised. Abruptly he stepped over the scattered reefers and opened the door. Katherine was outside about to come in.

"What's going on? What's all this shouting about?" she demanded, seeing Sabina prostrate on the bed.

"She'll tell you," Karl said and left the room. He made his way downstairs, still shaken, and headed for the kitchen dresser. There was a bottle of schnapps there. He poured a generous measure into a glass, thought about pouring some back, then drained the glass anyway and sat down to wait for the shaking to stop.

Richard came in from the living room where he had been watching television with Paul. He saw the open bottle on the table and his father's white face. Sensing trouble he hastily withdrew to the living room. Like his mother he had heard the shouting, but knew better than to get involved.

Katherine came down eventually and she too noticed the bottle of schnapps. "Alcohol can be as addictive as drugs," she said pointedly.

"I know." He pushed the empty glass away. "How's Sabina? I know I overreacted, but I was frightened for her. I kept imagining her in the same state I'd been in. That's why I needed this." He gestured at the bottle. "I can't face drugs. Even now, after all these years."

Katherine sat opposite him at the kitchen table, and poured a small measure of schnapps into the glass. She took a sip. "Sabina realises that. She knows you couldn't help being so angry."

There was a long silence. From the living room, the sound of applause disturbed their private ruminations, bringing them back to the present.

Katherine screwed the cap on the bottle and put it back in the dresser. Standing behind Karl's chair she leaned forward and put her arms round his neck, resting her chin on his head, to show she forgave him his loss of temper with Sabina. "What are we going to do about Alex? Someone's got to tell him what he's smoking."

"If he doesn't already know." He could feel the warmth of her breasts on his back. It did more to calm him than the schnapps.

"You think he does?"

Karl shrugged under the weight of her arms. Enveloped like this by her he felt safe. He had forgotten how deep-seated his terror was. She began to move away, but he held onto her arms, keeping her there a moment longer so she would realise how much he needed her. Then he let her go. She sat on the chair beside him, and began drawing circles with her finger-tip on the grained and pitted table.

"I suppose I ought to tell Audrey," she said. "We can't tell Andrew. He'd throw the boy out or do something equally extreme."

"All right. You tell Audrey. Alex must be stopped. I don't want him coercing Sabina into trying anything stronger."

"She wouldn't, Schatz. You know she wouldn't."

*

After Katherine's phone call, Audrey summoned Alex into the drawing room.

"Close the door and sit down, Alex," she told him.

290

Alex followed his mother's instructions, knowing he was in trouble for something, but wondering why it wasn't his father doing the reprimanding.

"I've just had a very worrying call from Mrs Driesler. She says you gave Sabina cannabis to smoke which you got from school. She said she wasn't sure whether you knew it was cannabis. Did you?"

Alex was outraged, not only by the revelation that he had smoked cannabis, but also by the lie Sabina had apparently told. "*She* gave the cigarette to *me*! She said she got it from someone in Germany. How dare she blame me!"

Audrey believed him. His outrage was too convincing to be faked. "Then I regretfully suggest, Alex, that you have nothing more to do with young Sabina Driesler, if that's the road she's heading down."

Alex hardly heard her, his thoughts already drifting away from Sabina's treachery to the memory of how good he felt smoking the cannabis. It was definitely worth another try. He couldn't wait to get back to school.

CHAPTER TWENTY-THREE

Katherine stepped into the gloom of the hall to check the post and newspaper delivery. With two weeks to go before the start of the summer examinations, the house was like a morgue. Richard was in his room studying for his O'Levels, and Sabina for A'Levels in hers. Paul should have been working for his end of term exams too, but had managed to escape into the sunshine to help his parents with the sheep dipping. Paul sought any excuse to leave his books, and Karl did not seem to press him about it. Someone had to help around the farm after all.

Katherine picked up the local newspaper from the front door mat. A familiar face caught her eye. She glanced at the headline, gave a gasp of horror, read a few lines then called up the stairs.

"Sabina! Come down! Quickly!"

Sabina clattered down to see what was so urgent. Her mother simply pointed to the headline.

"Boy found dead in school grounds," Sabina read out loud.

"It's Alex!" Katherine whispered.

"What!" Snatching the paper from her mother, Sabina saw the photo then read the details. The cause of death was not yet known but there were no signs of foul play. The report hinted at suicide, suggesting the pressure of impending A'Levels may have proved too much for him. There was to be a post-mortem today.

"I can't believe it!" Sabina whispered, her hands shaking so much that the newspaper rustled as she stared at the photo of Alex staring grimly into the camera. "But I knew he was dreading the O'Levels. He was only interested in sport. Why he ever went on to do A'Levels, I don't know!"

"No doubt his father pushed him into taking them," Katherine suggested. "Come and sit down in the kitchen, treasure, and let's have a cup of tea. We've had a nasty shock."

As the rest of the family gathered for refreshments they were told of the news.

"Poor Audrey must be devastated," Katherine concluded. "Andrew too, though more from the shame of having a suicide in the family than love of his son, I would imagine."

Karl nodded his agreement. He was glad to see Sabina was not too grief-stricken at the news. It was the last thing she needed at such a crucial time. He mentioned it later to Katherine when they resumed sheep dipping.

"I'm just glad she's got Wolf," he said, after shunting yet another sheep into the yellow dip. "Being so far away he can't keep her from her studies and he seems to have drawn her affections from Alex. What if she'd still been great friends with him?"

"This might not have happened," Katherine said above the noise of the sheep and swishing water, but quietly enough so Paul, in charge of penning sheep at the other end of the dip, could not hear. "I think Alex was hurt rather badly by Sabina's defection to Wolf."

"Really? I hope Audrey and Andrew don't blame her then."

*

Audrey *did* blame Sabina. She blamed her husband and Sabina Driesler in equal measure for the tragedy. Immediately after hearing the results of the post-mortem Andrew had driven off to the boarding school in a rage, but Audrey had other intentions. It was late afternoon. Sabina should be home from school. As Audrey stepped out of the Jaguar at Lane Head Farm, a sudden breeze caught her black skirt. The breeze brought with it the scent of May blossom underlain by the pungent aroma of freshly dug earth. It made her think of her son's grave, soon to be dug in the churchyard in Penchurch. Angrily she wiped a tear from the corner of her eyes and slammed the car door.

At the sound, Katherine popped her head up over the garden hedge where she was hoeing.

"Audrey! What are you doing up here?" She noticed Audrey's grim expression. Perhaps she wanted a friend to pour out her heart to. "Come into the garden and I'll get us a drink."

"It was Sabina I wanted to see."

"Oh? She's in her room, studying. Take a seat under the pear tree and I'll go and fetch her."

Audrey entered the garden by the picket gate and followed the aubretia- and alyssum-bordered stone path to the centre of the lawn, where the old pear tree shaded a new wooden garden seat. One of Karl's creations she supposed, although the rest of the garden was largely Katherine's handiwork. It was a scented, peaceful place where the buzzing of bees and the delicate song of a lark soothed her, easing her grief. She reflected a moment on how much Alex had loved coming up here, how he had found in the Drieslers the companionship he could not find at home. They had made him happy until Andrew put a stop to it all. *He* was the one who made Alex so miserable, had forced him to study and stay on for A'Levels when Alex really had no aptitude. It was Andrew who had turned him into a rebel.

She saw Sabina approaching from the opposite side of the garden, still wearing her school summer dress. As she came nearer Audrey noticed how pale and dark-eyed she looked. Alex's death must have shocked her too.

"Hello, Mrs Kellett." Sabina sat on the garden seat. "I'm so sorry about Alex. You must be feeling so sad."

Audrey nodded.

"You wanted to see me?" Sabina prompted.

"Yes. I ..." Audrey came abruptly to the point. "Alex died of a heroin overdose."

Sabina gaped in disbelief. "Heroin!"

Audrey nodded. "You introduced him to drugs, so I wanted to blame you for his death."

Sabina swallowed fearfully. "Why do you think that?"

"When your mother told me about you both smoking cannabis, Alex said *you* had given it to him. He was angry with you for blaming him, so I left it at that. I decided not to tell your parents. It was your word against his, and we could have argued for months. I didn't want another dispute to come between us." She looked away, only too well aware that Sabina knew her reasons for keeping good relations with the family. Karl's daughter was a sensitive girl and saw much with those grey eyes of hers. With an effort Audrey made hers meet them again. "I never told my husband about the cannabis, of course. He still doesn't know. If he ever found out, he would make your life hell. And all the rest of your family's."

As she watched, tears shimmered in Sabina's eyes. It made her own eyes brim over. She rummaged in her handbag for a handkerchief and dabbed gently at her own tears then at Sabina's. "I came here ready to condemn you today, but something about this place changed my mind. Now I just want to warn you about taking drugs yourself."

"Don't worry, Mrs Kellett," Sabina said firmly. "I won't. I know from what Da ..." She broke off abruptly as she realised what she was about to say. No one outside the family knew of her father's experiences except Robert Murdoch. "As soon as I knew what they were, I told the person who gave them to me I didn't want any more."

Audrey looked concerned. "Who did give you those reefers?"

Two years on and her love for Wolf was stronger than ever. Without hesitation, and without realising the underlying truth of her words, Sabina replied: "Siegfried." She knew everyone could and would believe it of him. Audrey evidently did.

"Ah. I see. Now I understand." She gave a deep sigh. "You watch out for that half-brother of yours. He's dangerous."

"He helped kill your son."

Sabina's bald statement showed she was racked with guilt. Audrey put her hand over the weeping girl's. "No. It would have happened anyway, some other way. Alex was not happy."

"But I can't help feeling it was partly my fault! If I'd never given him one of those –"

"It wasn't your fault, Sabina. It was my husband's for being so hard on Alex. He hated that school. Taking heroin must have seemed like a way of escaping it."

Sabina sniffed, unconvinced. She felt more than partly responsible; she felt wholly responsible. Alex had fallen out with her over that incident. She knew he had been far keener on her than she was on him. It had left him feeling betrayed.

Audrey squeezed her hand. "I wanted you for my daughter-in-law, you know."

Sabina nodded.

"Talking to you has helped me. I know what my true feelings are now. I'm determined not to let Andrew ruin Alan and Angela's lives too."

Sabina looked up. "You're going to leave him?"

Audrey actually laughed. "No! Life's too cosy for me here. No, I'll just make his life such hell, he'll stay away of his own accord."

Sabina had a nasty suspicion. "You won't involve my family, will you, Mrs Kellett?"

Audrey's blue eyes grew wistful. "No. I respect them too much. Speaking of which," she said, rising to her feet, "I'd better go and pay my respects to your mother. She'll think me awfully rude for ignoring her."

They both headed for the back door. Katherine was busy in the kitchen, placing biscuits on a plate. A jug full of iced lemon squash stood on the table, while the kettle was just beginning to whistle.

"How are you, Audrey?" she greeted her guest, quickly removing the kettle from the range and filling the waiting teapot.

"All the better for coming here. Still shocked, of course, but ... well ... you know what it's like to lose someone close."

Katherine gave her a hug. "Yes. I know." She turned to Sabina. "Can you tell everyone drinks are ready, please."

While Sabina was away, Katherine had a few moments to chat quietly to Audrey. "When is the funeral?"

"I don't know yet. After the inquest. Whenever it is, will you come?"

Katherine looked surprised. "Yes, of, course, if you want us. I rather thought you might want to avoid any awkward confrontations at such ..."

"I'd rather you and Karl were there. I know the children can't make it, what with the exams and everything. But you were his friends. Andrew can be damned."

"Are you sure, Audrey? We wouldn't want to upset –"

"I want you there. Please. Sarah too if she can possibly make it. I just feel I need my friends around me at the moment."

"Of course. I understand."

Paul was the first through the door. In the middle of a growth surge, he was always hungry, but the sight of Mrs Kellett halted him in his tracks before he could reach the biscuits. He glanced down at his manure-stained jeans, then across at his mother. Katherine mouthed the word 'hello' to him and nodded at Audrey.

Paul shuffled his feet awkwardly, uncertain how to speak to someone recently bereaved.

Audrey recognised the symptoms and helped him out. "Hello, Paul. Don't mind me. You go on and grab a biscuit."

Paul smiled shyly. Without further ado he took a couple of garibaldis and stood munching them by the sink as Richard made his entry from upstairs.

"Oh. Hello, Mrs Kellett." He too looked as awkward as his brother.

"Hello, Richard. You busy revising too?"

"Yes. But I'd rather be outside."

"I know," Audrey sympathised. "Who'd want to study on a lovely day like today? Alex certainly wouldn't." Mentioning his name hurt, but not as much as she had feared. "He enjoyed helping here. He would have done well at farming, but Andrew wanted him to study law."

Her bitterness told them all a lot about her relationship with her husband, but Karl and Sabina's arrival instantly lightened her mood. Karl went up to her and took her hand in both his.

"You have my deepest sympathy, Audrey."

She had been coping well until then, but the touch of him and the concern in his eyes brought fresh tears to her own. She desperately needed a male shoulder to cry on. Andrew had not obliged. She stood up and thrust her head against Karl's chest, feeling his hands rise to her shoulders.

Sabina watched in amazement as Mrs Kellett sobbed in her father's arms. She had promised not to involve Sabina's family, and here she was straightaway in a close embrace with Daddy. Sabina glanced at her mother, but she seemed unconcerned. Embarrassed by the scene, Richard and Paul left the room, but Sabina wanted to observe any goings on.

After a minute, Karl passed Audrey over to Katherine. Seeing her cling to another woman, Sabina's fears subsided. She supposed when you felt such grief you sought comfort from anyone who was prepared to give it.

Audrey felt better after a cup of tea and repeated her request for their presence at the funeral.

Sabina saw her chance. "I need to say goodbye to Alex. If I've not got an exam that day, I'd dearly like to come too."

Katherine and Karl looked at Audrey. She shrugged to signify she had no objections.

As she left, Audrey smiled at Sabina. No mention had been made of the post-mortem or of Sabina's part in introducing Alex to drugs. There was no point.

*

As she watched the coffin being lowered ceremoniously into the ground, Sabina knew she would always feel guilty, no matter what Mrs Kellett said. The grave would be a constant reminder of her part in Alex's death. It made the finality of death so real. She would never see Alex again.

She found her thoughts turning to Wolf. What if something happened to him and she never saw him again? The thought clutched at her heart. It wasn't enough only seeing him during her brief holidays in Germany. She wanted to be nearer him. She remembered something Wolf had suggested in one of his recent letters. At the time she had glossed over it, thoughts of exams uppermost in her mind. Now she saw sense in it, but she needed to ask someone's advice, someone close who knew about careers.

While the mourners were filing back to their cars, she sought out her Aunty Sarah. "May I have a word? In private?"

Sarah looked up at her statuesque niece in surprise. "What, now?"

Sabina nodded. "We'll never have the chance later at home. You know what it's like."

"All right. What's the problem?"

They were standing on the verge as cars began to leave the church's congested driveway.

"I'm not sure I want to go to university now. I think I would learn more actually working in Germany."

"You don't want to be a teacher?"

"No. There are plenty more things I can do with German than teach the same old verbs, day in, day out."

"Well, then. I think it's a splendid idea. How will you find a job?"

Sabina smiled. "Siegfried's stepfather. He's bound to have somewhere in his construction empire he can make use of me!" She grew more serious. "Will you back me up when I put it to Mummy and Daddy?"

"Of course."

Sabina collared her parents directly they all got into the Land Rover. "What would you say, if I were to forget about university and went over to work in Germany instead?"

Dead silence greeted her question, then both parents spoke at once.

"What's suddenly put that idea –"

"You can't be serious!" Karl glanced at Katherine and nodded to let her go on.

Katherine turned round to face the back. "Have you thought about this carefully, treasure, or is it a spur of the moment decision? What would you do? Where would you live? At Medebach?"

The answer came without hesitation. "No. With the Zopfs. I could –"

"No!" Karl butted in. "You're not living with *them*!"

"But I've stayed there so many times! What's the difference?"

Karl drove on up the valley road behind the funeral cortege, his mind searching for reasons for his instinctive refusal. "Because they'd be wholly responsible for you, and ..." And I don't trust them, he wanted to say, but knew he had no grounds for doing so.

Sarah picked up on his hesitation. "Come on, Karl! Admit it. You're just frightened of letting your little girl go off into the big wide world. She'd be doing that anyway at university. At least the Zopfs will be able to keep a good eye on her for you."

He did not reply. There was probably an element of truth in what Sarah said. He was relieved when Katherine stalled for him.

"Give us some time to think it over, Bina. You have rather sprung it on us, you know."

Sabina smelled victory and grinned at her aunt. Her mother at least had no objections. Her father could be persuaded by subtle pressure. She knew exactly how to handle *him*!

299

CHAPTER TWENTY-FOUR

The autobahn exit for Iserlohn was approaching. Siegfried slowed the open top Mercedes a fraction, dodged behind a lorry and nipped into the inside lane. Beside him Wolfgang hung onto the door as he read out a section from Sabina's latest letter.

> *"Guess what! Daddy has finally asked the Zopfs if I can live with them. From what Margit says, there shouldn't be any problem! Come August I'll pack my bags and journey to the land of my forefathers.*
>
> *I feel so at home in Germany, especially when I'm with you. That magical day we spent in Dortmund together on my last visit will stay with me for the rest of my life."*

Wolfgang folded the wind-rustled letter. "It starts to get personal here, but you can see how keen she is to come over. We'll make a true German of her yet!"

Breaking sharply for a junction, Siegfried made a rapid gear change, pulled out ahead of a slow-moving coach, then settled the car south for Iserlohn. "Patience is something I've learned over the years, Wolf. I'm pleased you've learned it too. When I asked you to do this for me, I knew it would be a long-term project. I hoped you'd stay the course."

"Couldn't have been easier. I really like her. Don't have to pretend." He squinted into the bright sunshine, camouflaging his frown. "I hope my father's not too disappointed I couldn't find a pure-blooded German girlfriend." He grinned at Siegfried. "Talking of which, how's Ulrike?"

"Gone. Too pushy. It's Ellen now. Bit more classy." He loosened his tie and undid his top shirt button. "Warm, isn't it? How about a beer?"

"Suits me. Let's start the weekend now!"

Siegfried pulled into the car park of the next pub, a dark brick building, its windows already swathed in geraniums. "At least it won't be full of bloody Turks! Not like the one near my office. Can't get in the place for them. Not that I'd want to. Noisy brutes." He slammed the car door.

They strolled into the dingy bar and ordered a *Dortmunder* each. The barmaid smiled warmly at Siegfried. "Nice car," she said, handing over his foaming glass. "This year's model, is it?"

Wolfgang sipped his beer, listening to Siegfried's conversation with the barmaid. It was always the same, wherever they went. He lapped up attention, seldom returning it in kind. Wolfgang wondered whether Ulrike had got fed up with Siegfried's arrogance and walked out voluntarily, rather than been sent packing as Siegfried made out. He seldom kept his girlfriends long. Whereas Sabina and he ... Over two years now.

"What are you grinning about?"

Wolf drained his glass. "You and women. I'm glad I've got Sabina." His smile slipped. It was now or never. He must face up to Siegfried before it was too late. He lowered his voice, but the barmaid was busy with another customer. "You can forget the dope, Siegfried. I know it was a large part of the plan, but it's not going to work. She was fooled at first, but then she was only sixteen. Now with this friend of hers dying, she's wary. She'll never take anything stronger ... and I don't want her to."

Siegfried ran his finger round the rim of his glass. His grey eyes bored deep into his friend's. "You've gone soft, haven't you? I'm disappointed. I expected you to be more persuasive with her."

"She won't have anything to do with the stuff, Siegfried! I can hardly force her. I'm amazed she's still so fond of me, after finding out what I was giving her."

Siegfried ground his teeth in irritation. He decided to make light of it. He needed Wolf's cooperation.

"Never mind. Maybe it's just as well. If you were caught by the police with that stuff ... You get on and enjoy her. Marry her even, if that's what you want. Just turn her into a good German. For your father's sake. Has he met her yet?"

"No. He was out both times she came round. He knows she's your sister though, so he ought to approve."

"Half-sister." He finished his beer. "Let's be off. I promised my mother I'd be back in time for cocktails. They've got guests this evening."

301

"Important ones?"

"Yes. That kind. I'm keen to meet them." Outside bright sunlight hit them. They both donned sunglasses. "You could come along too. Your parents are invited."

"Great. It's always nice to forget I'm only a humble apprentice during the week."

"Don't belittle yourself, Wolf. You'll be boss of your own factory, driving your own Mercedes soon, you'll see!"

"With your sister at my side."

"Half-sister!"

"Whatever."

*

Ilse guided her elegant young companion through the throng of guests towards Siegfried. She tapped him on the arm and he excused himself from the rest of his group.

"Siegfried, let me introduce Sophie Wendt. Sophie has just returned from a fact-finding trip to Berlin. But I'll leave her to tell you all about it. If you'll both excuse me?"

Ilse squeezed Siegfried's arm as she left. She loved him so much. Sophie was a nice girl. A good German. Siegfried was sure to like her.

Sure enough, half an hour later, he was still talking to her. Wolfgang's mother, Claudia Garisch approached Ilse, vodka-martini in her spindly hand. "Looks hopeful, doesn't it, Ilse. Like my Wolfgang and Siegfried's sister. If those two married, our families would be sort of united. I just wish I could convince Josef he should meet Sabina, but he won't have it. He should be welcoming the British into Europe, not turning them away."

"De Gaulle doesn't want them. Why should we?"

"To counterbalance the French, of course! We don't want their influence to be overpowering, do we?"

Ilse twirled the olive in her drink. "Leaving politics aside for a moment, Claudia, did you know Sabina's parents have asked if she could come to live here from August?"

"No! Wolf will be thrilled. When did you hear that? He hasn't told me!"

"Only this week. Once she's finished her school exams she'll come and work for Paul. It seemed more useful than studying German at

302

university when she's already got a good grasp of the language. She'll learn about business ... and be nearer Wolfgang. That had a lot to do with it, I think!"

"I *am* pleased. The poor boy does mope so inbetween her visits. I must go and tell Josef. He'll *have* to take an interest in her now."

Ilse watched her scuttle across to her husband's side. He immediately frowned, not sharing his wife's pleasure. Poor Claudia, caught in the middle between father and son. Ilse glanced towards Siegfried and smiled in satisfaction. He was deep in conversation with Sophie. She left them to it.

*

Sophie turned her back on the intense young man approaching from her right. Her hint was taken and the potential interloper moved on. It was time to broach more personal topics with her quarry. "Your reputation for ruthlessness has reached Berlin, you know."

"I'm pleased to hear it."

"Your reputation with women too."

Siegfried's eyebrows raised in half-hearted apology, but he made no comment. Sophie was a plain-speaker, and he wanted to listen. Her almond eyes held his, with no shyness or false coyness. He liked what he saw, but more importantly, he liked what he heard. No feather-brained goose, this one!

Sophie played her ace. "I've been asked to organise a reception for about twenty of our new recruits in Dortmund next month. Since you live there, perhaps you could be of help in finding a suitable venue for us. You know of course where we would be ... welcome."

"Indeed I do. Perhaps you'd like to accompany me there one evening beforehand for dinner. Then you can see for yourself what the facilities are like, choose the menu ... whatever."

She smiled in a business-like fashion, then broadened it as she quipped: "Your reputation is true."

"Which reputation are you talking about?"

"I'll leave you to guess. But perhaps I'd better warn you. They call me 'The Snow Queen'."

"I can't imagine why. But who do you mean by 'they'?"

Her trill of laughter sent a shiver down his spine. "Just friends." Her fingers flew to her lips. "That reminds me. While I was in Berlin

I met an old friend of yours who asked to be remembered to you. Gustav Halstrup."

"Gustav! Well I never! I was only a boy when I last saw him. What's he up to now?"

"Doing fine. He's quite influential amongst the acting community, and pretty high-up in our hierachy."

"That doesn't surprise me. He taught me a lot, did Gustav. Like how to hide my true feelings and manipulate people."

"Like me?" she joked, laying her fingers playfully on his wrist as she studied his face to see if she was right. His gaze never wavered. He was either a supreme actor or sincere in his dealings with her. She hoped it was the latter. She already rather liked Siegfried Driesler. His name reminded her of another matter. "Before I forget, Gustav particularly wanted to know how things stood between you and your 'traitor' of a father." Her smile changed abruptly to mock reproof. "He can't have meant Herr Zopf."

Siegfried's eyes iced. "Paul's the only father I acknowledge. The other *is* a traitor. Lives in England. He's learned to avoid me, although his daughter's coming over to live here soon." His expression warmed again. "I'll have fun then."

"Oh? Why?"

"Wolfgang Garisch and I are trying to make her see our point of view. That would *really* make my father mad! I want to see him disown her like he disowned me."

"But surely his daughter will resist our ideas. Especially if she's English – I mean half-English or whatever."

"She's young, impressionable. And you'd be surprised what love can do. She listens to Wolf. Anyway, we'll take things very slowly, very gradually. Show her some of the worst sides of the *Gastarbeiter*. Move on from there. That's another thing Gustav taught me. Patience. I'm in no hurry. I get nearly as much fun from planning ways to hurt my father as from seeing him hurt."

Sophie did not seem shocked. "Have you hurt him much already?"

"A bit. Not as much as I'd like." His voice was tinged with regret. "I broke his leg and once almost stabbed him. I nearly managed to drown his wife." He grinned at the memory. "I still carry the knife Gustav gave me, to remind me of my mission. Here!" He reached into his jacket and produced the small penknife, cradling it lovingly

304

in the palm of his hand. "Perhaps one day I'll get to use it. I always promised myself I would, although I can't while he and Paul are still friends. That's why I'm concentrating on Sabina, his daughter, since she'll be accessible." He tried to look modest. "Actually it was my idea for her to live over here, although I don't think anyone else realises that. Not even Wolf."

Sophie laughed. "Ruthless indeed!" She touched his lapel. "If I can be of any help with this Sabina, just ask."

Their eyes met in conspiracy, sending tingles down Siegfried's spine. It was the first time he had met a woman who fully understood him, was even willing to take risks for him. He sensed his mother's eyes watching him and turned round to smile his appreciation of her matchmaking.

*

Their dinner engagement was perfect. Sophie had chosen to wear an opalescent blouse and plain blue skirt, reasonably informal as the restaurant was not top class, but beautifully cut to express her own good taste and enhance her classic looks. Siegfried was proud to introduce her to the manager, whom he knew well.

"Fräulein Wendt wishes to book a reception here soon," Siegfried told him. "I'm sure you can offer her a good deal, Helmut."

"I'm sure I can, Herr Driesler," the manager replied with an understanding nod, showing them to their table.

They sat down and studied the menu. After Sophie had made her choice she looked across at Siegfried. "One thing I can't understand. If you hate your father so much, why do you keep his name?"

"That's my mother's fault. She insisted I kept it even when I came back to Germany to live with her and Paul. She's always hoped I'd make it up with him. I've just got used to living with it and people know me by it now, so what's the point? Besides, it's a constant reminder of him and how much I want to seek revenge."

"You must have had a truly awful experience to hate him so much."

Röbel's assaults were something Siegfried never spoke about. To anyone. Such humiliation was impossible to share. Ignoring her comment, he signalled to the waiter to come and take their order.

Sophie understood his reluctance to talk, but even so spent the remainder of the evening learning more about the man she had set her sights on. Gustav Halstrup had been right. Siegfried was headed for the top, and she wanted to be there with him. It was time to shed her 'Snow Queen' image and inject a bit of warmth into a relationship. It wouldn't be difficult for a man as perfect as Siegfried.

After dinner he took her back to his apartment. Sophie was unprepared to make her commitment so soon, but Siegfried seemed to expect it. Rather than spurn him, she let his fingers slip inside her blouse as they sat together drinking cognac on his leather sofa.

"Siegfried," she whispered, as he put down his glass and approached her more directly. "I've never –"

His lips closed over hers, allowing no protest. Sophie let go her inhibitions. This was to be her moment of sacrifice and she intended to enjoy it. She kept her eyes open throughout, relishing the sight of those determined eyes so close to hers, the feel of his soft hair against her breast, the touch of his lips on her body. He was *the* Siegfried. The hero. And she was his.

As he took her, their eyes locked. It was combat, a duel. She submitted and he was master. Each thrust made her gasp as he entered deeper, overpowering her senses, numbing her body as it merged with his. She watched as his moment of victory came; teeth bared, his breathing harsh, a growl. *Sieg*. Victory. *Fried'*. Peace. He grew still, staring down at her.

"You'll stay here tonight."

She knew it was not a question.

CHAPTER TWENTY-FIVE

Karl unloaded the last suitcase from the hired car. "Just as well the rest of the family stayed at home, the amount of stuff you've brought," he told Sabina.

"Some of it's yours," she playfully reminded him. "Anyway, you shouldn't have insisted on buying me those new outfits."

"I couldn't have you looking like a tramp to start work," he teased her.

A maid he did not recognise helped him in with the cases as Sabina disappeared off with Margit to inspect her new room.

Ilse stood waiting in the cool of the hall. "Leave those there, Karl. I'll have someone take them up in a minute. Come and have some refreshment."

He followed her out to the terrace where they sat under a large sunshade. Cold beers stood waiting. They toasted their continuing friendship then Ilse got down to business.

"I know you're anxious about her, Karl, but I promise we'll take care of her, like one of our own daughters."

"I'm sure you will, Ilse. It's really her and Wolf I'm worried about. He is four years older than her, and you know what young men are like."

"Yes, I remember you well!"

Karl smiled. "We had fun together, didn't we? Twenty-seven years we've known each other!" He shook his head. "Unbelievable!"

Their eyes met fondly, past differences annulled, lost in memories of earlier times, until Karl began to feel uncomfortable with the intimacy of her gaze.

"What about Siegfried? He won't be here, will here?"

"No. He's been living in Paul's old apartment in Dortmund for some time now. He's got his own life there, friends and such-like. He and Wolf see quite a bit of each other at various social events." She smiled proudly. "Paul's very pleased with Siegfried's efforts in the

307

business. He seems to have a flair for tough negotiating – knows what he wants and gets it."

"I can imagine he would. Single-minded is Siegfried. And ruthless."

Ilse knew he meant it as criticism, but pretended to understand it as praise. "A lot of people say that about him. Including his girlfriend, Sophie. A charming girl. I introduced her to him when I thought he would never find a suitable partner. They've been together nearly two months now. A record for Siegfried, I think." She smiled wickedly. "I've asked them both over for dinner tonight. I thought you might like to meet her."

Karl's heart sank, but he kept his feelings hidden. "As a potential mother of my grandchildren?"

"*Our* grandchildren, you mean. I hope so. Sophie's very sensible. She knows how to handle Siegfried. Won't stand any nonsense from him. Unlike me and Paul."

Karl heard the regret. "Oh? Still got his girlfriends, has he?"

She nodded. "I try not to mind. It's always been his way, but when I hear how young some of them are ..."

"You're still a very attractive woman, Ilse. I'm sure Paul wouldn't want anyone else as his wife."

"Wife, yes. If only he spent more nights here. He's away 'on business' tonight. Sends you his apologies." She drew her chair closer to his. "How is it I can talk so easily to you, Karl? It's always been like this between us, hasn't it? Years go by, but when we meet again it's just like yesterday."

"We know each other well enough to speak our minds, that's all. It's the same with Katherine's sister and me. She always pours out her troubles to me." He sensed her lack of interest and returned to more immediate concerns. "What if you took a lover? Would Paul object?"

"I don't know. I've never met anyone I liked well enough ... except you."

Karl was silent, the feeling mutual.

Encouraged rather than disheartened by his silence, Ilse pressed her case. "Siegfried says I ought to sleep with you again, if that's what I want."

Karl was taken aback by her forthrightness. "Seems a strange topic for him to discuss with you."

She laughed at his shocked expression. "He's always known I still wanted you. From that time in the ruined church in Dortmund when he was only eight. You remember? You kissed me in front of him."

"I remember."

"Don't you feel the same? You've always had Katherine with you before. Perhaps this time ...?"

A shout came from an upstairs window. "Mutti! Can Sabina come with us to the opera next week. She says she's never been before."

"Of course," Ilse called back to Margit. She murmured a quick aside to Karl. "We must continue our little talk later. In private." She raised her voice again. "Do you two want a drink? There's some here getting warm."

"We'll be down in a tick."

Karl raised his glass to his lips with a wry smile. Ilse never gave up hope. He set his glass back down on the white wrought-iron table. "Opera? What are you seeing?"

She accepted the change of subject. "*Tristan und Isolde*. Better than the Rolling Stones, wouldn't you agree?"

He shrugged. "Depends on what you're used to. Wagner was always one of your favourites. Sabina's more used to pop music, though perhaps the Stones aren't quite her taste either. Don't get me wrong, though. We do listen to more serious music at times."

Ilse was dismissive. "We'll soon educate her. We always take the children. Music is so important for them. If Sabina's going to live here, she must learn about German culture, mustn't she?"

"Of course."

"Another beer? Sounds like the girls are just coming."

"Please."

*

Karl straightened his tie in the mirror. A meeting with Siegfried was always traumatic, but if his girlfriend was with him, he might behave himself for once. Wolf would be there too for Sabina. There was no keeping *him* away, now Sabina was here. It would be interesting to see Wolf again. He had only met him the once at Siegfried's twenty-first, but he had heard a lot since from Sabina. Too much at times. He sighed heavily, happy that Sabina was turning out such a fine girl, yet sad she was leaving home. Inevitable, he told himself as he left his room.

Downstairs Ilse was waiting on the terrace with Margit and the two other girls. None of them had left home yet, he thought with a pang of regret. He sat down next to Margit. "Where's Sabina?"

She pointed to the front of the house. "At the end of the drive looking out for Wolf's taxi. She wants to greet him in private, I should think."

Ilse handed Karl a beer. "I seem to remember you having a need for some decent beer last time you visited us. Are things still as bad in England?"

"Thanks." He took a swift gulp, licking the foam from his lips. "Getting worse, if anything. The big breweries are buying up the small traditional ones. Mass-produced bilge-water's the result."

"Like the music?"

"You're showing your age, Ilse."

Voices came from the house. Ilse went through to the hall to greet the latest arrival. She appeared a minute later with Wolf and a highly excited Sabina in tow. After they had all greeted Wolf, a car drew up. Siegfried and Sophie. Karl tensed, feeling threatened. Taking a deep breath he tried to relax as Siegfried led Sophie across the terrace towards Karl.

No wonder Siegfried found Sophie attractive! She had the same looks and physique as his mother. Her fine blonde hair was swept up and back into a loose bun, framing her delicate features. Her crisp, embroidered blouse and full floral skirt spoke of tradition rather than the latest mini-skirted fashion. Karl could not help but like her. He took her hand. It was soft, with long, clear nails, unsullied by varnish. Her voice was light and friendly.

"We meet at last, Herr Driesler."

"At last? I didn't know you existed until today. I don't hear from Siegfried, as you probably know."

"Yes, I know. A shame. We must do something about that, mustn't we, Siegfried?"

Siegfried nodded, but without enthusiasm. Ignoring his father, he took Sophie's arm to introduce her to Sabina. "I expect we'll be seeing quite a lot of you now, Sabina. You and Wolf will have to come round to my flat in Dortmund, meet a few friends, and sample some of Sophie's wonderful cooking. Not like the English muck you're used to."

Sabina was used to Siegfried's rudeness. "That would be nice. Thank you. Do you live in Dortmund too, Sophie?"

"No. In Soest. But I'm planning on moving there in the near future."

"In with me!" Siegfried proclaimed loudly for all the family to hear.

Ilse and Karl exchanged pleased parental glances. Maybe Sophie was just what Siegfried needed to settle him down and help him forget his traumatic childhood.

"Well, let's get everyone some drinks," Ilse declared. She beckoned the maid over to oblige. "We'll eat out here since it's a lovely evening. Such a shame Heinrich's not here too. You don't have national service in England any more, do you, Karl?"

"No, thank heavens. I wouldn't want Richard or Paul to have to go off. I need them too much on the farm."

"What about their wishes?" Siegfried interjected, thrusting his beer glass aggressively towards Karl, slopping a quantity onto the terrace by his feet. "Don't they want the chance to experience something other than being farm-boys?"

"Not at the moment. They're only sixteen and fourteen. When they finish school it's up to them what they want to do next, but I hope at least one of them will stay on at the farm. There's enough for us all to do."

"Business booming?" asked Ilse.

Karl nodded.

Siegfried saw an opening for gentle provocation. "You won't mind what they do, so long as they stay out of the drugs scene. Am I right?"

Sabina's guilty eyes dropped suddenly, but her father did not notice, intent only on dodging a skirmish with Siegfried. "They all know the dangers of drugs."

"Of course. You told them your own experiences. You know what it's like to be a junkie."

"Yes. I do," he admitted painfully. He switched his gaze to Sophie's, in apology for his confession, but her face was expressionless. Siegfried must have told her all about his traitor of a father. In case he had not, Karl added for Sophie's benefit: "That's to say, I know what it's like to be forced to become a ... junkie. It wasn't my choice as you well know."

311

Ilse rescued him. "No one's blaming you, Karl. It was that man ... what was his name?" She looked to Karl for help.

"Goslar."

His tone chilled her. "Yes. That man Goslar's fault. He should never have done such a thing to a fellow countryman."

Siegfried gave Sophie's hand a light squeeze. He felt her respond. Good. He had been worried she would be charmed by his father, as women so often were, but Sophie was steadfast.

Throughout the evening meal Siegfried constantly baited Karl to ensure Sophie fully understood his hatred of his father. The rest of the family did their best to interrupt or tone down his worst excesses, but as the nine of them sat over coffee and liqueurs, bathed in humid, honeysuckle-scented air, Siegfried continued to apply relentless pressure on his father.

"I can't understand why you agreed to take British citizenship. That's betraying your birthright!"

"It was simply accepting my choice of home," Karl replied as patiently as he could. "I wanted to be entitled to participate fully in life, to vote and so on. Besides, we were ... recommended to take it."

"Forced you mean! What kind of democracy is that? You've become part of a nation which imposed its will on half the world's population."

"And we're all part of the nation which imposed its will on the other half," Karl countered. "Don't spoil the evening with your desire for one-upmanship, Siegfried. It's not appreciated by anyone; not even Sophie."

He had seen Sophie's brief unguarded look of impatience with Siegfried. Perhaps at last she was finding Siegfried's performance unwarranted.

"Sophie can speak for herself!" Siegfried snapped.

Ilse stood up. "Well! It's getting damp out here. We ought to move inside and let Beate clear away." She looked pointedly at Siegfried, who took the hint and offered his arm to Sophie.

"Fancy a stroll around the grounds?" he asked her.

The pair wandered off into the darkness, while the rest of the family came in out of the falling dew. The younger members disappeared off to the games room for table tennis, leaving Ilse and

Karl in the living room. Karl sat on the sofa, expecting Ilse to take her usual fireside chair. Instead she joined him.

"I'm sorry. He can't leave you alone, can he? But you were right. Sophie might do something for him. You never know what influence we women can have on our men."

Her stressed 'our' told Karl it included him. He carefully reminded her of her marital commitment. "So where's Paul tonight? Business you said."

Ilse reached for a silver box of cigarettes, lit one and blew the smoke carefully away from Karl. "Düsseldorf. A conference with some of his construction friends. Boring as hell. I'm well out of it." She turned towards him, her knee brushing his. "I'd far rather be here. With you."

"And a house full of children," he pointed out.

"It's a big house. We don't get in each other's way. They'll be playing table tennis and snooker for hours yet. Margit will see to that."

Karl sensed danger. "Ilse ..."

"Yes?"

"It's been a long day. I think I'll go on up."

She smiled. "Of course. You go."

She watched him leave the room, unsure whether she was interpreting his signals correctly. She knew what *she* wanted. Ever since that first glimpse of him in 1950 at the station in Winterberg, she had known. The feelings had taken her by surprise, made her angry with herself that she should still want him so badly. Over the years the feelings had never diminished. She would always remember how he looked after her when Erich threw her out, had shown her enough tenderness to tell her he still cared. That was fifteen years ago. He cared for her still. She was sure of it.

She stubbed out her cigarette and made her way upstairs.

*

Karl had already removed his shoes and shirt when he heard his door open. It could only be one person. An unexpected tingle of excitement coursed through his veins as his eyes confirmed it was Ilse.

She slipped through the half-open door, carefully closing it with the merest click of the latch. She walked towards him, barefoot, her body loosely encased in a white satin wrap. A smile was on her lips;

a smile of eagerness and anticipation; a smile he recognised from long ago which sent the blood rushing through him just as readily as when they were young lovers.

He put up his hands to ward her off. "Ilse, you mustn't tempt me."

She gave a warm, throaty chuckle. "So you *are* tempted! I knew you would be." She walked right into his hands, her breasts fitting perfectly like a train into buffers. She had come home.

Karl's fingertips did not recoil. Of their own accord they curled over the smooth satin, feeling the roundness of her, his palms pressed by her nipples. It was an easy matter to slip his fingers under the cool satin to the warmth beneath. Twenty-four years since he last held those breasts, twenty-four years since his lips had sought their softness. He bent his head down, feeling her fingers grasp his hair as his own undid the cord of her wrap and let it fall to the floor. Her hands were running over him now, re-familiarising themselves with his chest and back. He sensed the pause as she encountered the long, raised scars there, but she had seen them before, ignored them now, continued on her way down to undo his belt.

Their mouths joined at last, eyes drinking in the proximity of the other's face, nose savouring the other's smell, tongue tasting the sweetness of youth rediscovered. Time had gone backwards. They were as they had been that last Easter in 1943, so much in love, wanting each other ... regardless.

Karl tipped her gently sideways onto the bed, removing the rest of his clothes as he admired her sprawled body below him. Her hands reached up to receive him and he was on her, the length of his body feeling her skin against his. Grey eyes met blue as he regained possession of what was once his.

"I love you, Schatz," she breathed into his ear. "I love you. I love you. Love you. Love you. My Schatz, my Schatz, my Schatz."

Just as in days gone by, he kept time with her at first, but gradually increased his rate until her words came in gasps. His shoulders felt the familiar tightening of her grasp, until he carried them through as she moaned their arrival. After a moment to regain his own breath, he brushed a strand of golden hair from her damp face and kissed her.

"Still as noisy as ever, aren't you?"

"Only with you," she assured him. "I never got into the habit of it with Paul. That was always our little ritual."

He didn't like the reference to Paul. It reminded him too much that he also had a marriage partner. Now it was all over, the flood of guilt and remorse followed the ebb of passion. Ilse had no such doubts, snuggling into him, showing no inclination to go back to her own room.

Well, it's too late to throw her out now, he decided as his earlier tiredness began to catch up with him. He turned out the light, closed his eyes and tried not to worry that Ilse slept by his side.

CHAPTER TWENTY-SIX

"While you're over here, you must come and meet my parents," Wolf told the man he was rapidly considering as his prospective father-in-law. The two were alone at the breakfast table, lingering over coffee, while the rest of the household lazed in bed.

Karl topped up their coffee cups from the percolator. "What time are you going? I could drive you home."

"I was planning on leaving it as late as possible." Wolf took a contemplative sip of the hot, dark brew. "But on second thoughts, it would be nice if you could come for lunch. Tell you what," he said, pushing back his chair, "I'll give my parents a ring now, before they go off to church, and see what they say. My mother always gets in twice as much food as we need."

He disappeared off to the telephone. Five minutes later he returned just as Siegfried appeared, clad in a white towelling dressing gown, hair still wet from the shower.

"Morning, Siegfried," Wolf said breezily. "You and Sophie sleep well?"

"On and off. I'll be glad when my mother decides to give us a room together. You and Sabina sleep well?" he retaliated.

Wolf glared, then smiled reassuringly at Karl. "Don't worry. He's only joking."

Karl made no comment. He did not even look at Wolf, but out of the corner of his eye saw Siegfried watching closely. Did he suspect anything? "What did your parents say?" he hurriedly asked Wolf.

"Vater was a bit cagey when Mutter asked him," he warned Karl. "He's not really accepted Sabina yet, I'm afraid. But Mutter insisted, and, surprisingly, he agreed. Perhaps he's beginning to accept the inevitable at last. He even went and invited Siegfried and Sophie too." He turned to Siegfried. "I said you'd come. I hope I was right?"

Siegfried nodded. "Fine. I like your father. We've always got on well."

"What time are they expecting us?" Karl asked.

"Midday. It only takes half an hour from here, so there's plenty of time yet."

Karl looked at his watch. It was late. Almost nine. "I'd better wake Sabina up for some breakfast, or she won't want any of that lunch your mother's cooking."

"Wolf can go and wake her," Siegfried lewdly suggested.

Karl ignored the provocation. "It's all right. I'll go."

As he passed Ilse's room she appeared at the door, as before her satin wrap loosely draped around her. She was in the middle of putting on her make-up, her face powdered and eyes mascaraed, lipstick case in her hand.

She blew him a kiss. "Morning, Schatz. Am I the last one up?"

Karl paused in his tracks. "No. I was just coming to wake Bina. We're off to Wolf's parents for lunch. I hope that's no inconvenience to you?" Edging closer, he lowered his voice. "Ilse. Don't call me 'Schatz'."

"Sorry. Slip of the tongue." She smiled fondly at his back as he walked away up the landing.

*

They set off in two cars towards Dortmund, Siegfried soon speeding ahead in the open-top Mercedes with a headscarfed Sophie at his side. Wolf gave directions to Karl, who eventually pulled up alongside the Mercedes in the driveway of an old suburban house, its frontage entirely renovated with new stonework and modern windows to hide the bullet holes and bomb damage of old. Ornamental conifers ensured privacy of entrance and exit. The front garden was neatly tended, with weed-free beds and tile-edged borders, although the conifers gave it a gloomy aspect, even on such a bright summer's day.

"The house where I grew up," Wolf told Karl, leading him and Sabina up the three steps to the front door. His mother had been watching out for them and opened it immediately.

"Herr Driesler! Sabina. Welcome." She offered her right hand. Karl was careful not to squeeze it too hard, it seemed so fragile. "I'm so pleased Wolfgang thought to invite you. Please, come in."

Sabina, who had met Frau Garisch on several previous occasions, handed over a bunch of assorted blooms bought on the way.

"How kind." Frau Garisch pointed down the hall to where a back door stood open. "Siegfried and Sophie are already in the garden with my husband. If you'd like to join them, I'll bring us all out a beer." With a sudden thought, she touched Karl's sleeve. "Don't mind Heinzi, the Alsatian. He looks fierce, but he's very obedient."

"That's all right, Frau Garisch. I'm used to dogs."

The sun burst upon them as they stepped through the door into the secluded garden. Dazzled, they blinked until their eyes adjusted to the glare, finding themselves on a stone-flagged patio. Sophie was sitting on a garden chair; standing by her was Siegfried. Opposite them Karl could see the angular silhouette of a man flanked by an alert, large dog. Karl stepped aside to avoid the direct sun. As he did so, Josef Garisch's face became clear – the face which had haunted Karl for the past twenty years.

"Goslar!"

As Karl spat out the name, he saw Garisch/Goslar's hand darting under his jacket for the Luger pistol held in his waistband. Instinctively Karl attacked. Going straight for the Luger, with a twist and a yank he had it out of Goslar's hands and in his own. Stepping backwards and breathing hard, Karl raised the Luger in both hands. He aimed between Goslar's eyes, holding his foe to a challenging glare as he fought to steady his hands.

Goslar realised he had seriously underestimated his opponent. His memories were of a pathetic, tortured man, grovelling to obey his slightest command. His eyes flicked towards his son for help, but Wolf dared not make a move towards Karl. He was not close enough. Then Goslar noticed Siegfried. He was edging behind his father, out of his line of sight. In his hand was an open penknife, but he needed time. Goslar set out to distract the man opposite him whose index finger curled so confidently round the trigger.

"What are you trying to do, Driesler? Get yourself into more trouble?"

The Alsatian heard and smelled fear. He also saw the flick of his master's hand, giving the signal to attack. The dog's rumbling growls exploded into a snarl as he leaped at the man threatening his master. His teeth bit deep into Karl's right arm, dragging it down. As the gun passed Goslar's chest it fired. Karl saw Goslar fall as the dog's momentum knocked him off his own feet. He hit the stones of the patio just as Heinzi's teeth met bone. Karl tried to transfer the gun to his left hand, but before he held it securely, the dog shook his arm violently, sending the Luger spinning away out of reach.

Sabina watched in horror. Wolf was already at his father's side, oblivious to Karl's danger. Siegfried seemed unable, or unwilling, to react. Heinzi still hung grimly to Karl's arm, worrying at the flesh, refusing to let go despite Karl's frantic punches and kicks. Fear for her father's life brought Sabina courage. She lunged at the dog, grabbing it by the collar, desperately trying to haul the snarling beast off her father.

"Help me, someone!" she screamed.

Her cry broke through Wolf's grief. He reached forward and grabbed the gun off the ground. "Let go!" he yelled at Sabina. She sprang back instantly. Wolf took quick aim and fired twice at point blank range.

The dog dropped like a stone on top of Karl, it's jaws still locked around his arm, its dead weight pinning him down. Once again Sabina grabbed its collar and tried to haul it off. Wolf stuck the Luger in his own waistband and gave assistance. Once the dog was clear of him, Karl was able to sit up. He leaned against the wall bordering the patio as Sabina rushed to his side. His sleeve was in tatters but he seemed more shocked than in pain. She turned angrily to look up at Siegfried.

"Why did you just stand there? Why didn't you do something?"

Siegfried came and towered over her, realising she had not seen his earlier intentions. "If you want me to do something I'll look at his arm. I know some first aid." Roughly he pushed her aside and began to remove his father's jacket, revealing a shirtsleeve stained with blood.

Sabina shuddered and turned her eyes away. They fell on the lifeless body of the man she had known as Josef Garisch. At the sound of the shots, Frau Garisch had come running. She now crouched at her husband's side, moaning his name over and over as he lay dead in her arms, a neat bullet hole in the centre of his chest.

It was inconceivable he could be Goslar, Sabina thought. Yet he had drawn a gun on her father. Was he *really* Goslar? If so, then Wolf was Goslar's son! She watched him, now comforting his grieving mother. How could it be possible? How could Wolf come from such a terrible father? A gasp of pain brought her attention back to her own father. Siegfried was busy doing something to his arm. There seemed to be a lot of blood about. She looked round for Sophie, but she had disappeared. Couldn't stand the sight of blood, probably. Gritting her teeth, Sabina edged forwards.

"Can I do anything?"

Siegfried had a penknife in his hand and was using it to cut away the mauled shirtsleeve. "No! I can manage."

Wolf looked up from his mother and noticed the scene behind him. Pale-faced, he came over for a closer look. "Shit! That's bleeding a lot. I hadn't realised it was so bad. I'd better call an ambulance."

As Wolf ran into the house, Sophie emerged. Siegfried turned to Sabina. "You can help. Go into the kitchen and find clean towels or something. Anything to mop up blood."

Sabina did as she was told. The instant she was gone, Siegfried raised the penknife again. He looked at his father's face. He was staring at Garisch's body, seemingly oblivious to what Siegfried was doing. Carefully Siegfried inserted the blade of the knife into a particularly gaping wound. Finding a vein in amongst the mess was not easy, but the blade was very sharp. Against the background pain, Karl seemed not to notice. Blood began to pour down his hand as Siegfried lowered it to drain freely.

"Now all we need is a bit of time," Siegfried muttered with a satisfied smile. He turned round to grin at Sophie. "Go and distract Sabina."

She smiled back and nodded, rising obediently to her feet.

*

By now Wolf was busy at the front door holding back neighbours who had run round on hearing shots and the dog's snarls. Sophie went into the kitchen and gently took a bundle of tea towels from Sabina. "You'd better phone your mother, Sabina, and tell her what's happened. It may be difficult once the police get here."

"Police?" It came as a hammer blow. Her father had just killed a man. A politician no less. Of course the police would come. "Yes. You're probably right. Thanks, Sophie."

Sophie returned outside with the tea towels. She spread them on the growing pool of blood on the patio to make it look like they had been used. She appraised Siegfried of the situation in the house. "I also phoned Ilse. I thought she ought to know. Warn Paul."

"Good. You've done well, Sophie." He had put away the penknife, not daring to use it too freely. Questions were going to be asked about Garisch's connections. No suspicion must fall on himself! He studied his father. He seemed dazed, almost euphoric, as though high on something, unaware of the consequences of what he had done. Or perhaps it was loss of blood? His father was certainly reacting strangely, was distracted. Elsewhere.

He remembered the stories heard whispered in the back of English classrooms about his mad father. Siegfried smiled. If he doesn't die from loss of blood, Siegfried thought happily, I'll make sure he's committed for life to a looney bin. *That* would be an even more fitting revenge!

Karl sat quietly, feeling very calm and relaxed now the panic was over. Goslar was dead. With him went Karl's own guilty past. He could truly forget it all now; feel at peace with his soul. Past wrongs were righted, debts paid. He would go home a healed man.

For the first time since Heinzi's attack he looked down at his arm. He was surprised at the blood still flowing. He had thought Siegfried was doing something about it. But he must have. Blood-soaked tea towels lay nearby. Karl reached slowly forward, picked one up and pressed it down hard over the most gushing wound.

"Here. I'll do that for you," Siegfried said, hearing the sound of approaching sirens, and cursing their promptness.

*

The phone was ringing at Lane Head Farm but there was no reply. Sabina suddenly remembered it was Sunday and that England was an hour behind. Her mother was most likely on her way from church to the Murdochs' for Sunday lunch. Hastily she broke the connection and re-dialled the operator, this time giving the number of Yew Tree Lodge. The phone rang several times then she heard a familiar voice.

"Hello. Robert Murdoch speaking."

"Uncle Robert! It's Sabina. Is Mummy there?"

Robert heard the urgency in her voice. "Yes. In the garden. Is something wrong?"

"Yes. Daddy just killed Goslar!"

"*What!* How? Where?" He realised he was wasting time. "Never mind. You tell your mother. I'll go and get her. Hold on."

Sabina listened to the crackling line until her mother's slightly breathless voice came down it.

"Bina! What's this Robert tells me? Is it true?"

"Yes. It's just happened. And Daddy's been mauled by an Alsatian, but I think he's going to be all right. It was only his arm. But the worst thing is, Goslar was Wolf's *father*!"

"Slow down a bit, Treasure. I can't take all this in."

Sabina made herself calm down and explain properly. "Herr Garisch seemed to be expecting Daddy to recognise him," she concluded. "He had a gun. Daddy wrenched the gun off him. The Garisch's Alsatian attacked Daddy just as the gun went off."

"And Goslar was killed?"

"Instantly."

Despite the shock, Katherine could think clearly enough to realise the situation Karl now faced; not just that he had killed a man, but that the man was Goslar. He would be in a vulnerable state of mind. It was just as well Robert was here with his family for their annual holiday. Alice could look after the farm, with all the boys' and Werner's help. She made her decision. "I'll be over as soon as I can. Hopefully with Robert. Where can we contact you? At the Zopfs'?"

"Yes. No!" Sabina hesitated. "I'm not sure we'll be very welcome there any more. Herr Garisch was a good friend of theirs. And –"

"Daddy was right not to trust them. They're probably all still in cahoots as Nazis. Don't go back there, Bina. Stay away from them. Go to Oma and Opa. I'll find you there."

"What about all my belongings? And Daddy's?"

"We'll sort all that out. Don't worry. Just stay clear of the Zopfs. And Wolf."

"Wolf? But –"

"No 'buts', Bina. Do you understand?"

Sabina did not want to make any promises on that score. The sound of sirens saved her. "I can hear the ambulance coming. I'd better go. See you soon. 'Bye."

As she put down the receiver, Wolf called to her from the open front door. "They're here. Police and ambulance." He stepped back inside, partly closing the door.

"Bina," he said gently. "This was between our fathers. It's nothing to do with you and me. Right?"

She flung herself into his arms in relief. "Right!"

They only had a moment before they had to direct the ambulance men and police through the inquisitive crowds building up in front of the house. Sabina shrank into the background as the authorities took charge.

"This way." Wolf hustled them down the hall to the patio where Siegfried was still applying first aid to his father's arm, and Sophie was comforting Frau Garisch on the chairs. Siegfried stood to make way for the professionals.

Sabina wanted to go with her father when they were ready to take him to hospital, but an officious policeman told her to stay.

"Take care, Daddy," she called to him. "Mummy's on her way."

He turned his head on the stretcher and waved weakly back.

Sabina watched the ambulance drive away under police escort, then prepared herself to face the questions. Her stomach growled in hunger. It was going to be a long afternoon.

The questioning seemed interminable. When the police and Goslar's body finally left the scene, they all realised how hungry they were. Frau Garisch had retired to bed with a sedative, so the four of them sat at the dining table, picking at the now cold roast pork, discussing in muted voices what all this would mean.

Sabina was feeling increasingly nervous in their company. If Herr Garisch was prepared to kill, he was ruthless, probably still a Nazi. If her mother was right, it was highly likely Wolf, Siegfried and the Zopfs shared his diabolical political leanings. She couldn't continue to stay with the Zopfs. Not now she suspected what they were like – and what they might do to keep her quiet. Even here, now, she felt at risk, alone with Siegfried and Wolf. Could she believe Wolf's avowal of love? She felt rising panic as she remembered it was Siegfried who had introduced her to Wolf, who had promptly introduced her to cannabis. Wolf was in league with Siegfried; was obeying his instructions!

What could she do? She had a small amount of money in her bag. Enough to get her to Medebach. But how to escape from Wolf?

"What's the matter? You've gone very pale," Wolf said, putting his arm around her.

She stopped herself from shrugging it off. He mustn't suspect anything. "No. I was just thinking. Perhaps I'll stay at my grandparents'. Makes more sense. My mother will probably go there. But first I want to see how Daddy is at the hospital. If you could call me a taxi to get me there, I'll be fine."

"Siegfried could drop you off, I'm sure."

That was the last thing Sabina wanted: to be alone with the devil himself. "No. It's OK. He's got Sophie to take home. A taxi's fine."

"I'll take you then in my father's car."

"No!" Sabina tried to quell the panic. "You must stay here with your mother. She needs you. I'll go and call a taxi myself." She hurried into the hall before he could object and found the number in the directory. The taxi would be there in ten minutes.

A glance out of the front window made her recoil in horror. Reporters and a television crew were gathered there, waiting to pounce on the first person to leave the house. She also noticed the hired car her father had driven here. What would happen to that? Her father had the keys, so she couldn't drive it. She would have to get them off him and come back here for it. She shuddered. There was too much to cope with.

She heard footsteps behind her. It was Siegfried. What could he want? Fear gripped her as she remembered the knife in his pocket. She would rather face the reporters than him. Flinging open the front door she stepped out onto the driveway. There was an immediate flashing of cameras, and reporters jostled up to speak to her. To her astonishment, Siegfried was close behind. He stepped past her to pre-empt her dealings with the press.

"I'm prepared to answer your questions if you ask them one at a time," he shouted above the clamour. The television crew assumed priority, asking who he was.

"I am Siegfried Driesler, a friend of the family. It was my father who shot Herr Garisch. Since the war my father has suffered from er ... mental instability."

As the reporters surged around to listen to him, Sabina was squeezed out of the limelight. She tried to recapture their interest. "It's not true!" she yelled. But nobody was listening to her.

Nobody except one old hand who preferred finding his own sideline to a story.

324

"And you are?" he asked, taking her carefully to one side, away from the others.

Quickly, Sabina began telling him all he needed to know.

When her taxi arrived she made a run for it, then realised she had not brought her handbag with her. The leech-like reporter got in with her. "I'll pay," he said. "Just keep talking."

*

There was a strong smell of disinfectant. Karl hated that smell. It reminded him of hospitals. He opened his eyes, saw blank walls, a wash basin. He groaned. He *was* in hospital. He remembered now what had happened. He had killed Goslar. The memory brought back that surge of euphoria, dispelling the gloom.

A brusque female voice spoke to him. "Herr Driesler? Can you hear me?"

Karl turned his head to his left. As he did so a rush of nausea came over him. The efficient nurse held up a bowl for him.

"The effects of the anaesthetic," she explained mechanically, as he sank back limply onto the pillows. She left the room to deal with the bowl, passing a policeman sitting attentively by the door of the private room.

Karl looked across at the policeman, aware now of the throbbing in his right arm. He tried to ignore it, studying his guard instead. The policeman's hair was longer than was usual on British bobbies, brushing the collar of his mustard-coloured shirt. The revolver in its holster was disconcerting too. The young man was watching him keenly. Karl quickly dropped his gaze.

It was madness! He had done Germany a favour killing Goslar, and now he was going to be punished for it. The euphoria shattered as the all too familiar depression took hold; one of the black moods which had plagued him since the war. He thought about Katherine. She was always there to comfort him when he felt like this. He needed her now. He remembered Sabina's last words. Would she already be on her way?

The nurse returned, her wide-winged hat brushing the door. "Feeling better now, are we?" she asked without interest. She automatically took out a thermometer from her apron pocket and stuck it in his mouth, taking his pulse at the same time. After filling in his chart she left without another word, except to ask the young policeman if he would like a cup of coffee. He declined.

There were voices in the corridor. The door opened and two plain-clothes policemen walked in. No long-hairs these; these were senior detectives. The young uniformed policeman hastily stood up to give them his chair, then dragged over another from beside the sink.

First came the formal charge with murder and warnings about his rights. Karl nodded listlessly. Then the interrogation began. "How long had you known Herr Josef Garisch?"

Karl looked into the guarded eyes of the man who had introduced himself as Hauptkommissar Heitmann. This man was no fool. He would listen to reason.

"I met SS Sturmbannführer Goslar in 1943. In Yugoslavia." Karl watched for surprise to show on the pockmarked face, but Heitmann remained impassive.

"What proof have you that Herr Landminister Garisch was this man Goslar?"

Karl's reply came slowly, lethargically, the anaesthetic still having its effect. "He drew a gun on me. He knew I recognised him."

"You have no tangible proof?" The question dismissed Karl's statement as insufficient. "No one else who could confirm your allegation?"

Karl shrugged. "There must be plenty around who knew Goslar during the war, who could identify him now."

"Herr Garisch was a politician. Hardly someone who would keep his face hidden. Yet no one has ever questioned his identity."

Karl gave a long sigh. He was none too sure he was thinking clearly. Yet he had to get his point across. "He most likely killed all his victims. There's no one left alive to identify him. Except me."

"What about colleagues, acquaintances, neighbours," Heitmann barked. "Are you implying he killed all of them too?"

"His colleagues were SS," Karl replied tersely. "Of course they wouldn't grass on him."

"Not necessarily. Nevertheless, you have no means of proving your allegation."

"Except that he drew a gun on me!"

Heitmann calmly nodded as his colleague silently jotted down notes. "Have you previously been convicted of assault, Herr Driesler?"

How did they know that? Siegfried! Karl swore inwardly but tried to keep his cool. "That was in 1947. Twenty years ago, for heaven's sake!"

Heitmann read from some notes on a pad. "Two assaults on the same man over a short period. It seems like you had it in for this Englishman. Was he really someone else too? Another SS officer in disguise perhaps?"

They didn't believe him. Were hunting for a motive. He had to make them believe. "Tell me. Why would Garisch draw a gun on me? I was a lunch guest. His son is my daughter's boyfriend. It was supposed to be our first meeting. So why the gun?"

"Just answer *our* questions, Driesler."

Karl tried to remain unruffled. They're only trying to do their job, he told himself. Garisch was a politician, had a high profile. It did seem impossible that such a man could escape detection for so long. It meant his new identity was watertight. Until I showed up. He shook his head wearily. Katherine's God is unforgiving. This is my punishment for betraying her, for sleeping with Ilse. I'll be paying the penalty in prison for the next twenty years.

"Answer the question!" Heitmann snapped.

Karl had begun drifting off to sleep. "What? I'm sorry."

"How many people would you say you have shot in your life?" Heitmann repeated.

"That's not relevant! You can't expect to –" He broke off in disgust at their tactics.

"Shooting is your preferred method of killing," Heitmann baited. "Your military record states you are an accomplished sniper. Who paid you to do it?"

Karl stared in disbelief. "It was *his* gun. He was going to kill *me*."

"Three witnesses say otherwise. You drew the gun on him. So who gave it to you and who paid you to do it?"

Three witnesses. Siegfried, Sophie ... and Wolf! Karl felt too tired to argue. He turned his head away and stared at the wall, ignoring all further questions. After a few more unproductive minutes, the two detectives got up and left the room.

"I want a lawyer!" Karl yelled at their backs. And Katherine, he thought with an anguished sigh.

A different policeman sat glumly by the door when the night nurse showed Sabina in.

"Is it all right if he has a visitor?" the nurse asked. "It's his daughter."

"S'pose so," the policeman replied, with an interested look in Sabina's direction.

Karl glared at him, then quickly welcomed Sabina. She gave him a kiss on the cheek.

"No physical contact!" the policeman warned.

Sabina blanched, unused to police authority.

"Don't worry about him, Bina," Karl soothed her. "He'll go back to sleep in a minute."

His words did the trick. She smiled. "How are you, Daddy. How's your arm?"

"Hurting like hell, but all stitched up. The police want me out of here in the morning." He omitted to add 'and in jail'. "How about you?"

"Frightened. Mummy told me to stay away from the Zopfs ... and from Wolf. He's all right though, but I won't be –"

"No he's not!"

"What do you mean? He promised me it was still all right between us, even though you –"

"He lied to the police."

She stared, aghast. "Lied? What about?"

"They told me three witnesses said *I* drew the gun. Three. That's Siegfried, Sophie and Wolf. He lied."

Her face crumpled. Ignoring the policeman, Karl reached for her hand to comfort her. Stifling her tears eventually, Sabina returned the comfort in kind.

"Mummy said she'll be over as soon as possible. Hopefully with Uncle Robert. I suppose they'll have to get his passport sent down from Edinburgh." She looked hard at him. "Why's it so important for Uncle Robert to come? Because of what he knows about you, or in case you need him?"

"Both, perhaps. Mummy's not taking any chances. She knows me too well. I'm all right though." He nearly believed it himself.

Sabina remembered her own predicament. "I was going to stay with Oma and Opa, but I haven't any money. I left my handbag at the Garisch's. If you can give me some and the hire-car keys, I can drive there."

"In my jacket." He looked around for it. There was a small cupboard in the corner. "In there, perhaps."

Sabina looked inside, found his other clothes, but no sign of the jacket. "Blast! I remember now. Siegfried took it off you. It must still be at the house. Or else the police have got it. What on earth am I going to do now?"

"Phone Oma. Get Onkel Rudi or someone to come and fetch you."

"Of course." She smiled in relief. "There'll be some change in your trouser pockets." She hunted around and produced a handful of coins. "I'd better go and do that now. It'll take them quite a while to get here. Be back in a few minutes."

On her way down the corridor she met Wolf clutching her handbag and her father's jacket. She stopped. He looked friendly enough. He could do nothing in the middle of a hospital.

"You went without saying goodbye," he rebuked her. "And without these." He held out the jacket and bag.

"Thank you," she said coldly, stepping aside to pass him.

Puzzled, he grabbed her arm. "Why the shut-out? What have I done?"

"What have you done?" she stormed. "You only lied about my father to the police. You only condemned him as an assassin."

"Oh." He bit his lip, looking down at her with regret. "It seems I have a conflict of interests. If I've got to choose between my father and yours, it has to be mine. I'm sorry. It looks like it's over between us."

"It most certainly is!" She brushed past him and down the corridor to the bank of public telephones at reception.

Wolf stood and watched her dial. He was on dangerous ground with Sabina. He loved her but he had to let her go. Regretfully he walked out of the hospital and drove back home.

Siegfried and Sophie had stayed at the house, awaiting his return. Wolf found them calmly sitting in the dusk on the patio where his father had died.

"Would you mind if we went indoors?" he asked. The bloodstains from both men had been scrubbed off the patio by Sophie. Nevertheless, he did not feel comfortable sitting there.

"Of course not." Siegfried led the way back inside to the living room. "Don't want anyone overhearing us. It's just as well we had a few moments to get our stories straight before the police came, but we need to go over the details."

Siegfried sat on one of the leather armchairs, beneath a portrait of a turn-of-the-century businessman Wolf had been told was his grandfather, Georg Garisch. It seemed that relationship was now in doubt. Wolf cleared his throat nervously.

"Before we start, Siegfried, I'd just like to ask if you knew what my father intended doing with the gun. He could never have shot your father without causing one hell of a stink." Enlightenment dawned as he spoke. "That's why he invited you for lunch too, isn't it? He wanted extra help around. He must have warned you there might be trouble."

Siegfried nodded. "You're right. Your father said he couldn't keep avoiding mine. They were bound to meet some time, so it might as well be on his terms. He asked me to help as he knows my reputation for arranging ... accidents."

Sophie knew Wolf would quickly realise Sabina had been a danger too. She set about distracting him from that train of thought. "So your real name is Goslar, Wolf. What do you make of that?"

"I can't believe it. Vater was supposed to have been a Wehrmacht officer during the war. We've got all his documents, photos, medals. I never suspected for one moment he was anyone other than who he claimed to be."

"Your mother must know the truth," Siegfried observed.

"She won't say anything. Not even to you, Wolf," Sophie declared. "She's worked too hard to keep their cover. She's not going to blow it now. I bet she denies everything."

"And you must too, Wolf. For your mother's sake," Siegfried warned. "We never heard my father call him 'Goslar'. Agreed? You didn't mention that to the police, I hope?"

"What do you take me for?" Wolf scorned. "Sophie passed me your message. I told them Herr Driesler suddenly drew a gun, unprovoked."

"Good. Of course Sabina will back up my father's version. The police will expect that. But it's three against two. And who can believe what my father says? He's a known head-case." He laughed. Sophie joined in, but Wolf was quiet.

"What about fingerprints on the gun?" he asked. "If they find any of my father's, then our story's obviously a lie."

Siegfried grinned. "Herr Garisch was always a careful man. He was wearing gloves for that very reason. I removed them while you were busy meeting the police."

After going through their version of that day's events once again, to make sure they all agreed on details, Siegfried looked at his watch. "I'd better get back to Iserlohn. Paul should be home by now and we'll need to organise a few things." He stood up. "I hope your mother doesn't take this too hard, Wolf. She'll get all the support she needs. You know that."

"Yes. Thanks, Siegfried. I'll tell her."

Wolf showed them to the door. A few press late-comers still loitered outside. Siegfried gladly gave them the story he wanted them to hear, before ushering Sophie into the Mercedes and driving off. Wolf shut the door on the outside world and sat down again in the living room, staring at the portrait of Georg Garisch.

*

Haus Fichtenblick was awash with inquisitive neighbours and the inevitable press when Rudi Driesler drove up after fetching Katherine and Robert from Düsseldorf airport.

"It's been like this ever since yesterday evening when the news broke," he told Katherine. "It's the biggest news story we've had round here since the war. As boys I was forever the one in trouble. I'd never have believed then that my big brother would be the one to cause us so much worry."

As she got out of the car, Katherine reflected that trouble had really started for Karl the day he met Goslar. Now Goslar was dead, but trouble had not gone away. She was grateful that Rudi shielded her and Sabina from the press as they made their way inside. Robert, whose knowledge of German consisted almost solely of Freudianisms, was immune to the barrage of questions flung at them. Safe inside Katherine greeted Karl's parents with a warm hug. His normally robust mother looked ill with worry.

Dieter Driesler was particularly effusive in his welcome to Robert, holding the handshake long to express what words could not – his gratitude for Robert's help in the past. Robert looked into the seventy-year-old man's eyes and gave an unspoken promise to do his utmost to help this time. Dieter nodded. Language was superfluous when emotions ran deep.

"Well," Katherine said once they were settled out of prying eyes. "What news of Karl? Is he still in hospital?"

"No," Anna told her. "We called just after lunch and they said he'd been taken back to police headquarters in Dortmund for more questioning. The one o'clock news report confirmed he's been charged with murder."

Katherine looked at Sabina hopefully. "There's no question he did it?"

Sabina grimaced. "I don't see how there could be. What is in question is whose gun it was. Siegfried, Sophie and Wolf are saying Daddy brought it with him."

"You're joking!" Katherine was stunned into silence.

Robert picked up the conversation with a few questions of his own. "Until then, Karl had never met this Garisch fellow? You're absolutely sure?"

"Yes. He was supposed to come to Siegfried's twenty-first party but never showed up. He must have had a suspicion about Daddy even then. It's probably why he's been trying to avoid me, too."

"Probably. So the instant they meet, Garisch produces a gun. Was it simultaneous recognition?"

Sabina thought back. "No. We had the sun in our eyes. But as soon as Daddy said his name, Herr Garisch reached for the gun." She still had trouble thinking of Wolf's father as Goslar.

"What you're telling me then is that virtually Karl's first sight of Goslar includes a gun. He's immediately threatened."

"Yes, I suppose so."

Karl's family sat patiently during Robert's questions. They knew it was important he understood the facts. He knew Karl's mind better than any of them, even Katherine.

"What do you think, Robert?" Katherine asked him. "Did he know what he was doing?"

He was noncommittal. "I'll have to speak to Karl."

332

CHAPTER TWENTY-SEVEN

His shirt was too tattered to wear. They had given him a blue one from some store. Then the usual treatment. No tie or belt allowed. Mugshots taken, fingerprints. They'd not exactly been gentle with his right arm. Now there was to be yet more questioning. He'd spent all afternoon with them and his lawyer. What more could he say? Once again he was led to the interview room.

Instead of the two detectives, Katherine and Robert were seated at the table, waiting. They were both clearly intimidated by the surroundings, their greetings muted. He smiled bleakly and sat down opposite them.

"Thanks for coming." He laid his bandaged arm carefully on the table. "What a mess!" he said with a nod at it. "More scars for the collection!" He was finding it difficult to look Katherine in the eye, his light-hearted conversation a decoy for the turmoil inside.

"How are they treating you, Schatz?" Katherine asked.

"Like a murderer," he replied. "Have you seen the newspapers yet?" Both Katherine and Robert shook their heads. "Siegfried's been busy telling them my mental history; how unstable I am. Everyone's convinced I'm mad. Except the police. They seem to think it's a Communist plot, that I'm a hired assassin or something. I expect Sabina's told you what really happened."

"Yes," Robert said. "But I want to hear it from *you* now. What do you think happened? What was in your mind when you grabbed the gun and pointed it at Goslar?"

"Nothing when I grabbed the gun. That was instinct. Survival."

"But then?"

"Intense anger. I was remembering all the people I knew he had hurt or killed."

"So you weren't immediately thinking of killing him."

Karl's brow furrowed in thought. "I don't know. I'm not sure."

"Did you intend pulling the trigger?"

"I don't know."

"Is that what you told the police?"

"No. They didn't ask the questions like that. I hadn't really thought whether I meant to do it."

"It makes a big difference, Karl. Whether you knew what you were doing, or not."

"Whether I was in control, you mean. Are you going to try to make out I'm mad too, Robert?"

"It's a defence."

"Well I don't like it!"

"It could mean the difference between life and a few years."

"It's not going to wash as long as Siegfried maintains I brought the gun. I'm up against him and the rest of his lot. *I* can't prove it was Goslar. The court will decide one way or the other, and I bet I know which way."

"The police might find something," Katherine said. "They'll be looking very carefully into Garisch's past now. I'm sure they'll find something that doesn't add up."

"You underestimate Siegfried's lot, Schatz. They're very thorough. And influential. Whereas I'm a nobody. A German who traded his nationality to become English."

Robert could see this line getting nowhere. "Tell me, Karl. How did you feel when you realised Goslar was dead?"

Immediately Karl's face lit up. "Wonderful. Like the weight of the world was off me. Like I was before the war; me with no history."

"Why don't you feel like that now?" Robert saw Karl's eyes flick across to Katherine then back to himself. "Are you ashamed of what you've done?"

"I'm not ashamed of killing Goslar."

"But you're ashamed of something else. Of what Katherine thinks of you, perhaps?"

"I'm not ashamed of you," Katherine butted in before Karl could reply. "I understand totally why it happened."

Robert's trained eye had seen something else; Karl had some kind of a problem with Katherine. "Perhaps it would be best if I had another meeting with you tomorrow, Karl. What do you think?"

"If you want."

"Good. I'll try and arrange it. In the meantime, I'll get in touch with Sam Goldberg. He's living in America now, but we still correspond. He often asks after you. His opinion as your former psychiatrist might be needed at some stage."

Karl pulled a face. "I've just thrown all that overboard. I don't want it all dredged up again in court, Robert."

"Unavoidable, I think."

*

The directors of Zopf Construction were discussing strategy behind closed doors. Paul had spent Sunday evening double-checking that all evidence of neo-Nazi activity was concealed, after Siegfried had briefed him on the events of that afternoon. At work the following morning, Paul and Siegfried shut the door of Paul's office to discuss the way forward.

"Naturally everyone keeps a low profile for the moment," Paul began, "but there are to be no sudden cancellations. Any events organised are still attended but purely on a social level. Nothing of any significance is to be discussed. The police must find no reason to believe Garisch had Nazi connections."

Siegfried sat erect, thoroughly enjoying planning the campaign of war. "I've had confirmation that everyone is aware of the situation. Neptune was out of the country yesterday, but is now implementing the agreed procedures." His fingertips joined as if in prayer as he prepared to deliver his plan of action. "It seems to me, Paul, that our chief purpose should be to discredit anything my father says, so that his evidence is inadmissible. The best way of doing that is to prove he's mad."

"But he's not mad!"

Triumph gleamed in Siegfried's eyes. "Oh, but he is. Ask Katherine. She knows! I've watched how she protects him. I've seen for myself his sudden loss of control. I *know* he had to have psychiatric help after the war. If we play our cards right, he's going to need it again. Only this time they won't be letting him out."

Paul was interested but sceptical. "How do you propose to achieve that?"

Siegfried gave a wicked smile. "Sophie gave me the idea. It was on Saturday night when you were away. If you have any remaining loyalty to my father you'll forget it when you've heard this."

"Get on with it then!"

Siegfried drew a deep breath. "Sophie is convinced, and I agree, that my father spent Saturday night with my mother. The whole of it." He paused, waiting for comment from Paul. None came; only a blank stare. More detail was required. "When we went upstairs Sophie noticed Mutter's bedroom door was open, the light out, but there were voices coming from *his* room. Sophie got up later in the night to check. Mutter's door was still open." He made himself sound regretful. "I'm sorry to have to tell you this, Paul. But under the circumstances it could prove very useful to us."

"How exactly?"

"Tell Katherine, and also let Karl know we've told her. The added stress at a time like this is sure to send him over the edge."

Paul sat stunned by Ilse's cuckoldry. He would never have believed it of her with any other man. But Karl was different. She had always retained a soft spot for him. He studied the nails of his left hand, manicured for him by a delightful brunette called Gabriele. He supposed Ilse had every right to Karl. But Karl must be punished for murdering Garisch. "I see. How do you plan on telling them?"

"Katherine won't believe it coming from me. Mutter must admit to it herself."

"You'll be punishing your mother, making her do that. Is that the idea?"

"No. I only suggest her because she has most chance of persuading Katherine it's true."

Paul was not so convinced this was the right step to take. "Let me think this over, Siegfried."

*

Paul called Ilse into his study the moment he got home that evening. He shut the door behind her, his face stern.

"I'll come straight to the point, Ilse. It's been brought to my attention – never mind by whom – that you spent Saturday night with Karl. Now – don't interrupt! – I know you've always turned a blind eye to my little indiscretions, so I'm willing to do the same for you." Here he paused, allowing her visible emotions of fear then relief to settle. "However, as a direct result I must call on you to perform a duty for the cause. An unpleasant duty which I can't permit you to refuse."

Ilse sat dumbstruck, unable to keep up with Paul's brisk manoeuvring.

When he told her what she had to do she broke down in tears.

"I can't do that to Karl – or Katherine!"

"You've no choice," he told her firmly. "You should have thought of that before you slept with him!" He suddenly smiled and drew closer, taking her hand gently in his. "I understand what he means to you, Liebling. But you and I mean more, don't we? Siegfried too. We've got to guard our backs against attack. You can see that, can't you?"

Ilse hung her head. She had to choose between Paul and Karl. She knew she could never permanently win back Karl.

"All right. I'll do it."

*

Robert returned alone to Dortmund police headquarters the following morning. It was only a short walk from the Gasthaus where he, Katherine and Sabina had stayed overnight. Sabina had offered to come with him to translate, but Robert felt confident he would find someone who spoke English.

He was told he could have half an hour alone with Karl prior to the initial hearing before the magistrate. Then he was shown into the interview room where Karl was already waiting under guard.

"How are you feeling today?"

"Lonely. Depressed. What do you expect?"

Robert sat down. "I thought we were supposed to be alone."

Karl looked across at his guard. "He'll go now."

As he spoke the policeman left his post by the door and went outside. Robert relaxed. "I don't like seeing those guns they carry. It's enough to make anyone nervous. Anyway, enough of me. I rather felt there was something you wanted to tell me yesterday, and couldn't."

"Was there?"

"Something to do with Katherine?"

Karl looked away. It was crazy. He could admit to murder but not adultery. "No. Nothing. I was just anxious about how she would take all this, but she was wonderful. I couldn't have asked for more support. Tell her that, will you?"

"All right. But you'll be seeing her again. Now, about your feeling depressed."

"I've every right to feel depressed! It looks like Siegfried's achieving his aim in life. I always thought it would be that knife of his which finished me off, but now I can see he's far more devious than I expected. He's going to have me put away as a madman, and you're helping him, Robert!" His voice rose. "I don't want Goldberg brought into this!"

"All right, all right! Keep calm. I can only advise your lawyer on what I consider to be the facts. It's up to him what line of defence you take, but there's no way you're admitting to murder. I'll see to that!"

Karl was silent, trying to cool his anger. The last thing he wanted was to alienate Robert. He had to explain. "I know I'm not mad, Robert. Pointing that gun at Goslar was the most logical thing I ever did. This was my big test. All those times in the war when I failed to carry out my convictions, when I gave in to survival. At that moment I could ... redeem myself. I no longer mattered. What mattered then were all those people he had killed. I was thinking of them!"

"That's what you believe?"

"Don't sound so sceptical. I *know* that's what I was thinking when I faced him with the gun. His crimes won't pass unnoticed. If I must be punished for killing him, then it will be for the truth, not some pretence of madness!"

"Think of your family, Karl. Wouldn't it be easier –"

"Think of the truth, Robert. I'm not going to lie to anyone. I'm *not* mad."

Patiently Robert explained: "That's for experts to decide."

"So you believe it too." Karl sat back on his chair, arms folded, and stared at the door.

Easy does it, Robert thought. He waited a few moments before speaking again, his voice calm and reassuring. "I have to tell the truth as I see it, Karl. I can't lie either. I don't believe you're mad, but there again, at that particular moment, I don't believe you were fully in control of yourself."

"The safe British compromise, eh?" Karl managed a smile and looked back at his friend. "All right. I'll compromise too. I'll go along with whatever you think. You know me best."

"Good. I'm glad we've sorted that out. Now, was there anything else you wanted to tell me?"

A slight hesitation preceded an emphatic "No".

Robert instantly detected the lie. "Are you sure?"

"Quite sure," Karl said firmly.

With a sigh of frustration Robert tried again. "If there's anything troubling you, Karl, anything at all, you know you can tell me and it won't go further."

"Believe me, Robert. You know all there is to know."

Despite the assurance Robert did not believe him.

All too soon the half hour was up and the guard returned to take Karl off to his cell. Robert returned defeated to the Gasthaus ready to accompany Katherine and Sabina to court.

"He's holding something back and I'm not sure what it is," he reported. "It's most unlike him not to tell me everything. It worries me."

"I'm sure he will eventually," Katherine reassured him, finding her handbag and shoes ready to go out. "He was probably too worked up about the court proceedings to think about anything else. Try again tomorrow."

"He'll probably be in a remand prison somewhere. He's not going to like that. He'll be even less likely to open up."

"Let's just wait and see," Katherine said optimistically.

Robert and Sabina caught each other's doubtful eye.

At the court they met up with Rudi and his parents. They all tried to smile their support to Karl when he was brought in, but as they sat through the proceedings each one of them grew increasingly dispirited. Siegfried was there, along with Wolf and Sophie, sitting well apart from Karl's contingent. Sabina refused to look at Wolf as his evidence added weight to the case against her father. The case was referred for trial. No bail was granted.

Katherine was crying as she watched Karl led away out of sight. Sabina joined in. Gisela too cried for her son. What made it worse was they all knew he had indeed killed a man.

Outside the court, Siegfried approached them although Wolf hung back with Sophie. "My mother wants to know whether you'll still be staying with us, Sabina. She says you're still welcome."

Sabina shrank back from him, as though he carried the plague. "No. I've decided to stay in Medebach."

"In that case she'll bring your belongings to your Gasthaus, along with Vater's. Where is it you're staying?"

Sabina was loath to give the name of the Gasthaus, but at least it would be Ilse, not Siegfried, coming there. She watched Siegfried as he rejoined Wolf and Sophie, visibly gloating over events. "He disgusts me," she burst out.

There was a general murmuring of agreement as they made for a restaurant to revive their flagging spirits.

"The first thing to do is find out where they're taking Karl," Rudi said, after ordering drinks for them all, "so Katherine can visit him before she goes. How long do you intend staying over here, Katherine?"

"I can't stay long. I really don't want to leave him, but I'll have to get back to the farm and the children. It could be months before the trial."

Gisela put her hand over her daughter-in-law's. "We'll visit him and tell you how he is, don't you worry."

When their drinks arrived, Robert spoke quietly to Katherine. "I can see you're worried about him being in prison, aren't you? Don't worry. Karl's a lot stronger than he was after the war. He knows he's got your support and backing. That'll see him through."

"Yes, but for how long? What if he's given a life sentence, Robert? I'm not sure even I could cope with that."

He squeezed her hand. "You've got all your family and friends. Use us."

Sabina had been listening. "I'll stay in Germany, Mummy. I can visit Daddy too. He'll have plenty of visitors. But why are we all being so pessimistic? They'll listen to what he says about Goslar, they'll hear Dr Goldberg's evidence. They can't commit him of murder after that!"

"Thank you, Treasure. But we can't ignore the fact that Daddy killed a man. There's bound to be some penalty to pay."

Throughout the remainder of the meal no one was very communicative, each wrapped up in worries about the future. When it was time to leave, Rudi took his parents back to the car, while Katherine returned with Robert and Sabina to the Gasthaus.

Ilse turned up a couple of hours later.

*

Sabina had gone out for a walk, while Robert was in his own room when Ilse knocked on Katherine's door. She stood surrounded by baggage, accompanied by the Gasthaus owner's teenage son to help carry it. Suppressing qualms about Ilse's supposed allegiances, Katherine tried to sound welcoming.

"Ilse! Siegfried said you would call. Please come in."

"Thank you." Ilse beckoned to the boy to bring in the bags, herself picking up a small case with Karl's raincoat draped over it. She tipped the boy generously and allowed him to leave before setting down the case and coat in the room. Katherine noticed her lingering touch, almost a caress of the coat, as if she did not want to part with it.

"I'd just got him back and now I have to let him go," Ilse complained softly. The scent of expensive perfume moved across the room with her as she went to the window then turned round to confront Katherine. She spoke slowly and clearly for Katherine's benefit. "Of course, I shouldn't be telling you this, but it hardly matters now, does it? He'll be sent to prison and neither of us will have him."

Katherine's heart skipped a beat. "Neither of us? What do you mean?"

Ilse seemed to brace herself for a difficult task. "I just want you to understand Karl's needs at such a difficult time for him. He still loves me. He demonstrated that very clearly on Saturday night. I know it's hard for you to accept that he and I are lovers, but –"

"Get out!" Katherine wanted to say more, but her command of German suddenly failed her. She pointed to the door. "Get out!"

Her mission accomplished, Ilse beat a hasty retreat. "I'm sorry, Katherine."

Curiously enough, she sounded as though she meant it. Katherine stood, too stunned to move, going over Ilse's words in her mind, making sure she had understood. She knew she had. And it was too painful to contemplate. With a cry of despair she flung herself onto the bed.

When Sabina returned from her walk she found her mother curled up on the bed, engrossed in a novel.

"It's a lovely evening out there, Mummy. You should have come too."

Katherine did not look up from her book. "I had to wait in for Ilse, remember?"

"Oh, right. I see she's been." Sabina went over to the suitcases stood against the wall. "What'll we do with all Daddy's stuff?"

"Take it over to Medebach. He might need some of it. You never know."

Sabina flopped down onto her bed and lay staring up at the ceiling. "You know, I can't believe Wolf could do such a thing. I thought we loved each other. It really hurts."

"Yes, Treasure. I know it does."

"He obviously prefers his Nazi friends to me." A muffled sob came from the other bed. Sabina looked across at her mother, whose eyes had never left her novel. "Are you OK, Mummy?"

"Yes. Fine." She sniffed. "How about you? I expect you feel more hurt than angry."

Her mother's voice sounded tight, as though she were holding back tears. Sabina supposed the strain of events was getting to her. Her own troubles with Wolf were paltry compared with her mother's. She got up and sat on the bed beside her, laying a hand gently on her arm. "It's all right, Mummy. You can cry if you want to. I might have a good cry too."

Katherine flung down the novel and turned to Sabina, burying her head on her shoulder. The ferocity of her sobs surprised Sabina so much her own never came. She held her mother tight, wondering what could have brought on such feelings of despair.

There was a gentle knock at the door. Robert came in and promptly took over the comforting from Sabina, rocking her in his arms until Katherine was quiet once more.

"It's going to be very hard on you, Katherine, but we're here. You won't be alone."

Katherine looked bleakly over his shoulder. They misunderstood and she was glad. She could never tell them the real reason for her tears.

342

*

"How did it go?" Siegfried asked his mother upon her return to his flat.

"It was awful. Don't ever ask me to do such a thing again. I only managed to get through it by thinking of you. Poor Katherine was devastated. I wish I'd never slept with Karl now. Not if this does to him what you're hoping for."

"You're too soft." He sidled up to her and tenderly kissed her cheek. "It's him or us. Don't forget that."

Ilse put her arms round him and held her son close. "I know. It's always been that way."

Escaping her embrace, Siegfried went to the dresser and poured them both a schnapps. He raised his glass. "Here's to the next stage. My visit to jail."

"*You're* going to tell him?"

"You bet! I wouldn't want to miss visiting my father in prison! I can't wait to see his expression when I tell him Katherine knows all about his little indiscretion," he said jubilantly. "I'd better tell him before she sees him again. If she ever does!"

Ilse sipped at the schnapps. She could never face Karl again. Not after betraying him like this.

"When's Sophie moving in here?" she asked to take her mind off recent events.

"Next weekend. She's given a month's notice on her flat, but she's not waiting to see it out. We'll move all her stuff out then."

Ilse nodded, feeling a bit happier. "You're really keen on each other. I'm so pleased, Liebling. She's such a nice girl. You will treat her well, won't you? No messing about with other –"

"When I commit myself to someone, I do it totally. You know that, Mutter." He looked her squarely in the eye. "I don't permit myself to have divided loyalties. Unlike some people I know."

His criticism hit home. Ilse thought about Siegfried's words as she drove back to Iserlohn. Divided loyalties. It was true.

CHAPTER TWENTY-EIGHT

The prison regime was less severe than Karl had been used to in the labour and prisoner of war camps. He had a cell to himself, and the food was not lacking in quantity. Boredom was the usual problem, but there were newspapers available, so he could study the differing reports of the events concerning himself. Of particular interest was the one based on Sabina's account. The reporter had taken a sympathetic stance; hardly surprising considering the left-wing tendency of the newspaper he was writing for. Other papers scoffed at suggestions of Nazis infiltrating politics, giving far greater emphasis to Karl's mental history as supplied by Siegfried. He guessed Germans preferred reading about lunatics than skeletons in their own cupboard.

He was in the middle of reading such an article when a warder approached the table where he sat.

"You've a visitor."

Karl smiled. Katherine at last, he thought, then shivered at the sudden surge of trepidation. He was afraid to meet his own wife. Guilt was a powerful emotion. It had ruled his life before and now it would rule it again. How could he have been so foolish as to sleep with Ilse? But love was a force to be reckoned with too. He had never stopped loving her, yet he loved Katherine as much, if not more. Two women to whom he owed his sanity, two women who loved and cared for him in return. But he still should not have slept with Ilse. Another of his fatal moments of weakness which would blight his life forever. Unless he confessed.

Karl followed the warder through numerous locked doors down unfamiliar corridors to the visitors' room, his mind tackling his dilemma: whether to confess to Katherine or not; whether easing his conscience would irretrievably wreck his marriage. It was with considerable gloom and no decision made that Karl entered the already crowded visitors' room.

"*Scheiße!*" Karl stopped dead.

"Come on. You've not got long," the warder snapped.

"I don't want to see him."

"Well he wants to see you. So get moving."

Reluctantly Karl moved to the table where a boldly smiling Siegfried waited. He sat down opposite his son, rapidly adjusting his emotions from guilt to anger. "Come to gloat?"

"Yes, and I'm enjoying every second, seeing you here under guard." Siegfried affected pretend concern. "How's the arm?"

"Shot full of antibiotics. That dog was as poisonous as you! I've been reading what you told the press."

"Well, it's true, isn't it?"

Karl's anger flared. He banged the table hard with the side of his hand. "It may be true but it's not relevant. You've really stuck the knife in me with this, haven't you?"

Siegfried's teeth flashed in a triumphal grin. "Yes, and now I'm going to twist it too." He paused, savouring the moment before delivering the *coup de grâce*. "Katherine knows about you and my mother."

The blood drained from Karl's face. The decision had been made for him. He could barely speak. "How?" he croaked.

"My clever Sophie guessed," Siegfried bragged.

His son's self-satisfied sneer had a strangely steadying effect on Karl. Fear for his marriage evaporated under the intense heat of a searing but controlled rage. "So you came here to tell me and enjoy my pain," Karl said quietly.

"Yes." The sneer was plainer than ever.

"There's an English saying," Karl said so quietly that Siegfried had to lean forward across the table to catch his words, "about being hung for a sheep as a lamb." With that he grabbed Siegfried's hair with his left hand and slammed his son's face into the edge of the table. He managed it once more before a warder reached him, closely followed by a second. He was swiftly hauled out of the room and back to his cell.

Groggily Siegfried raised his head off the table to watch his father's departure. If he could have smiled he would have, but it felt like he had a broken nose and other damage. A small price to pay for the satisfaction of seeing his father dig himself into an even deeper hole.

"Are you all right?"

A solicitous hand on his back told Siegfried to play this for all it was worth. He turned to the warder, blood streaming from his nose. "He's mad!" It came out satisfactorily muffled. Siegfried allowed himself to be ushered away to a first aid point, where it was decided he ought to go to hospital for an X-ray. As he was helped out to the waiting ambulance, his right eye already closed and his face swollen, Siegfried caught sight of Katherine and Robert approaching the prison entrance. He hastily turned his head away, not wanting them to see him in such a state. They would be hearing all about it in a few minutes anyway. Half his face couldn't help smiling.

*

"What do you mean, we can't see him?" Katherine asked the warder in charge of visitors. "When my daughter rang this morning, you told her we could." She put down her handbag heavily on his desk.

"You can't now, Frau Driesler. He's not allowed any more visitors."

"*More* visitors? Has he had some already?"

"Yes. His son ... your son? ... had to be sent to hospital after your husband attacked him. I'm very sorry we couldn't –"

Katherine turned to Robert in a fury. "Siegfried's been here causing more trouble. Now they won't let us see Karl."

Robert stepped up to the desk, stabbing at it with his finger. "I'm Herr Driesler's doctor. I insist on seeing him at once."

Not to be bullied, the warden pretended ignorance of English. Katherine explained in German.

"Look here. We're flying back to England tomorrow. If I'm not allowed to see him, please let Dr Murdoch here talk to him. Dr Murdoch is his psychiatrist."

With a reluctant sigh, the warden picked up the telephone on his desk and conferred with a superior. When he put down the receiver he looked at Robert with more respect. "All right. Herr Dr Murdoch may see him. You must stay here, Frau Driesler."

To her surprise she felt relieved at not having to face Karl. Since hearing Ilse's disclosure she had gone over her last meeting with Karl, remembering how he had avoided her eyes, how Robert had sworn he was holding something back. He had slept with Ilse all right. Why, she couldn't understand. She didn't want to talk about it, preferred to ignore it. This new situation gave her the chance.

"You go on in, Robert. I'll wait for you outside. It's too intimidating in here."

He nodded. "Do you want me to tell him anything? Any message?"

Katherine hesitated. She knew what she ought to say, for Karl's sake. "Only that I love him."

To her ears it sounded dutiful rather than sincere, but Robert did not seem to notice. He smiled. "I'll tell him."

He was taken to a small room with a steel mesh partition separating its two halves. Robert sat at the table that formed part of the partition and watched the doorway on the far side. After a wait of ten minutes, Karl came in, with a warder who would not have looked out of place in a wrestling match. The first thing Robert noticed was fresh blood seeping through the bandage on Karl's right arm. Karl sat on the other side of the screen. Robert could see he was worried.

"Where's Katherine?" Karl asked before Robert could open his mouth. "Why hasn't she come?"

"They wouldn't let her in. She's waiting outside. She asked me to tell you she loves you."

"Does she think I'm in doubt?" he asked cautiously.

"No, of course not."

His glib answer told Karl that Robert was unaware of the events with Ilse. Katherine had not confided in him. If she hadn't, he wouldn't either. It was a personal matter.

"How's she coping?"

Robert's hand gave the 'so-so' waggle. "She was rather upset yesterday evening after Ilse brought all your stuff back. I think it must have hit her then, you wouldn't be home for a while."

Ilse. The mere mention of her name stabbed Karl's guilt-ridden heart with a pain no knife of Siegfried's could ever have inflicted. He fiddled with a straggly edge of the bandage, eyes downcast. "Like possibly twenty years," he muttered. "Do you think she'll wait that long?"

"For God's sake, Karl! What's brought this on? She's not going to leave you. Far from it!" Robert saw disbelief on Karl's face. Only Katherine could persuade him, and she wasn't allowed to see him. "Listen to me, Karl. Much as I regret it, I have to get back to England tomorrow. I have commitments I can't possibly ignore. I promise I'll come back over to see you, and speak to your lawyer before the trial. You must stay calm and whatever you do, don't go getting into any more scrapes like this. Do you understand?"

"Siegfried came to gloat. I only gave him what he deserved."

"Yes, and look what good it did you!" Robert recognised Karl's growing despair. He had to offer him reassurance. "We're all on your side, Karl. Remember that. You've got all your family over here who'll come and visit you; Sabina too. Katherine will come over when she can."

Karl said nothing.

The patch of blood on the bandage was growing, Robert noticed. "I think I'd better go so you can get your arm looked at again. Just don't forget, Karl. We're all with you."

He stood up, signifying an end to the conversation. The wrestler wasted no time in leading Karl back to the doorway. Robert watched him leave, a vision of hopelessness. He too felt depressed when he returned outside into the sunshine to find Katherine.

"How was he?" she asked.

"In a strange mood. A bit remote, and still holding back. I don't like the look of it coupled with these violent episodes. It's too reminiscent of before. You *must* get to see him before you leave."

Katherine put a hand to her forehead, hiding her eyes and the swelling tears.

"I'll try."

*

Siegfried was rather proud of his battle wounds. The orbit of his right eye had a hairline fracture, and his nose was definitely broken. Sophie drove him back from the hospital to his flat, ready to nurse and feed him with painkillers. Siegfried had insisted on discharging himself, despite the casualty doctor wanting to keep him in under observation.

"God, I hate those places," he said settling down on the leather sofa. "No privacy, everyone staring at you. It's twice as bad when your father's a notorious murderer."

Sophie brought him a glass of schnapps, then very tenderly stroked his battered face. "How do you feel?"

"Great!" He tried a smile. "This is the start of what I've been waiting for all my life. Complete and utter revenge on my father. You know, Schatz," he made a grab for her hand, pulling her onto the sofa beside him, "I feel so great, I want you. Right now."

Sophie read the signs. Siegfried was in domineering mood. With his face in such a condition there would be no affectionate kisses. He would take her and be done. She loved him when he was like that: powerful, masterful. Meekly she let down her hair and undressed in front of him, his slave, then took off his clothes for him. The young god stood proudly in front of her, and she worshipped him. With an imperious command he pointed to the floor and she knelt down on all fours, ready for him. His vigorous thrusts drove her to cry out as all too quickly it was over.

Resting his hands on her haunches he slowly withdrew. "We work well together, you and I," he commented. "We should stay together. Permanently."

She turned her head to look at him over her shoulder. "I agree."

They had only just finished in the shower when the buzzer sounded for the apartment block front door. Siegfried went to the intercom in his dressing gown.

"Yes?"

"Liebchen, it's Mutter and Paul."

"Come on up." He pressed the door release button and stood waiting at his own front door. They appeared from the lift half a minute later.

Ilse went straight up to her son, her expression one of horror at the state of his face. "We only just heard on the news what happened. Why on earth didn't you tell us?"

Siegfried ushered them inside. Sophie had managed to quickly dress herself, although her hair was still damp at the edges. There was no hiding the recent activity, not that Siegfried wanted to.

"We were too busy celebrating." He looked towards Sophie. "Weren't we, Schatz?" He turned back to his mother, a smile breaking through despite the pain. "Sophie and I are going to get married."

Ilse gave a squeal of delight and hugged her son. "That's wonderful news! Isn't it, Paul?"

As Ilse went to give Sophie a hug, Paul gave Siegfried's shoulder a fatherly squeeze of congratulation. "Well done, *Junge*. I'm proud of you. It all seems to be working out very smoothly so far."

Siegfried knew he was not talking about the engagement. "We're not home and dry yet. But I don't see how he can wriggle out of this. I think he's convinced the warders he's unstable. Now we've got to persuade the shrinks and the court. Easy when his personal psychiatrist comes running to him at the first sign of trouble!"

Paul's hand slipped from Siegfried's shoulders as an unwelcome twinge of guilt tugged at him. All this was really Garisch's fault. The man should never have allowed Karl to see his face. But it had happened and it was Paul's duty to cover it up. He shrugged off the guilt.

"I don't suppose you're in a fit state to come out and celebrate properly, looking like that! What do you say to me going to find a bottle of champagne to bring back here?"

"Fine."

Paul went back out to the car, giving Ilse the chance to have a word with her son while Sophie finished drying her hair in the bathroom. She watched Paul from the window as she spoke, keeping her back on Siegfried so she did not have to see his eyes. She would never speak her mind faced with those intimidating orbs.

"I know how much you hate your father, how you've always wanted to punish him for what you had to suffer from Erich, but this time you've hurt me too, Siegfried. I slept with Karl because I still love him. I don't like having to destroy him now. I'm only doing it out of loyalty to you and Paul." Ilse finally turned to her son. "You deserved what you got today." She let her words sink in, then mellowed her tone. "But I won't speak of it again. Now you know what love is, perhaps you'll understand how I feel."

"All right, Mutter. You've made your point. You love the bastard so I'll leave you out of this if I can."

Ilse nodded. It was the most she could expect by way of apology from her arrogant son. She had to admit it. He *was* arrogant and self-centred; had been ever since he found comradeship in Paul. She wondered whether Sophie found it attractive, or whether she just tolerated it. Whatever, she was going to have to live with it. Nothing would ever change Siegfried.

*

After seeing Robert off to the airport, Katherine went with Sabina to the remand prison the following morning, only to be told once again they could not see Karl.

"He's up before the magistrate again this morning for assaulting his son," the warder told them. "Open and shut case. He'll probably be sentenced today, so won't be coming back here." He looked apologetic. "You couldn't have seen him anyway. Inmates are only allowed an hour's visiting a week. He's had his lot already."

"But I live in England," Katherine exclaimed. "Surely you can ..." She ran out of German.

"... make an exception," Sabina supplied.

They both knew from his expression what the answer would be, even before the man opened his mouth. "Rules are rules. Can't break them. Not even for the English."

He might as well have said 'especially for the English'. In a flurry of impatience, Sabina took her mother's arm. "Let's dash to the magistrate's court. At least we might get to see him there."

They arrived there to find Sophie and Siegfried waiting outside. At least they assumed it was Siegfried behind the swollen, discoloured face.

"Look at him!" Sophie said to Sabina, pointing to Siegfried. "Your father's just got eighteen months for doing that."

"We're too late!" Katherine moaned, yet experiencing a huge sense of relief. She ignored the pair in front of them. "This is turning into a wild goose chase."

Siegfried was not to be ignored. "Don't worry, Katherine," he said with a leer. "My mother will visit him in jail for you. She can say she's his wife!"

Katherine exploded. "Don't you dare mention your mother to me!" she said in English. "You're all as bad as each other."

There was a camera flash as a lurking reporter spotted news, recognising Siegfried from the court. Katherine's tirade was cut short by Sabina.

"Come on, Mummy. Let's go and find out where they've taken Daddy."

Katherine gave Siegfried a last glare then followed Sabina inside. It took them some minutes to get the information they wanted and when they had it they were not pleased. "But that's miles away!" Sabina groaned.

Katherine felt too dispirited to comment. It was not so much the distance that concerned her. It was more the nature of the prison. A high-security jail. They obviously considered Karl dangerous. As Sabina made more enquiries of the court official, Katherine sank wearily onto a nearby chair. At length Sabina joined her.

"It's no good, Mummy. He said we wouldn't be allowed to see Daddy for at least a week."

Katherine hardly heard her. Something Siegfried had said was bothering her. She tried to think what it could be. Then it hit her. He knew about Ilse! How? Why? She began to smell a rat. If Siegfried was somehow involved in all this, then maybe Karl was not so much to blame. Why had he assaulted Siegfried? Perhaps he'd not slept with Ilse after all. Perhaps it was all a lie engineered by Siegfried. She gave a long sigh, confused and bewildered by too many events. What was she to think of it all? She needed more time to learn her own mind. And if she couldn't speak to Karl for another week ...

She stood up abruptly. "There doesn't seem much point in me staying here, Bina. I'm needed at home, now Alice and Robert are off back to Edinburgh. Besides, I've got to start rustling up some money to pay Daddy's lawyer. Oma and Opa have offered to help out. Robert too, very kindly. Even so, it's going to be tough finding it all."

"When I get a job, I'll chip in what I can," Sabina promised. "Come on. Let's get back to the Gasthaus. You'd better phone home and tell them the latest news."

As they headed outside, Katherine's uncertainty over whether the Ilse incident was true resurfaced. "I must write to him," she told Sabina. "If I can't see him, at least I can tell him we're all doing our best for him." Around them people bustled about, interested only in the next court case or their own private dramas. Katherine suddenly felt very alone. "Oh, Bina. Somehow I don't think our best is going to be enough."

She found pen and paper the moment they got back to the Gasthaus, but agonised over what to write. Eventually she got started.

My Schatz,   *Thursday, 10th August 1967*
This is a very difficult letter for me to write. I had hoped to be able to visit you, but I've been told it will be at least a week before I'm

*allowed. In the meantime I must return home and attend to the farm
– I can't let that go to rack and ruin, can I? Not when we have your
legal fees to cover. Do you have any suggestions for raising
sufficient money? I've a few thoughts but I'll wait to hear what
you've got to say.*

*Now for the hard part. Ilse told me something when she brought over
your belongings, and I don't know whether to believe her. She told
me you still loved her. She wasn't explicit, but I guessed you spent
the night with her. I hope this isn't true, just another of Siegfried's
plots to drive a wedge between us, but the way you've avoided
looking at me since all this happened makes me tend to believe it is
true. I imagine Ilse made herself irresistible to you, as I'm sure she's
well able to do. I know how much she meant to you all through the
war, and because she's the mother of your first child. I'm not
excusing you; just trying to understand.*

*You've hurt me deeply, Karl, but I'm willing to pretend it never
happened. We must concentrate on surviving whatever life throws
at us over the next year or so. To do that we need each other's love
and support. You have mine. Do I have yours?*

*I won't say anything else until I hear from you. You're in my
prayers, Schatz, and constantly in my thoughts.*

Your ever-loving Katherine.

She read it through, satisfied it struck a balance between admonition
and encouragement. She folded the letter and put it in an envelope.
It took her a moment to screw up her courage and address it to the
prison where he was held. The address only served as a bitter
reminder that Ilse could easily visit him, whereas she could not.

353

CHAPTER TWENTY-NINE

Karl held Katherine's letter in his hand. He dreaded having to read it. She had not been to see him. She would only have written because she didn't want to see him again. It was too much to expect of her to forgive him after everything else that had happened.

His cellmate poked him in the ribs. "Aren't you going to read it? You've been staring at it for ten minutes now."

Karl had taken an instant disliking to Willi Auer, a nightclub bouncer who had overzealously removed a client, breaking the unfortunate man's neck in the process. It had not been the first incident of this kind. Auer was a night owl and frequent jailbird. Karl had nothing in common with him, except knowing what it was like to kill a man. Eighteen months confined with him was unimaginable.

"I'll read it when I'm ready."

"Who's it from? D'you know?" Auer edged closer to look at the sender's name on the back of the envelope, but Karl sat on it.

"Mind your own business," he said tersely.

With a swipe of his paw, Auer knocked Karl off the chair. "Listen, matey. You're the new boy here. What I say goes. And I say this goes!"

He grabbed the letter from the chair and started ripping it to shreds. With a yell of rage, Karl threw himself at Auer to retrieve the letter, but Auer's bulk was formidable. Tossing Karl aside he reached across and flung the contents into the toilet, flushing it before Karl could get anywhere near.

Karl watched the torn pieces of paper slip away. He looked up angrily at Auer, then backed off. Survival conditions prevailed. Karl knew when to make a tactical retreat. Glumly he sat down at the tiny table.

Satisfied he had made his point, Auer became instantly friendly again. He opened a packet of cigarettes and offered one to Karl.

"I don't smoke."

"Suit yourself." Auer lit up. "This is your first time inside, isn't it? I can tell."

"How?"

Auer smiled. "You're prickly. On edge. You'll soon learn to relax." He puffed smoke across the table into Karl's face. "They don't usually put common assaults in here. You must have done something else to upset them."

Karl waved the smoke away. "I'm awaiting trial for murder. Garisch, the politician."

A new respect came over Auer's face. "Ah! That's what I like to hear. You got rid of one of those pompous bastards. That's all right then. You're one of us. Shot him, didn't you?"

"He was shot."

"You're saying you didn't do it? I thought the papers said there wasn't any doubt you did it."

Karl leaned his chin on his hand. He had been over and over that scene in his mind many times since the killing. How could there be any doubt he did it? "I was holding the gun. I suppose I shot him."

"You don't remember?"

"I was being attacked by a dog at the time." He gave a wave of his bandaged arm. "It's all a bit hazy. But I must have done it."

Auer grunted. The technicalities didn't interest him. He'd just remembered something else the papers had said. "Your son says you're mad. Are you?"

For the first time since his arrest, Karl felt like laughing. "You worried I'll kill you in your sleep, Auer?"

The bouncer gave a weak grin. "Course not."

An uneasy silence fell.

"Sorry about the letter," Auer said eventually.

"That's all right. I think I know what it said." Karl looked around the cell. "Do you know where I can get some writing paper? I need to write back to her."

Auer nodded. "I've got some. Prison issue. Never use it myself." he rummaged around on his shelf and handed Karl a piece of headed notepaper. "Fancy stuff this!"

Karl took it. "Got a pen?"

Auer grinned. "You need to get yourself kitted out, you do." Again he rummaged on the shelf and found a blunt pencil. "Best I can do, I'm afraid."

Hoping Auer would leave him in peace, Karl began to write.

My beloved Katherine,

I received your letter but was prevented from reading it by my friendly cell mate. I can only guess what you wrote after you heard about Ilse and me – probably that living with a murderer is bad enough, but with an adulterer impossible. I would dearly love to make excuses for myself, to say it was all Ilse's fault. But how can that be true? I betrayed your love and your trust for a night of self-indulgent nostalgia. I can only beg your forgiveness, and promise it will never happen again as long as I live.

But what good is such a promise when I may not be living with you ever again? If I'm convicted of murdering Goslar, I could well die in here before my release. If you want to commence divorce proceedings, then you have my permission, if not my blessing. I would rather only one of us sat alone waiting. I give you up because I love you, and want you to be happy. I have always taken more than I gave. Now you can stop giving, stop worrying about me. Don't feel you have to come to the trial. It will be long, tedious and in German! The farm and the boys need you. I have my memories to sustain me. I don't want to see that same hurt in your eyes I saw once before, long ago.

He paused to think, realising Auer was watching him closely.

"Difficult, is it?" Auer asked with a trace of concern.

Karl nodded and carried on writing.

I only ask of you that you don't tell the children about my foolishness; but perhaps Sabina already knows? Was she there when Sophie told you? No doubt she and Wolf are having problems themselves over all this. It is a difficult time for us all.

I await your decision with an anxious heart. You must do as your heart dictates.

Yours for ever,
Karl

He had seen from the envelope's return address she was staying at a Gasthaus in Dortmund. He addressed it to her there.

*

Werner, Alice and the boys had kept the farm ticking over in her absence, but there was a stack of correspondence waiting for Katherine upon her return. Fortunately she and Karl had always run everything as a joint venture, so there was nothing she could not sign or deal with. Only tree-felling and coppicing jobs were beyond her, unless Werner was willing to undertake them with Richard's help.

The national news had made brief mention of Karl's arrest. It was quite like the old days, Katherine found, with most villagers supportive and the rest quick to condemn. Loyally she defended him, not allowing anyone the pleasure of saying: 'I told you so!' Her cousin Evelyn phoned to hear the juicy details, likewise Sarah.

"Please let me help with the legal expenses, Katherine," Sarah urged as soon as she realised the severity of the situation. "I've got a bit tucked away you could have."

"Thank you. We're going to need help. All these trips back and forth will soon mount up." Remembering that Sarah had once experienced the trauma of an unfaithful husband, she sought her opinion on the matter. "Sarah, this is a little delicate and I'm not sure whether what I want to ask you about is true or not. I have a suspicion it is, though I'm not a hundred per cent sure."

"Go on."

"I think, or rather Ilse told me, she slept with Karl."

"No! I can't believe it. He'd never ..." Sarah paused. "Ilse, you said?"

Katherine knew Sarah was revising her opinion. "Yes. If it *were* true – and that's an 'if', remember – if it were true, what do you think I should do?"

Sarah's resentful voice swiftly came back down the line. "You can't ask me! Only you can decide." Despite her last words, Sarah gave herself a moment to ponder the facts, before going on: "But I think I'd remember all the many times he could have been unfaithful and wasn't. And I'm telling you, Katherine, there *were* many! Ilse is a very different kettle of fish for Karl. Not so cut and dry. I know that's not very helpful, but you asked for my opinion."

"No, you have been helpful. You think I should stick by him."

"It's your decision." Sarah played the card she knew would make Katherine dig her heels in and hang on. "If you don't want him, I'll have him!"

"You're forgetting he's in prison, Sarah," Katherine said quietly.

*

Richard's reaction to his father's eighteen-month sentence was drastic. "I'll leave school," he declared the morning after Katherine's arrival home. "I'll have to work on the farm now."

"I don't expect you to," she replied. "We can always hire a labourer."

"No we can't. We'll need the money for Dad's lawyer."

Katherine ruffled his hair affectionately, grateful he was willing to sacrifice his education for the sake of his father and the farm. Pulling him into her arms she gave him a hug, a rarity since adolescence bloomed. He did not shy away as he would have done before. He sensed her need for reassurance.

Paul, much more his father's son, missed Karl dreadfully. Katherine recognised the symptoms: moodiness, withdrawal of affection, uncommunicative. It seemed to be the same with Karl now. She had expected a reply to her letter by now. The delay was explained the following week, when the post brought an envelope bearing Karl's writing. It had been forwarded on by the Gasthaus; even the extra postage paid. Paul brought the letter to her from the postman outside, as eager as she was to read it. Katherine took it from him, hoping he wouldn't try to read it over her shoulder. She suspected it was not for his eyes.

"Give me some space, Pauli. I'll tell you what's in it later."

Grudgingly Paul went off to continue with the chores, leaving Katherine alone in the silent kitchen. She sat in the rocking chair, looking at the envelope, not daring to open it. She had asked him for his love and support. Was she going to get it, or was he going to cut himself off from her as he had before in times of trouble, and sink into his own mire of despond? She opened the envelope and read his letter.

By the end tears poured onto her lap. It was all true. He freely admitted it. What was worse, he hoped she would divorce him, thus leaving him free for Ilse. She would never give him that satisfaction. He might want someone else, but she didn't. How could he think she

358

would ever leave him? She set about writing an immediate reply, hoping that this time he got to read it.

When she had finished she called Paul in from mowing the lawn. "Can you get on your bike and take this down to the Post Office? I want it to catch the second post."

Even at fourteen he was already a shade taller than her. She was beginning to feel dwarfed by her family. He looked down into her eyes.

"You've been crying, Mum. Is everything all right?"

She squinted up at him into the sun. "Your father's a bit depressed. It's only natural in the circumstances. I've sent him everybody's love. You can write your own letter to him, but I want that one to go today."

"You bet!"

She watched the gangly, blond figure disappear off to fetch his bicycle. So like his father. The most like him of all his offspring. Except Siegfried.

*

Auer noticed an immediate difference once the next letter arrived. His cellmate became almost cheerful, especially when the letters kept coming. There were letters from his parents, his children individually, more from his wife, and several from 'a friend in Scotland'. There was a visitor too, his daughter. Auer could imagine the meeting, especially after being shown a photograph of Driesler's entire family taken at his parents' home.

"If anyone asked for my opinion whether you're mad or not," he told Karl on the day he was to be assessed by two independent psychiatrists, "I'd tell them you're perfectly sane, and lucky with it to have such a large family. Can't you get them to write *me* a letter sometime?"

"I'll ask them," Karl smiled. "Wish me luck for this. My future could depend on it!"

"Do you want them to think you mad, or not?"

"I wish I knew. Which is better: twenty years in jail, or an unknown period in a mental institution?"

"God, what a choice! Jail, I think."

"Then I'm sane. I've got to convince them of that."

"You shouldn't have any trouble. But good luck anyway."

The two assessing psychiatrists looked friendly enough, Karl decided as he was led into an office near the prison governor's. They had cups of coffee on the desk in front of them. There was no spare cup, Karl noticed, but it was hardly likely he would be offered one. The warder went out, shutting the door behind him. Karl was glad of the privacy now, even though everything he said would probably come out later in court. He tried to relax, look confident. Robert had sent him a letter with tips to prepare him for this interview. What he wasn't prepared for was the depth of their knowledge about him. They had all his files from his time as a POW. Karl recognised the faded buff covers. There also seemed to be equally old files with the eagle of the Third Reich stamped upon their covers. He wondered what secrets they contained.

By the end of the session Karl felt drained. The questions often demanded much soul-searching. What was it about the Hitler Youth he had most enjoyed? Why had he first obeyed the order to torture the Partisan woman? What was he thinking when he attacked Kellett at the roadside? What were his motives for adopting Siegfried? Why did he punch the eight-year-old Siegfried on the jaw? The questions were endless, largely based on the more violent episodes in his past. Upon his return to the cell they revolved round and round in his head. He examined each answer he had given. Was it the right one? Was it the truth or self-justification? Could they spot which?

Auer interrupted the turmoil. "Well, are you going to tell me what they thought?"

"I've no idea. They didn't tell me whether I'm sane or not."

Auer looked sympathetic. "The more you tell me about that son of yours, the more I think he's the one who's mad."

*

Paul Zopf was reading a letter from an American business colleague over his breakfast coffee. He put down his cup in dismay. Barely four weeks since Garisch's death and now *this* had to happen!

"It seems Karl's been giving people ideas," he told Ilse, who was concentrating on Siegfried and Sophie's list of wedding guests. With the wedding fixed for mid-November, time was growing short.

She looked up from the list. "Why's that, Schatz?"

"Some nutter's shot George Rockwell, founder of the US Nazi Party. Killed him."

The news frightened her. "We're safe though, aren't we? No one can associate us with the Party, can they?"

"No. We've been too careful. They won't believe Karl's delusions that Josef was this chap, Goslar. Apart from that, there's nothing to link us with the Party. Nothing at all. We can safely invite appropriate friends to Siegfried's wedding. Even Karl come to that." He put down the letter. "Has he thought of inviting Karl's family? They won't come, but it would show we have nothing to hide."

"No, and I didn't suggest it. Since Karl's in prison we rather thought he wouldn't be able to –"

"Compassionate leave. They'd bring him under guard."

"Paul, I don't think I'd want Karl there. Nor would Siegfried. I'm sure Karl wouldn't want to come either."

"Perhaps you're right. We won't suggest it to Siegfried. Don't want to spoil his day, after all." He looked quizzically at her. "You still hanker after Karl, don't you? It's all right. I don't mind," he added when she averted her eyes.

"Yes. I do. That night I spent with him was an echo of the past; the way things used to be. Still could be if it weren't for Goslar. I understand the way Karl feels about the man."

"Even if that man was Garisch?"

"You don't think he was, do you, Paul?"

If Ilse had not just proclaimed her sympathies for Karl, Paul would have told her Siegfried's account of what really happened on the day Garisch was murdered. As it was, he felt it best to lie. "No. Couldn't possibly be." It was time to move on. "I'm glad Wolf and Claudia are invited to the wedding. Give them something to look forward to. Poor Wolf's been very downhearted since his father ... died. Although breaking up with Sabina has something to do with it, I think."

"Do you think she should be invited?"

"She won't come. She suspects the truth about us, even if she can't prove it."

"Shame. I'd grown to like her. Margit's certainly going to miss her. I don't suppose we'll see her again. Except at the trial."

And I'll see Karl again, Ilse thought, the tragedy of his predicament threatening to overwhelm her.

361

CHAPTER THIRTY

Sabina had not expected to meet the Zopfs again either, until one cold, grey day in November her grandmother went down with the flu. It quickly became bronchitis. The doctor was called but the next night Gisela's condition suddenly deteriorated and she died in the early hours.

The whole household was stunned. Sabina sat with Monika, Lothar and Tante Anna over a late breakfast the following morning, although no one was eating much. Opa had gone for a walk alone in the forest; Onkel Stefan and Onkel Rudi were down at the sawmill office organising things already.

"We'll have to get a message to Uwe in Stockholm. His first business trip away and something like this happens!" Anna lamented.

"What about my father? Who'll tell him?" Sabina asked her aunt.

"We'll send a telegram. You'd better phone your mother so she can begin to make preparations to come over for the funeral."

Sabina was surprised when her mother proved hesitant about coming. "But they're expecting you and the boys, Mummy. You've got to come! And you haven't even been over to see Daddy yet."

"I know, Treasure, but you know what a busy time of year this is, what with tupping and the apples to harvest."

"Well you can't have any more excuses, Mummy. That must all be finished by now. Werner can hold the fort as usual for a few days. You get yourself over here with Richard and Paul in time for Oma's funeral."

"Yes, dear," Katherine meekly replied with a smile of amusement at her daughter's newly found self-confidence.

*

The church of St Peter and Paul, Medebach was almost full by the time Karl arrived, discreetly handcuffed to a sober-suited minder. The funeral party had not yet arrived to fill the pews left empty at the front. Karl nodded towards the altar, indicating he wanted to be in the thick of things, not skulking in shame at the back. The minder obligingly agreed. It was the first time Karl had got his own way. He had asked to be taken to his home, so he could see his mother before the coffin was closed. Permission was refused. His request to travel with the funeral party was met with another refusal. His own mother's funeral and he was a mere bystander. He was determined to make his presence felt.

He walked up beside the pews, the minder in step with him, their footsteps echoing on the familiar honey-marble floor. He made a point of searching out faces amongst the mourners, receiving nods of recognition and sympathy in return. Seated near the transept were Margit and Peter Witter, next to them the all too familiar faces of Ilse, Paul, Siegfried and Sophie. Keeping his face impassive he passed them, sliding into the first empty row, his back firmly towards them. It was only a matter of minutes before his family arrived, processing behind the coffin borne by Rudi, Stefan, Uwe and Richard. Seeing his son where he himself should have been cut Karl to the quick, serving to underline his fall from grace.

The coffin was placed on a draped trestle and the mourners took their seats. Anna sat next to her father, holding his arm while the rest of the family filed in beside and behind them. As Katherine took her seat she turned. Karl looked into her eyes for the first time in almost four months. Expecting a smile he was astonished when she looked away. In disgust? Surely not? Her letters held no hint of animosity. She had spoken of forgiveness and the future. So what had that look meant?

Karl found himself distracted from the service by thoughts of Katherine. She had not yet acknowledged his presence, unlike everyone else in his family. It was a definite cold-shoulder, and it frightened him.

Once the Requiem Mass was over the whole congregation was to follow the coffin bearers through the churchyard, down Kirchstraße and across Ostwall to the cemetery, situated on the edge of town. Karl felt his place was at Katherine's side in the procession, and managed to drag his minder over to her and the children. Paul greeted him enthusiastically, Richard more soberly, Sabina with a quick kiss. Katherine hung back, waiting her turn, her hat shielding her face from him. He ducked down to peer under it.

"Schatz. It's good to see you. I've missed you so much."

Katherine looked past him to the blank-faced man at Karl's side. His presence was intrusive. She could not say what she felt but gave a watery smile as she looked up at her husband.

"Hello, Karl. I'm glad they let you come."

His hand reached for her cheek. The moment he touched her, felt the soft warmth of her, he realised the reason for her previous discomposure. He had been sitting right in front of Ilse. No wonder she didn't want to look in his direction. Her gloved hand went to his, all too briefly, a momentary display of affection before they had to move on to follow the coffin.

Around them the procession thinned, as if respecting their few moments together. It was less than a five-minute walk, but Karl treasured every second at Katherine's side. Once in position by the grave Karl could see her tears flowing freely as the interment began. He stood close, holding her hand until she drew it away to reach in her bag for a hanky. She did not return her hand to his.

Karl looked out over the bowed heads, across the neatly planted cemetery and the memorial to those who never returned from Russia, across the meadows beyond to the distant forest. Forgiveness was a difficult thing to find in your heart. He had never forgiven Goslar. Never wanted to. Would Katherine ever entirely forgive him?

Over the heads his eyes met Siegfried's. Gloating as usual. In another few days Siegfried would be marrying Sophie, so Sabina had told him on her last visit. Another event he was unable to participate in. Not invited. Sophie was watching him too. He knew now it was Ilse herself who had told Katherine, but it was Sophie who found out in the first place. A miscreant and troublemaker. An ideal partner for Siegfried. The children of that union would be blighted indeed.

He looked at his other children. Sabina, Richard, Paul. All three intent on the ceremony, momentarily oblivious to their father, although the time would soon come when they must say goodbye. He dreaded that moment, dreaded the thought of breaking down in front of them, letting them see his frailty. He must be strong for their sakes.

He watched his father throw a handful of earth on the coffin. As eldest son he was next in line. He stooped, twisted by the restriction on his left wrist. Straightening up he cast the soil into his mother's grave. He heard her voice speaking to him just as she had when he was a small boy: "Be brave, my son. Be brave."

"I will," he promised her.

As everyone began to drift away from the grave ready to head for the nearby *Zum Österntor* for refreshment and commiserations, Karl's minder gave a tug towards the church where their car awaited them.

"Time's up. Say your goodbyes."

It took him ten minutes. Everyone wanted a few words, the funeral temporarily forgotten. When he finally came to his children they each hugged him hard. Then it was Katherine's turn. Her reticence to talk was plain by the downward tilt of her head. Abandoning his chosen words of farewell, he bent close to her ear and delivered others, sotto voce. "Forgive me, Schatz." Then he kissed his fingertips, placed them on her lips, and walked away.

Tight-lipped Katherine watched him go, aware of Ilse's eyes upon him. It had all been far worse than she had expected. Ilse's presence had spoiled it all, seeing her directly behind Karl in the church, her familiarity and freeness with the townsfolk. She belonged here and Katherine did not. Ilse had been Karl's first love. And the last to share his bed.

Anna stepped up to her and put an arm round her. "You look lost, Katherine. Let's go with the others now."

Katherine felt herself gently steered up the path to the cemetery gates and over the road. It was she who ought to be comforting Anna in her loss, she thought. Not the other way round. No one else but Siegfried and the Zopfs knew of her real problems. She must not give anything away.

At the reception she kept well in the background watching Sabina deal confidently with the good wishes of the townsfolk, wishing she could slot so easily into this alien environment. All she wanted was to get home as quickly as possible.

To her consternation she saw Siegfried approaching, accompanied by Sophie. Katherine looked around for an escape route but she was hemmed in by tables and people. His resemblance now to the Karl she had first met was uncanny, his voice too, except for its unpleasant undertones.

"Greetings, Katherine! You haven't met my fiancée, Sophie, soon to be my wife. Very soon in fact. Next Saturday."

"Congratulations. I hope you'll both be very happy," she said automatically.

"Unlike you and my father, eh? Doesn't surprise me him going back to my mother like that. He's wanted to since the time he kissed her in the ruined church back in ... let me see ... 1952 it must have been."

"I don't want to hear this." Katherine pushed past them straight into Richard standing behind. His expression told her he had heard every word Siegfried said.

"Don't listen to him! He's a liar." Katherine grabbed her son and propelled him forwards to where young Paul stood chatting to Lothar. Out of the corner of her eye she could see Ilse deep in conversation with Anna and the wife of the sawmill driver, Peter Witter. Katherine's deficiencies in German had always prevented her from holding much more than slow, superficial conversations with her German relatives. They had all known Ilse since the beginning of the war, accepted her as part of the family, albeit by default as Siegfried's mother. Katherine felt the fires of jealousy burning deep as Siegfried's words came back to haunt her. 1952. The year of her miscarriage. Had Ilse been in Karl's arms as she was losing her baby?

The crowd of people around her was oppressive. Katherine felt over-hot and weak at the knees. She moved closer to the door, wanting to get out into the fresh air, escape the clamour of German in her ears. She stepped out onto the street, turned right and headed back to the small cemetery.

It was so peaceful there. A sparrow twittered in the bare branches of a silver birch planted in memory of some burgher of Medebach. She strolled down to the newly filled in grave, covered now with wreaths and flowers, a candle in a red glass bowl already burning in memory of Gisela Driesler. As she stood there she felt again Karl's hand in hers.

He had often stood with her, holding hands by her father's grave in Penchurch. Now she stood alone by his mother's. Was this how it was going to be from now on? Alone? It was almost as if Karl himself lay dead in that grave. He was gone. She must get used to the idea. He would not be back for a long time – if ever.

A cold gust blew across the meadows from the east, tugging at her coat. She shivered in the growing gloom then walked slowly through the graves up to the road.

*

As he changed out of his suit back into prison garb under the watchful eye of a warder, Karl felt the ever-present weight of depression sink even more heavily onto his shoulders.

Auer noticed it too. "I know you've been to your mother's funeral, Driesler, but it's not the end of the world. For God's sake, you'll have me crying next!"

Karl said nothing but went to the box where he kept all Katherine's letters. He sat down and read them through from beginning to end. There was nothing in them to indicate she didn't want him back. So why the cold shoulder today? Was what she wrote different from what she felt? He was beginning to suspect it was. She was under instructions from Robert not to let him get depressed. She was willing to pretend forgiveness knowing the chances were she would never actually have to put it into practice. If that were the case, he would be better off spending the rest of his life in prison than having to face up to a life of freedom but starved of Katherine's love.

"Cry if you need to," Auer said. "You look as if you should."

"No. I'm all right." He put the letters away. "You're turning soft in your old age, Auer. Quite motherly, in fact."

"It's you, Driesler. I've learned the softer side of life from you. Never experienced it before. Families and all that. Makes me wish my life had been different now. Still, it's too late for all that. Never have a woman now, will I? Or children."

"I saw Siegfried today."

Auer's eyebrows shot up inquisitively. "And?"

"He's getting married this weekend as you know. Made me wonder what his children will be like. My grandchildren, heaven help them!"

"Well you can comfort yourself they won't necessarily be like their parents. My parents were missionaries, so I'm told. Killed in South America. That's where I was born. I was sent back here to a church orphanage, but look how I turned out!" He pulled a gruesome face to illustrate the point.

Karl had to smile. "Do you believe in God, Auer?"

"No."

"Neither do I." He wondered whether to confide in Auer and decided to. "But I heard my mother's voice today, at her graveside. Clear as day."

"Hearing voices? You must be mad then." Auer lit a cigarette. "What did she say?"

"She told me to be brave."

"Sound advice. I should take it." He grinned. "Perhaps she knows something you don't."

"Perhaps she does."

*

Richard spoke to Sabina in the quiet of the barn at Haus Fichtenblick.

"I know now why Mum's so upset, Bina. I overheard something Siegfried said to her today."

Sabina was scornful. "You can't believe Siegfried! But go on. What did he say?" She sat on a bundle of hay near the open door to the house. The rest of the family was safely ensconced in the warmth of the living room. She was wishing she was there too, but Richard had insisted on speaking to her alone.

"He said Dad had gone back to Ilse. That he'd always wanted to, ever since 1952."

Sabina was ready to hotly deny the truth of such a thing, but the memory of seeing her father and Ilse laughing and chatting on the terrace at Iserlohn, of Ilse fawning over him, made her stop to reconsider.

"Well?" Richard prompted. "What do you think? Could it be true?"

"No, of course not. It's Siegfried up to his wicked lies again."

Richard breathed a huge sigh of relief. "That's what Mum said, but I thought you might know Dad better than me. You've always been closer to him than I have." He headed for the door and the warmth. "You coming in?"

"In a minute."

She sat on in the cold and dark. Another nail in Daddy's coffin. Her fists clenched until her nails dug into her palms. Damn Siegfried and his mother!

CHAPTER THIRTY-ONE

Sabina was not sure why she had come to Soest, why she had gleaned the details of the wedding from Ilse at Oma's funeral. But here she was, standing in the cobbled square in front of the curious pale green church of St Petri, awaiting the end of the wedding service. She had not wanted to enter the church, not wanted to participate in the ceremony in any way. She had noticed that St Petri was a Protestant church. Immediately behind it stood the equally green, Roman Catholic cathedral of St Patrokli. Siegfried's religious upbringing would have been a mixture of the two: Protestant in England and Roman Catholic in Medebach. She doubted either denomination meant anything to him. It was all a demonstration of respectability for the public-show about to begin, as the organ piped up for the final bridal procession.

The open church doors revealed Siegfried in traditional grey and green loden leading Sophie on his arm. She wore a princess style bridal gown, extravagantly embroidered in silver threadwork. Her silver-blond hair was adorned with a circlet of myrtle leaves and white rosebuds, partner to the large bouquet of roses and myrtle she carried. Behind them followed Margit, Edeltraud, Roslinde and Sophie's younger sister decked out in emerald and ivory shepherdess dresses; then came Paul escorting Sophie's mother. Her outfit was of sapphire blue bordered with old gold, while Ilse had chosen a suit and hat of jacaranda blue. The whole entourage looked stunning.

Sabina caught her breath as she noticed Wolf amongst the numerous guests pouring out into the square. He saw her at the same moment, his smile abruptly vanishing. He was quickly hidden from her view as Siegfried and Sophie led the procession across the square, past the Town Hall and down the cobbles of Rathausstraße in a shower of flowers, rice and applause from the assembled onlookers. As Ilse passed the spot where Sabina stood she did a double take, hastily lowering her eyes in shame or embarrassment,

369

Sabina was not sure which. She was glad to have unnerved the woman who had dared to ensnare her father.

A moment later she herself was unnerved. A hand grasped her elbow and an all too familiar soft voice asked: "Why did you come?"

Sabina spun round, shaking off the hand. In glacial tones she replied: "I have nothing to say to you, Wolfgang *Goslar*. Not until you speak the truth about what happened that day."

You might as well ask me to fly to the moon, his sorrowful eyes told her. "I still love you, Bina. I miss you."

"Then you know what you have to do to get me back," she retorted, turning away from him with aching heart. She pushed her way through the crowds, knowing he would not follow. His loyalties were directed elsewhere, to his murdered father and the participants of the procession.

With a heavy heart Wolf watched her go. Wolfgang Goslar. It wasn't right. He was a Garisch. Always had been and always would be. No matter what her father said. He rejoined the procession making its way to the market square and its picturesque hotel, *Im Wilden Mann*.

After the wedding banquet there were plenty of Sophie's friends to dance with, but they found him poor company that evening. Even Siegfried noticed his melancholy and took time off from dancing with his bride to have a quiet word in a dark corner.

"You spoke to her?"

Wolf nodded. "I didn't realise you'd seen her."

For once in his life Siegfried found sympathy for someone else. "I'm sorry I got you involved with her, Wolf. I admit it's not worked out quite how I planned. You've had more than enough trouble from that lot." His sympathy reached its limits as his prevailing emotion, anger, dominated once more. "My father seems to side-step round every trap I lay. But not this one! He's going to need a damned good lawyer to get him out of this."

"You think he stands a chance?"

Siegfried gave a hollow laugh, and patted his friend's shoulder. "No worries there. The police would have taken action by now if they'd found anything. There's nothing *to* find. No. We're just going to have to answer carefully in court and keep to our story. Trust me,

Wolf. And stop looking so worried! Enjoy yourself! Go and dance with Margit."

Wolf watched Siegfried wander back through the smoke-swirled, music-filled room to Sophie's side, the epitome of the happy bridegroom. If only I could free myself from my father as easily as he has from his, Wolf thought bitterly.

Since that fateful day in August, he had searched the house for evidence to prove or disprove Karl's claim, although the police in their searches had found nothing. The old photographs taken before and during the early stages of the war were not clear or close-up enough to categorically prove his father's identity. Even his Wehrmacht papers were not much help. Josef Garisch had gained a lot of weight and lost a lot of hair since his youth. Who could say for sure whether the photographs were of the same man? There was enough of a resemblance for Wolf to believe they were. Except for what had happened on that day. There was no doubt his father feared recognition. He *was* Goslar, the murderer and torturer.

Wolfgang Goslar. Sabina's words haunted him. Her careworn face too. The ordeal she and her family were going through was as bad as what he and his mother had suffered. If not worse. He liked Karl; knew Sabina adored him. She would have to see her father rot in jail for the rest of his life.

"You look glum, my Liebling," Claudia Garisch rebuked her son, her wineglass tilting dangerously in her hand. Wolf recognised the first signs of tipsiness.

"I was thinking of Vater, wondering how he got away with it for so long."

His mother smirked. "They should look where he fell." She took another large sip of wine. "Come along, Wolf. Relax! You've got to get over that Driesler girl. There are plenty here to choose from. You quite liked Margit Röbel at one time, didn't you?"

"I suppose so." Wolf allowed his diminutive mother to drag him back over to the dance floor where a traditional polka was in progress. A handful of the youngsters present were having trouble dancing to the accordion tune, but most guests were enjoying themselves immensely. Dutifully Wolf sought out Margit for the start of the next dance. He had to admit she looked quite pretty

371

today, with her dark hair curled in ringlets, and her normally pallid complexion flushed by the heat and excitement of dancing.

"I saw you talking to Sabina," Margit said the moment the accordion started up again. "What did she want?"

"I don't know." He guided her around Ilse and Paul into a small space on the dance floor. "Just came to witness the event, I think, since nobody from her side was invited."

Margit looked directly at him. "I hope you don't think me insensitive or anything, Wolf, but I do hate the thought of Karl in prison. He's such a nice man. I had quite a crush on him when I was younger. I just can't understand how he could have done such a thing ..." Her voice trailed off. "I'm sorry. You don't want to talk about that, do you?"

"I'm going to have to in court. We all are. We'll all lie through our teeth and send Karl away for life."

He felt her stiffen. "Lie?"

"Yes, Margit. Lie. It's him or us. Didn't Paul tell you?"

She missed her step and he trod on her foot. "Sorry. No, he hasn't said a word except to tell us to think twice before saying anything. We all know what's at stake, but why should you have to lie in court? There's nothing to incriminate any of us. The subject shouldn't come up."

"Of course it will! Karl's lawyer will use every argument there is to try to get him off with a lighter sentence."

"Don't be daft, Wolf! Karl murdered a politician. There's no way he's going to get off with anything. That's what's so awful. I'm sorry, but it is. I can't help the way I feel about him."

"I know. I like him too."

"Really? Even after ...?"

"Yes. Even after he killed my ... father." He hoped she had not heard the doubt in his voice, a doubt that had grown since his mother's careless words.

*

After filling the rest of the afternoon and early evening with sightseeing and having a meal, Sabina found her feet turning once again towards the half-timbered hotel where she could still hear music and voices as the reception continued in full swing. At that time of the evening, as a young woman on her own, she did not feel right entering the hotel alone. Instead she hung about outside, getting colder and colder, yet unable to leave. Eventually at ten o'clock, the bride and groom emerged to be whisked away to a secret destination as the guests waved them off.

She had watched and waited, her heart bitter and angry at the dancing and revelry, in stark contrast to Oma's funeral a few days before, and to her parents' anguish. The more she watched, the more disheartened she became. They were so powerful. So careful too. In all the time she had known them and stayed with them, she had not seen a shred of evidence to link them with the neo-Nazis. Her father didn't stand a chance. Her anger and frustration came to the boil when she saw Ilse and Paul about to re-enter the hotel.

"Bitch!" she shrieked at Ilse. "How dare you try to steal my father!"

A lurking police car cruised slowly towards her, window down, as Paul ushered Ilse inside out of earshot. "All right, that's enough of that kind of talk," the policeman warned, getting out of he car. "Move along now."

Sabina obligingly turned aside, but the light of a street lamp fell full on her face, a face which not so long ago had endured the attention of the press; an attractive face which the young man remembered.

"Hey! Aren't you the daughter of Herr Garisch's killer? What are you doing here?" The policeman took hold of her arm. "You'd better come with me. Don't want you causing any more trouble."

A softer hand took her other arm. "It's all right. I can vouch for her. I'm Wolfgang Garisch."

The policeman hesitated a moment until he recognised Wolf too. "Very well, sir, if you're certain the young lady's not going to be a nuisance."

"She'll be fine," he assured him. "I'll see to that."

They both stood and watched the policeman drive off, Sabina still fuming at his treatment of her. "I suppose I did ask for it," she said eventually, when Wolf seemed disinclined to talk.

"Perhaps." He already knew the facts from Siegfried but decided to feign ignorance. "What did you mean though? Why the sudden outburst at Frau Zopf?"

Sabina didn't really want to talk to Wolf, but decided spreading the truth about Ilse might be helpful. "Siegfried was taunting Mummy at Oma's funeral. He said Daddy had gone back to Ilse, had wanted to ever since 1952. I didn't want to believe it, but I think it's true. Ilse didn't want to meet my eye today. She feels guilty about something."

Wolf was growing tired of aiding and abetting in Siegfried's blood feud. "Whether it's true or not, you can guarantee Siegfried's milking it for all it's worth. I'm sorry. Your mother must have enough to worry about without this too." He noticed her shivering in the cold night air. "How long have you been standing out here? You look frozen. Where are you staying?"

"Nowhere. I was going to drive back to Medebach earlier, but I've ended up staying here later than I expected. I don't know what I wanted to achieve. What I did, I suppose. Hurl abuse at her."

"Well it's too late to drive all that way now. You'd better –"

"No it's not." She didn't want him making any offers to her. She sensed he wanted to make up for his lies. "I need to get back. I'll be taking Mummy and the boys to the airport tomorrow."

Without even a goodbye, she turned her back on him and strode off to where she had left the car borrowed from Opa. It hurt to leave Wolf. Despite what he had done she thought she still loved him. And it was transparently obvious he still felt a great deal for her. He wasn't bad. Not like Siegfried. Just misguided.

The long drive back to Medebach was uneventful on the almost empty roads. Haus Fichtenblick was in darkness apart from the welcoming front door and hall lights left on for her. She crept in and up the wide staircase to the room which had become hers since August, but which she was temporarily sharing with her mother. She undressed in the dark, then climbed into bed, snuggling under the feather quilt that was such a welcome feature of staying in Germany. She lay awake, remembering the feel of Wolf's hand on her arm, comforting rather than alarming as the policeman's had been. She knew now why she had stayed so long at the wedding. It was to catch glimpses of Wolf; to see but not touch. Yet she had touched – been touched rather. But he was a Nazi.

She rolled over onto her side. The room seemed strangely quiet. She could hear no sound from the other bed; no breathing or gently whistling nose. She opened her eyes. The closed shutters made the room totally dark, despite the moonlight outside. She called out quietly: "Mummy?"

There was no reply. Stepping out from under the quilt she felt her way across the gap to the other bed and carefully laid her hand upon it. It was empty.

Puzzled, she got back into bed. Mummy had been to the prison in Düsseldorf to see Daddy today. It was a longish journey, but she should have been back. She had borrowed Onkel Stefan's car, was not used to driving on the right. Perhaps she'd had an accident and no one else in the house knew about it yet. Or they were all out at her hospital bedside already? No. They would surely have left a note for her, clearly visible by the front door. Perhaps she should check anyway.

She got out of bed again, pulled on her dressing gown and crept downstairs, only turning on the hall light when safely down. She scouted around. Sure enough there was a note, propped up against the telephone at the foot of the stairs. Sabina's heart began to pound with fright as she picked it up and read it.

CHAPTER THIRTY-TWO

Katherine felt like a prisoner herself, subjected to security checks and locked doors. As she sat with the other visitors waiting for the prisoners to be brought in, her spirits plummeted. She had thought after seeing Karl at his mother's funeral that a visit would help. She had not had the chance there to speak properly to him, to find a sense of reconciliation with him. Ilse's presence had soured the day. Now she needed Karl alone.

Alone was impossible. There were at least ten others waiting within the grey-painted walls, seated one side of a long line of tables. It was not the easiest place in the world to re-float a marriage that had suddenly and inexplicably run aground. Karl's last words to her gave her hope that everything would be all right. He had asked for forgiveness, now she must give it. She looked around her, at the motley selection of people, mostly women, waiting with her. There was a respectable, middle-aged woman like herself, who looked as anxious as Katherine felt. Perhaps this was her first visit to a prison too? What crimes did she have to forgive?

At last the door opened and the men filed in, each searching out his visitor. It was hard to smile when she saw Karl near the back of the line in the unfamiliar garb, his face pale and drawn. Four months they had been apart and he was a stranger already.

He sat down carefully, and the face that eventually looked into hers was etched with the furrows of nagging pain.

"You look awful," she blurted out. "Are you ill?"

Karl tried a smile. "Just the gripes, that's all."

"Since when?"

He gave a slight shrug, as if to do more would have been too painful. "A week or more. I'm not sure. It wasn't too bad at the funeral. Just happens to be worse today."

"Have you seen a doctor?"

"You have to be at death's door before they do anything in here."

"I don't believe that, Karl," she rebuked him. "You must demand to see a doctor straight away. You've lost weight. You've not been eating properly, have you?"

"Only because of my mother's death and everything. It's nothing, Schatz. Stop worrying."

The corners of his mouth twitched as a flicker of pain crossed his face. Significant pain. Katherine could see he was having trouble hiding it from her. There was no thought now of discussing their problems. He was in no fit state. Her old protective instincts jumped into gear.

"I *am* worried. Your face looks grey. Whereabouts is the pain?"

His right hand automatically fell to cover the lower left of his abdomen, but she knew his body too well.

"Your old bullet wound?" she asked.

"Maybe." He gave a gasp as another wave of pain caught him by surprise. "It never rains but it pours," he said through clenched teeth as the spasm gradually passed. "This is all I need right now. I was coping quite well with it all until this started up."

"All the more reason to insist on seeing a doctor. Promise me you'll do that as soon as we've finished here."

He nodded, biting his lip as another spasm caught hold, his right arm curling protectively over his belly.

Katherine was beginning to feel frightened. She looked around for a warder to call. Suddenly Karl doubled over in agony, clutching at the table with his left hand. Ignoring instructions to the contrary, Katherine reached for his hand, unable to cross to the other side of the table. A warder was promptly upon them.

Fortunately he immediately realised something was seriously wrong. He did not need Katherine's urgent pleas for a doctor to convince him the prisoner was not faking. "Call the doctor!" he yelled to the guard at the door.

Katherine was beside herself with fear by now. Karl's head had dropped to the table, where he lay panting, trying to control the intense pain. Katherine leaned right over to caress his face, which felt clammy to her touch. He was not looking at her, his eyes fixed on some point behind her. She saw her own fear mirrored in them.

"It's all right, Karl," she tried to soothe him. "A doctor's coming."

The other prisoners and their visitors stared at the drama unfolding before them. The warder was busy loosening Karl's collar as his gasps became more laboured and his eyes rolled in fear and pain. Unable to stand helplessly by any longer, Katherine clambered over the table in an undignified scramble to be closer to him. His shoulders shuddered as he tried to ride the pain.

"Oh God! I can't believe this is happening," Katherine moaned, holding his head to her breast. Briefly his eyes met hers, but he was beginning to lose consciousness. "Somebody do something!" Katherine screamed in English.

Urgent footsteps approached behind her and a hand pushed her aside. It was the prison doctor, a young man, who looked as though he qualified only yesterday, still with all the zeal of his training. Deftly he felt Karl's pulse, noticing the pallor and failing consciousness.

"Get him on the floor!" he snapped. Between them, he and the warder lowered Karl's rigid body to the ground. On the way, Karl went limp and his eyes closed. The doctor instantly rechecked his neck pulse. Katherine saw his fingers move a fraction, feel again. Her own heart missed a beat and she felt sick as she heard the doctor call for an ambulance.

She knelt by him watching in horror. "Karl! Don't go! Oh God, don't take him from me, please!"

The doctor looked across at her. "His pulse is weak and unsteady. We need to get him to hospital quickly. Can you tell me what happened?"

Fighting back her tears, Katherine tried to tell him, but the German words eluded her. "Stomach pain," she managed to say, knowing it wasn't his stomach at all. She laid her hand over the exact spot. "Shot in the war." It would have to do. She was shaking and crying too much now to be of any use. She saw the doctor was pulling out Karl's shirt from his waistband while maintaining a finger on his pulse.

"Undo his trousers," he told her. "I need to examine him."

She quickly did as he asked, feeling the heat from the taut and inflamed area around the old scar. Whatever he'd done, she could never live without him.

She bent down by his head, kissed his closed eyes then whispered in his ear. "Schatz, I love you. I need you. Stay with me, please!" She grabbed the doctor's arm. "Don't let him die!" she begged in English.

The doctor patted her hand. "We'll do our best," he promised, but he saw his words held no comfort for the distraught Englishwoman.

The warders had decided to clear the room, much to the disgust of the prisoners, who felt they were being short-changed by missing out on such excitement. There was some scuffling and muttering, but eventually they were all herded out to make way for the ambulance men. They arrived as the doctor finished inserting a drip into Karl's arm. On their way out to the ambulance the doctor put Katherine more fully in the picture.

"Your husband's in shock. Blood pressure's falling." Deciding to be totally honest, he added: "They'd better get a move on."

*

Katherine sat alone in the hospital waiting for news. She had been there two hours already, had relived the scene at the prison over and over in her mind. What chance was there the doctors could save him? While there was still hope she had not telephoned anyone. She dared not disappear in case the doctor came to find her to tell her ... tell her what? That Karl had died? She remembered the strange feeling by his mother's grave that it was Karl in there. A premonition maybe?

It never rains but it pours, Karl had said. How right he was. His whole life had followed that pattern; long periods of sunshine and then a hurricane devastated his life, followed by floods and tidal waves, one after the other. At least if he died he wouldn't have the ordeal of the trial to go through ... and whatever came after. The thought was surprisingly calming. Although he had said he had been coping well until the pain started. Robert, too, had been pleased with Karl's state of mind, all things considered; had said he felt confident Karl could stand up to questioning in court. But what they said and what turned out in reality could easily be totally different. Karl hated talking about the war, about Goslar. Even now, after all Dr Goldberg's and Robert's help to come to terms with it. It was forbidden territory. It was re-opening old wounds. Katherine bit her knuckles in anguish. Old wounds. Old flames. All that business about Ilse was a nothing, a nonsense, whipped up by

379

Siegfried into a drama whose sole purpose was to unnerve his father, to prevent him coping with the trial. Siegfried wanted to see him certified insane. Or dead.

For the twentieth time she looked at her watch but her thoughts were now focused elsewhere. The wedding was about to start. What if Karl died? Should she try to get a message to the wedding party? She decided against it. She would deny Siegfried the pleasure of that particular wedding gift. But even if Karl lived, Siegfried was still going to have the satisfaction of knowing his father's life was ruined.

Either way, she could not face the future. Her lower lip began to tremble, her vision blurred and she gave way to the sobs that had been building up for the past two hours. A passing nurse sat beside her to comfort her as all the pent-up worry of the past four months poured out.

The nurse made her a cup of coffee once the tears subsided. Katherine tried to drink it, but her throat felt constricted. Her sodden handkerchief was of no further use and the residual tears streaked her face. She should have been used to grief. First her mother, then father. A number of elderly relatives and villagers. Alex Kellett. Gisela.

She remembered the emptiness when her father died. Her life was like that now, without Karl. Four months she had slept with the bed empty beside her. Four months of imagining Karl with Ilse, of hating her, sometimes him. But all that meant nothing when the other side of the bed might never be occupied again.

At least she had the children. They ought to know what was happening.

"I must use the telephone," she told the nurse who was about to return to her interrupted duties. "If there is any news of my husband, please tell them where I am."

"Of course."

She spoke to Anna. It was a difficult conversation trying to explain everything in German, especially since Katherine had no details to give except a promise to keep them all in touch. She returned to her chair outside the operating theatres, prepared to wait as long as necessary.

She realised someone was standing by her. She looked up and saw a rather dumpy surgeon. Ominously he sat down beside her, his glasses glinting, hiding what news he might bring.

His voice when he spoke was grave. "Frau Driesler? I'm Dr Langen. I understand you're English so I'll tell you what the situation is as simply as I can."

She nodded, her eyes transfixed by the movement of the surgeon's scrubbed hands as he illustrated his words.

"We have had to remove a section of your husband's large intestine. Because of the poor repair of his previous injury it had twisted, then recently become inflamed which led to the crisis today." He smiled. "But he is basically healthy and strong. If he recovers he should have no more problems."

That small word grabbed at her heart, making it lurch with fear. "If?"

His head moved and now she could see his eyes behind the glass, kindly, encouraging, but the firm set of his mouth betrayed his caution. "We have rejoined the bowel, but in cases like this the main worry is infection. I'm afraid he's not out of danger yet."

"When will you know for sure?"

"Tomorrow, the day after, maybe. Not too long." He knew she was on the verge of breaking point, and tried to offer some comfort. "You can see him shortly, if you like. He'll be waking soon, and when he's comfortable a nurse will come to find you. Don't expect him to talk much. Just let him know you're there."

"Thank you, Dr ..."

"Langen," he reminded her. "My pleasure."

Katherine watched him go back to the operating theatres. Dr Langen. She wanted to remember their names, the doctors who saved Karl's life. Despite his warnings of infection she felt more hope. Karl would fight to live, as he always had.

It was another twenty minutes before a nurse of about Katherine's own age appeared.

"I'm Sister Voß. I'll be looking after your husband, Frau Driesler. Would you like to see him now?"

She led Katherine to a single room where Karl lay, drip tube in one arm. Everything about him looked grey, from his hair to his face. The only originally grey part of him, his eyes, were invisible to her under closed lids.

The sister pulled up a chair and left Katherine to him. Reaching for his limp hand, she asked: "Karl, can you hear me?"

His eyelids fluttered open briefly then closed again, his hand moved slightly in hers. He could hear her. But what should she say? She didn't want to talk about anything that had happened, all the trouble and worries. She must give him positive thoughts. The words of her old favourite Bing Crosby song came to her. Accentuate the positive. She began to hum the tune. Karl had told her shortly after their marriage how much that song, which she had so often sung, meant to him. He responded now with a firmer squeeze of her hand. She stopped humming, knowing what to say.

"Do you remember the first time I danced with you? Formal dancing, not the Scottish country dancing at Donald and Gertie's that New Year's Eve. I think it was at a fund-raising do for the new village hall, shortly after your release. I remember feeling so proud to have the handsomest man on the dance floor. It took us a little while to forget that everyone was staring at us. And now I watch Richard and Paul growing up so fast. They'll be taking all the girls by storm soon, you'll see. The Driesler boys will be the subject of many a Penchurch girl's dreams."

He opened his eyes. For a moment she saw her old Karl, with no guilt about Ilse to spoil their relationship. She gave his hand an extra long squeeze, which he returned in kind.

He looked so old all of a sudden, so frail, his normally tanned and healthy face bleached by the months in prison. What would he look like at the end of twenty years behind bars?

"Of course Sabina isn't short of admirers in Medebach now," she prattled on. "Anna tells me the young men are queuing up to take her out. There's one chap in particular, Volker Schaaf – I think his father's something to do with the forest office, am I right?" She saw him nod. "Won't take no for an answer. Practically forced her to go bowling with him. And she went. Anna says he's a nice enough young man, if a bit of a show-off. But aren't they all? Young men, I mean. I well remember you showing off to me in the early days, with your skiing. Then there was that time on the river in the summer you lost your memory. You were showing off swimming until Robert dunked you and part of your memory came back. It was funny at first, seeing you sitting there in the water like a –"

She suddenly realised his hand lay limply in hers. Panic-stricken she reached across and put a hand on his chest. It rose slowly with his indrawn breath. He was asleep. She sank back onto the chair, her knees weak with relief. However was she going to survive the next few days?

She sat on in the chair beside him, unwilling to leave. Every moment with him now was precious. She wanted to absorb every detail of him, every crease, wrinkle and scar on his face, even the scars on his right hand and arm, the legacy of traumas both old and new. The hand was from broken glass in a prison camp cell, the arm from Goslar's dog. Karl carried his history visibly on him.

Sister Voß returned to check on her patient's condition. "I expect he'll sleep for a while now, Frau Driesler. You ought to go and have some food, get some rest yourself."

"I can't leave him. We may have so little time together."

*

During the night his temperature soared. Katherine kept vigil while the night staff gave antibiotics and cooled him with electric fans and ice packs. By dawn there were signs his temperature was dropping once again as he responded to treatment. Dr Langen appeared briefly at eight and seemed pleased with progress.

"Please, Frau Driesler," he told her after examining his patient. "Go and get some rest. There's a hotel down the road; the Hirschmann. You'll be comfortable there. We'll call you if there's any news."

Reluctantly Katherine looked at Karl. He was quiet now after his restless night. It would be best if she had some sleep herself. But what if something happened and she didn't get here in time? "No. I'll go and get some food, then I'll be back. I can't leave him."

Dr Langen smiled at her devotion. "I understand your position. You want to make the most of being with him, before he goes back to prison. I'll try and keep him here for you as long as possible, but he'll have to return to the prison hospital sometime, you know."

Katherine felt a surge of relief. "He's out of danger?"

Dr Langen glanced at his patient. "It's early yet, but I think so."

Suddenly she felt utterly exhausted. "Perhaps I will go to that hotel. The Hirschmann you said?"

"That's right. Sleep well."

Before leaving, Katherine kissed Karl's lips, cooler now the infection was under control. "Sleep well, my Schatz. I'll be back soon."

Her first stop was at a telephone. Sabina answered immediately.

"Mummy! How is he?"

"Pulling through at last, thank God. I don't know when I've prayed so hard in my entire life."

"Me too! When I read Tante Anna's note last night I nearly died of fright. I was all set to drive straight over, but Tante Anna came down and told me to wait until morning and bring Richard and Paul too. We were only waiting to hear the latest news on the radio. Tante Anna said it was mentioned last night. Do you think Siegfried knows?"

"I doubt it, and I don't care if he does. You just get yourselves over here as soon as you're ready. Is Opa all right? I hope this hasn't upset him too much so soon after Oma's death."

"He's as shocked as the rest of us, but otherwise OK."

"Good. I'm going for a rest at a hotel nearby, but I expect I'll be back at the hospital by the time you arrive. I don't suppose you slept much last night, so drive carefully, Bina."

"I will." Sabina was about to say goodbye when she realised she had a question. "Mummy?"

"Yes?"

"You've forgiven him, haven't you? I can tell. Your voice ..."

"Yes, I've forgiven him."

"Good. I'm so glad."

"So am I, Treasure. So am I."

CHAPTER THIRTY-THREE

Sabina was not the only one to listen to the radio news that morning. Wolf too had been up all night. After leaving Sabina and escorting his mother to her room in the hotel in Soest, he had driven all the way back to his home in Dortmund. He had immediately changed into an old pair of work trousers and a warm pullover, and set about ripping up the paving slabs of the patio. It was a backbreaking job. Underneath the concrete slabs was a layer of sand, beneath that compacted soil. He had dug most of the night before he found what he was looking for near the wall. 'Where he fell.' His mother's clue was wholly accurate. The sturdy green metal box sat on its waterproof bag in front of him on the kitchen table, locked fast. Before attempting to open it, he decided he needed a reviving cup of coffee and a bread roll, stale if necessary. He plugged in the percolator, switched on the transistor radio, then listened in open-mouthed astonishment to the newsreader's voice.

> ... Driesler's English wife spent the night at his hospital bedside. His condition was described by the hospital authorities this morning as stable. It is hoped this illness will not delay the trial, scheduled for March next year.

The percolator bubbled noisily as Wolf stood stupefied by the news. His immediate concern was for Sabina. What state was she in at the moment, with the father she adored nearly at death's door? He felt a need to go to her, but recognised it as pointless. He wouldn't be welcome, his presence intrusive at such a time.

Wolf poured the brewed coffee and dunked the stale roll he had found in the bread bin. No, he must set about opening the box and discovering what secrets it contained. First thing was to find the key.

It took him half an hour of searching through the heavily carved bureau in the living room before he came across the tiny drawer he missed first time round. His father had never shown it to him, and it was by sheer luck, when a bulldog clip snagged on it and dragged it open, that he found it. Inside was a pillbox containing a key small enough to fit the lock on the box. He took the key into the kitchen, sat at the table and inserted the key into the lock. It turned with only a slight effort. Wolf prised open the lid. Inside was exactly what he was hoping to find – a bundle of documents.

Nervously he lifted them out and began to examine them. Within five minutes he had discovered all he needed to know about Josef Garisch and Johann Goslar.

Relaying the paving stones was no easy task. He had to level off his excavations, then try to leave the slabs themselves looking undisturbed. It gave him the time he needed to digest and deal with what he had learned. By the end he was physically and mentally exhausted. His mother back at the hotel in Soest must be wondering where on earth he had got to. He left a message at reception for her saying he would collect her that evening, then went upstairs for a shower and some rest. Not even the box's startling revelations could keep him awake for long.

When he woke it was five fifteen. As he dressed, niggling doubts began biting at his conscience. He went into the living room, sat in an armchair, and gazed up at the portrait of Georg Garisch who now represented the truth. Until now his life had built on lies: lies about his parentage, lies about the glories of National Socialism. Sabina had told him what her father had suffered at Nazi hands. He only believed her because he knew she had no reason to lie. Yet what unspeakable fate might befall himself – and her – if he betrayed his friends?

His hands gripped the chair in fear at the sudden image of Sabina mangled by one of Siegfried's 'accidents'. No. He couldn't take the risk. He would keep quiet.

He was about to rise from the chair when he caught Georg Garisch's reproachful gaze, which became Sabina's as she realised he could have told the truth about her father, maybe even kept him out of jail. Then he knew what his decision must be. If only he had the courage.

*

Katherine walked tentatively into Karl's room and immediately her spirits soared. Instead of the greyness of the morning, there was a golden glow to the room now, as the early afternoon sun poured through the window, highlighting the remaining blond of Karl's hair and giving some colour to his face. His more alert eyes twinkled in a smile of greeting. She laid a bunch of chrysanthemums on the bed and bent to kiss him.

"My word, you're looking better, Schatz," she told him, taking off her coat. She turned to put it on the back of the chair then noticed the armed guard by the door.

He saw her hesitation. "Don't mind Schulz there. He's only a formality, aren't you, Schulz?"

If Karl was able to joke then he must indeed be better. She sat down and asked him anyway. "How are you feeling?"

"Sore and weak, but I'm dosed up with morphine so it's not too bad. How about you? I gather you were here all night. Have you had any sleep?"

"I snatched about three hours but couldn't stay away any longer. I can't believe the difference in you since this morning."

He gave another weak smile. "Well I won't be dancing for just a while, but I'm certainly trying to 'accentuate the positive'."

Katherine smiled too. "So you remember all that. I wasn't sure if you were awake. You certainly gave me a fright when you dropped off."

He reached for her hand. "I know. You seem to be coping with all this so well. If it was you lying here instead of me, I'd be panic-stricken."

"I was. You just didn't see me. Still," she said, determined not to be morbid, "just look at you now, all bright-eyed and bushy-tailed. The children won't know what all the fuss was about by the time they get here."

"They're coming here?"

"On their way. Sabina was all for setting off last night, but fortunately Anna dissuaded her. She'd already driven back late from Soest."

"Soest?"

"She went to watch Siegfried and Sophie's wedding."

"Oh, yes. I'd forgotten. So we have a daughter-in-law. Fancy that."

They both reflected on the thought. "I hope Sabina won't want a grand wedding after seeing Sophie's," Katherine said after a few moments. "Her wedding fund will be rather reduced now it's being used for a good cause. But with any luck, at least she'll have you there to give her away."

"It won't need luck. As long as she marries in Germany, the chances are I'll be there – in handcuffs."

It was as though her own guts were twisted, the pain his words made her feel. "You mustn't lose hope, Schatz." Her eyes could not meet his to prove her own faith in her words.

He stroked her hand. "Don't worry about me, honestly. I'm not going to let Siegfried see me go to pieces. I can stand up in court and tell the world what happened. You'll see." He was no longer looking at the top of her head as her eyes met his. "Mud sticks. Even if nothing is proven, their reputations will never be the same."

"What about your reputation?"

He gave a rueful smile. "My reputation has always been bad. The people of Penchurch know my chequered history only too well."

"But not the people of Medebach."

"Oh yes they do," he assured her. "They never say anything, but they all know."

Sister Voß stuck her head round the door. "Your children are here, Herr Driesler. Shall I send them in?"

He nodded, but both she and Katherine could see he was tiring.

"Just a few minutes though," Sister Voß warned.

Paul was first in, rushing to his father's side, closely followed by Richard. Sabina seemed to hang back as though frightened at the prospect of seeing her frail father. She looked exhausted too. Katherine stood up to make room for her daughter. They exchanged sympathetic glances, each fully aware of the other's nervous state.

Karl gamely chatted to his sons, but his words were coming more slowly. Katherine was glad when Sister Voß kept to her word and turfed them all out after only a few minutes, but with a promise they could return later. The moment they were all safely out of the door, Karl's eyelids dropped as he let Morpheus embrace him.

*

Doctor Langen allowed no more visitors that day. Disappointed, Wolf returned to the Opel he now drove and sat behind the wheel, undecided about his next course of action. He had really wanted to discuss things with Sabina's father. Now he felt very much alone. There was no one else he could turn to for advice. At least he could tell Sabina of his intentions. She deserved to know.

He found a call box and rang Haus Fichtenblick to find out where she was. When he was told she was at the Hirschmann, he discovered it was only just down the street. Leaving the Opel in the hotel car park, he went inside where the receptionist told him she thought the Drieslers were all in the restaurant for the evening meal. She directed him down the corridor where he soon spotted them in the half empty room. A waiter approached him.

"I'm with the Driesler family," he said authoritatively, threading his way through the tables and chairs.

Sabina saw him approach and frowned, but he forestalled her protests.

"I have very good news for you. Do you mind if I sit and share it with you?"

How could they refuse such an offer? Katherine pointed to an adjacent chair. "Sit down and tell us."

They were nearly at the end of their main course, but none of them continued eating, all sitting expectantly for his news. Wolf cleared his throat but spoke quietly so only the Drieslers would hear.

"Last night I found unequivocal proof the man Karl killed was never Josef Garisch. I've seen the papers which identify him as Joachim Goslar."

There was a rush of indrawn breath from both Katherine and Sabina. "Where are they?" Katherine demanded.

"Safe at the moment, but I would like to put them into the hands of the police as soon as possible. I'll take them there first thing tomorrow. I was hoping to visit Karl today but –"

"I'm afraid we tired him out," Sabina volunteered. She was more than ready to speak to Wolf now he had begun to see sense. "Does this mean you'll finally confirm what really happened the day your father was killed?"

Wolf hesitated. "It's not easy for me, all this. I was brought up to honour and respect my father, and obey him. That's why I stood by his memory. Now, however," he watched her intently as he spoke and knew his decision was the right one, "now I know my true father died in the chaos at the end of the war. The man killed was not my father. It makes all the difference. He was an impostor, who wooed my mother into helping him take over my father's identity. That's why he was so successful. She must have given him all the paperwork, history and backup he needed. He and my father looked sufficiently similar for people to be fooled. If Frau Garisch said that was her husband, he must have been."

"You'll tell all this to the police?" Katherine asked. She felt she had to point something out to Wolf, even though it might jeopardise his decision. "Your mother could go to prison. And what about Siegfried and Paul? There must be a lot you can tell the police about them!"

The waiter, thinking they had finished, came to take their plates, but Katherine waved him away in irritation at the disturbance.

Wolf waited till he was well away from their table. He was about to betray everything he had believed in and he needed a moment to summon the strength. "Yes. I know everything. I can tell the police where to find any evidence they need. Of course, I'll be incriminating myself too, but that doesn't matter now. My mother has betrayed my trust in telling me lies, and I just want to honour my true father's name. I don't want it sullied by the likes of Goslar any more." He smiled at Sabina, who seemed almost bursting with happiness. "You were wrong when you called me Wolfgang Goslar. I'm no such person!"

Sabina took his hand in hers. "You can't imagine the relief I feel, Wolf. I'm so pleased. And grateful to you!" She stood up and kissed his cheek.

"It's worth it just for that," he grinned, ignoring Paul's snigger. "I must say, I'm mighty relieved too. It worried me to think I was descended from a monster like that."

Katherine had more practical considerations on her mind. "Those papers, Wolf. I hope they're in a really safe place. There's no chance of Paul or Siegfried hearing you've found them, is there? Or your mother, even? If they found out ..."

"I covered my tracks pretty well. I doubt my mother will notice anything."

Katherine shook her head. "Doubt isn't good enough, Wolf. With people like this, you must be sure."

There was silence round the table. Four pairs of eyes bored into Wolf.

"You're right. I'd better go and hand them in at once."

"You have the papers on you?" Katherine asked, startled.

Wolf nodded. "I don't want to get them out in case anyone here sees and guesses. I've been brought up to be cautious."

"Good." Katherine remembered their half-finished meal. "Let's eat up then all go to the police. Safety in numbers. I want to make sure they *do* something!"

*

Sophie draped her towel over the rail on the villa balcony, her svelte body exposed to her husband's appreciative gaze. After only a day spent naked on the private beach she had regained some of her summer tan. She ran her fingers over her golden arms, feeling the fine grit of sand and dried salt under her fingertips.

"I'm going for a shower," she told Siegfried. "Are you coming?"

"In a minute." He poured himself a Bacardi and Coke and leaned on the rail to watch the sun setting through the palm trees over the sparkling Caribbean. The secluded villa on the island of St Lucia was proving a perfect honeymoon location. They had total privacy, except for a maid who would come in each morning to tidy up and bring fresh fruit and provisions for breakfast. Yesterday they had enjoyed a superb evening meal of spicy fish at a small restaurant over in the next bay. Siegfried could not remember ever feeling so happy before. Sophie was a treasure, so perfectly able to fulfil his every need. He did not need to ask anything of her, however demanding or bizarre. She knew instinctively what he wanted; their minds were so finely tuned. Likewise, he knew there was nothing he would not do for her. If she had asked for his father to be at their wedding, he would have agreed. But of course she had not.

Swilling down his drink before the ice melted he followed Sophie into the shower. The sight of her firm breasts dripping with lather stirred him again. Earlier in the day he had felt tender, protective, when making love on the beach. Now he felt the familiar aggression generated by thoughts of his father. He grabbed hold of her wet hair to raise her mouth to meet his. Her startled eyes quickly read his mood and she submitted to his onslaught of probing tongue and fingers, relishing the variety of forms their lovemaking took. Her excitement quickly caught up with his, the stinging force of cool water on their skin and in their eyes and mouths adding to the sensual experience. She braced herself against the wall, clutching the shower attachment to steady her as he plunged into her, his muscular body gleaming and slippery as an eel. Heaven could hold no angels as magnificent as him, she thought, her ribs crushed by his weight. Her breath came in short gasps, all she could manage with her constricted lungs. Siegfried's breath too was short, then came a long growling hiss. Sophie let out a wail of pleasure as her whole body celebrated his embrace.

Siegfried stood, still leaning against her, but the pressure eased slightly as he relaxed. The shower water fell full on his back, cascading in a waterfall down his taut buttocks. "God, I love you, Sophie," he told her, planting a more tender kiss on her lips. "You make me so happy."

Sophie eased herself away from him and flexed her bruised back. "I'm in heaven. Nothing can be better than this!"

"Except dinner. I'm starving!" He found a towel, went into the bedroom and began to dry himself. The air felt muggy after the cool of the shower. He glanced out of the window and noticed clouds piling high into the sky. A thunderstorm was brewing over the island. It would be as well to set off early for the restaurant this evening.

By the time they were ready to leave the storm clouds overhead emitted ominous rumbling noises.

"Should we wait for it to blow over?" Sophie asked.

"No. It's only my stomach you're hearing!" Siegfried laughed.

The storm broke on the way, rain gushing down in an almost solid sheet. The windscreen wipers on the jeep couldn't cope. Siegfried pulled in under a stand of palms at the side of the flooding track, until the storm abated. The jeep rocked as a gust of wind caught it, drowning the rattle of the flailing palm fronds. Sophie clung to Siegfried, aware there was only a canvas top between them and the leaning trees. The moment the rain eased a fraction she urged him to continue driving.

Siegfried tried to pull away but the sticky mud sucked onto the wheels, holding them fast. "You drive while I push," he told Sophie.

He climbed out into the howling wind and braced his back against the rear of the jeep. "Ready!" he yelled.

Sophie revved steadily and let out the clutch as Siegfried pushed. The jeep lurched forward just as a sudden squall uprooted a tree beside them. With a splintering crack it fell across the jeep.

CHAPTER THIRTY-FOUR

It was like something out of *Götterdämmerung*. Mud-spattered, rain-drenched and windswept, Siegfried stared in disbelief, then relief, at the crushed bonnet of the jeep. Another metre on and the palm would have fallen over the cab and Sophie. A second later Sophie began to scream. Siegfried's blood ran cold at the agonised sound. He rushed to the driver's door, forcing it open. The gods had not been kind.

"My legs!" Her face was pinched with terror. "Can't move!"

Siegfried leaned inside the jeep. The steering column was compressed down over her legs. Beyond that he could not see. He cautiously tried shifting the obstruction, fearful of worsening the situation, but it was hopeless. There seemed nothing he could do to get her out safely.

"I'll go and get help. I'll be as quick as I can." He planted a kiss on her hair, but she grabbed hold of his dripping shirt.

"Don't go!"

Forcefully he uncurled her fingers and backed off. "I must. Be brave, Schatz. I won't be long."

He ran at full tilt, slipping and sliding down the track. He guessed he had about two kilometres to cover before he reached the hamlet where the restaurant stood. The storm had crossed the island, was venting itself on empty ocean, by the time he arrived, gasping for breath, at the wooden veranda where they had sat and eaten so carelessly the previous evening.

Never before had Siegfried been so grateful he could scrape together some rusty English as when he stood, chest heaving, in front of the restaurant owner.

"Help me, quick! A tree on our car. My wife ... inside."

The owner immediately recognised Siegfried as the wealthy customer from the previous evening. Without further ado he yelled to the loitering young waiter. "Go get Jonas and his truck. There's been an accident. Might need cutting gear. Hurry, man!" As the waiter sped off, the owner looked up at the distraught German. "Ambulance?"

Siegfried nodded, watching in relief yet impatience as a rescue team was quickly assembled, together with a tow truck from the tumble-down garage. All Siegfried could see of the rescuers were flashing eyes and teeth in the darkness as the whole hamlet rallied round in support. A young nurse, home visiting from London, crammed herself next to him in the truck as it sped back to the stricken jeep.

"Don't worry, man," she tried to reassure him. "We'll get your wife out, no problem."

Helpless, Siegfried's imagination took over. He could see Sophie's once shapely legs, now crushed and bleeding. Tears streamed down his face, tears he had not cried since he was a boy. If Paul could see him now, weeping on a black woman's shoulder!

All was quiet when they reached the jeep. The truck's headlamps showed the silver of Sophie's head slumped forwards onto her chest.

"Sophie!" Siegfried called out in terror. He ran to the door, thrusting it open, fearing the worst.

She stirred, groaning faintly. His relief brought fresh tears pouring down his face as he caressed her face.

Judy, the nurse, pulled him gently aside so she could assess the situation. "Sit down, man, over dere. Dere's nuttin' you can do at de moment."

Siegfried refused to sit still, involving himself in helping fix ropes to the tree so it could be hauled clear by the truck. Others had already begun cutting away the wing of the jeep. Someone called out that Sophie was asking for him. He hurried to the opposite side of the jeep, murmuring words of encouragement to her as work progressed agonisingly slowly. An ambulance from Castries, the capital, arrived at the scene well before the rescuers freed Sophie's legs.

Torch beams swung about wildly in the darkness as people clamoured round to see once she was lifted free of the wreckage. Siegfried was in amongst them, ready to hold her head and comfort her as she was moved onto a stretcher. Blinded by the lights, Siegfried swore at the helpers.

"*Um Gottes Willen*! Make the light on her legs!"

He could see dark streaks he knew must be blood, but then Judy's back obscured his view. Siegfried concentrated on holding Sophie's hand, which clutched his tightly, her sharp nails digging into his skin.

"Don't worry, Schatz," he told her. "You'll be all right." He spoke as much to reassure himself as her.

Throughout the nightmarish journey to Castries, Siegfried held her now limp hand, cursing every bump and jolt which could further damage her legs. They were still bleeding profusely. The activities of Judy and the ambulance man told him as much. Whereas he had enjoyed seeing his father's mauled arm, he could not look at the horror of his wife's shattered legs. Suddenly, for the first time in his life, he knew what it felt like to want to pray. The words formed unbidden in his head. *Please let her be all right. I'll do anything as long as she's all right.*

He felt a hand on his shoulder. Judy's gentle voice penetrated his misery. "Are you feeling OK? For a white man you look awful pale."

The warmth of her hand penetrated his sodden, bloodstained shirt, right through to the deepest part of him, almost as though his prayer was being acknowledged. He looked up and gave her a weak smile. "Yes. Thank you." It was all he could say right then, but she seemed to know he meant more.

"Good. You stay that way. She's going to need you."

*

Ilse sat drinking her mid-morning coffee, flicking through the contact prints of the wedding, sent over by Sophie's parents. She had intended choosing about a dozen of the best ones, but quickly realised there were so many she really liked she would end up ordering the complete set. It had been a truly memorable day, with everything organised perfectly, down to the minutest detail. She held up a print of Siegfried and Sophie standing under an archway of lilies and ivy at the reception. Her special son, married at last. And to the girl she had chosen for him. Things couldn't have been better. Except for Sabina's outburst.

The distant ringing of the telephone brought Beate to the door a minute later. "Telephone, madam. It's Herr Zopf."

Ilse put down the prints and picked up the extension at her side.

"Hello, Paul. I was just looking at the wedding photos. They're –"

"I haven't got long," he interrupted briskly. "Just called to let you know I'll be late home this evening. The Finnish consignment's gone astray. See you when I do. 'Bye."

The buzzing of the line in her ear confirmed he was gone. Although his tone had been perfectly natural she knew the importance of the code. 'The Finnish consignment's gone astray'. He'd had a tip-off the police were onto them. Slowly she replaced the receiver in its cradle.

The world was shifting under her feet. It would never be the same again. Paul's business would have trouble surviving a major scandal such as this. There would be no more local government contracts. Developers would be unwilling to ally themselves with suspected Nazi sympathisers. And what of Paul and Siegfried? Would it mean jail for them? Paul had said 'See you when I do.' Vague in the extreme. Was he already making a run for it? And what of Siegfried? She must get in touch with him and warn him.

At that moment the phone rang again in the hall. Ilse immediately picked up the extension before Beate could answer it. There was the crackle of a long-distance line.

"Hello. Ilse Zopf speaking."

"Mutter!" Siegfried's voice sounded strained. "Listen! Sophie's in hospital. Her legs were crushed when a tree fell on our car. I've no idea yet how bad it is. They're operating on her now. I want you to contact the health insurance and get everything set up to fly her home as soon as she's allowed, and into the best orthopaedic unit there is."

It was as though the storm which had lashed St Lucia was buffeting Ilse right now. She felt devastated, winded by yet another blow so soon after Paul's news.

"Mutter? Are you all right?"

Ilse collected herself together, made herself think rationally. "Yes, Siegfried." That would alert him. She almost never called him by his name. "I'll do what you asked. I won't be able to tell Paul the terrible news just yet. He's going to be late home this evening. The Finnish consignment has gone astray."

It was Siegfried's turn to be struck dumb, but he quickly recovered, his voice giving no hint that he understood the significance of her statement. "That's a nuisance." He gave himself a

397

moment to reconsider his plans but decided against it. "Don't forget to contact the insurance for me. We'll be home soon, with any luck."

Ilse cursed this talking in code, in case the phone was tapped. She longed to pour out her heart to her son. At least she could commiserate properly about Sophie.

"Keep in touch, Liebling. Tell us as soon as you have any news of Sophie, and give her our love and best wishes for a speedy recovery. I'll send some flowers through Interflora. What hospital is she in?"

She jotted down the details with a shaking hand. When Siegfried had gone, Ilse sat motionless, staring blankly at the pile of prints on the table beside her. There was Sophie standing so proudly next to Siegfried. In the three days since that picture was taken the world had totally changed. She had heard on the news on Sunday that Karl had nearly died and was in hospital. Now Sophie was also in hospital. And where was Paul? A fugitive somewhere? Siegfried sounded as though he was coming back with Sophie, whatever the risks to his personal liberty. At least Ilse could feel proud of her son for thinking of Sophie's needs before his own. Now she had to think what to do. Act normally. Health insurance claim and flowers. Sophie came first. At least it'll take my mind off everything else for a few minutes, Ilse sighed.

She had made the first call when Beate appeared at the door looking unusually concerned. "Excuse me, madam, but several police cars have just pulled up outside."

Ilse took a deep breath and straightened her skirt and blouse. "Let them in, Beate. Let's see what they want."

The house was turned upside down. All Paul's diaries and personal papers were taken, Ilse's passport confiscated. She knew they would find nothing incriminating in the house, but this was more than the formal enquiries of before. Now the police had a search warrant.

Ilse silently raged as she was led out to a waiting car. Someone had betrayed them. And she meant to find out who.

*

Wolf went with Sabina to visit her father in hospital. Karl's condition had stabilised, but he still required careful monitoring and drip-feeding. Katherine and the boys had visited him earlier in the afternoon, leaving the evening session free for Wolf and Sabina.

They both felt anxious about the meeting. They could not be sure how well he would receive Wolf, despite the latest turn of events.

Sister Voß's night-time colleague, Sister Pöllmann, took them aside before allowing them in his room. "If he shows any signs of becoming agitated, I want you to leave and call me. We can't risk his blood pressure rising."

After such a warning Wolf and Sabina stood outside his door in trepidation. Sabina gave a brief knock then walked in, past the guard. "Do they expect him to escape?" she commented to Wolf, then noticed her father was well enough to listen to the radio through headphones. He removed them as soon as he saw his visitors. Sabina took them from him and hung them up on the bed head, switching off the radio.

She gave him a kiss. "Hello, Daddy. I've brought you another visitor. I hope you don't mind."

"So I see." He nodded amicably at Wolf. "I don't mind. It was a brave thing to do, Wolf."

"Thank you," Wolf said, rearranging the furniture to allow them both to sit by the bed. "But it was surprisingly easy, once I discovered he wasn't my real father, and I'd been lied to all my life. I hope this might make a big difference to the outcome of your trial. They'll believe your version of events now. Not Siegfried's."

"Possibly. I might get ten years instead of twenty."

Sabina flinched. Although he kept saying how well he was coping with the situation, she could see her father growing more depressed as time passed. The reason soon became clear as he spoke again, to her this time.

"Since the trial is in March, I told Mummy not to come over. She's been away from the farm too much this year as it is, without risking the lambing. I had to be firm with her. I hope you see my point, Bina. Persuade her it'll help me more, knowing the farm's in good hands. She wouldn't understand all the German at the trial anyway."

"I'll try, " Sabina promised.

Karl turned his attention to Wolf. "I hope you realise the danger you're in now. They won't let you get away with this." His words made Sabina reach anxiously for Wolf's hand. It told Karl all he needed to know. "If you want to come back to England out of their way, I'm sure we can find a home for you."

"Thank you, but my home will always be in Germany. Sabina's too, I hope."

Karl looked anxiously at his daughter. She nodded.

"I'm staying here with Wolf. Siegfried doesn't frighten me! Besides, I want to be able to visit you if ..."

There was no point saying what they all knew was likely. They had all seen him fire the gun at Goslar.

There seemed little to talk about after that. Sabina and Wolf soon took their leave. Before going, Sabina replaced the headphones over her father's ears and switched on the radio.

On the news a few minutes later, further developments in the Garisch murder enquiry were announced: Ilse's arrest, Paul's disappearance and Sophie's accident. Despite himself, Karl felt sorry for the two women. But he drew the line at feeling sorry for Paul or Siegfried.

CHAPTER THIRTY-FIVE

"I've stopped the bleeding and immobilised her legs, but your wife really needs the attention of a specialist," the surgeon explained. "She's going to need several operations and months of physiotherapy, I'm afraid, before she'll walk again. But I'm reasonably confident she *will* walk again."

Siegfried stared blankly at him, finding it all beyond his powers of concentration and comprehension. Judy came to the rescue. "I'll explain it to him later, Mr Simpson. He's still very shocked. Right now he needs to rest and get some food inside him. He'll be at my home if you have any news for him."

The surgeon beamed at her. "Ever the ministering angel, aren't you, Judy? I can't remember the day you haven't had some lame dog or other to care for. Well, you'd better take him and get him out of that wet clothing. We can't have him falling ill now, can we?"

Mr Simpson was already being called away as Judy took Siegfried's elbow and led him outside to hail a taxi. Siegfried could do nothing but submit to Judy's ministrations. He felt totally numb, unable to make any decisions for himself. With a great effort of will he tried to focus his thoughts. He had contacted his mother; there was nothing else to do now but wait. He heard Judy chat to the cheerful driver, who seemed to know her. Everyone seemed to know Judy. And like her. She was warm and generous ... and black.

In this alien environment Siegfried's defences were down. From the moment Judy first sat next to him in the rescue truck he had felt her warmth trickling under the barricades into the frozen wastes of his inner being, gently thawing his icebound soul within. He was now experiencing the first stirrings of its crumpled wings flexing, pumping blood into the new being – a metamorphosis. That word – black – held no significance any more. Judy was Judy. A friend.

They called first at the beach house for him to get changed, then went on to Judy's home. Her parents welcomed him into their shack – Siegfried could not truthfully call it anything more than that – and fussed over him. With a glass of cheap rum in his hand he watched the large family rally round to feed him, make up a bed for him in a hammock on the veranda, cosseting him like an orphaned lamb. A dim memory of just such an animal at Lane Head Farm returned to mind. He saw his father and stepmother wrapping the skin of a dead lamb about an orphan to deceive the bereaved ewe. What matter the outer covering? It was still a lamb inside, needing a parent ... as a parent needs its offspring. Gazing at the distant stars from his hammock, warmed by the generosity of Judy, her family and the rum, he thought about that for a long time.

A crowing cockerel woke him as dawn broke. Through the string of the hammock he could see it strutting about, beautiful in its colourful plumage, ridiculous in its self-importance. Carefully he eased himself out of the hammock, stretched his cramped limbs, and watched the sun rise above the silent palms in dawn's stillness and brief rosy glow. Germany felt a million miles away.

The house door opened and Judy popped her head out. "Ah. You're awake, Mr Driesler. I've brought you some coffee." She handed him what was obviously the household's best china cup and saucer. "Did you sleep well?"

"Yes. Thank you," he lied.

"Good. We've got a busy day today. You'll be wantin' to go visit your wife, and I'll arrange for your belongin's to be brought over here, ready for when you leave. But first you'll be wantin' a good breakfast inside of you."

And a shower and a shave, Siegfried thought. Immediately images of his last shower with Sophie flooded back. He clenched his jaw and blinked to hold back the incipient tears. Judy saw his distress.

"Come on in, man," she said gently guiding him through the door.

*

That evening at the airport, where a heavily sedated Sophie had joined them by ambulance, Judy took both Siegfried's hands in hers as they prepared to say goodbye.

"Now you jus' remember to keep in touch, Mr Driesler. You promised to let me know how Mrs Driesler's doin'. And if you're ever in London, you knows where to find me."

402

"Yes. St Thomas's hospital. Thank you, Judy. You are a ... an angel." He stooped and kissed her black cheek, knowing in that simple action he was betraying everything he had always believed in.

With Sophie settled on the plane, he sat in a nearby seat and let his exhausted mind merge with the clouds below, wisps of thought appearing, bubbling up then disappearing; his whole life nebulous, in a state of flux, reshaping out of his control.

His arrest the following morning in Germany completed the process. He sat poker-faced in the police car as the gentle drizzle and grey skies of home gradually began to impinge on his consciousness. He scraped the dirt of the journey out of his fingernails and wished he could shave. As honeymoons go, this took some beating. The charge of being a member of a banned political movement was trifling compared with what Sophie had got to go through. He might get six months imprisonment, but it was those very six months she would need him most at her side.

As he watched the hoardings, traffic and dreary streets slip by, Siegfried thought of Judy. What would she think when she heard he had been arrested as a Nazi, who reviled the likes of her and her race? Disgusted? Betrayed? But why should he worry what Judy thought of him? He need never see her again. The thought left him feeling strangely empty.

Once safely within Dortmund's police headquarters he had more problems to contend with. The casually dressed police officer sitting opposite him in the interview room looked unaccountably sympathetic. Convinced the worst had happened, Siegfried blurted out: "Something's happened to my wife?"

"No. Not as far as I'm aware." The policeman's face remained concerned. "It's your parents, I'm afraid." Köhler was used to imparting bad news, but it never got any easier.

"What about them?"

Köhler had the grace to look apologetic. "Your mother is here in Dortmund, under arrest. Your stepfather, Paul Zopf has probably fled the country by now. Your father ..." The immediate frown on the prisoner's face surprised him. "Your father is in hospital recovering from major surgery. I gather his condition is beginning to improve."

Despite his long hours of contemplation in the hammock and on the aeroplane, Siegfried was unprepared for the effect the news had on him. In his mind's eye he could see Sophie in hospital, her face gradually melting and remoulding into that of his father. His feelings for Sophie seemed to carry over to his father. Throughout Köhler's subsequent interrogation he remained silent, his mind numbed into confusion by exhaustion and conflicting emotions.

Later in the confines of his cell, lying on the hard bed, he brooded on what cards Fate had dealt him. He had always gone his own way, chosen his own path, often against the advice of his mother ... and father. When he had finally achieved true happiness with Sophie his idyll had been cruelly shattered. But the experience was also teaching him to value help, friendship, love when it was offered, no matter by whom. All these years he had spurned his father's love, even when pressed to accept it by his mother.

It was like a stone dropping from his heart. Suddenly his beliefs meant nothing, seemed unreasonable even. His parents still loved each other, after everything they had gone through. Thanks to Sophie, he understood now what that love was. He gave a long sigh and rolled over, turning his back to the wall and his old beliefs.

The following day when Köhler interviewed him again, he answered all their questions and added some information of his own. Towards the end of the session, Köhler was joined by another man, who immediately dominated the proceedings.

"Change of heart?" Kommissar Wach asked, his broken front teeth giving a distinctive whistle to his words. No one ever laughed at the speech impediment, or at the expressionless, yet intimidating shark eyes staring out of the cadaverous face. "You've certainly seen the light, haven't you, sunshine?"

Siegfried's eyes flashed but he bit back the retort, forcing himself to reply meekly. "I want clemency. My wife needs me. I want to be with her."

"And you reckon what you've just told us will get you off the hook?" Wach asked in disbelief.

"It's got to."

Wach was silent, tapping what was left of his teeth with his pen. At length he focused his obsidian eyes back on his prey. "Your wife is of course implicated in all this. We can't ignore that fact. It might be to her advantage if you could persuade her to divulge her Berlin contacts. Could you do that?"

Siegfried understood. The bargaining was commencing. "Can I see my mother too?"

Wach's teeth smiled. "We might be able to manage that."

"And my father?"

Wach scowled. "Don't push your luck, sonny."

*

Ilse seemed philosophical about Paul's decampment when faced with Siegfried's concern. The promised meeting had been quickly arranged, held in a secure room at the Dortmund police headquarters.

"I've denied all charges, of course. Paul's still tied up with the Finnish consignment. I haven't heard from him yet. I don't expect he's heard the news."

She was still talking in code because of the guard, but Siegfried had had enough.

"I'm pleading guilty," he warned her.

She couldn't have been more shocked if he'd slapped her round the face. "Why?"

He licked his lips, not liking having to betray her. "Because the game's over. It's time to grow up. My responsibility is to Sophie and she needs my help. I can't give it to her in jail. I've asked for clemency." It suddenly occurred to him how he could possibly sway her. "And told the truth for Vater."

Ilse's heart skipped a beat. Her delicate eyebrows puckered in a frown. "What do you mean, 'the truth'?"

"That Garisch *was* Goslar."

The significance of his admission was not lost to her. At a stroke Siegfried had deliberately destroyed years of careful planning and political manipulations. It was hard to comprehend. Paul would never forgive him. But she had seen the softer light in her son's eyes when he spoke of Sophie, and she was glad. Her enthusiasm for Nazism had waned over the years, only kept alive by Paul and Siegfried's zeal. Now she had to choose between keeping faith with her husband or going the way of her son. She had ditched Karl for not being a Nazi. Should she now betray Paul because he was one?

"I suppose whatever happens now it's the end for us," she said sadly. "You look after Sophie and be happy. You don't need me anymore. I'll stick with Paul. He's always been good to me. I can't desert him now."

Siegfried smiled tenderly "It's all right, Mutter. I understand. Before I met Sophie I wouldn't have, but she's changed me. Only she doesn't know it yet."

Ilse sat bolt upright in concern. "You mean you haven't discussed it with her? How can you be sure she'll understand your change of heart?"

Siegfried gave a long drawn-out sigh. "I can't. That's the problem. I can't be sure."

*

It was no use broaching the subject now, Siegfried decided as he stood looking at Sophie's prone figure. The police would have to wait for their information. It would break her spirit enough to know he'd been arrested and couldn't freely visit her. With both her legs pinned and undergoing major reconstruction, he couldn't inflict additional pain. Gustav Halstrup and his friends would have a reprieve. Siegfried's assistance to the police only went so far. He couldn't betray *all* his old friends.

She saw him standing there and gave a pain-wracked smile. "I gather I'm back in Germany," she mumbled slowly.

He stooped to kiss her. "You're in the best hospital we could find." He knew he couldn't stay long. He must get to the point. "You've got to be very brave, Schatz. I won't be able to visit you much. Nor will your parents or mine. We're all under arrest. Someone blew the whistle on us." He stroked her feeble hand, watching her try to understand and fail. "I'm trying to limit the damage to us. What I'm doing is for you, Schatz. It's for the best; the only way we'll survive together. Trust me."

She was too weighed down by her own problems to question his judgement. "Whatever you say," she said.

Siegfried smiled encouragingly. The lead sheep had turned aside and she was blindly following. The precipice no longer beckoned.

He sat with her a few more minutes, talking about their wedding, about people they knew who would come to visit her. "When I get bail I'll be able to come too," he told her as their time drew to an end.

"I'll have to visit my father in hospital too, if they'll let me. I've a few things I need to tell him."

She did not understand yet, of course. It was no use attempting to explain now. With a last caress of her hand and a kiss on her dishevelled hair, he left the room.

*

Once bail was granted, Siegfried sought permission to visit his father. Dr Langen was hesitant about letting such a potentially troublesome visitor see his patient. Siegfried was surprised but relieved when permission was granted once Karl was transferred to the prison hospital. Christmas was approaching; the season of good will even amongst heathens such as themselves. Perhaps that would help. He just hoped his father would find it in his heart to listen to him.

He was shocked when he finally saw his father, propped up on his bed in the austere prison ward. There seemed nothing to him, so wasted and drawn was he after his illness. There were other men in bed in the ward, but Siegfried only had eyes for his father's condition.

The warder left them together, called away by other duties.

"They told me you were coming," Karl said quietly. "Come to gloat again, have you? I'm surprised they let you in after what happened last time."

Siegfried towered over his father, wanting to come down to his level but there were no chairs, only the bed. Cautiously he perched on the end. Now they were eye to eye, in body if not in spirit. He'd tried to prepare this speech, floundering at each attempt. Now he had to say something, and it was almost impossible.

"Vater," he began, hoping that would set the tone immediately. But suspicion instantly sprang in his father's eyes and Siegfried knew his task was going to be far harder than he anticipated. He battled on. "How old were you when you turned against Nazism?"

The question caught Karl completely by surprise, although his mind automatically made the calculation. "Er ...Twenty-three. Why?"

"Because I'm twenty-three. For a few more days."

Karl looked hard at him. "Your birthday's when? Wednesday, is it?"

"That's right."

"So what are you trying to say?"

"I wish I knew. Except that some things don't seem as important as before."

"Before what?"

Siegfried sighed. His father was dragging it out of him, bit by bit. But it was no easy thing to admit that he'd been wrong. "Before Sophie's accident."

There was an uncomfortable silence before Karl spoke. "If I understand what you're trying to say, I'd like to believe you. But I have no faith in your ability to speak the truth."

"With reason. I know. But surely your lawyer's told you I've changed my statement about Garisch. I'm supporting your version now."

"Yes, I'm aware of that. I was wondering what new scheme you'd come up with. So it's first Wolf, now you changing your spots."

Siegfried smiled. "So it *was* Wolf!"

Karl blanched. So *this* was what Siegfried had wanted. The name of the informer. "Damn you! You'll never change, will you? Why do you have to –"

"Hold on, Vater! Give me a chance to explain."

Father and son's eyes locked, Karl's in anger, Siegfried's in placation. Reluctantly Karl backed down and gestured for him to continue.

Siegfried bared his soul. "I think for you it was the Yugoslav Partisans with their hatred that opened your eyes. For me it was the love of the people of St Lucia. They showed me the error of my beliefs, my arrogance. I realised love was a more powerful force than hate, especially when those you hate don't deserve that hatred." He sought his father's eyes. "What I'm trying to say is, I'm sorry. Sorry for being such a fool."

Karl was not ready for this, was totally unprepared to receive Siegfried's apology. Or grant forgiveness. Was too used to having the wool pulled over his eyes by Siegfried. But he had to say something. "How is Sophie?"

It was enough. Siegfried recognised his father's difficulty, expected nothing less considering the pain and anguish he had caused him over the years. "Making progress, but it's going to be a long haul." He saw his father's eyes soften at last.

"Give her my love and best wishes when you next see her."

Siegfried had one more thing to explain. "You know it was she who twigged what you and Mutter were up to. I've always felt jealous of Mutter's continuing love for you, but when I nearly lost Sophie, it didn't seem to matter any more. Nothing mattered except her and me. Now she's on the mend, I find there are other things – relationships – which need mending. I hope I've made a start today." He gave a rueful smile. "Do you know when I first realised how grateful to you I was?"

"Grateful? No."

"When I had to summon help and explain everything in English. Not immediately then, but afterwards, when Sophie was first in the hospital and I had nothing to do but wait. The thought shocked me and I tried to throw it aside, but it lingered and set other chains of thought in motion. This is the result today."

Karl smiled at last. "You must take Sophie to visit England when she's on her feet again. Show her where you used to live."

"That's if I can persuade Sophie to see my new point of view. I'm not too sure how she's going to react. I've rather avoided the subject so far."

"I see." Karl shifted against the pillows. The question: 'What if she doesn't see your point of view?' demanded to be asked, but he decided against it for the moment. He did not want to cause Siegfried to have second thoughts so soon. Instead he took the initiative in another direction. "Of course we've got to persuade Katherine to love you again too."

"And to love Sophie after what she let slip about you and Mutter." Siegfried immediately wished he'd held his tongue. It was not particularly tactful to keep mentioning his father's indiscretion.

"It's all right," Karl reassured him. "It wasn't Sophie she had to forgive. But you're right. We can't always assume Katherine's soft heart. How she puts up with us all, I don't know!"

They both smiled, the hatchet buried at last.

CHAPTER THIRTY-SIX

A month after their first meeting, Siegfried sought another with his father. It was a new year – 1968 – a year which would probably see many changes in their lives.

After being checked in, he was directed to the normal visiting room. It meant his father was out of the prison hospital at last. He was glad, not only for his father's sake, but also because the background chatter would make their conversation together more private. He sat at a table and anxiously waited for the prisoners to be brought in, reminding himself that he was to blame for his father's incarceration in a high security jail rather than in the less severe regime of a remand prison. He had given a lot of thought to this meeting, fearing his father might have begun to doubt the sincerity of his last visit. On past experience, his father had every reason under the sun to suspect his motives for wanting a reconciliation. Never had Siegfried given him the slightest grounds to trust a word he said.

Casting impatient eyes towards the wall clock, Siegfried dismally chewed on a thumbnail, experiencing an emotion so alien to him until recently. Remorse.

Karl's mood was quite different. For the first time since finding the young runaway Siegfried at Medebach, he felt pleased to see his eldest son. So it was with some surprise that he noticed Siegfried perched anxiously on his chair, hands clasped tightly on the table in front of him as if in prayer. As he crossed the room towards his son, Karl casually put up a hand in greeting.

"First time I've been in here since my spot of trouble." He sat down and beamed at Siegfried. "Well! This is an unexpected treat."

Siegfried's relief was tangible. His hands unclasped and he relaxed in the chair. "I had to come. I've got a lot of catching up to do. And I was worried you'd forget about the change in me. Or not believe it."

"How could I forget? Rather miraculous, I grant you. But what you said about age twenty-three convinced me. I was just the same – convinced of the rightness of the cause ... until disaster struck. You and I are very alike – in many ways."

"Too many, I think," Siegfried replied more seriously than Karl expected. He seemed hesitant about carrying on, looking and listening to see if anyone else could overhear, but the occupants of the adjacent tables were well wrapped up in their own business. It was still with a visible effort, Karl noticed, that Siegfried began to reveal what was on his mind.

"From what I've heard let slip by Sabina and Margit, I know you poured out all your troubles to Robert Murdoch. I've never had anyone like that, not even Paul or Wolf. I've always felt I had to seem strong – invincible." He had tried not to let self-pity creep into his voice, but knew it was there nonetheless.

Karl held his breath, hardly able to believe his proud and wayward son was about to confide in him. "Now you've found me, you think I'll understand?" he prodded cautiously.

Siegfried shrugged. "Maybe." There was a long pause. Karl waited patiently until Siegfried went on. "People have done things to you – horrible things."

Karl could see where this was leading. "And someone's done things to you?"

There was a faint nod from Siegfried. Words were not easy to find.

Karl longed to make it easier for him. "Can I guess who it was? Röbel, perhaps?"

The babble of voices around them was like a blanket cushioning them from the outside world. Siegfried drew strength from his father's gentle yet shrewd probing. "Yes. Him." All the hatred of years was uttered in that last word. A hatred which had tarnished all other relationships ever since. "At first he just used to beat me. When I was a bit older he started locking me in the flour store as a punishment. It was there that he ..." Siegfried faltered, looked down at his hands on the dirty Formica table. He couldn't go on.

Karl felt intense anger welling up inside him. His intuition told him exactly what Röbel had done. "The bastard! I'd kill him if he wasn't already dead." But more anger was not what Siegfried wanted. He'd had over eighteen years of repressed and silent anger.

Understanding and compassion were needed now. Karl had to prove he understood. "You're right. We're *very* alike."

It was the way he said it, with such emphasis on 'very', that made Siegfried look squarely at him. "You too?"

Karl nodded. "During the war. Yugoslavia."

"Oh." Siegfried knew how difficult this was – for both of them. He tried to keep the conversation rolling, put his own emerging thoughts into words. "I wanted to kill him, but never got the chance. So when you came along, I picked on you instead. Paul had Erich killed in the end, but that left my need for revenge unfulfilled."

Karl felt total understanding. "Like me with Goslar. I've been a different person since I saw him die. No more hang-ups. What Goldberg really intended but didn't quite achieve, I think."

"But it's not necessary to kill someone to do that," Siegfried pointed out, amazed he shared his father's innermost thinking. "Sophie's accident sorted me out."

"Count yourself lucky." His son's instant sadness made him regret his flippancy. "I'm sorry. To see someone you love hurt is devastating enough. How is she?"

Siegfried accepted the apology. "Incredibly brave. She's more screws and metal plate than leg now, it seems. The left leg's worse. They weren't sure whether they could save it at first, but the flesh is starting to heal. Once the bones have knitted she'll probably only have a bad limp, if that. If we're lucky."

"So many 'ifs'," Karl commiserated.

Siegfried realised he had been remiss. "But I haven't asked about you. You look a lot better."

"Yes. I gave myself, and Katherine in particular, a nasty fright, but I'm well on the mend. My body's had enough practice at patching itself up over the years."

Siegfried found himself blushing like a schoolboy. He had a confession to make. "You know when you broke your leg? That was my fault. I made the ladder fall."

Fortunately Karl could laugh about it now. "And there was me thinking I was getting careless in my old age!"

"It was the only time one of my plans to hurt you succeeded," Siegfried admitted shamefully. "You seem to have a magic shield protecting you from harm."

"You've more to confess? What else have you done to me?"

Memories flashed through Siegfried's brain: of himself continually trying to set Katherine and his father against each other; spiking Katherine's drinks so she would drown in the lake; introducing Sabina to drugs then, when that failed, intending to wean her onto Nazism; telling Katherine about his mother and father's night of indiscretion. Not one plan had worked. In all of them, somebody's love had got in the way. "I think they're best forgotten. Don't you?" he suggested. "I'll only admit to one other. Gustav's knife. You always thought I would use it on you. And I did. I made the dog bite worse, but the ambulance came too quickly."

"I see. Perhaps that was your catharsis, using the knife. You didn't need to do anything more after that."

"But I did."

Karl worked it out for himself. "Ilse and me, right? You made Ilse tell Katherine."

His father's total lack of vindictiveness allowed Siegfried to smile. "Do you remember me ribbing you about not having mistresses like Paul?"

Karl thought back to the holiday in Bavaria. "Yes."

"Well I understand now. I love Sophie. She's all I want."

Karl chuckled. "Good for you." His smile faded. "I wish I could boast the same with a clear conscience."

"It's clearer than mine, I can tell you!"

"Want to bet?"

It was good to laugh together. Siegfried left the prison in lighter mood than he had known possible. Until he remembered there was still the magistrate to face.

*

The string of court hearings began. Siegfried and Wolf were first. Their pleas of guilty to membership of a banned political movement resulted in merely a hefty fine and a caution. Ilse's diminished role in politics got her off too with a simple caution.

Siegfried relayed the good news to Sophie at her hospital bedside. "You see, Schatz? Nothing to worry about. Our parents were a bad influence on us, and we virtually get away with it. It'll be the same for you."

413

Sophie was still to be persuaded of her husband's new outlook on life, but she had her own adjustments to make. She had put her lack of periods down to the trauma of the accident, but a recent test confirmed the alternative. Their honeymoon had been brief but productive.

"I couldn't go to prison anyway," she told him. "Shouldn't rather. There's no way I want our baby born in jail. It's bad enough all his grandparents likely being there." She laughed at Siegfried's expression. "Don't look so shocked, Liebchen! We're married now. Such things are perfectly possible."

"Yes, but I didn't think we were going to ..." It was not the appropriate response. "You've rather taken me by surprise. Give me a minute to get used to the idea and I'll be pleased."

"It's just what we need," Sophie said to help persuade him. "A new start, a new way of life. I know I've not been at all happy about your sudden change of heart, but lying here day after day with not much else to do but think, I've decided to try to see your point of view. Whatever my loyalties to my parents and own ideas, I'll go along with you for the sake of our happiness ... and the baby. It seems the biggest deception of my life, but I'm prepared to do it for you. But I won't betray anyone else to the police. That I utterly refuse to do!"

Her fighting spirit pleased him. It was part of the reason he loved her. He couldn't deny her rights to her own beliefs. "I can live with that. Now Paul's safely in Uruguay, I expect Mutter will follow as soon as she's able. The running of the company will fall to me. I've got to be Persil white to regain clients' confidence. And so have you."

She squeezed his hand in reassurance. "You can trust me."

He grinned, but then his eyes grew troubled as he thought about the implications of her pregnancy. "It's going to be tough for you, trying to get up on your feet again, carrying all that extra weight."

She laughed. "You really are an old softy now, aren't you? I never thought I'd see the day."

"I'm only soft to you," he promised. "I haven't changed that much."

"Oh no?"

"No!" he growled in jest before turning deadly serious. "Honestly, Schatz, I thought I'd lost you when we drew up in the truck that night. I saw my life ahead, alone, in misery, without any

414

purpose. Now you've given me a double purpose in life. You and the baby."

She looked at him curiously. This was most definitely not her old Siegfried. But perhaps she could grow to like this one even better. She cast her eyes down the length of the bed, at both her damaged legs. For Siegfried's sake as much as the baby's, she was determined to get up on them again as quickly as possible. "You once told me you caused your father to break a leg. I think you can call this quits, don't you?"

"It ought to be me lying there, not you," he protested.

"No. If it were, you wouldn't have been able to make your peace with him, would you?"

"How did you know I had? I never mentioned it."

She took his palm and traced his heart line with her middle finger. "Because the hatred has gone from you."

"You witch!" he teased, pulling her finger to his lips.

She withdrew it reprovingly. "Why didn't you tell me about you and your father?"

"Because I didn't want you to put a curse on our new relationship," he teased.

"As if I'd do a thing like that! It's about time you two were friends," she grinned. "See! I'm growing soft too. It must be because I'm pregnant. I want our child to have grandparents who'll love him like we will."

*

Siegfried drove straight back to Iserlohn to share the news of his impending fatherhood with his mother. His arrival at the old familiar house coincided with that of an estate agent's. His mother's world was crumbling yet again and there was little Siegfried could do about it. He waited in Paul's old study, sifting through the remaining documents left by the police, until his mother was free. At last she came in to find him.

"Liebchen! I'm sorry it took so long." She planted a kiss on his cheek. "There's so much to organise before I go. Fortunately Margit's taken charge of selling all the furniture, and Heinrich's sorting out an apartment for the girls to live in. If there's anything you want from the house, take it. You and Sophie might want a bit more furniture some time."

415

"Like a cradle!"

Ilse's jaw dropped. "You mean ...?"

"Yes. Sophie's expecting. Due in August."

Ilse gave a cry of joy and flung herself into his arms, but Siegfried soon realised her cries had becomes sobs. He held her close. She was the one person he had always loved unreservedly, and now he was going to lose her.

"Mutter. Do you have to go to Paul? Can't he come back and face whatever happens?"

Ilse made an effort to stem the flow of tears. She stood back to face her son, eye make-up ruined. "No. He won't get off lightly like we have, what with his previous conviction for war crimes. Then he'll be under constant surveillance. It's all over. The time's not yet right here. But he can keep going in Uruguay. He's got good contacts there." She brushed a tear off his lapel. "You can revive the business, divert a few funds our way occasionally."

"Only for your own personal use," he warned her.

For a moment she seemed peeved, but then smiled. "Another turncoat. Another Karl. You'll have to get together with him, you know."

"I already have. We understand each other very well now."

Ilse couldn't believe what she was hearing. "You mean you're friends at last?" She grew wistful. "I'd love to see you two together before I go, but it's impossible."

"Why? It could be arranged."

"No. I can't see him again. That's partly the reason I'm joining Paul in Uruguay, to get as far away from Karl as I can. I'm a danger to him. It's not fair on the rest of his family."

"I'll send you a photo of us then."

"No. That would be too painful for me." She pulled a handkerchief from her cuff and wiped her eyes. Straightening her back she faced Siegfried, more composed. "You must send me plenty of the baby though!"

"We can visit you, surely?"

A shadow fell across her face. "I'm not sure Paul would have you."

For a moment he felt angry. Why should politics come between a family? But then he remembered it was because of himself and Wolf that Paul was forced to flee. "It really is exile for you," he said sorrowfully.

"Margit and the others will visit," she said brightly. "Perhaps I'll return once in a while and see you ... and my beautiful grandchildren. I know they'll be special. Like you."

She seemed to remember something, delved in the safe by Paul's desk and pulled out her maroon velvet jewellery box. Opening it, she lifted out three layers of trays full of glittering gems, before finding what she wanted at the bottom. It was a wooden hair clasp, carved in the form of interlocking wild roses. She handed it to him.

"If it had any intrinsic value I would have sold it long ago to feed us. Now I wear my hair short and don't use it. Give it to Sophie for her to wear and make sure your father sees it. He made it. It's the only memento of him I have."

"Then why don't you keep it?"

"I've got to forget him."

Siegfried looked at the exquisite carving, at the tiny detail of the flower centres, absorbing the love that had gone into the piece. He carefully put it back in the jewellery box. "I'm sure he would rather you kept it. There's a lot of him that loves you still. Sophie wouldn't appreciate it. But I'll tell him you showed it to me."

Ilse didn't argue. Siegfried was right. "When I no longer need it, I'll make sure it goes to a daughter of yours."

He smiled at her sentimentality as well as his own. "All right. I'll let you do that." His fingers went out to touch the hair clasp one last time. "Perhaps I ought to make something like that for Sophie and our new baby."

Ilse held onto his outstretched hand. "I'm so glad you're happy at last, Liebchen."

He looked at her. "I just wish you could be too, Mutter."

CHAPTER THIRTY-SEVEN

The courtroom of the *Landgericht* in Dortmund was full to capacity with observers and reporters. Amongst the forest of strangers, Karl was able to pick out very few familiar faces. At the front sat his father and Rudi, behind them to the left were Margit and Roslinde Röbel. They were all he recognised. Katherine and the boys were back home occupied with the lambing, Anna and Stefan were holding the fort in Medebach, while Siegfried, Sabina and the other witnesses had to remain outside. He turned his attention to the court officials. At the bench sat the three judges and two jurymen who would decide his fate. The presiding judge, gowned and capped like his two fellows, nevertheless seemed to dominate them with his massive figure and luxurious black eyebrows which met over his hooked nose. Of the two jurors forming the remainder of the panel, one looked too young to really remember the war and all it entailed. It might be difficult to win his sympathy, Karl thought ruefully. But courts were not about sympathy; they were about justice, he reminded himself, and for that he was relying on his lawyer, Hans Zimmermann. Karl already knew Zimmermann's sleepy-owl appearance belied the strategic awareness of a champion chess player. If he had any hope at all, it was thanks to this man. But hope was a transient emotion, become even more ephemeral now he was finally appearing in court.

Opening statements were made, the calling of witnesses begun. Karl listened to the police and forensic reports without much interest. Fingerprints on the murder weapon, time and cause of death; all were established facts, clearly pointing the finger of guilt at Karl. The crux of the prosecution case therefore was to prove intent and motive for murder, and perhaps more importantly, that the defendant knew what he was doing at the time. The first part of this process was to establish the true identity of Joseph Garisch.

There was an expectant hush around the court as Wolf was called. He cast a reassuring glance at Karl, knowing his evidence could not

418

do any harm. Wolf boldly explained his finding of the documents from clues given by his mother. A document expert was then called to validate their authenticity. Finally, Claudia Garisch herself, in the face of such incontrovertible evidence, admitted under oath that her former husband's identity had been assumed in 1945 by SS Sturmbannführer Johann Goslar.

The significance of this identity was now to be revealed. Karl shifted anxiously in his seat as prosecuting counsel, Konrad Mittermaier, called one of the panel of psychiatrists who had assessed him. Mittermaier reminded Karl of a heron, with his plume of black slicked-back hair, sharp eyes and long, probing beak, as Mittermaier fished for ever more damning answers from the authoritative psychiatrist. Quoting from wartime Wehrmacht and SS files, as well as his own report, Karl's experiences at the hands of Goslar and the doctors at Dachau were told in cold, clinical detail. Karl saw the five men at the bench accept the portrayal of himself as a man suddenly faced by a lifelong enemy; a man known to lose his temper easily; a man trained from childhood to use a gun; a man used to killing. Despite the reported mental breakdown in 1947, the psychiatrist was in no doubt the defendant was now completely sane.

Karl was relieved. Zimmermann had told him of the psychiatrists' findings, but now they were made public there could be no lingering doubts. What was still in doubt was whether Zimmermann's tactics would work.

*

Robert waited anxiously as each question to him and his own answer were translated. He knew his evidence could be crucial, yet he had to tell the truth. At Zimmermann's request, he recounted the nature of Karl's breakdown and the necessary psychiatric treatment provided by Dr Goldberg. Robert was careful to create more sympathy for Karl than the German psychiatrist had shown. He thought he had done quite well until the prosecution's cross-examining began.

"Let me get this straight, Herr Doktor Murdoch," Mittermaier posed. "You are in fact agreeing that the defendant had good reason to want to kill the man he knew as Goslar."

There was the usual translation during which Robert sensed he had to be extra careful now. "Not necessarily. Although it was Dr

Goldberg's intention, through hypnosis, to make Goslar a scapegoat for all the defendant's misfortunes. The fatal consequences of a meeting between the two might seem inevitable."

"Come now, Herr Doktor. You're not trying to tell me a hypnotist can instruct one man to kill another, are you?" Mittermayer turned in exaggerated disbelief to the judges. "Every murderer from here to Timbuctoo would claim he'd been hypnotised to kill!"

Robert winced. "No. I'm not saying that." He cast an apologetic glance at Karl, knowing his supposed help could backfire. "It would need a predisposition on the part of the person undergoing hypnosis to *want* to kill the potential victim. But Dr Goldberg did not instruct the defendant to *kill* Goslar – only to hate him rather than anyone else for all his physical and mental torment. As you well know, wanting to kill someone and actually doing it are very different matters."

"But there he was, faced with this man, a gun in his hand. Could he resist the temptation to fire?"

It was the question Robert had been dreading. "I don't know. How can anyone be sure what they would do in such a situation? I think most people would assume they would not go so far as to pull the trigger."

"We're not talking about *most* people, Herr Doktor Murdoch. We're talking about a man who has won sniper's badges for the number of kills achieved!"

Karl thought Mittermaier had won that round.

*

The following day saw Sabina called. She was a bag of nerves, her first words catching in her throat, but Zimmermann took great pains to put her at her ease, before making her relate the events of that August day.

"How long would you say your father held the gun before it fired, Fräulein Driesler?"

Sabina thought hard, desperate to be accurate in everything she said and not be caught out. "Er ... about five seconds, I would guess. It seemed ages at the time."

"So your father had plenty of time to pull the trigger if he'd wanted to."

"Yes."

420

"Now, did the gun fire before or after the dog got hold of your father's arm."

"After."

"You're quite sure about that?"

"Definite."

"Thank you, Fräulein."

Mittermaier was not so soft on her. "You said, and I quote," he consulted his notes, " 'It seemed ages at the time'. But it could have been shorter. Isn't that what you're saying? In other words, your father was simply taking careful aim."

Sabina did not know how to reply.

"May we have an answer, Fräulein Driesler?"

Sabina tried not to panic, but her mouth was dry. She caught her father's eye and felt comforted. "It was a long time. More time than he would need to aim at such close range."

She found she was shaking. Had they believed her? It was bad enough giving evidence. What on earth must it feel like to be on trial yourself?

Siegfried too found it a nerve-breaking experience. His original statement to the police, like Wolf's, was revealed as a lie. But unlike Wolf he had no obvious grounds for deciding to tell the truth. He was made to seem fickle, unreliable. All he could do for his father was to assert that Garisch was a covert Nazi who feared recognition. Prompted by Zimmermann he explained the plan Garisch had devised to dispose of the threat.

"While we were waiting for my father to arrive at the house," he told Zimmermann, "Herr Garisch told me of his fears about my father and asked me to help get rid of him." He waited for the murmurs of the spectators to die down. "He said we would force him to eat the meal and drink sufficient wine to make him drunk, then contrive a motor accident in which he and Sabina would inevitably be killed."

"And Garisch had no qualms about contemplating such a plan of action?"

"None whatsoever." And neither did I, Siegfried shamefully recollected. He looked at his father and knew he was thinking the same.

Zimmermann straightened his back and gripped both lapels to make his next point. "What you're saying is, that your father's – and your half-sister's – lives would have been forfeit, if your father had not wrestled the gun from Garisch's hand."

"That is correct."

"What were you doing while your father stood pointing the gun at Herr Garisch," Zimmermann asked next, almost casually.

"I was moving behind my father to overpower him."

"What prevented you?"

"The dog got there first."

It was this point that the ever-probing Mittermaier in his turn took up with fervour. "You stated you did not have time to overpower your father, as the dog attacked and Garisch was shot too quickly. Does this not imply that it was a very short period of time between your father gaining control of the gun and shooting Herr Garisch?"

Siegfried thought hard. It was possible to put any interpretation on the events, depending on one's point of view. "My father had more than enough time to simply aim. I needed three or four steps to get behind him. If he intended firing he could have done it almost immediately."

Mittermaier was not convinced. "A guard dog seeing a man grapple with its master," he argued, "would hardly delay in attacking that man. You say yourself you were concentrating on overpowering your father. Can you be absolutely certain how long the gun was in your father's possession? Or whether he was about to pull the trigger, thinking about pulling the trigger or merely aiming at Herr Garisch?"

"I can't be specific how long it was, and I certainly can't guess what my father intended doing," Siegfried snapped back, annoyed that he could be no more neutral than that.

Mittermaier's beady eyes gleamed. "So you also cannot hazard a guess as to the interval between the dog's attack and your father firing the gun?"

"It was instantaneous. The gun went off as the dog attacked."

"We heard earlier that it definitely fired after the dog attacked."

Siegfried cursed his lack of accuracy. "A split second after. Virtually instantaneous."

The prosecution's eyebrows soared into his black plume, demonstrating to the judges a point made. "In other words, the

422

dog's attack did not prevent him firing. It could even have prompted the event."

"Or caused it!" Siegfried countered. He saw Zimmermann smile. So that was where Zimmermann's questions had been leading. Crafty devil! He had delicately and circumspectly planted the idea earlier while questioning Sabina, allowing it to mature and apparently spontaneously blossom from a witness's mouth rather than his own. It had certainly flattened Mittermaier.

"No further questions."

*

The courtroom hushed as the presiding judge straightened his gown, donned his glasses, then read his statement. "Karl Dieter Driesler, the court finds you not guilty of the charge of murder. There is sufficient doubt as to your intention to fire the gun to render a guilty verdict unsafe. The shot could be wholly attributed to the actions of the dog. The court is also of the opinion that you have served sufficient of your current sentence and should be released forthwith. Court dismissed."

A roar of applause and cheering erupted from the whole Driesler contingent, now allowed into court to hear the verdict. After Siegfried's testimony and Zimmermann's adept summing up, the verdict was not wholly unexpected. But nobody, least of all Karl, would have wanted to bet on the outcome. He stood motionless, staring in stupefaction at the five judges. They were already preparing to leave the court, his life no longer any concern of theirs. Yet he owed them his freedom. He did not know himself whether their verdict was right. He suspected it wasn't, but had gone along with Zimmermann's line of defence as his main hope. The man had certainly earned his fees in suggesting the dog killed his master.

Karl found himself surrounded by his family, all wanting to kiss him or slap him on the back at once. No policeman or court official told them to stand back. He could step down and mingle with them, a free man. The first person he spoke to was Wolf.

"I doubt this would be happening if it weren't for you. Thank God you found that box!"

A figure pushed its way from the back of the family gathering, past Dieter Driesler busy congratulating his son. Dieter stepped aside when he saw who it was.

Siegfried stood before his father, closer than he'd ever been before. It took only a moment before both clasped each other tightly in a silent but heartfelt embrace. The rest of the family looked on, then, one by one, joined in the embrace, publically receiving Siegfried back into the fold.

If only Mutter could see this, Siegfried thought wistfully. And Sophie. She would be pleased too. A breath-taking hug from Sabina brought his mind back to the court.

"Well done, Siegfried. You clinched it for us!"

Siegfried realised there was something else he wanted to do. Once the furore had died down and Karl was sorting out some administrative details with the court officials, Siegfried made his way inconspicuously to Zimmermann, who was busy collecting his papers together.

"Well done, Herr Zimmermann," he said shaking him heartily by the hand. "If I'm ever in trouble again, I'll know where to come." He stepped closer, lowering his voice. "Please send your bill to me. And don't tell anyone who's paying it. Our secret, right?"

Zimmermann regarded him closely, a frown of suspicion quickly changing to a smile of complicity. "Agreed, Herr Driesler. And well done yourself."

Siegfried smiled too, then spotted Wolf and the other Drieslers hustling his father out of the court. He ran after them, through the waiting journalists and flashing cameras, as they all headed towards the first bottle of champagne they could find.

Karl was feeling bemused, swept along with the tide of events. After months of passivity there were at last decisions he could make. "Just a moment," he said, suddenly digging in his heels. "Phone."

There was a public booth not far off, although a queue of journalists stood outside. Sniffing the opportunity for more photos, they allowed him next in line.

He made a reverse charge, overseas call.

When Katherine heard who was making the call, she couldn't give her consent fast enough. As soon as she heard his initial 'Hello', questions flew to her lips.

"Karl? What's happened? Where are you calling from?"

"Outside the court!"

"*Outside*? What do you mean?"

"I'm free, Schatz. Free! I can come home!"

In Dortmund there was a popping of flashbulbs as photographers saw their shot. But Katherine was oblivious of the scene, oblivious to anything but the sound of Karl's voice.

Also by Caron Harrison:

Shades of Grey

Who is truly free?

Katherine Carter believes she is. With all her life spent on her father's Herefordshire farm, her future seems mapped out – until she meets Karl.

Karl Driesler has little freedom. His future is bleak. Still a prisoner of war eighteen months after Germany's surrender, he suffers nightmares, and his fiancée has just married another man.

Robert Murdoch, the village doctor's son, also suffers nightmares. A former prisoner of the Japanese, he finds freedom unexpectedly hard to cope with – until he meets Karl.

These three find their growing bonds of friendship and love tested to the full as Karl's past catches up with him. Denied the freedom to love, Karl's world is shattered, while Katherine's is thrown into turmoil.

ABOUT THE AUTHOR

Caron Harrison was born and raised in Epsom, Surrey. She was educated at Rosebery Grammar School and the University of Durham before commencing a short period of work with British Telecom. Marriage to an RAF doctor brought numerous house moves and overseas postings to Cyprus and Germany whilst trying to write *Shades of Grey* and its sequel, *Divided Loyalties*. She is now settled on the Isle of Man with her husband and two daughters.